In Deadly Fashion

Books by Rosemary Simpson

WHAT THE DEAD LEAVE BEHIND

LIES THAT COMFORT AND BETRAY

LET THE DEAD KEEP THEIR SECRETS

DEATH BRINGS A SHADOW

DEATH, DIAMONDS, AND DECEPTION

THE DEAD CRY JUSTICE

DEATH AT THE FALLS

MURDER WEARS A HIDDEN FACE

DEATH TAKES THE LEAD

IN DEADLY FASHION

Published by Kensington Publishing Corp.

In Deadly Fashion

Rosemary Simpson

kensingtonbooks.com

This book is a work of fiction. Names, characters, businesses, organizations, places, events, and incidents either are the product of the author's imagination or are used fictitiously. Any resemblance to actual persons, living or dead, events, or locales is entirely coincidental.

To the extent that the image or images on the cover of this book depict a person or persons, such person or persons are merely models, and are not intended to portray any character or characters featured in the book.

KENSINGTON BOOKS are published by

Kensington Publishing Corp.
900 Third Avenue
New York, NY 10022

All Kensington titles, imprints, and distributed lines are available at special quantity discounts for bulk purchases for sales promotion, premiums, fund-raising, educational, or institutional use. Special book excerpts or customized printings can also be created to fit specific needs. For details, write or phone the office of the Kensington Special Sales Manager: Kensington Publishing Corp., 900 Third Avenue, New York, NY, 10022. Attn. Special Sales Department. Phone: 1-800-221-2647.

KENSINGTON and the K with book logo Reg. US Pat. & TM Off.

Library of Congress Card Catalogue Number: 2025937917

ISBN: 978-1-4967-4108-0
First Kensington Hardcover Edition: November 2025

ISBN: 978-1-4967-4111-0 (ebook)

10 9 8 7 6 5 4 3 2 1

Printed in the United States of America

The authorized representative in the EU for product safety and compliance is eucomply OU, Parnu mnt 139b-14, Apt 123
Tallinn, Berlin 11317, hello@eucompliancepartner.com

"O beware, my lord, of jealousy!
It is the green-eyed monster which doth mock the meat
it feeds on."
Othello by William Shakespeare

CHAPTER 1

The wedding was set for mid-September.

Josiah Gregory had reserved the church, seen to the invitations, approved the music and the flowers, hired a photographer, and selected the luncheon menu at Delmonico's. He'd also booked for Mr. and Mrs. Geoffrey Hunter a luxurious suite aboard one of the White Star Line's fastest oceangoing vessels. Except for the dress she would wear when she walked down the aisle of Trinity Church, Prudence MacKenzie had turned all the planning and decision-making over to her and Geoffrey's highly organized company secretary. Josiah would see to it that every element was perfect.

He had assured them that the September 16th date would allow for a long honeymoon visiting European capitals and sailing on the Mediterranean before returning to London for Christmas with Prudence's aunt Gillian, Dowager Viscountess Rotherton. At which time they could expect to be presented to the Prince of Wales and lavishly entertained by Lady Rotherton's titled friends. Luncheons, dinners, balls, nights at the opera and the theater. Stalking on someone's estate. Perhaps even a trip to Scotland, though winter weather in the north was nothing to look forward to. The secretary had done his research.

"Josiah wants us to go over all the lists one more time." Prudence nibbled on her toast and sipped at her coffee.

"Does it matter? We know there won't be anything to add or change." Geoffrey leaned across the dining room table to kiss her lightly on the forehead, thinking how beautiful she looked in the early morning hours. How perfectly the black equestrian habit she was wearing flattered her slender figure, light brown hair, gray eyes, and pale skin.

"His feelings will be hurt if we don't." She handed her fiancé a sheaf of papers covered with Josiah's perfect penmanship. "You don't have to read them. Just put your initials at the bottom of each page. Scribble something appreciative, like *Well done!* He's put so much time and energy into this. I don't know how we would have managed without him."

"I should have taken you up on your suggestion that we get married by a justice of the peace." Geoffrey scrawled a few words on each page, initialed all of them, and considered it a task duly completed.

"I'm glad you talked me out of it," Prudence said. She took for granted her assured place among New York City's wealthy social elite, and seldom bothered to worry about following the inflexible customs demanded by that high and exclusive society. But Geoffrey and Josiah had been right to insist that a wedding was not something to be dismissed. She'd been so focused on negotiating the terms of a contract she'd been drafting—her first commission as a member of the New York State Bar—that she'd been willing and eager to push everything else aside. Even an event as momentous and life-changing as her own nuptials. She really would have to find exactly the right words with which to thank Josiah for all he'd done.

"The carriage has pulled up out front, Miss Prudence," announced Cameron, the MacKenzie family butler hired long ago by the late Judge MacKenzie, Prudence's father. Tall, with the posture of a soldier on parade, not a hair or a thread out of place, Cameron had seen to the efficient running of the household since before his current employer was born. He thoroughly approved of Geoffrey Hunter, especially since Miss Prudence had a habit of getting herself into situations from which she had to be extricated before serious harm was done. Hunter was educated, financially well-off, the scion of a distinguished Southern family, and an ex-Pinkerton agent. Ideal husband material for the young woman the butler loved as though she were his own daughter.

Cameron smiled to himself as he stepped into the hallway and Prudence gathered her veiled riding hat, gloves, and crop from where she'd tossed them onto the table. Ladylike restraint had never been a lesson easily learned. She tended to walk too quickly, say almost exactly what she meant instead of what she should, and do without a corset when she thought she could get away with it. She'd taken up detecting and the law, neither of which were suitable activities for a female of her station, and she was as close to being a magnet for danger as a human being could get. He wondered if becoming Mrs. Geoffrey Hunter—and eventual motherhood—would have any calming influence on her at all. Probably not.

Prudence and Geoffrey had gotten in the habit lately of riding in Central Park several times a week, less for the New York convention of being seen in the right place at the right time than because they both enjoyed the exercise. It helped that Geoffrey had been given two fine horses by a Long Island breeder whose case he had argued in open court. Until they married, Geoffrey would continue to live and take most of his meals at the Fifth Avenue Hotel, but on the mornings they didn't meet at the stables, he joined Prudence for coffee and conversation before her carriage took them to the park.

"I've got to stop by Madame Régine's salon on the way," Prudence said. "Do you want to check on the progress the contractors are making upstairs before we go?" Geoffrey had it in mind to build a large mansion of their own on Fifth Avenue sometime in the next few years, but for the foreseeable future they'd agreed to live in Prudence's family home on the corner of Fifth Avenue and Twelfth Street. The rooms that had once belonged to her parents and then to Prudence's father and his second wife—of bitter memory—were being refurbished to suit the more modern tastes of the soon-to-be-married younger couple.

"All I really want to know is whether they're on schedule." Geoffrey folded that day's *Times* and slipped it into the lawyer's leather briefcase he carried with him everywhere he went. His meticulous attention to the legal details of the cases he undertook was what made him one of the most sought-after attorneys and private inquiry agents in the city. He'd learned to pace himself, but there were days when every spare minute was given over to reading briefs and studying investigative reports.

"We've a meeting with the architect and the builder later on this afternoon," Prudence reminded him. "Cameron says that judging by the number of workers in the house and the noise from the second floor, things seem to be moving along pretty much as promised. That's a bit of a miracle, given all the construction going on in the city. Are you ready?"

"Isn't it too early in the morning for a fitting?" Geoffrey had learned a great deal about women's couture in the past few months. If it wasn't Prudence giving him updates on the all-important wedding gown, it was Josiah tut-tutting over the difficulty of scheduling appointments for a society belle who refused to act like one.

Prudence opened a blue velvet jewelry box that had sat beside her riding gear. "My mother wore these," she said, lifting out a triple strand of perfectly matched pearls. "The bodice of the wedding gown will have pearls sewn on in a waterfall pattern, and there will be more pearls on the sleeves and the skirt. Madame Régine needs to be able to match the color of the pearls her seamstresses will be using to the necklace."

"They're white," Geoffrey said, as if that solved the problem.

"Do you have any idea how many shades of white pearls can be?" Prudence asked, only half-seriously.

"I give up. We'll tell Kincaid to stop by Madame Régine's on the way to the stables. Are you sure someone will be there?"

"Positive. Madame Régine herself is meeting me. She'll put the pearls in her safe after the head seamstress has found a match for them."

It was something of a minor scandal that Prudence MacKenzie's wedding gown was not being designed by Charles Frederick Worth's Paris salon. Lady Rotherton had telegrammed her shock at the news that an upstart, no-name American woman—of all things—had been chosen to create the most important dress her niece would ever wear. And which would be described in minute detail by the *New York Times* and every society rag worth its name. She'd followed the telegram with a letter that Prudence had skimmed, then refolded and returned to its envelope. With a chuckle. Aunt Gillian could always be counted on to volunteer her opinion, even when it hadn't been asked. She'd apparently forgotten that she, too, had once been called an upstart American—whose father had bought her a title.

The truth was that the gown Prudence had originally intended wearing *had* been created by the House of Worth, lovingly stored away the day after Sarah Vandergrift married Thomas Pickering MacKenzie. It hadn't occurred to Prudence that the carefully preserved dress would have deteriorated so much over time that there was no possibility of restoring it. Preoccupied with the theatrical rights contract she was negotiating between her friend Lydia Truitt and the Broadway impresario David Belasco, Prudence had left the matter of the dress too late. A hasty trip to Paris was out of the question. Even Charles Frederick Worth's celebrated couture house could not perform miracles.

It was Josiah who came to the rescue. One of his many theatrical costumer friends knew of a young dress designer who'd trained in the House of Worth and recently come to New York to open her own salon, an almost unheard-of enterprise for a woman. Females sewed for a living, adapted fashionable patterns to the figures of their clients, and operated small, boutique operations. They did not challenge the male world of high fashion and salons that boasted palatial reception rooms and squads of seamstresses adept at the art of fine beadwork and exquisite embroidery.

To make things worse, Madame Régine wasn't even French. She was a relatively recent American whose deceased parents had immigrated from Ireland to the tenements of the Lower East Side. How she got to the House of Worth was a mystery best not looked into. But she was back in America now, ambitious, talented, and determined to make her way in a field where success depended on the fickle whims of women who had never soiled their fingers with work of any kind. For an independent individual like Prudence MacKenzie, Madame Régine was the perfect choice.

She was honest, too.

"My name is really Regina Healy," she told Prudence at their first meeting. "But while I was at the House of Worth in Paris, everyone called me Régine—and it stuck."

Her French was impeccable and her English without a discernible Irish accent. She'd made herself over to better take on the world she was bent on conquering. Régine had learned who was who in New York City: who was important and might be persuaded to frequent her salon, who unapproachable and therefore not worth the trouble.

And she'd heard the story of the frequently gossiped about society girl who'd become a private investigator and then had the gall to sit for and pass the New York State Bar exam.

When Prudence recounted the tale of her mother's unsalvageable wedding dress and described what she wanted in its place, Régine sketched a gown that left her new client breathless.

"How did you do that?" Prudence asked, touching the drawing paper with an admiring finger, careful not to smudge a single line. "It's exactly how I imagined it would look."

"Not quite," Régine said. "You'll want small changes here and there as we work on it. Trust me, there's a huge difference between what you see on paper and how a gown looks when a fabric has been chosen."

"Silk?" Prudence asked.

"The finest silk we can find," Régine agreed. "We'll decide on the thickness once we see how the various types of silk fold."

"We don't have much time," Prudence reminded her.

"Then it's fortunate I don't have many clients yet."

Both women had burst into spontaneous laughter.

"I'll wait in the carriage," Geoffrey decided, handing Prudence onto the pavement in front of Madame Régine's salon. He looked admiringly at what had once been a substantial family home constructed of square cut gray stone, transformed now into a dignified business venture with a discreet brass plaque beside the shiny black front door. "I thought you said she was just starting out. This looks as though someone has sunk a very decent amount of money into the enterprise."

"It does, doesn't it?" Prudence agreed. "And it's even more impressive inside. Turkish carpets, heavy velvet drapes, furniture that may not be but certainly looks antique. I'd say it's on par with anything to be found in Paris."

"I forgot that you and Lady Rotherton have been to House of Worth more than a few times."

"She more than I. She goes over at least once a year. Monsieur Worth keeps all the measurements of his clients in files that he stores in a locked vault. As long as a lady doesn't change her figure too drastically, it's not always necessary to be fitted on the premises."

"I'll ring the bell for you." Geoffrey extended his arm, assisted Prudence up the stone steps, and pressed a gloved finger on the recessed doorbell beside the brass plaque. He waited, half turned to go back to the carriage, then frowned as the door remained closed. No sound of anyone approaching from inside. "I thought you said Madame Régine was meeting you here."

"We may be a few minutes early." Prudence looked in both directions along the empty street, then nodded as a hansom cab turned the corner from Fifth Avenue. "There she is. Right on time."

The woman who descended from the hansom cab was strikingly beautiful. Taller than average, with shining black hair, dark blue eyes, and skin as pale as the pearls Prudence had shown Geoffrey that morning. She was impeccably dressed in the latest Parisian style, but with a certain distinctive difference that would draw every woman's attention. It was a graceful elegance that Madame Régine sought to impart to each of her creations, what she thought of as her signature panache. Impossible to quantify or explain, but unforgettable in its élan.

"Brenda Leavitt should be here," Madame Régine said after being introduced to Geoffrey, who stood to one side as she produced a key from her reticule and inserted it into the lock. "If she's all the way in the back sewing room, she may not have heard the bell." The door swung open on a dark hallway. "That's odd. I would have thought she'd have turned on the gaslights. She knows what time we planned to be here. I reminded her yesterday. Will you join us, Mr. Hunter?"

Even before Madame Régine's invitation, something about the darkness of the salon's interior and its utter stillness had made Geoffrey decide not to wait in the carriage after all. He didn't really expect anything to be amiss, other, perhaps, than a seamstress who had overslept and failed to arrive on time. But Prudence had a way of walking into trouble that made him conclude it might be better if he did not leave the ladies alone.

"Straight through along this hallway," Madame Régine directed. "The workrooms are upstairs, for the light. I had all the rear wall windows replaced and enlarged. Gaslight isn't always bright enough for the most delicate work."

She started to call out Brenda Leavitt's name, but Geoffrey shook his head. Their own footsteps were the only sounds in the building.

Geoffrey heard a scrabbling sound behind him. Prudence had opened her reticule and was reaching inside it for the two-shot derringer he insisted she always carry. She, too, had picked up on the vague sense of wrongness that seemed to permeate the building like a bad smell.

"The fitting rooms are along here, to the left," Madame Régine said. "But I told Brenda we'd meet in my office. I want to put your pearls into the safe right away, as soon as we've matched them with one of ours. Then you can be on your way to the park."

"I shouldn't have suggested we do it this way," Prudence apologized. "It seemed logical at the moment when we planned it, but I'm beginning to think it was a bad idea. I could just have easily made time during the day to bring the pearls by, and you wouldn't have had to go to this extra bother."

"It's no trouble." Madame Régine was used to catering to the odd whims of her clients. It was part of keeping their business.

The door to her private office was closed and locked.

"Brenda isn't here yet," Madame Régine said. "She would have opened for us if she were."

"Your head seamstress has a master key, including one that

opens your office?" Geoffrey asked. His question made it clear he considered that type of arrangement less than trustworthy.

"Not usually. But I gave her a copy of my office key yesterday. I didn't want to keep you waiting in case I was late."

"If she's here, where would she be?" Prudence asked. She'd been to several fittings with Brenda Leavitt, who had never been late to a single one of them.

"She could be upstairs, in the workroom where the gowns that are nearly finished are stored in individual wardrobes overnight," Madame Régine said. "She might be getting a piece of the fabric to bring down with her so we can see the effect of your pearls and ours against the silk." Logical, but she sounded dubious.

"Shall we?" Geoffrey asked.

Madame Régine led the way to the employee staircase that opened onto an enormous second-floor sewing room with floor-to-ceiling windows and worktables in orderly ranks throughout the space. All of the finer work was done by hand, but there were sewing machines for hidden seams and the creation of muslin patterns. Six of them, shrouded in canvas covers to keep the needles and surfaces dust free. At the far end of the room stood a row of cedar-lined wardrobes, each one labeled with a client's name.

"Brenda? Are you here?" Madame Régine's voice echoed through the vast space. She stood in the doorway, Prudence and Geoffrey beside and a little behind her. It was a moment before she stepped over the sill, as if even before she saw the disaster, she had become afraid of what she would find. "Brenda?"

A woman's body lay face down on the floor. Blood so fresh it was still bright red and liquid spattered her back, the floor, and the legs of the sewing machine she must have been trying to get behind. She had been bludgeoned multiple times, the splintered shards of her skull clearly visible through the tangled mass of her hair. Beside her lay one of the heavy glass weights used to secure fabric to the surface of the cutting table. Smears of blood, hair, and brain identified it as the murder weapon.

Someone strong had attacked her, had chased her halfway across the workroom, battering repeatedly at her head and body as she tried to escape and finally fell.

Atop the body and scattered all around it were ribbons of white silk. A snowstorm of white floating in a pond of scarlet.

A name was embroidered on a fabric label the killer had positioned just above the dead woman's waist.

"My dress," whispered Prudence, unable to tear her eyes away from what she was seeing. "Cut into pieces and tossed over her as she lay dying. The poor woman. Who would do such a thing?"

"If that's Brenda Leavitt, she's the chance victim here." Geoffrey turned Prudence away from the scene, holding her closely against him, pressing her face against his chest, stroking her back to quiet the trembling he could feel running up and down her spine. "The real target was you, my love."

And by her sobbing, he knew Prudence believed him.

CHAPTER 2

Detectives Stephen Phelan and his younger partner, Pat Corcoran, were assigned to the dressmaker case, as it was called around the Mulberry Street Station House.

Not until they arrived at Madame Régine's salon did Phelan discover that the victim had been sewing a wedding gown for the annoying young socialite turned amateur inquiry agent, Prudence MacKenzie. Phelan had no patience with women edging their way into professions properly reserved for men. He'd more than once had to choke back what he would have liked to say to the late Judge MacKenzie's daughter. She had an infuriating way of turning up before him at a murder site, always accompanied by the ex-Pink Southerner she was now about to marry.

The bride-to-be, decked out in an expensive riding habit and sipping a cup of tea in Madame Régine's private office, glanced at him as though she and her intended had already taken charge of the crime scene. Phelan felt his ears flush red. Geoffrey Hunter was an experienced investigator—and a man. But he was also wealthier than Phelan could ever hope to be and welcomed by virtue of his birth into a society that would forever exclude an Irish copper. Phelan loathed both of them. He'd promised himself that one day he'd teach them what it felt like to be a working man in this city.

"Detective Phelan." Geoffrey Hunter rose to his feet and extended a gentlemanly hand. "I wondered if you and Detective Corcoran would be here this morning. Have you been filled in on the details of what's happened?"

"I have. You and Miss MacKenzie will remain here until I'm ready to question you. Madame Régine will come with me." Phelan acknowledged Prudence's presence with a stiff nod; that was as much as he was willing to concede to the bare bones of civility.

"We were together, the three of us, when we found Brenda Leavitt in the workroom," Madame Régine protested. "We've been in one another's company ever since arriving. I met Miss MacKenzie and Mr. Hunter on the front steps and led them inside. I don't understand why you think you have to separate us."

Another woman attempting to dictate terms of behavior to a man whose instructions she should follow without question. Phelan didn't bother arguing with her. It was beneath him to explain the rules for interrogating suspects that Chief Thomas Byrnes insisted all of his detectives follow. Strictly speaking, the ex-Pink and the MacKenzie woman should also be kept apart, but Phelan knew he didn't have enough uniforms assigned to the case to accomplish that.

"Out into the hallway," he snapped at Madame Régine. He consulted the small notebook in which he kept his case notes. "The building is deeded to a Regina Healy. I assume that's your real name?"

"I'm known professionally as Madame Régine. That's how I would prefer to be addressed."

"Step outside, Miss Healy." He wasn't going to yield anything. "I'm putting an officer on the door, Mr. Hunter. Don't try to leave this room for any reason. That goes for Miss MacKenzie, too." Phelan held out his hand for the ring of keys Madame Régine wore at her waist, locked the office door from the outside, and gave instructions to the beefy young policemen he stationed there. "Remember, they don't come out no matter what."

"Yes, sir."

"All right, Miss Regina Healy, take me to this workroom where you found the body." Phelan toyed for a moment with a pair of handcuffs, letting them dangle from one finger. "Do I need to use these?"

Madame Régine's eyes blazed with a fury she was barely able to contain. The handcuffs looked as though the cold steel would dig into her skin, and she had no doubt that the detective would not be gentle as he fastened them around her wrists. She'd learned the hard way—as most tenement dwellers did—that arguing with a policeman would get her nowhere. She was years away from that hardscrabble childhood, but she'd never forgotten the lessons of the past. *Do whatever they tell you when you have no other choice.*

"I don't suppose we're going to leave this case in Detective Phelan's less-than-capable hands." Prudence had set down her empty teacup and found paper and pencil in Madame Régine's desk. "I might as well write down everything we saw and can remember. It looks as though we'll be stuck here for a while with nothing better to do."

She frowned in concentration, covering the piece of embossed letter paper with line after line of perfect penmanship, the product of hours of practice under the tutelage of demanding governesses. Every now and then she paused, tapped the pencil on the desk, and asked Geoffrey a question. It wasn't that she didn't trust her own memory, but Prudence was aware that despite everything her partner had taught her, she couldn't match his ability to read a scene and draw logical conclusions. That came only after years of experience.

"Would a glass weight like the one used on the seamstress be left out on the cutting table overnight?" Geoffrey asked. He nodded approvingly as Prudence sketched the weight from memory. Neither of them had touched or moved it, but both had memorized what it looked like and the spot where it lay.

"When I was working in the costume shop at the Argosy Theatre the cutting table was always cleared at the end of the day." Prudence absentmindedly rubbed the healed but still sensitive palm of one hand. She'd gone undercover on the Argosy Theatre case and been badly injured. "Once in a while a weight would be forgotten, but they were usually kept in a basket under the table. The fabric shears—like the one Brenda Leavitt's killer used to destroy my dress—were stored in a locked drawer because they're much more expensive than ordinary scissors. The costume mistress said they should never be used on anything but material. Cutting paper or cardboard with them was a cardinal sin. Don't ask me exactly why. It has something to do with the way the blades are sharpened."

"That answers one of my questions. Our killer came unarmed. He would have used a gun if he'd had one. Instead, when his victim ran from him, he picked up the only weapon at hand—a glass weight in plain sight on the cutting table—and chased her across the room. He was bigger, stronger, and faster than Brenda Leavitt, but it couldn't have been a swift or painless death."

"If, as Madame Régine suggested, Brenda had come upstairs to get a piece of silk to match with the pearls, she probably unlocked whatever drawer the fabric shears were kept in. They weren't on the cutting table or her attacker would have used them instead of the glass weight." Prudence was reenacting the death scene in her mind. Just as Geoffrey had taught her. Placing herself there as an imaginary witness. "I don't think a knife could have made those even cuts in the silk. It would have slashed raggedly through the fabric."

"So perhaps Brenda had already cut a piece of the silk, then set the shears down somewhere out of the killer's sight. She ran because she was trying to get to them to defend herself." Knives were common street weapons. Odd that this intruder apparently carried neither a gun nor a blade.

"Except for the glass weight, there was no other weapon anywhere near the body," Prudence said.

"Master chefs take their personal knives with them to whatever restaurant they work in," Geoffrey mused. "Would a seamstress have bought her own fabric shears?" He wasn't sure where he was going with the question, but he was puzzled by the absence of shears that had clearly been used to shower the dead woman with remnants of the garment she'd been working on. Some killers were known to collect souvenirs of their crimes. Personal objects belonging to their victims.

"They're too expensive," Prudence said. "If a *salon de couture* operates at all like the costume shop at the Argosy, the seamstresses are provided what they need. They're not paid enough to be able to invest in the kind of high-priced shears needed to cut silk, velvet, and satin."

"So if the shears weren't left behind, it was because whoever took them knew their monetary value or prized them as a keepsake."

"There's another way to look at this," Prudence said. "If it was someone who was familiar with the way a salon's sewing room is organized, the killer might have already been here, perhaps was in the act of destroying the dress, when Brenda Leavitt discovered him. He might have dropped the shears or she snatched them out of his hand and threatened to call the police. The weight was close by, so he picked it up. She ran. If she was holding the shears in one hand, they could have fallen under her body when she went down. The dress was already in tatters, so he didn't need them anymore. They might still be there."

"The end result is the same," Geoffrey said. "The only difference is whether one of Madame Régine's workers is involved."

"We'll have to question all of them," Prudence said. "If only to find out whatever can be learned about Brenda Leavitt." It seemed callous to be talking about the dead woman as though she were something less than human, but emotions got in the way of logic. And it was always logic that solved a case.

"I suppose it's possible she was working with a confederate who turned on her." Geoffrey paced the small office, plainly becoming impatient with their enforced stay.

He turned abruptly and Prudence rose to her feet as they heard the key turning in the lock.

Detective Pat Corcoran smiled at them from the doorway. "We won't need to resecure the door," he told the uniformed policeman who stood in the hallway behind him. I'll be responsible for Mr. Hunter and Miss MacKenzie. The rest of the staff will be arriving soon, if they haven't already gotten here. You go see what needs to be done with them."

"Detective Phelan said I wasn't to leave my post, sir."

"I'll square it with him. You won't be in any trouble."

The policeman touched a forefinger to his helmet and disappeared toward the front door.

"The only good thing about having Phelan on the case is that you're here, too, Pat," Geoffrey said, shaking hands with the young Irishman. It was common knowledge that Corcoran was the only detective at Mulberry Street who could put up with Stephen Phelan's idiosyncrasies. And the only partner Phelan would tolerate. "It's good to see you again."

"Miss MacKenzie." Corcoran smiled and tipped his hat.

"I think married life must agree with you, Detective," Prudence said. She liked Pat Corcoran. Was it a year ago he'd mentioned that he was engaged? Longer than that? Their paths didn't cross socially, of course, but he was a kind and decent man. The New York Police Department could use more like him.

Corcoran patted the small bulge on what had formerly been a flat stomach. "That's kind of you to remember, Miss MacKenzie. She's a lovely cook, my lass. And there'll be three of us soon." The tip of his nose turned red. "That's enough about me and mine," he said before the conversation could get any more personal. "Phelan is wringing every last detail out of Miss Healy; he's left the two of you to me. We'd better get on with it so you won't have to come down to the station house."

He waved them toward the seats they'd vacated, pulled up another chair for himself, and took out his notebook and stub of pencil.

"Start at the beginning?" Geoffrey asked. He grinned. It was how interrogations always began.

"What time did you get here?" Corcoran asked.

"I don't know what good it will do, but I told that horrible detective everything I know about Brenda Leavitt." Madame Régine looked drawn and tired, as though Phelan's questions had used up the last bit of energy she possessed. "The body is gone, and I've ordered the floor to be scrubbed. And everywhere else where a drop of blood might have landed. The seamstresses are drinking tea now, but they need to get to work. Sitting around doing nothing is the worst possible way to recover from a tragedy like this. It's best to stay busy." She took a handkerchief from her skirt pocket, holding it tightly in her clenched fist. "I offered to give them the rest of the day off, but they all refused."

"I'd like to see the workroom again before it's cleaned," Geoffrey said. "I can find my way there. You don't have to come along if it's too much for you."

"You forget that I grew up in a tenement," Madame Régine reminded him. "This isn't the first time I've been around a bloody death." She pressed her hands against her skirts, then led the way from her office toward the staircase to the second floor work and storage rooms at the rear of the building.

The main workroom—atelier as it was called in Paris—was empty except for two brawny women attacking the blood-stained floorboards with scrub brushes and pails of water that smelled heavily of lye. Two windows along the back wall had been opened wide to dissipate the odor and sheets had been flung over the wardrobes where clients' dresses were hanging.

"Except for draping the cupboards and the cleaning you've started, has anything else been done in this room since the police left?" Madame Régine asked them.

"Nothing, madame," one of the women said, getting awkwardly to her feet. It was clear that she'd spent most of her forty odd years of life doing hard manual labor. Her fingers were callused and knobbed around the knuckles, shoulder and upper arm muscles as well developed as a man's, flushed skin pitted with the ravages of smallpox. "We came in when the Bellevue boys were loading poor Miss Leavitt onto a stretcher."

"All right, then. Take yourselves off to the downstairs kitchen and tell whoever's down there that I said to give you a cup of tea. I'll send someone to let you know when we've finished here."

"Begging your pardon, Madame Régine, but what exactly are you looking for?" The woman who asked the question was the younger of the two. Her eyes were brighter, skin clearer, hair still untouched by gray.

"Anything that can help us figure out who killed Brenda," Madame Régine said. "Miss MacKenzie and Mr. Hunter are private inquiry agents. They'll be questioning the staff later on."

"She didn't die right away. I can tell you that much," the younger cleaning woman said.

"What makes you think that?" Geoffrey asked.

"You can see where her fingers dug into the wood of the floor." The woman beckoned them over to where she was standing and pointed downward. "There's no place else where the wood is scratched and dug out like that. She was trying to crawl away, and then when she knew it was too late, I think she started to write something. Just one letter was all she managed, and not even a whole one, at that. No more than a straight line in her own blood. My guess is she meant to do more but didn't have the strength."

"Do you read and write, Ellie?" Madame Régine asked.

"The hedge priest back in Ireland taught us what he could, though he wasn't all that well educated himself."

"Is it possible that what you're showing us isn't really a letter, but just an involuntary movement made by the hand of a dying woman?" Prudence needed to be sure she understood what the scrubwoman was saying.

"It was a letter, miss. I scrawled enough of them in the dirt of the road to know what they look like. We didn't have chalk and slates," Ellie explained.

"If you had to guess, do you think you know what letter she was trying to write?" Geoffrey spoke in the mellow, encouraging tones that few women could resist. He was interested in what she had to say, valued it, and waited patiently for a reply.

"It would be a letter with at least one straight up and down line," Ellie finally managed. No fine gentleman had ever addressed her with kindness and respect. "Wouldn't it be, sir?"

"Anything else?" Madame Régine asked. "Did you notice or find anything you didn't expect to be here?"

"To be specific, a pair of fabric shears," Geoffrey said. He didn't like leading a witness, but there didn't seem any way to avoid it. "Perhaps under the body when the Bellevue men picked it up."

"Nothing, sir," the older scrubwoman said. "We clean this workroom every day and there's always bits of sewing, pins, ribbons and such on the floor. We left it clean as a broom could make it last night, and there was nothing new this morning except the blood. Nothing you could use to cut up that dress the way it was sliced all into ribbons." She crossed herself and muttered a prayer under her breath. "The police put the pieces into a bag and took them away."

"Go get yourselves that cup of tea now." Madame Régine looked to Geoffrey and Prudence for confirmation that the women could leave. She pretended not to see Geoffrey slip a few coins into their hands, as gracious a smile on his lips as though they were his social equals.

Prudence had dropped to her knees, taken off one of her gloves, and was running bare fingers over the wet wood. Tiny splinters clung to her skin. "She must have been desperate, in those final minutes. But if there was ever anything to find other than what Ellie described to us, it's gone now."

"If the cleaning women were wrong, and the police found the fabric shears, I assume Phelan took them with him," Geoffrey said, eyes on the floor as he paced from one side of the room to the other. Quartering, it was called. Dividing a location into four equal parts the better to scan the area for clues.

"Which cupboard was my dress being stored in?" Prudence asked.

"The third from the end, on the right." Madame Régine pulled off the sheet that was blocking the smell of lye from penetrating into the interior of the closet and opened the door. "There's nothing inside so there's nothing to protect now."

But she was wrong. Where a pair of evening shoes covered in the same shade of silk or satin as the dress would have stood, there was instead a delicate gold chain. Just a chain, coiled around on itself like a magical snake. No cross or heart-shaped pendant, no cameo or precious stone set in elaborate scrollwork. Just the chain.

"Look at this, Geoffrey," Prudence said, lifting it from the floor of the armoire, letting it dangle from her fingers. "I wonder what it means."

She thought his slightly olive-toned skin paled, but she wasn't certain. Geoffrey was often hard to read. All those years of

Pinkerton training had taught him to wear an inscrutable face when it most mattered.

"I don't recognize it," Madame Régine said. "Shall I put it in my safe?"

"No," Geoffrey said, taking the chain from Prudence and slipping it into his watch pocket. "We'll take it back to the office with us."

"I suppose I'll have to tell Detective Phelan," Madame Régine said. "It's obvious that his men didn't do a very thorough search."

"They don't have to know about what they didn't find," Geoffrey said quietly, as if speaking only to himself.

"I suppose not." Madame Régine, like most dressmakers, knew and kept more client secrets than their lady's maids.

How odd, thought Prudence.

CHAPTER 3

Nearly four hours had passed since the discovery of Brenda's body.

Madame Régine spoke individually to each of the seamstresses as they filed into the workroom and picked up where they'd left off the day before. One of them closed the two windows the cleaning ladies had left open. They all glanced surreptitiously at the damp spot in the center of the room. No one stepped anywhere near it. Gradually, as the last of them joined the others, a low hum of conversation banished the heavy silence. Questions and answers, consultations over a hem, the placement of a button, changes that might have to be made to a pattern.

"It's like a hive of very busy bees," Prudence commented. "They work to heal themselves and take the place of the one who doesn't return."

"Some salons forbid any talk whatsoever in their workrooms," Madame Régine said. "I've always thought that a silly idea where women are concerned. We accomplish more when we can consult and help one another."

She smiled her thanks at the seamstress who carried over a bolt of white silk to the cutting table.

"This became available after we'd settled on something else." Madame Régine unrolled several yards of the shimmering silk. "It's thinner and more finely woven than the fabric we were using before. Very hard to get hold of. More expensive, too, I'm afraid."

"You know that doesn't matter," Prudence said. She let the silk slide off her hand. It felt as smooth and cool as spring water. "Can we use the same design? With this type of silk, I mean."

"It will be even more beautiful. The skirt, especially," Madame Régine assured her.

Prudence took her mother's necklace from its case and laid it atop the folds of the wedding dress fabric. The pearls nestled into the silk as though they had sprung fully formed from its threads.

Madame Régine brought a box of single decorative gems to the table, spilling a handful next to Sarah MacKenzie's necklace. She slid each pearl aside until only one remained, a perfect match in color and sheen. "These are dressmaker quality, but they'll do very nicely. I'll order them today."

"I can't help but feel as though it's a sort of sacrilege to be planning a new wedding dress before the floor is dry where Brenda bled out her life." Prudence's glance traveled around the room until it lit on Geoffrey. Hands clasped behind his back, her partner was strolling among the seamstresses, stopping every now and then to smile and exchange a few words. It was like watching a magician charm his audience.

Madame Régine closed and put away the box of pearls. "I don't mean to be unfeeling, but Brenda was such a private person that none of us knew her very well. She came with references and a sample of her work only a few months ago. The way she was killed was a horror we won't forget, but Brenda herself was a relative stranger. It's almost as though I read about the murder in a newspaper and then pictured it in my mind."

Prudence nodded agreement. "It still seems cold that Geoffrey and I will continue to plan for a future together when Brenda has no future at all. We'd only had two fittings together, but I feel I should be mourning more than I am. The only thing that helps is to remind myself that her death won't be left to the police to solve."

It helped to put into words what she knew had to happen in the coming days. There would be fittings for the new dress, of course, but Prudence had already decided that she would spend every spare moment on this case until she got to the bottom of it. Geoffrey had said that she, not the dead seamstress, was the target. She knew he meant that someone with a vicious grudge against her had taken out his—or her—rage on the dress because the woman was unreachable. Brenda had had the misfortune to step into a tragedy.

Yet the more Prudence thought about it, the less likely that theory became. It made more sense if the pieces of wedding gown strewn over the dead woman's body were meant to show the bitter spite of the murderer toward his victim. Brenda Leavitt's beautiful workmanship cavalierly destroyed and left to float in her blood. It made the crime so much more personal than if the seamstress had simply been in the wrong place at the wrong time.

Madame Régine, supremely practical and ambitious, would ensure that Prudence's new gown would be one of the most beautiful ever worn at a New York society wedding. The designer's future in the world of high-quality couture was riding on it. So with the same confidence she had in Josiah Gregory, Prudence resolved to leave the execution of the dress in Madame Régine's capable hands. Not to worry over it.

She would turn her mind to murder, resolutely shutting out everything else.

* * *

The last time Geoffrey Hunter had watched a seamstress at work had been as a small boy on the North Carolina plantation where he'd grown up. The war was over, the family's slaves had been freed, and he was soon to leave for the northern boarding school his father had chosen for his eldest son. The military academy in Savannah that generations of male Hunters had attended closed its doors permanently when faculty and students alike volunteered for the Army of the Confederacy. Nearly all of them had died in battle.

He remembered trailing alongside his mother as she chose from among the fabrics the seamstress had brought with her, debated the decoration of a bodice, the size and swing of a skirt. The dressmaker stayed with them for a week, leaving for her home and shop in New Bern only after the plantation's mistress and her daughters were satisfied with their choices, promising to return with the completed gowns and to make final adjustments.

It didn't occur to Geoffrey to wonder how his family had managed to escape the widespread devastation so many Southerners suffered. The former slaves who remained to work the fields were paid a small wage—and charged for the cabins in which they had always lived and for the food that was exactly like what they had eaten before Emancipation—but otherwise, life on the several Hunter plantations did not seem to have changed. It was only after he'd grown to manhood in the North that he understood what his family's prosperity meant. And the backbreaking labor on which it was built.

Sometimes, as was happening today, Geoffrey allowed himself to slip for a very short time into a past he found difficult to discuss, even with Prudence. The sound of needles slipping through fabric, the rattle of a button box, the swish of ribbons unwinding, the rustle of expensive fabrics. He put the memories aside. The family estrangement had lasted for years and might never be resolved.

He moved slowly around Madame Régine's workroom, stopping to admire some particularly fine hand stitching or embroidery, always politely asking if the woman over whose workstation he bent minded if he watched for a few moments. No one ever refused him. They smiled and blushed at his nearness, inhaling the scent of the sandalwood cologne he wore and the faint aroma of the cigars he smoked. He began to ask questions.

"Did you know Brenda Leavitt well?"

"Not well, and only here in the workroom. She didn't talk much about herself. I know she lived with her mother and an invalid sister. She mentioned them, but not often." Fingers twisted a thimble, pushed it more firmly down a vulnerable joint.

"Did Brenda Leavitt ever speak of walking out with anyone? Had she ever been married?"

"I think there was someone, but she never mentioned a name. It was more an impression I had than anything definite. Sometimes you can just tell when a girl feels that way."

The woman who thought the dead seamstress might have had a beau ducked her head. Walking out was usually discouraged. It meant a girl might marry and start having children. Then she'd lose her job, except for piecework done at home in overcrowded, underlit rooms.

"I only saw her for a few moments, and under the worst possible circumstances, but I had the impression she could have been in her late twenties or early thirties." It was the least intrusive way Geoffrey could manage to ask the question of age.

"She might have been, sir. Madame Régine would know for sure." A very young seamstress seemed confused by the question. All the women who labored in the workroom seemed old to her. She'd lied about her age and was terrified someone would find out she was only fifteen. She had a gift for the needle, but more experienced seamstresses would resent her crowding them out. This was the first decent work she'd been able to get, and she was determined not to lose it.

"Did you ever see her wear this gold chain? Perhaps with a locket or a cameo on it?"

Geoffrey always asked his questions in a soft, intimate tone of voice, as though the woman with whom he was speaking would be doing him a rare personal favor by answering. Bit by bit he stored away the few facts her fellow laborers knew about the deceased Brenda Leavitt.

Talking seemed to ease their shock at what had happened to her, and as the scrubbed spot of bloodied wood dried and began to look like the rest of the floor, shoulders relaxed, the hum of conversation picked up, and the answers to his questions came easier. They began to speculate, remembered a word here, a phrase there, a look in her eyes or on her face. By the time Prudence and Madame Régine beckoned him to rejoin them, he thought he had about as good a portrait of the dead woman as could be expected at this stage of investigation.

He returned the gold chain to his watch pocket. He'd shown it to all of the seamstresses, but none admitted to having seen it before. All were certain that Brenda had never worn it. Not in the workroom, at least. Several of them held out a hand, and he'd deposited the chain into their palms.

"Lovely," one of them commented, softly stroking the perfect links.

"I'd say this cost a pretty penny," another added.

"I wouldn't mind having something like this myself." Handing it back with a slight show of reluctance.

He turned for one last look around the workroom before escorting Prudence and Madame Régine into the hallway.

Detectives Phelan and Corcoran had left, the body had been removed to the Bellevue morgue, and the floor showed not a trace of blood.

It was as though the shockingly violent death of Brenda Leavitt had never happened.

* * *

"Pat Corcoran was given the task of notifying Brenda Leavitt's family of her death," Prudence told Geoffrey as they walked with Madame Régine back to her office.

"I'm surprised Phelan didn't decide to do it himself. He's always struck me as the type of detective who doesn't mind seeing people suffer," Geoffrey said. "I've heard victim's relatives say that Detective Corcoran was as compassionate as a priest when he brought them the bad news. He'll have been to and left the Leavitt house by now."

"Then Brenda's mother will have been informed of what happened to her daughter. I wasn't looking forward to being the one who first broke the news to her. There's a sister, also." Madame Régine unlocked her office door and reached for a shawl and hat as soon as she was inside. "I've told my assistant designer where I'll be and that she's to take charge until I get back."

"As I said before, I'd like to come with you." Prudence slipped on her gloves and resettled the long hatpin holding her bonnet in place.

"I'm glad to have you with me. This isn't going to be easy."

"We can take my carriage. Kincaid moved it down the block to let the morgue wagon and the police vehicles approach the curb, but I told him not to leave the area."

The tree-lined residential street where Madame Régine had opened her salon was nearly empty of traffic, its cobblestones continuously swept clean of horse droppings by a squad of street urchins paid by the householders. It took only a few minutes to reach the spot where Kinkaid had parked Prudence's carriage.

"I'll go up to Fifth Avenue and catch a hansom to the office," Geoffrey said.

"Do you still have the gold chain? I want to ask Mrs. Leavitt if she's ever seen it."

Geoffrey hesitated, but when Prudence held out her hand,

then cocked her head at his delay, he coiled the chain into her waiting palm and watched it disappear into her reticule. He touched his hat with one gloved hand and began to walk toward Fifth Avenue.

"We'll stop at a florist on the way," Madame Régine decided as she and Prudence settled themselves into the carriage. "And I'll order food to be delivered later from one of the nearby restaurants."

Prudence nodded approval. Flowers and food. It was what you did, in addition to offering condolences. "I'd like to pay for the food, at least. After all, it was my dress she was working on when she was killed."

"This feels so strange," Madame Régine said. "Yesterday afternoon I was telling Brenda how good her workmanship was. Every stitch she put into your dress was perfect, Prudence. She was so looking forward to sewing on the pearls. And now, today, I'm going to a house I've never been to before to tell a woman I've never met that the daughter I hired was murdered in the atelier where she should have been as safe as in her own home."

"We won't need to go into the details. Corcoran will have answered all the mother's questions," Prudence said.

"Poor woman." Madame Régine took a small brown bottle from her reticule. Laudanum. "I always carry this with me. Clients sometimes need calming down." She tipped a few drops into a tiny silver spoon attached to the bottle by a crocheted cord and offered it to Prudence.

The acrid smell of the drug filled the carriage.

Prudence shook her head. No matter how difficult the task or how challenging the situation, she could not afford to let laudanum get its addictive claws in her again.

The woman who opened the door to their knock was thin, gray-haired, rigidly upright. Dressed in black, with not a single piece of white lace to relieve the starkness of her mourning dress. She wore spectacles that failed to hide reddened eyes, and clutched a black bordered handkerchief, crumpled and tear-stained.

"I'm Madame Régine. I'm here to offer my condolences and ask if there is anything I can do to help you in your grief."

The woman—Brenda Leavitt's mother—stood aside and beckoned them into the house. "That's very kind of you," she murmured. Visitors may have been the last thing in the world she wanted, but etiquette demanded that she receive them politely. "Please, join us in the parlor. My younger daughter will want to thank you for coming."

The house was narrow, three stories tall. Staircases to the right in the hallway, a single closed door on the left. Prudence knew that when rooms opened into one another in a line they were called railroad rooms, a common arrangement in the city's tenements and many of its modest single-family houses. The rug beneath her feet was clean, but threadbare, the walls free of fingerprints but badly in need of a coat of fresh paint. A faint smell of baking hung in the air. She wondered if the house had been purchased at a more prosperous time in the family's history, perhaps when the husband was alive. A daughter sent out to work, even at a respectable occupation, was something a middle-class family only embraced as a last resort.

"The police have already been," Mrs. Leavitt said as she opened the parlor door and gestured them through. "So I've been told what happened."

Prudence interpreted the statement to mean that Brenda's mother was asking them not to remind her of the brutality with which her daughter had been attacked. She knew. She would have to go to Bellevue to identify the body. Prudence tried to remember whether there had been wounds anywhere but on the seamstress's head. Her hands? Perhaps her face if she had turned to face her attacker? All Prudence could see in her mind's eye was the white shirtwaist saturated with blood and the snarled strands of hair drenched in the gore of a battered skull.

Mrs. Leavitt introduced the young woman sitting in a wheeled chair as Nessa, Brenda's younger sister. Her arms and fingers were stick-thin, the bones of her face like a skeletal mask, her dark eyes bright with fever. She was clearly dying, and had probably been ill for most, if not all, of her life. But she had a sweet, childlike smile, and it was obvious that visitors, even on so unhappy a call, were a treat. Her hands reached out for the bouquet of flowers Madame Régine was carrying. Nessa buried her face in their fragrances as one by one her fingers loosened their hold and the blossoms fell to her lap.

"I'll put them in water," her mother said. Moments later she returned from the kitchen with a green glass vase that she placed on a small side table beside a framed photograph of a young child. "Brenda was five years old when we had her portrait taken," she informed them. "Her father insisted."

"She was a beautiful young girl," Madame Régine said.

"We had high hopes for her, but it wasn't to be." Mrs. Leavitt turned away from the picture of her dead daughter. Smiled sadly at the young woman in the wheeled chair. Soon she would be mother to two deceased children.

"I wonder if you could tell us about Brenda's friends," Prudence began. She handed one of her business cards to Mrs. Leavitt. "Particularly any male acquaintances."

"I didn't know women could be inquiry agents." Mrs. Leavitt stared at the card then passed it to Nessa.

"I'm sure you've heard of the Pinkerton National Detective Agency," Prudence said. "They've been using lady operatives for a number of years."

"In my day, young women stayed in their homes, where they belong." Mrs. Leavitt touched her handkerchief to her eyes. "A respectable young lady like my Brenda would never have put herself out to work."

"She was a very talented seamstress," Madame Régine said. "Her skills were greatly appreciated."

"Friends? Male acquaintances?" Prudence prodded the grieving mother back to the central question. "Especially anyone she may have met recently."

"There weren't any," Mrs. Leavitt declared in a firm voice. "Brenda spent all her spare time taking care of her sister and helping me look after our home and our boarders. She wasn't inclined toward casual or inappropriate liaisons."

"How many boarders do you have?"

"Four at the moment. Two older ladies—cousins—occupy one of the second-floor bedrooms, and two gentlemen rent the bedrooms on the third floor. All of them came with good references from their previous landlords. I provide breakfast and dinner."

Four boarders. In addition to what Brenda had earned working for Madame Régine. The Leavitt family finances must be precarious indeed. Prudence wondered how quickly Mrs. Leavitt would clear out her murdered daughter's bedroom for another paying guest. "I'd like their names, please."

"Surely you don't mean to question them," Mrs. Leavitt protested. "They have nothing to tell you that will bear on what happened to Brenda. My daughter's death is entirely due to the circumstances of her employment." Tears no longer stood in eyes that now gleamed hard and determined. Death could not be allowed to interfere with the difficult and exhausting business of living.

"I assure you I'll be brief and respectful," Prudence promised. "But you must understand how important it is that we—and the police—find out all we can about anyone who might have had a connection to your daughter."

"I hope the food I've ordered delivered for your dinner this evening will be to your liking," Madame Régine said smoothly.

Mrs. Leavitt's face froze, then gradually unthawed as she appeared to consider the savings that the dress designer's gift represented. "I'm sure it will be a week or more before I'll be able even to think about planning or preparing meals."

"Of course. I can easily make arrangements with Maurice's Restaurant to supply you with meals for the next seven days. If their food doesn't please, I can engage another establishment. For you, your daughter, and the four boarders."

"There was one man Brenda mentioned." Nessa's voice from the corner where she sat was thready and so soft it was almost a whisper.

"What man?" her mother snapped.

"She told me about him one day. I don't remember exactly when. Not very long ago. She meant to keep him a secret, which is why she didn't let it slip to anyone but me. He never came to the house. She met him in the park. They walked together and sometimes he brought her violets. Once he gave her a book of poetry. She kept it in a drawer of the table beside her bed."

"I've never seen a book of poetry," Mrs. Leavitt said indignantly. "That's inappropriate reading for an unmarried woman."

Nessa shrugged. "She knew you wouldn't approve. It doesn't matter now, does it? And anyway, I don't think their walks together lasted very long. Didn't you think she seemed sad this last week or two, Mother?"

"Women of good family don't wear their emotions on their sleeves," Mrs. Leavitt declared.

"Did she tell you his name?" Prudence asked gently.

"No. I asked, but she just smiled and shook her head." Nessa's fingers played with the fringe on the blanket that covered her legs.

"You said she walked with him in the park. How often was that?" Prudence wished she had thought to get a box of chocolates when they stopped for the flowers. She was certain Mrs. Leavitt considered candy an unnecessary expense, even for a dying child trapped in a wheelchair.

"Whenever she had errands to run."

"How would she let him know when that would be?" Prudence didn't like the increasingly sour expression on Mrs. Leavitt's face. There was no telling how much longer it would be before she showed them the door.

"I don't know that, either." Nessa's face fell. "It can't really matter though, can it?"

"You said Brenda only spoke of him once." Prudence flashed a glance at Madame Régine, hoping she was listening intently to the conversation and would remember all the details. "But then recently you sensed a change in your sister. Could it have been because she was no longer meeting her friend in the park?"

"I thought something must have made her unhappy, but when I asked, she said she didn't want to talk about it."

"I think that's enough." Mrs. Leavitt rose from her chair and opened the parlor door. "Nessa is tired. She doesn't need to be plagued by more questions." She stood there like a sentinel who would not move until her unwelcome visitors had passed in front of her.

"Only one more." Prudence drew the gold chain from her reticule, displaying it on her lace-edged handkerchief. "Has either of you seen this before? Did it belong to Brenda?"

Nessa shook her head. Mrs. Leavitt made a sound of disgust, as though Prudence had suggested her daughter accepted gifts no unmarried lady would consider keeping. She swung the parlor door open wider. They had no choice but to move into the dark hallway.

Prudence and Madame Régine were out on the sidewalk again almost before they realized it.

"Did you get all of that?" Prudence asked.

"There's a man in the story," Madame Régine said. "And I'll lay odds that sometime in the last couple of weeks he told

Brenda that whatever was developing between them was over. Or he just didn't show up for their walk in the park and she never saw him again."

"Whoever he was, he had to have worked or still be working somewhere close by. There's no other way Brenda could arrange for him to meet her."

"We don't know his name, what he looks like, or what he does for a living."

"I'll ask Geoffrey to hire one of his ex-Pinkertons to find him."

"You sound more confident than I feel," Madame Régine said.

"I'm a private inquiry agent." Prudence tugged on her gloves. "Pinkertons say they never sleep, and the Canadian Mounties boast that they always get their man. I'm somewhere in between, but I haven't given up on a case yet."

"You're getting married in barely more than two weeks."

"Your job is the dress," Prudence said. She smiled the way she always did at the beginning of an investigation. "Mine is catching a murderer."

CHAPTER 4

Amos Lang was tempted to turn down Geoffrey's offer of a new case, but he needed the money. Years ago, he'd quit the Pinkerton National Detective Agency with empty pockets, skills that had earned him the respect and admiration of every operative with whom he ever worked, and a nickname. They called him the Ferret because he was quick to arrive on a scene and quick to disappear into a crowd. No one ever remembered exactly what he looked like. Back then he lived in rented rooms, had no bank account, and dosed himself with measured drops of laudanum to get to sleep at night. There'd been a woman once, but he'd taught himself never to think of her. It was the only habit at which his self-discipline consistently failed.

"We can do a flat fee, or you can bill the agency by the hour," Geoffrey proposed. It was an offer he made to all of the ex-Pinks he employed, most of whom were rolling stones who wandered through life without ever settling down.

"I have a new form for the reimbursement of monies spent and the reporting of billable hours." Josiah Gregory took the document from the folder marked *Régine* and handed it to Amos.

The for-hire inquiry agent glanced at it, grimaced, and handed it back. "I'll let you know what you owe me as I need it."

"Good enough." Geoffrey had known and worked with Amos since both of them were Pinkerton agents. It was always easier to fall in with whatever plan the Ferret proposed. Stubbornly independent and prone to taking only those cases that intrigued or challenged him, Amos reminded him of himself. He knew that some people thought Prudence had softened him, but Geoffrey wasn't ready to concede yet that marriage could change a man. He'd find out whether that was true or not in slightly more than two weeks.

"About the victim, Brenda Leavitt. We don't know her presumed suitor's name, what he looks like, where he lives, or what he does for a living," Amos said. He liked puzzles that other agents considered impossible to solve and had been known to take on conundrums that experienced Pinkerton operatives had turned down. He quit the agency because Allan Pinkerton made a fortune hiring out his men to break the emergent power of striking workers. When Amos knew himself to be on the wrong side during the violent confrontations, he resigned.

"Whoever he is, he has to be located somewhere near the Leavitt house," Prudence said. She liked Amos because he was the most honest man she'd ever met, and perhaps the only one who had never tried to sweet-talk her. He also carried his own lidded tin box in which to expectorate. Most tobacco chewers expected offices to supply them with spittoons.

"Something happened a week or two before the murder. The sister didn't know what it was, only that Brenda grew despondent and withdrawn." Geoffrey repositioned the pens on his desk, something he usually did only when he was also rearranging his thoughts. "We may be putting too much importance on a change of mood, but it's all we have."

"The mother denied that her daughter had been seeing anyone." Prudence drew the gold chain from the velvet pouch where she'd begun keeping it. "Then there's this. We think it may be connected to Brenda, but we don't know how. None of the seamstresses who worked with her admitted to having seen it before, but it was found on the floor of the armoire where my dress had been hanging."

"What about the sister? And the mother? Did they recognize it?" Amos asked.

"Same thing. They both claim that it couldn't have belonged to Brenda. The mother was adamant that her daughter would never have accepted such an inappropriate gift."

"Looks expensive." Amos held it up to the light streaming through the window. "I don't think I've ever seen links like these before."

"Geoffrey and I are taking it to Tiffany," Prudence said. "They should be able to give an estimate of its value and perhaps even some idea of where or when it was made."

"Have you considered that if Brenda Leavitt wasn't the real target, whoever destroyed Miss Prudence's wedding dress might strike again?" Amos wrapped the gold chain around the fingers of one hand, admiring the way the links fell into perfect alignment.

"High fashion isn't a world that willingly opens its doors to women designers," Prudence said. "If she makes a success of her business, Madame Régine will undoubtedly earn herself the enmity of her male competitors."

"I'd say it's likely one or more of them would want to deny her the chance of succeeding. Knock off the challenger before she gets any stronger." Amos handed the chain back to Prudence. "Finding a dead body and a wedding dress in tatters in a designer's workroom is something the newspapers will jump all over. Madame Régine could be facing bankruptcy before we find the murderer."

Geoffrey nodded. "Brenda could have been supplying her mysterious gentleman with information about Madame Régine's business, gossip gleaned from the workroom where she was a seamstress. Companies spy on one another all the time. The other thing to remember is that seamstresses always know the identity of the designer's clients. They hear all the latest tittle-tattle while they're pinning hems."

"I'll start with the boardinghouses and bars closest to the Leavitt house and work my way outward." Amos closed the small tin box into which he'd been discreetly spitting and returned it to a jacket pocket. He glided out of Geoffrey's office with the smooth, swift gait of his namesake, leaving nothing behind but the faint fragrance of well-masticated chewing tobacco.

"I doubt you'll get him to fill out one of your forms." Prudence greatly admired Josiah's administrative skills, but she thought that in Amos Lang he might have met his match.

Josiah shrugged. He already knew that he'd be the one to complete the form while Amos laconically recited his hours and expenses. The Ferret didn't mind signing a document; he just didn't like filling in the blank spaces. It reminded him of the reports he'd had to write for the Pinkerton Agency.

Prudence MacKenzie was a familiar and valued client of New York City's premier purveyor of fine gems, exquisitely designed jewelry, and objets d'art. MacKenzie women had worn Tiffany creations since well before the war, passing them from one generation to the next while always collecting new pieces ordered by husbands and fathers. The spectacular diamond engagement ring on Prudence's left hand had been a Tiffany commission. Geoffrey had stipulated that the stone had to be flawless. Neither he nor anyone associated with Tiffany had ever mentioned price.

"What can you tell me about this gold chain?" Prudence had chosen to meet with the jeweler she'd worked with on a case that had involved the theft of diamonds once destined for Queen Marie Antoinette. They'd been replaced with well-crafted and hard-to-detect imitations. Tiffany had as much care for its reputation as it did for the stones it guaranteed.

The jeweler stretched out the chain on a bed of black velvet, positioned a loupe against one eye, and bent over the piece to examine it. His fingers caressed each link with delicacy and knowledge. He would write out an appraisal if Miss MacKenzie and Mr. Hunter asked for one, but this initial inspection would be both accurate and unchanging. His whispered comments were voiced too softly to make out, but it was obvious to both Prudence and Geoffrey that he was pleased by what he was seeing.

"The craftmanship is exquisite," he said, laying his loupe beside the velvet and polishing two more of the small magnifying glasses with a soft, lint-free cloth. Miss MacKenzie and Mr. Hunter weren't only valued clients, they were also skilled inquiry agents. And they'd examined gemstones and gold objects before. He clucked instructions as first Prudence, then Geoffrey positioned a loupe against one eye and held it in place with a strong squint.

"This particular pattern of chain is unusual," Geoffrey said, choosing his words carefully.

"Alternating curb and bobble links," the jeweler told him. "Victorian. I'd tentatively date it from around 1850. Definitely made in England. Twenty-two carat gold. If you look very closely at the clasp you can see signs of wear. This is called a box clasp because one part, called the tongue, slips into the other and is caught and held in place by a small latch. The box clasp is flat whereas the barrel clasp is round, but the locking design is otherwise the same."

"Is there any way to trace its ownership?" Prudence asked.

"Not unless you have the original bill of sale." The jeweler ran one experienced finger along the length of the chain. "Sad to say, we have many fine pieces of unknown provenance consigned to us for appraisal. Sometimes we can identify the individual jeweler or company that might have created them, but unless there is paperwork or family history passed from one owner to the next, many lovely designs go unauthenticated. There's no maker's mark anywhere on this chain."

"Do you think it's one of a kind?"

"I doubt it. Most chains conform to a specific named pattern. Watch chains, for example. For women, a chain is usually meant to display a pendant, perhaps a cameo or a stone set in a matching gold setting. This chain probably belonged to a woman. If you look very closely you can see where a pendant rubbed against the links." He positioned one finger at the approximate center of the chain. "The links here are slightly worn. That indicates to me that it was more likely the pendant was a gemstone rather than a cameo."

"My mother had a cameo brooch that she always wore when she was informally dressed." Prudence touched a spot just below her throat. "Right here. She'd unfasten it from her shirtwaist and pin it onto my dress. I felt like a princess."

"Cameos are usually the first pieces of jewelry a young girl is given," the jeweler agreed. "They don't weigh as much as gold or gems, and they're certainly less expensive. It almost doesn't matter if the pin fails and they fall off and get damaged."

"We had a cat then," Prudence recalled. "I seem to remember being stretched out on the library floor reading and seeing her striding off with something in her mouth. I cried when I couldn't find the cameo. My mother comforted me on her lap and my father promised to buy me another one. Funny, I'd forgotten that until just now."

Geoffrey nodded at the jeweler, who unlocked a display cabinet and placed a tray of exquisitely cut cameos on the countertop.

"One should never leave Tiffany without one of their blue boxes," Geoffrey said. "I think a cameo is just what your secretarial suits need, Prudence."

He never failed to amuse and delight her. "What do you think of this one?" she asked, studying the array before choosing an onyx cameo with a pure white female head—delicately Roman—surmounted by a diamond-encrusted gold bail.

"We can make that into a brooch or a pendant, whichever Miss MacKenzie prefers," the jeweler said. "It's a very fine piece."

"Brooch," Prudence decided, picturing the cameo pinned to one of the severe secretarial suits she sometimes wore when actively pursuing a case. She set the cameo aside and picked up what she had started thinking of as *Brenda's chain*. "Is there anything more you can tell us about this?"

The jeweler shook his head. "I'm afraid not. If you'd like to leave it with me, I could ask one or two of our older, retired artisans to stop by and take a look. I can't promise anything, but it's remotely possible one of them might recognize the maker, although, as I said, I'm sure it's English in origin."

"What do you think?" Prudence turned to Geoffrey.

"It's worth doing as long as it's not out of our possession for more than a day or two." He put the chain back into its velvet pouch and handed it to the jeweler.

The woman who recreated herself as Madame Régine, couturiere par excellence, moved her family to an attached brownstone as soon as she was given the money to get them out of the tenement where her mother, father, three brothers, and a younger sister had been squeezed into two unheated rooms. No indoor plumbing, no gas lighting, no heat except for bits of coal found on the street that could be lit in the belly of a small stove. She'd been born and raised in tenement squalor for sixteen years herself, moving with her parents and siblings whenever the rent came due and there wasn't any money to pay it. The first thing she'd done when she found a patron was rescue them.

She'd had to have a protector, of course, a backer, an investor—a wealthy lover she'd met and entertained while working in one of New York City's most exclusive brothels.

"You don't belong here," Madame Jolene had told her after the first few months. "You've got more talent in that head of yours than my whole flock of girls and all of their nether parts put together. One of your clients will want to buy you out of the house and set you up somewhere. Take him up on it."

Régine worked hard, long hours, taking on as many johns as she could, always remembering Madame Jolene's advice. When Norton Meulenkamp fell in love with her, she accepted his offer and never looked back. Already in his sixties, he died after three years of what became almost a warm, comfortable marriage. Except that he was legally the husband of one of Mrs. Astor's acquaintances and therefore a member of the Four Hundred. Régine didn't have the benefit of his name, but she did receive a tidy sum conveyed to her by a closemouthed lawyer who presented papers that stated she would never reveal her connection with the deceased on pain of having to return all he had given her. She signed them, paid off the money owed on the brownstone, then set sail for Paris. Home of House of Worth and the competing salons of Jacques Doucet, Pingat, and a host of other haute couture designers; it had been the dream of her youth to work at dressmaking in that rarified atmosphere.

She started over again, one seamstress among many in every workroom she could convince to hire an American. Four years later, Regina Healy—now Madame Régine—had learned all that Paris could teach her. A new life in New York City had always been her objective. To clothe its wealthy women of fashion her highest aspiration. With what remained of the money Norton had generously provided, she opened her salon and set about making her mark.

And then a seamstress had been murdered on her premises a scant three weeks before one of the most talked-about society weddings of the year.

The only woman she knew who had successfully weathered scandal, near bankruptcy, murder in her house of ill repute, and the weekly payoff demands of the New York Police Department was her former employer and tutor in the ways of satisfying masculine flesh.

Madame Jolene.

An Irish immigrant like Regina Healy herself, Jolene—who took the name off a packet of perfumed soap—managed to convince an intake officer that the Irish she spoke was really a French dialect. Every man alive knew that Frenchwomen were more talented in the bedroom arts than any other nationality.

Madame Régine sent a note to the decorous mansion recognized as a house of pleasure only by its clients and waited for a response. It came by return messenger.

> *I heard about your trouble. Come whenever you like.*

The signature was an elaborately curlicued *J*.

Chapter 5

"The new house is as grand as anything on Fifth Avenue," Madame Régine said, savoring the fine port Madame Jolene had served in tiny crystal glasses.

"I didn't sell the old one, you know," Madame Jolene said. "Owning property in New York City is as profitable as a gold mine. And a lot less risky."

The brothel was quiet, its residents keeping to their beds, sleeping off last night's clients and resting up for the ones to come. The cleaning crew had erased all traces of alcoholic excess, and the laundresses had scrubbed, hung out to dry, then ironed sheets and lingerie. The cook was putting together an early evening meal and brewing large pots of coffee. Madame Jolene had strict rules about what needed to be done before she opened her doors every night to a clientele that expected and received only the best. She'd learned long ago that no business, whatever its product, succeeded without close attention to details.

Madame Régine settled deeper into the armchair that was as comfortable as a feather bed. Luxury was what Madame Jolene's establishment was known for—that and girls who were examined once a month by a doctor to ensure they stayed clean. For the space of a few breaths, the designer allowed herself to forget what had brought her to her former employer's private office. She studied Madame Jolene, nodding in satisfaction. Some people never allowed themselves to change. From the moment she'd bought the house where she'd once worked, Jolene had worn unrelieved, elegant black. Silk or satin, depending on the season, but always liberally embroidered and sewn with glittering jet beads. Coal-black hair, pale Irish skin, and the manners of a fine lady. She exuded confidence and aplomb, coolheaded poise and a warm intimacy that promised to respect your secrets. Régine had modeled her own conduct on that of New York City's most well-known lady of the evening.

"The only way out of your dilemma is to secure a client from among the Four Hundred." Madame Jolene lit one of the North Carolina bright leaf cigarettes she'd lately taken to allowing herself. The fragrant smoke curled above her head and filled the room with a hint of woody sweetness.

"Not a single one of the women in Mrs. Astor's crowd would admit to wearing a gown fashioned by an American designer. They're all House of Worth."

"Worth is expensive."

"Money is no object to the Four Hundred. The women especially. I saw them every day when I was working as a seamstress in the Paris fashion houses," Madame Régine said. "They never asked the price of a gown. Neither did their husbands. It was considered gauche."

"Some of the younger men have serious gambling problems. More than a handful run through their allowances faster than you can imagine. They live on credit and their fathers' liquidity until someone deposits the next check in their account or they snare a wealthy heiress."

"Black sheep?"

"Careless, arrogant ne'er-do-wells. Playboys. England is full of them, and New York City has its fair share. No titles, though, which is why our American society matrons are taking their daughters to London. There are also some older men among the Four Hundred who aren't as solidly fixed as they would have the rest of us believe."

"I don't understand where you're going with this." Régine waved a manicured hand through the smoke.

"Forget the young wastrels. One of my oldest clients is a Schermerhorn on his mother's side. A remote cousin, but a genuine Knickerbocker nonetheless. You may recall that Caroline Astor's maiden name was Schermerhorn. There are dozens of them in the extended family, not all as wealthy as the queen of New York society. The Schermerhorn I'm talking about has a very plain daughter of marriageable age. He's desperate to find her a rich husband—banking and investments preferably—but he's already spent her dowry, though he believes no one suspects it. The only marketable thing about the girl now is her lineage. Knickerbockers tend to marry among themselves, but this father won't be too particular. He needs a son-in-law whose pride won't allow his wife's father to fail. A safety net, in other words."

"What does this have to do with me and the dead woman in my workroom?"

"In order to attract a worthy husband, a young lady of the Four Hundred must be impeccably dressed throughout the winter season in the city and the summer season in Newport. Agreed?"

Régine nodded.

"And that, my dear, is where you come in. My Schermerhorn-related client can't possibly pay for the type of wardrobe his daughter needs for successful husband hunting. Not to mention elevate her sadly ordinary looks. She'll never be a beauty, but stunningly designed gowns could transform our ugly duckling into a fairly decent facsimile of the proverbial swan. Suppose the Schermerhorn daughter wears your creations and thereby attracts the attention her father so desperately wants. Even when not asked, she never fails to sing the praises of the wonderful Madame Régine, newly arrived from Paris to transform New York society women at a fraction of the cost of a visit to the House of Worth. A large fraction, to be sure, because the Four Hundred mistakenly believe money equals quality. Your reputation is saved, your business is launched, and little Miss Plain and Simple may find herself a spouse. What do you think?"

"Genius." Régine raised her glass in a toast. "Sheer genius!"

"It's who you know," Madame Jolene said. "The Schermerhorn cousin can't be allowed to outshine the bride at Prudence MacKenzie's wedding, but she can come very close to it. The Four Hundred will all be there, everyone who's in town. And for the weeks immediately preceding the wedding there will be luncheons, teas, dinner parties. A ready-made audience as hungry for something different as the women who crowd the Paris salons when the new lines are introduced every season. Time isn't on your side. Can you do it?"

"How do I make the contact?" Régine put down her port.

"You don't. I'll set it up tonight through the father. He's not good with money, but he's not stupid, either. He'll have his daughter at your salon tomorrow. I guarantee it." Madame Jolene paused. "One other thing. You'll have to front expenses yourself for a while. If we can reach an agreement, I'd consider the salon a good investment. I believe in talent as much as I do real estate."

Seamstresses were paid only if they worked. But if Régine offered substantially more than their daily wage, her most expert needlewomen would sew until they dropped from exhaustion. It was worth the gamble Madame Jolene's money would make possible.

Régine stripped the glove off her right hand, spit in the palm, and held it out.

"I haven't clinched a deal this way in years," Madame Jolene said as she met Régine's hand with her own moistened palm.

In the world these women had come from, it was as good as any written contract a lawyer could draw up.

"Tiffany is sending us one of their retired goldsmiths." Prudence handed Geoffrey the note she'd just read.

"I'm supposed to meet Amos Lang at a bar near the Leavitt house." Geoffrey reached for his cane and hat, slipping an envelope into a jacket pocket. "Cash," he explained. "An advance on what he thinks he'll have to spend buying drinks for men who may or may not have information about the man who walked with Brenda in the park. If that's what happened."

"Not to worry. Josiah and I will deal with the goldsmith. Is there anything in particular you wanted to ask him?"

"I drew up a list of questions," Josiah said. They were handwritten as the secretary rarely used the Remington typewriter he'd removed from his desk and set on a small table in the corner. He was not one for modern innovations.

Geoffrey scanned the paper, turned it sideways, and scribbled a few words in the margin.

Josiah winced.

"Was this pattern of links ever made in America? That's the only additional bit of information we might need." Cane in one hand, hat in the other, Geoffrey paused for a moment in the open doorway. "I'm briefing Danny Dennis on the case. He'll spread the word among the rest of the hansom cab drivers, especially the ones who work the neighborhoods around where the Leavitt house is located. If Amos can come up with a description of the man we're looking for, one of them might remember picking him up."

Danny Dennis, Irish to the core, was the acknowledged kingpin among New York City's hansom cab drivers. He wore a green feather in his hat, rode with a beautiful red-gold dog ensconced in the driver's seat beside him, and was on permanent retainer by Hunter and MacKenzie, Investigative Law. He'd named the huge white horse that pulled the cab Mr. Washington—for the animal's spectacular yellowed teeth. Danny had left his real name and the details of his life behind when he'd fled Ireland after surviving a stretch in Kilmainham Gaol. Like Josiah, he admired and respected Geoffrey Hunter and considered Prudence among the loveliest of womenfolk needing his protection.

"Have you made tea?" Prudence asked after Geoffrey had left.

"The water in the kettle is hot," Josiah said. "The goldsmith might prefer coffee." Most men did.

"We can question him in the conference room. I think my office might be a bit crowded for the three of us." Neither Prudence nor Josiah considered for a moment that she might interrogate the retired Tiffany jeweler on her own. Women didn't meet with men who were not family members without the presence of a third party to protect their reputation. Though she broke the strict rules of socially acceptable behavior whenever necessary—and relished doing so—it wasn't in Prudence's character to flout them without a good reason. She was a proud attorney at the bar and a skilled private inquiry agent, but both her parents had been of pure Knickerbocker stock. Which doomed her to a life of respectability and decorum.

Herbert Bennett would indeed have preferred coffee, but he resolutely turned down the offer of a hot drink. His hands shook, sometimes with a mild tremor, sometimes with an uncontrollable twitching that made it impossible to hold on to anything. A cup and saucer would have been out of the question. He'd stayed on at Tiffany until he could no longer conceal the palsy. They'd given him a gold watch and a modest pension. Whenever the trembling allowed, he fashioned gold jewelry of such delicacy that his private consignment pieces were sold almost as soon as Tiffany placed them in one of its display counters. He enjoyed the extra bit of cash, but nothing could compare with seeing one of his creations exhibited among other masterpieces of the goldsmith's art.

Prudence laid the gold chain on the velvet drawstring bag in which Herbert Bennett had brought it back to her. She and Josiah sat on one side of the long conference room table, their visitor on the other.

"Curb and bobble links. You don't see that very often, especially nowadays. Victorian, of course, but I'm sure Tiffany has given you all the particulars. Twenty-two carat gold. Tiny scratches here and there. It's a piece that was frequently worn. You can always tell when something has sat unused in a jewelry case. I always think that's such a shame." Bennett's hands might betray him, but his old man's voice was firm and knowledgeable.

"We were hoping you might be able to tell us something about who might have owned it," Prudence said.

"Not the name, if I ever knew it. My memory's not that good. But I do recall a gentleman bringing this chain, or one exactly like it, into the store for a very small repair. One of the bobble links had opened up just a fraction and he was afraid the chain might break apart. I was called from the workroom into the salon—highly unusual, I might add—and was able to confirm that we could effect the reclosure of the link while the gentleman waited. It's not something we ordinarily do, but he said that he and his family were leaving their hotel early in the morning and would not be returning in the near future. So we accommodated him."

"When was this? Do you remember the date?"

"1853? 1854 perhaps? Definitely not too many years before the war. The gentleman didn't say where he and his family were going, other than that they were to board a packet for the journey. I think he said packet. It might have been frigate. I've never been on a sailing ship, myself."

"May I ask what made you remember this client? Apart from being called from the workroom to examine the chain?" Prudence repressed a sigh. She'd been hoping for much more.

"The workmanship of the chain was so fine that I made a quick sketch of the design after I'd done the repair. I'm proud to say that drawing was used to create a Tiffany version of what the client had brought us. Very popular over the years, especially as a watch chain for gentlemen."

"Nothing else?"

"He was a man of means, of course. Exquisite broadcloth coat and beaver high hat. He sported a signet ring on the little finger of his right hand. I always notice whatever jewelry someone is wearing. Gold, with a raised gold crest. A family heirloom, perhaps. Dark beard and eyes. Now that I think about it, he was almost as dark as an Italian. Black hair. Black eyes. Taller than average. Very wide shoulders for a gentleman."

Prudence thought the description could fit any number of men. "Did he name the hotel where he and his family were staying?"

"The Astor House." Herbert Bennett's hands had ceased to quiver as he reached deeper into his memory for details of the client who might have owned the chain he stroked with steady, admiring fingers. "I don't know how we came by that piece of information, but I do remember thinking, after he'd left, that of course such a distinguished gentleman would stay at the Astor House. At that time, it was by far the most luxurious hotel in the city."

"We greatly appreciate your help," Prudence said. A short silence had fallen. She had no more questions to ask, and it seemed as though the goldsmith had nothing to add to what he'd already told them. "I'd like to offer you a cab to wherever you need to go."

"That's kind of you, Miss MacKenzie, but I think I'll walk a bit. It's a beautiful day and I've a mind to stop by the graveyard of Trinity Church and pay my respects to someone. Nobody recent, of course. Alexander Hamilton. He was a man who appreciated the value and beauty of gold." Bennett chuckled at his little joke.

Josiah reclaimed the chain, handing it to Prudence. Neither of them had done more than smile at the reference to one of the most famous men ever killed in a duel.

"I almost forgot," Herbert Bennett said. "One more thing. The man who brought his or his wife's gold chain to Tiffany all those years ago had a very pronounced Southern accent. I couldn't name the state, but he was very definitely not a Northern gentleman. I don't know if that's significant, but it's really the reason I remembered him so well. Especially after the war. I always wondered what became of that gentleman. Whether he owned slaves. Lived on a plantation. Died on the battlefield. I suppose we'll never know."

"It's not likely," Josiah said.

Prudence said nothing. She smiled a vague goodbye as Josiah walked the old goldsmith through the outer office. The door to the hallway opened and closed. She heard Josiah take a few steps toward the room she hadn't left, then change his mind and settle in at his desk. Papers rustled. The lid of his inkpot clicked open. The wall clock in Geoffrey's office bonged the hour.

Prudence sat at the conference table, staring at nothing, curb and bobble link chain dangling from her fingers.

Chapter 6

Absent any description of the man who walked with Brenda Leavitt in the park—according to the sister who never actually saw them together—Amos Lang retreated into the busy cavern of his imagination and past experiences to conjure up an image from which to work.

Brenda was a talented seamstress, which meant she would have an eye for the way someone dressed. He pictured Geoffrey Hunter's bespoke suits, gloves, meticulously brushed hats, polished boots, and the ever-present sword cane. It was a starting place, but Brenda was a working woman. Her park beau was unlikely to be a gentleman of Hunter's social standing and financial resources. Nor, on the other end of the scale, was he in all probability a laborer who dressed in the rough clothing of the construction or dockyard trades. Somewhere in between, Amos thought.

He added a celluloid collar and cuffs to the presumed ready-made pants, jacket, and broadcloth shirt that could be bought for around ten dollars at any of the men's clothiers that catered to clerks, accountants, and bank tellers. They were respectable but low-paying professions in which a man could spend his entire working life without ever earning more than just enough to get by. Slowly, but very possibly accurately, the man he believed might have broken Brenda Leavitt's vulnerable heart began to take shape.

Low-ranking clerks and accountants were clean-shaven, often of pallid complexion, and almost never as tanned or athletic as the wealthy yacht owners in whose offices they spent their days. Medium height, medium build. Drinkers of beer by the pint and cheap whiskey by the shot, though not the rotgut of the piers and Five Points. He would know how to speak well when he had to and tip his hat as a lady neared. He probably possessed all of his visible teeth and smelled of one of the cheaper brands of pomade or macassar oil. The lingering odor of a cigar? No. Too expensive. Spectacles perhaps. Either because he needed them or because a man wearing eyeglasses always seemed more trustworthy and less dangerous than one with good vision.

"I've got a rough idea of what he might look like," Amos told Geoffrey Hunter. "And I'm beginning to think he could be a professional. Possibly an inquiry agent or an ex-Pink. One of us, in other words. Hired by someone to find out what was going on in Madame Régine's salon. His friendship with Brenda and her subsequent death are too opportune and coincidental not to be related." He slipped a wallet containing the funds Geoffrey had brought him into an inside jacket pocket.

"Put yourself in his place. Walk in his shoes. See with his eyes. Think with his brain." Geoffrey spieled off the advice Allan Pinkerton had liked to give his operatives. "Have I forgotten anything?"

"I'll let you know as soon as I've found him," Amos said.

They'd arranged to meet at one of the entrances to the park where Brenda had walked with her mysterious admirer and where something happened within the past one or two weeks. The mysterious stranger either told her that whatever had blossomed between them was now over, or he hadn't shown up at all. That was as logical a supposition as Amos could come up with, and logic was always key to his investigations.

"It's small, for a public park," Geoffrey said as they strolled along one of the raked paths.

"Too hot today for anyone but dogs and children to be out," Amos commented. He could feel sweat prickling along his neck and beginning to dampen his shirt. "If you've seen enough, I'll double back to the Leavitt house. I want to get a feel for the street before I move on."

"Let me know if you learn anything." Geoffrey swung his cane at a dandelion that exploded into puffballs.

"It may take a while."

"Not quite three weeks. That's all the time we have before the wedding." He'd be a married man by mid-September, Geoffrey thought. The time couldn't pass quickly enough. Whenever he looked at Prudence he wondered if she was changing her mind, if the lure of independence would prove stronger than what he was able to offer. It was a haunting worry that he couldn't dispel.

Best keep busy.

Amos thought he'd probably spent half his investigative life hanging out under trees or lurking behind buildings—watching, waiting, spitting his chaw into the lidded tin box he was never without. If you smoked a cigarette, you pinched the butt between your fingers and rolled it back and forth until the bits of unburned tobacco dropped into the dirt where they could be ground to invisibility. The spit of a chaw was a little messier and easier to spot, so you learned to swallow as much of it as your stomach could stand and carried a leakproof container for the rest of it.

The Leavitt house was no different from the houses on either side of it, all of them attached one to the other, a narrow alleyway running behind the row for gardens and outhouses. He thought there was more than one boardinghouse on the block, and figured that the widows who ran them counted themselves lucky not to have been left with nothing but the clothes they stood up in. It was a working-class neighborhood, a couple of rungs up the social ladder from the tenements, hanging on to respectability by hard work and sheer determination.

Brenda Leavitt's mother had come out to sweep the front stoop, and then a second time with a market basket over her arm. Amos followed her to the corner, where small shops and produce wagons dotted the cross street. She'd bought potatoes, carrots, and onions. Stew, he decided, when she disappeared into a butcher shop whose fat-streaked display window was black with flies. Clouds of the buzzing insects swarmed the entrance every time the shop door opened. She was making stew for the boarders that night.

It was a Saturday, which for some workers meant just a half day's drudgery. He didn't know what was expected of seamstresses in a dressmaking salon, but whether they were paid by the hour, the day, or the piece, they'd only be at their tables or machines when there was work to do. So sometimes, perhaps on a day like today, Brenda must have had the afternoon off. Unpaid, of course. And rather than go back to the house with the dying sister, the stern-looking mother, and the upstairs boarders, she'd wandered down to the park. Sat on a bench and watched the pigeons. Envied the pretty girls strolling by arm in arm with good-looking young men.

She'd caught someone's eye. Or maybe he'd lain in wait for her, sitting patiently at the street window of a bar waiting for her to pass by. Amos walked both sides of several blocks, as he suspected the man he was looking for might have done. An experienced operative would have done it often enough to become a familiar figure in the neighborhood. Unnoticed after a while.

He didn't live in any of the several boardinghouses, Amos decided, committing to memory their details as he ambled by—

just in case he was wrong. Which seldom happened. A man who shadows a woman doesn't take chances if he wants to be successful. So he'd put a bit of distance between them until he was ready to make his move. The block the Leavitt house was on had a homey feel about it that must have been reassuring to Brenda when she ventured out alone to run errands for her mother. When she made those excursions into the park. When, later on, she hurried along its shady sidewalk to meet her beau at their prearranged special spot.

It was always at this point in a new case that Amos felt the tingle along his jawline that meant he was close to discovering that first clue, the initial confirmation that he'd picked up a genuine trace of the person he was being paid to find. After that, it was like arranging marbles in an alley for a game of ringtaw. You drew your circle, put down your clearies, polished your best shooter on your pants leg, and let fly. The ping of glass against glass was as exhilarating as stealing a mouthful from the whiskey barrels left unguarded on the dray while a delivery was being made to the corner saloon. Nothing in the world tasted as good or went as quickly to your head.

The trick was not to let the prey know you'd picked up his scent. The Ferret was as good at that as he was at managing his laudanum. He might make the mistake that finished him someday, but not for a while yet.

Even though it was more than a decade and a half later, living in faraway New York City in the late summer of 1891, Inez Rankin had never forgotten the July of her twentieth year. She could remember everything that happened, every word that had been spoken.

There was nothing special about the twenty-two-carat gold curb and bobble link chain except that it had been in the Rankin family for generations.

"Your great-grandfather bought it in London for his new bride," Clementine Rankin reminisced as she threaded an antique cameo onto the links and slipped the chain around her daughter's neck. She judged that Inez was old enough by several years to marry and begin reproducing the family line, although her children would bear the husband's name. Fortunately, she had three older brothers, all of them living. They had been too young to wear a Confederate uniform during the war.

"Is it certain Geoffrey is home from Harvard?" Inez asked, twirling slowly before the cheval glass in her mother's bedroom. She thought the curb and bobble link chain looked a little heavy above the lightweight summer dress she was wearing. Its pattern of pink roses on fine quality lighter pink lawn lent a glow to the pale skin she zealously guarded against a relentless North Carolina sun. The necklace was an heirloom; she was supposed to feel privileged to wear it.

"His mother sent a private note along with the invitation to dinner. His whole family wishes for the same outcome we do."

"Oh, Mother, I've wanted to marry him ever since we were children."

"Your father and I are very aware of that."

The two families, the Hunters and the Rankins, owned neighboring plantations, had supplied officers to the same regiment, and interbred their slaves for muscle and stamina until emancipation interfered with the way things had always been done. They were part of the burgeoning New South that would emerge in full glory as soon as the government in Washington, D.C., withdrew federal troops from the defeated states of the Confederacy. The war had been devastating for many, costly for all, but wealthy Southerners had always maintained financial interests in the North, even during the worst days of the conflict. They were biding their time, hoping that the upcoming election of 1876 would turn in their favor.

"Do you think he'll go back up north in September?" Inez played with the curls clustered around her face, tweaking them to frame her best features. High cheekbones, beautifully shaped lips, eyes bluer than the sky.

"He'll want to finish his degree, and right now Harvard is the best place to do that."

"Then law school. Three more years at least." Inez sighed.

"You'll be engaged," her mother said. It was almost as good as being married, especially if the ring was impressive and the two fathers drew up a contract that was both unbreakable and fair to both parties. A widow had to be protected from penury and a husband had to be assured that the children born to his wife were indeed his. Scandal always lurked just beneath the surface of their world. Gossip made life in the mosquito-ridden heat bearable, but no one wished impropriety for their own family.

"Do you really think he'll ask me?" Inez gasped. She'd had her maid lace her stays so tight it was an effort to take a deep breath.

"If not now, then the next time he comes home. It may depend on whatever conversations Geoffrey has with his father."

"Mr. Hunter has always liked me."

"He considers you as dear to him as his own daughters." The mothers had been planning this marriage since their children—born three months apart—had been placed in their cradles. Family bibles, with their detailed lists of births and deaths, kept close tallies of who married whom, ensuring that not too many close cousins were allowed to wed each other. It wasn't unheard of that neighbor should marry neighbor, rather a good thing when it meant plantations could be joined and fortunes substantially increased. There was no reason why Geoffrey Hunter and Inez Rankin should not become husband and wife.

Inez couldn't know that Geoffrey had already decided his future did not lie in the South.

Geoffrey waited until Amos Lang had disappeared from the park before leaving it himself. He'd told Prudence and Josiah that he was meeting the Ferret, but he'd purposely omitted naming the second person he planned to see.

Nathaniel Hunter was a distant cousin, so far along the convoluted family tree that Geoffrey wasn't sure exactly where to place him. Long before a nine-year-old Geoffrey was sent to Phillips Academy in Andover, Massachusetts, Nathaniel had earned his academic credentials in England, returning to the United States with the stellar reputation of an Oxford scholar. Which meant he had offers to join the faculties of multiple American colleges.

He chose the University of the City of New York for its location on Washington Square and reputation for academic innovation. He had decided that the South of his birth was a lovely place to visit, but not where he wanted to spend the rest of his life. Not surprisingly to anyone who met him, he taught literature. English literature, to be precise. He was also a fervent supporter of what had been christened The Lost Cause.

Within a year of the surrender at Appomattox Court House, the South had reimagined itself and recast its history. Confederates agreed that slavery had never been at the root of the conflict. It was something called states' rights, which certainly sounded loftier and more idealistic than forcibly taking away a human being's liberty because one of his ancestors had been born in equatorial Africa. Southern generals and their officer staffs became knights in shining armor, their wives and daughters delicate creatures to be gently nurtured and fiercely protected. The history of the Confederacy changed as memoirs and history books were rewritten. If you said something often enough, people eventually believed it.

When he chose, Nathaniel Hunter could resurrect so perfect a North Carolina accent that he sounded as though he'd never left his native state. He could also fool New Yorkers into believing he was English. If it hadn't been such an impossible way to earn a living—and an appallingly ignoble profession to boot—he would have chosen to be an actor. He never married, settling instead for a string of accommodating housekeepers who only left his employ when it became obvious they would never advance beyond the status of domestic servant.

"Congratulations are in order," he said when he'd settled Geoffrey into a comfortable armchair and placed a glass of whiskey in his hand. "You've done very well for yourself, my boy. It's not easy to catch a Knickerbocker these days."

Geoffrey frowned. He wouldn't contradict the elderly scholar with whom he hadn't spent any time in years—that wasn't done—but silence should warn the man off. Prudence—her lineage and fortune—was not a topic he was willing to discuss.

"To what do I owe the pleasure of this visit?" Nathaniel changed the subject. He'd gotten the point.

"I think you probably keep in closer touch with the state of things in North Carolina than I do," Geoffrey began. Southerners never came out and asked a direct question. They eased their way into it through rings of circumlocution.

"Politics, people, or economics?" Nathanial preferred the gossip of politics and people to the dry statistics of economics, but he prided himself on being well-versed in all three topics.

"People."

"One person in particular?" Nathaniel repressed a smile. He'd known more than one man about to assume the bonds of matrimony who inquired about the status of a past love. As if to reassure himself that she'd really and truly gotten away. Or that she was no longer available under any circumstances.

"A family, actually."

"You'd better come right out with it and give me a name." Nathaniel poured more whiskey and reached for his cigar case. When Geoffrey produced his own preferred brand of tobacco, Nathaniel trimmed and lit a dark flue-cured blend from Virginia, puffing clouds of fragrant smoke into the air. He'd had glass doors installed on all of his library shelves to protect the books from his favorite vice.

"Do you remember the Rankins? They owned a plantation to the east of ours."

"Still do. As far as I know. They came out of the war in a more precarious position than our family did, but they've more than made up for it. Each of the sons took over one of their outlying plantations. They all turned a profit within a year or two. Joined the Klan early on and worked their way up to leadership positions. They've coasted along without any trouble or opposition ever since."

The question Geoffrey needed to ask was one he could not quite bring himself to put into words. It revealed too much about the self he preferred to keep anyone from suspecting.

"That's not what you came looking to find out about, is it?" Nathaniel seldom forgot anything important. He ticked off the years before Geoffrey had quarreled with his father and disgraced the family by going off to join the Pinkertons. His leaving had been the talk of the county. Earlier than that. One of the summers when he'd come home from Harvard, his soft Southern accent ruined by harsh Yankee consonants and shortened vowels. Nathaniel had been in the habit of spending his Christmas breaks in the warmer climate of eastern North Carolina. It kept him in touch with everyone and everything that was going on, and the demands of his academic career meant that the visit could not be prolonged. He'd planned it that way from the start.

The bits and pieces fell into place slowly, but with the precision of a well-cut wooden jigsaw puzzle. Inez Rankin. He recalled an anticipated engagement that never happened. Inez's stay of several months with an aunt no one had ever heard anyone in the family mention. In Charleston, South Carolina. A later marriage that produced no children. The sudden death of Inez's Yankee husband. Fairly young, too. She'd never gone back home again. Stayed up North where she didn't have any kin.

There was no doubt in Nathaniel's mind that Geoffrey had sought him out for one reason only.

"Last I heard, Inez Rankin was widowed, well-off financially. Still living in the home she shared with her late husband. Henry Purcell was his name. No children. Pets, though. Rumor had it at one point that every time the late Mr. Purcell complained about one of her dogs, she bought another pup. No love lost there."

"Are your sources dependable?" Geoffrey's reputation as an inquiry agent and attorney who never missed an important detail of any case he was working was well deserved.

"I have meetings here sometimes. People like to get together and talk about what happened during the war and how we aim to fix what got broken. The movement has a name. The Lost Cause. I rather like the poetry of it." Nathaniel waited, but Geoffrey said nothing. "At any rate, one of the folks who came to a meeting knew the Rankins back home and has made a point of keeping up with Inez. As much as anyone can. That's how come I know she's still right here in New York City. To this day." Nathaniel's voice had taken on the cadence of his childhood. Bourbon and cigars often plunged him into the past.

Geoffrey set down the whiskey glass from which he'd taken only a modest sip and replaced his unlit cigar in its case. He nodded at the elderly gentleman lost in clouds of smoke and reminiscences, taking his time about saying his farewells, remembering how Southerners loved to stretch out a leave-taking. Then he showed himself to the door and stepped out into the fresh air and greenery of Washington Square Park.

He would have to tell Prudence what he'd learned.

He wasn't looking forward to the conversation, but he'd promised not to hide things from her.

Whatever the consequences, he couldn't go back on his word.

Chapter 7

Every bar and saloon in New York City had a distinct personality, though for convenience' sake you could group them by the trades of the men slouched against the counter or sprawled in scuffed captain's chairs around the tables. Sawdust on the floor, a mirror stretching the length of the bar itself, dartboards affixed to the walls, pool tables with hanging gas lights lurking in the darker depths of the long room. The smell of unwashed bodies, hard-boiled eggs, brined pickles, salted meats, sour beer, and unemptied spittoons smacked a customer in the face the moment he pushed open the door. For many a working man it was the scent of the end of a hard day, far preferable to the stench of diapers and cabbage that was likely to greet him in his overcrowded tenement room.

The clerks, accountants, and bank tellers among whom Amos Lang believed he'd find the man he was searching for frequented saloons that had a thicker layer of sawdust on the floor, relatively splinter-free wooden tables and chairs, whiskey that wasn't rotgut, and stronger beer on draft. The food they served was edible: slabs of beef and mountains of potatoes swimming in gravy, hog trotters nestled in a bowl of noodles and kraut, boiled corned beef from the barrels used as ship's ballast. Hearty portions that resembled the meals served in decent boardinghouses. It was a sad fact of life that many of the men who put on celluloid collars and cuffs every morning remained unmarried well into their thirties or forties. They couldn't afford a wife and the inevitable children that followed, not without slipping down an economic rung on the ladder they were struggling to climb.

The first and second saloons in which Amos Lang bought a beer for himself and a whiskey for the bartender brought him nothing but casual, uninformative conversation and the soothing, rhythmic click of pool cues and billiard balls. He'd deliberately begun his canvas of the neighborhood bars during that quiet time after lunch and before offices closed for the day. The countermen who poured whiskey and pulled beers were more likely to answer questions when there were few customers. As with most local bars, they knew by name all of the regulars who drank in their establishments and could recite the times they usually pushed through the pair of swinging doors. They knew how long the drinkers would stay, how many shots or pints they'd down, and whether they were likely to spend most of their weekly pay before that night was over.

Celluloid collar man, as Amos had begun to think of him, had probably hung around for as long as he was ingratiating himself with Brenda, then disappeared—abruptly and without explanation. Newcomers were rare beings, always noticed and cataloged. They didn't run up tabs. Paid by the drink for as long as the bartender made that the terms of service. Amos left a more than decent tip in each of the two saloons. To be remembered by in case he needed to come back.

The bartender in the third saloon downed the shot of whiskey Amos bought him and followed it with a beer chaser. A big man, he had the shoulders and heavy arms of an ex-boxer and a scarred and broken-nosed face to match.

"Used to work the docks for a while. Then I drifted into the ring until I couldn't dance around fast enough anymore to stay on my feet. Ended up here, my cousin's place. I double as a bouncer. Name's Bill."

He was obviously one of those Irishmen who loved to talk, for which Amos bought him a second whiskey, then asked the important question.

"I do remember that fellow. We don't get many newcomers. I've been wondering what happened to him."

"He left a girl in a bad way," Amos explained. "She won't give up his name, but the family wants to know, if you get my drift."

"I don't think I ever had a conversation with him that lasted more than a few minutes. He wasn't one to volunteer information about himself. Most of the men who come in here are friendly enough. A little more reserved than the boyos who drink down by the docks, but not standoffish. After a while they end up telling you their name and maybe where they work. Not this one you're looking for, though. You'd think words were gold coins the way he wouldn't part with them."

"Did he ever mention a young woman?"

"I'd remember that."

"And you didn't ever see him walking by, maybe toward the park, with a member of the fair sex on his arm?"

"Not once."

"When did he stop coming in?"

"A couple of weeks ago. Maybe a little less than that." Bill poured himself another whiskey and slipped a coin from the pile Amos had deposited on the counter. "Don't mind if I do." He smiled, revealing a mouth with missing and cracked teeth. "He's the only customer I had who showed up out of the blue, drank regularly, then went on his way without a word of explanation. Like maybe somebody was after him. Has to be the one you're looking for."

"You wouldn't happen to know if he lived around here?"

Bill shook his massive head, then slid a pint glass under one of the draft handles as a small man in a worn though well-brushed suit sidled up to the bar. "Here you go, Casey," the ex-boxer said, scraping a crown of foam off the brew and sliding the drink across the width of the counter.

"I couldn't stop from hearing what you were talking about." The man called Casey helped himself to some of the coins in front of Amos, his agile fingers so quick Amos couldn't tell how many he took. "I saw that fellow go into a boardinghouse once. Just happenstance. He was about a block ahead of me and I thought to catch up and have a friendly word, but he was walking too fast, and I didn't want to call out."

"Did you get the name or address of the boardinghouse?" Amos took a fifty-cent coin from his pocket and laid it beside the much-diminished pile of smaller coins. Anchored it with the spread-out fingers of one hand.

"I can take you there, mister, but it'll cost you."

"He's got a decent girl in the family way, Casey," Bill said. "This gentleman here is helping out the family."

The small man shrugged.

Amos handed him the half dollar.

"Your man's not as big as Bill. Not by a long shot. But he's taller than average. Got a decent beard on him, too. Brown hair, brown eyes. Ordinary looking. Clothes didn't look like he bought them secondhand." Casey set a quick pace, short legs eating up the pavement as he led Amos up one block and over two more.

"Name?" Amos asked.

"He never said. Never got chummy enough with any of us so's we'd ask."

"But you're sure he was around until a couple of weeks ago?"

"I don't remember when he first showed up, but yeah, he stayed around the neighborhood until a week or two back."

"You're sure you don't recall when it was you first saw him?"

"Bill could tell you that better than me. But maybe not. Somebody paid him to throw a couple of fights back in June and he got beat up pretty bad. Missed work right afterward. Nobody wants to see a boxer's messed-up face when he's drinking."

"How do you know he threw the fights? Maybe he just can't hold his own anymore."

"Word gets around. His cousin didn't fire him for not showing up. Flashed a roll of bills around. You get my drift?"

The more Amos learned about the man Brenda had believed was showing an interest in her, the more convinced he became that he was looking for a professional. The easiest and one of the best disguises in the world was a beard. Shave it off and you were unrecognizable. Clerks were usually clean-shaven, which made it all the more probable that his quarry had lied about what he did for a living. Especially if he'd told Brenda he worked in an office. Which always sounded safe. He wondered if the beard had made her uneasy at first, if she'd gotten used to it and assumed his employer didn't mind facial hair as long as a man did his job.

"That's it, right there," Casey said, stopping in front of a boardinghouse that boasted a handwritten ROOM TO LET sign in one of its front windows. He held out a hand, waited for Amos to put another fifty-cent coin in it, turned, and took off down the street.

It was too much to hope that the ROOM TO LET sign had anything to do with the man he was after, the bearded fellow who'd stopped going to his neighborhood bar as long ago as a couple of weeks. Landladies usually put a sign in the window as soon as a tenant gave notice or did a runner during the night, and professionals didn't hang around once a job was done.

The problem was that Amos didn't know what that job had been. Had Brenda been courted so she could be questioned about the fashions being designed in Madame Régine's workroom? Was it as simple as that? Spying on the competition? Or had murder always been what the killer had been hired for? Were there two crimes here, the one unrelated to the other?

Amos doubted you could be arrested for trying to find out how a competitor ran her dressmaking salon, but taking a life was definitely a hanging offense.

Staring at the ROOM TO LET sign, Amos reminded himself that it was always a mistake to start interpreting clues as soon as you gathered them. Bending what you learned to fit the hypothesis you'd come up with was the surest way to lose the real thread of a case. He pictured Josiah Gregory's neat office files, and mentally tucked what he'd found out about celluloid collar man into one of them, careful not to let it taint the image of a dead woman lying beneath a shower of pieces of white silk. Gather the facts. Store them away until they began to make sense. Don't jump to conclusions. All valuable adages for an inquiry agent, but hard to follow when the trail seemed to be warming up.

"I let my rooms by the week or the month," the landlady said, barring the front door with a broom in one hand.

Amos knew she was deciding whether the man on her stoop was trustworthy enough to allow in. He smiled his most inoffensive grin and tipped his hat respectfully. "Could be a month. Maybe not. Maybe longer. I just don't know."

"Pay by the week. Miss one payment and you're out. I don't extend credit to anybody." The landlady's hands twitched at her apron.

"No, ma'am. I can see that you run a respectable house here."

"All right, then. You can follow me up the stairs. The room's in the front. Two windows looking out over the street. Linens are extra. Laundry not included. Breakfast and dinner served on time. Miss a meal and you go hungry. No boarders allowed in my kitchen."

The stairs were newly swept, and when Amos ran a forefinger along the banister, it came off dust-free. This would be a well-run house, the kind where you knew the landlady poked through your drawers when you were out and clocked your comings and goings with the exactitude of a prison guard. If this was indeed where Brenda's friend had rented a room, Amos couldn't have asked for a better informant. If she had a loose tongue. Which most women who ran boardinghouses did. For a price.

"I'd like to know who just moved out of this room," Amos asked as the landlady unlocked the door to the vacant second-floor bedroom and beckoned him through.

"I don't believe I'll answer that question," she said. "He hasn't caused any trouble and cleans up after himself." She cocked her head to one side. "He paid for the room in advance. Two more days left to go, but he hasn't been using it regular, so I wasn't sure he was gonna stay. I figured I'd put the sign in the window. That's all I'm saying unless you're a policeman. And in that case, I'd have to see a badge."

He handed her a folded one-dollar bill.

"What's he done?" she asked. The money disappeared into her apron pocket.

"Walked out on a young lady who got left in a bad way." When you were making up a story it was always best not to vary it too much.

"You family?"

"I'm helping them out."

"He said his name was Walter Duncan." She shook her head. "Maybe. Maybe not."

"Did he tell you where he worked?"

"Claimed to be between jobs. But he wasn't short of funds, I can tell you that. He'd go out in the morning like he was looking for work, but I never heard tell of where he went. I saw him in the park once in a while, late in the afternoon and a couple of times on a Sunday."

"Was he with someone?"

"Respectable young woman. Lives a couple of blocks from here with her mother and a sister who's got the consumption.

The mother's a widow. Like me. Started taking in boarders after her husband died."

"Do you know the young woman's name?" Another bill changed hands.

"Leavitt's the family name. I only know that from reading the obituary when the mister passed. Everybody around here works too hard to be sticking their noses in somebody else's business."

He didn't tell her that the respectable young woman was dead now, too. She'd find out soon enough. "I'll need a description of the man calling himself Walter Duncan. That's not the name I was given to track down."

Brown hair, brown eyes. Beard. Decent off-the-rack suit. Celluloid collar and cuffs. The details matched what Casey had told him.

"What about his boots?" Sometimes a careless inquiry agent didn't bother changing his footwear to match the rest of a disguise.

"Now that's interesting. I might not have thought of it if you hadn't brought it up. He had him a pair of boots that cost a lot more than the suit he always wore. I've polished many a shoe in my day. Cheap leather has a nasty, stiff feel to it. Cracks a lot, too. Mr. Duncan—or whatever his name is—never bought those boots from any shop around here."

"Did he ever get any mail?"

"Not a thing. Most of my boarders will get a letter from family after they've been here a while, but this fellow didn't stay long enough for that. And if he was running away from a situation, like you said, he wouldn't want it known where he was. Would he?"

"When was the last time you saw him?"

"I heard the front door open and shut last night, leastways I thought I did. But he didn't come down for breakfast, and when I checked the room, the bed didn't look slept in. It's been four or five days since I saw your Mr. Duncan in person. I got the notion he was traveling, like maybe he'd gotten himself a job selling from town to town, and that's why he wouldn't show up every night. Like maybe this was a place to come back to if you get what I mean."

"Has he left anything behind?"

"I did up the room first thing this morning, like I said. If he'd left anything, I would have found it."

"And when did you say you put the ROOM TO LET sign in the window?"

"I didn't say, but it was just a while ago, as soon as I figured he might not be coming back."

"If he shows up or you think of anything else you can tell me about him, here's where you can reach me." Amos handed her one of the Hunter and MacKenzie business cards as the landlady shooed him out of the room he wasn't going to rent and led him downstairs.

"One of them Pinkerton men?" she asked. The card joined the bills in her apron pocket.

"Private inquiry agent but not a Pink." Not anymore.

When he looked back at the house from the street, she was standing at a parlor window, watching him through a starched white lace curtain.

CHAPTER 8

Katja De Haan had known from the time she was a very little girl that she was neither pretty nor talented. Everyone told her so.

Her mother had pined away and died from the mortification of bearing so unadmirable a child. Her father sighed every time he laid eyes on her. He grimaced whenever she entered the parlor where he sat reading the newspaper, smoking his pipe, and nursing his drink of the moment. It was an exhalation that breathed dismay and defeat.

Without a decent fortune, there would be no second wife for Leopold De Haan, and without a wife there would be no more children. He dined on a precariously distant cousinly relationship to Caroline Astor, but cash money seldom filled his pockets. The only bright spot in an increasingly drab life was that he was allowed to run up charges at Madame Jolene's brothel; ladies of the night were the only females who would tolerate him. He never questioned the largesse; he assumed it was because of Lina Astor's queenship of New York City society and accepted that one day he'd be asked to approach her for a favor. What that would be, he couldn't imagine, but some people liked to store up sources of influence the way others deposited money in banks.

So, when Madame Jolene approached him with a scheme to launch Katja into the social whirl and marriage market of the Four Hundred, he was set to comply. He hadn't had the wherewithal to buy his daughter a debutante season and he'd been too proud to go begging among the Schermerhorn relatives. He wasn't sure any of them would part with the needed sum and couldn't face the specter of repeated refusals. Katja had stayed home practicing her needlework and pounding on their out-of-tune piano while other girls of her age and family background displayed their marriageable selves at balls, dinners, the opera, and interminably boring but obligatory afternoon teas.

Madame Jolene's proposal was simple. Katja would be outfitted with the season's most fashionable wardrobe money could buy. All of it created in the salon of a new and exciting Parisian designer who had recently graced the city with her presence. It wouldn't cost Leopold a single dime of the money he didn't have. Madame Régine's services would be provided free of charge. Any expenses the designer couldn't afford to cover would be paid by Madame Jolene. Yes, the designer was a woman. And no, despite having a French-sounding name, she was actually American.

Which is where the Knickerbocker connection came in. Madame Régine needed someone of impeccable background to model her handiwork in all the right places. Someone who could drop her name into the most important ladies' conversations. An unfortunate incident had muddied Madame Régine's modest reputation; she was in need of whitewashing.

What was in it for Leopold De Haan? All he or his daughter had was their name. But with the Knickerbocker family luster and Madame Régine's magnificent dresses, Katja De Haan could catch more than one well-to-do young gentleman's eye. New money was hungry for the prestige of old blood. Yes, it was a bit like selling Katja to the highest bidder, but wasn't that what marriage was all about in their circle? The hidden gem at the center of the plan was the assurance that the well-to-do young gentleman who won Katja's hand would certainly never allow his father-in-law the embarrassment of frayed cuffs or clothes purchased off a rack. A generous allowance could be written into the marriage contract.

Leopold De Haan considered the proposition. For as long as it took to relight his pipe and send clouds of satisfied smoke billowing over his head. He agreed. No one bothered to consult Katja.

"We'll start with four or five day dresses," Madame Régine decided, circling a nearly naked Katja De Haan who was perched on a raised platform like a statue in Central Park.

Bloomers, a chemise, corset, and petticoat couldn't conceal the naturally voluptuous and well-sculpted body that indifferently constructed clothing had hidden. Katja, once outfitted in garments made specifically to highlight the finer points of her figure, would certainly attract the kind of attention that encouraged courtship. Shed of dreary brown, washed-out gray, and colors that were so drab as to be indistinguishable one from the other, she would glow like a newly lit candle. She had naturally blond hair, bright blue eyes, and the creamy skin of a Dutch milkmaid. None of it artificially enhanced in any way.

Her father had explained that a sudden windfall had come his way due to the untimely death of a cousin whose name he failed to provide. He had decided to lavish it all on his beloved daughter. She had the sense not to question him.

"Blue silk to bring out the color of your eyes, I think, and pale rose, daffodil yellow, and buttermilk tones to flatter your hair and skin," Madame Régine decided. A lady's maid skilled in the arrangement of hair would take up residence at the De Haan home. Paid for by Madame Jolene, who had personally retired the young woman from the brothel's main business. She hadn't the personality of a lady of the evening, but she was a genius when it came to arranging curls and creating hairstyles that defied gravity. She was already sketching out coiffures that ranged from simple to elaborate, all of which would flatter the shape of Katja's face and draw attention from her regrettably large nose and prominent chin. The superbly trained lady's maid could apply cosmetics so adroitly that no one suspected a face was painted.

It was the first time in Katja De Haan's life that anyone had fussed over her. A bevy of someones clucking their tongues, voicing suggestions, touching, pinching, smoothing, rearranging her into a person she had never dared dream of becoming.

"When will the first dress be ready?" Katja asked. She hadn't had the courage to suggest changes to what Madame Régine envisaged. Why bother, when nothing she could propose would come anywhere near the designer's level of perfection?

"We'll deliver the first box tomorrow," the head seamstress declared, as heads bobbed agreement around her. They'd work all night if necessary. Everyone could use the extra money, and there was something challenging and exciting about turning a frump into a beautifully plumaged swan.

Katja knew how to walk and sit with feet demurely crossed. She could supervise the laying of a formal dinner service and understood exactly where at table to place a bishop, a banker, a foreign dignitary. She'd been trained in the art of conversation, saying absolutely nothing in genteel vocabulary and beautifully formed sentences. She could ride sidesaddle, sketch and paint watercolors, decorate china plates, read uplifting books and listen to musicales without yawning, dance complex figures without a single mistake, and move food around on her plate instead of eating it. Had her father not had a gambling problem, had she not been plain-featured verging on unattractive, had her mother lived and grown to love and cherish her—Katja would have led a different life.

As it was, she was happy to be someone's pawn. At least it meant she was in the game.

* * *

"Miss Prudence is in the conference room." Josiah didn't wait for Geoffrey Hunter to ask where his partner was. "She's been sitting at the table with that chain in her hand since the Tiffany goldsmith left. Hasn't said a word. Shook her head when I offered to brew a cup of tea. Staring into space like she's lost in a bad memory. Something's wrong, but I don't know what. I've never seen her like this."

"Put a few extra pieces of coal on the fire in my office," Geoffrey instructed. "Then you can leave for the day."

He waited outside the closed conference room door, saying nothing more as Josiah tended the inner office fire and returned to his desk. Straightened the papers he'd file in the morning. Settled his hat on his head, picked up his gloves. Ran out of things to do to delay his leaving.

"I'll see to her," Geoffrey said in a quiet, assured voice.

Josiah nodded. Dawdled in the hallway listening for the click of the conference room door opening. Heard the key turn in the lock of the outer door.

Gave up and started home to his empty apartment.

Geoffrey knocked gently on the conference room door before turning the knob and opening it.

Josiah hadn't exaggerated. Prudence sat motionless, the curb and bobble link chain twined through the fingers of one hand. The soft gray eyes she turned in his direction were blank and unfocused, as though she were still caught in a vision she had found impossible to escape.

"Prudence?"

She didn't answer.

"I had Josiah build up the fire in my office." Geoffrey slipped an arm around her shoulders, brought her to her feet. The chain fell almost noiselessly to the table. He picked it up, dropped the gold links into the pocket that held his watch fob. Enfolded Prudence's hands in his. They were cold. "We need to warm you up." He stopped himself from calling her by one of the endearments that always brought a smile to her lips. He sensed that now was not the time.

She allowed him to lead her through the outer office and into the private domain that had once belonged to a former U.S. senator. In the three years since Hunter and MacKenzie, Investigative Law, had opened for business, Geoffrey had gradually transformed the space. The new furniture was expensive and comfortable, the wall hangings a mixture of framed credentials and landscapes belonging to what was called the Hudson River School. Dark green velvet drapes allowed for dimmed daylight or a view of the steeple of Trinity Church. The scent of Virginia pipe tobacco and Cuban cigars mingled with a faint whisper of men's sandalwood cologne. Geoffrey's workspace invited clients to place their trust in his experienced, ex-Pinkerton hands.

He seated Prudence in an upholstered client chair close to the fire, stirred the coals and burning logs with a polished brass fire poker, drew his own chair close and sat where Prudence could not avoid looking at him and he could hold both her hands in his as he talked. It was a long and painful story he had to tell. One that reached back into his past. One he had hoped never to have to think of again.

"The necklace we found in your dress cupboard at Madame Régine's salon once belonged to a young woman named Inez Rankin," he began. He took the chain from his vest pocket and laid it on the arm of the chair in which he was sitting. "There's probably no way to prove it's really the one she wore, because there isn't a maker's mark on the clasp, but if it didn't belong to her family, it's an exact duplicate." He waited, mutely urging her to fight through the stony melancholy that had clearly frightened Josiah.

When she spoke, Prudence's voice was studiously devoid of emotion, her words carefully chosen. It was as though she were reciting a narrative that had nothing to do with what he had begun to tell her.

"The Tiffany goldsmith who came here earlier today told us he made a sketch of the curb and bobble links chain. The Tiffany workrooms created and sold copies of it. Herbert Bennett is his name. Apparently, it was a popular piece for a number of years. There are probably dozens of them in existence."

Geoffrey had no doubt that there was only one chain that was of any consequence.

"Nevertheless, no matter how many examples of the Rankin family chain there are, I still need to tell you about Inez. She was a part of my life before I came north to stay. I had thought never to pronounce her name again and never to have to tell our story, but what happened in Madame Régine's workroom has changed that. A seamstress was brutally and callously murdered, and your wedding dress was viciously shredded. The chain was left in a place where we were bound to find it, like a calling card on a silver tray. I would be a fool not to suspect a connection." He paused. "Whatever else I am now or used to be, I've never been a fool."

"Tell me," she whispered. The gray eyes fastened on his nearly black pupils, a steady gaze that asked only to be told the truth.

"Inez and I grew up together on neighboring plantations, so we'd known each other since we were in leading strings. The way things were in those days, both sets of parents expected us to marry. We may have assumed the same thing, without ever giving the subject much thought. It was the way southern society was structured. Young men married their friends' sisters. Cousins married second or third cousins. Reciting family lineage was an absorbing pastime much beloved by our mothers. The South was a close and closed society."

"Not so different from the North," Prudence said. "Descendants of the original Dutch settlers—for generations—frowned on marrying anyone who wasn't one of them." Her hands were warming up, and her lips no longer felt stiff.

"It was the custom for those of us who went north to school

to come home for the holidays and term recesses. My first year at Harvard was also the last full summer I spent at my family's plantation in North Carolina. I fished and hunted with my father, brothers, and friends. Early in the morning, before the heat overwhelmed us. July and August are so hot and humid that no one not born in the South can long tolerate it. We spent the afternoons in the shade of our porches or under the ceiling fans indoors. Nights were for dinners and dances. Courting in well-chaperoned homes and halls. You have to understand that despite the war, despite the loss that was devastating to so many of us, despite Reconstruction—which was about to end—it often seemed that very little had changed.

"Inez was twenty that summer. So was I. I remember the chain because she wore it to a dinner my parents gave shortly before I took the train north again. One of the ladies at the table commented on the unusual design and the cameo that hung from it. Mrs. Rankin—Inez's mother—told the story of how it came to be a family heirloom, passed from one eldest daughter to the next. Sometimes so little happens in rural communities in the South that even as inconsequential a subject as a woman's necklace can become a topic of lively conversation. That's what happened that night.

"What Inez expected, although I don't think I realized it at the time, was that I would propose marriage, and we would become engaged before I left. What she didn't know, what no one in my family suspected, was that I'd already made up my mind that I wouldn't live the life they expected me to lead. My father, certainly, firmly believed I would devote myself to one or more of the plantations we owned. There were also businesses in which he had a partnership, investments here and abroad. The Hunter fortunes had been amassed over time; they were as secure as the Bank of England." He was meandering, his thoughts flitting into the hot, dark nights of his youthful past.

"So you didn't ask Inez to marry you?" Prudence's fingers trembled. The Tiffany diamond weighed down her left hand.

"I did not." Geoffrey smiled. It was a relief to pronounce Inez's name and know that he was as indifferent to her memory as he was to any of the women he'd encountered after he met and fell in love with Prudence. "I saw her once more, the following spring. She wrote me a desperate letter, begging me to come south when Harvard broke for Easter. I hadn't intended to go home, but the letter forced my hand. I'd already decided I wouldn't spend the summer in North Carolina but I'd yet to inform my father of my decision. So I had two good reasons to board a train that April—Inez's frantic plea and the confrontation with my father that I knew I couldn't avoid."

He let Prudence's hands drop into her lap while he stirred the coals in the fireplace, searching for the right words to say what had to be revealed. There weren't any.

"Inez was pregnant. The man who'd gotten her in the family way refused to take responsibility and had already sailed for a grand tour of Europe. She wanted me to marry her. She said I owed her that much, that I'd broken her heart when I didn't ask for her hand the previous summer, and so I was somehow guilty of landing her in the impossible predicament in which she found herself."

"You owed her marriage?"

"That's what she claimed. She screamed it, raged at me that I was a cad and a dishonorable seducer to boot. She accused me of misleading her through false pretenses of affection. She promised she would accuse me of raping her if I didn't give in to her demands. She threatened suicide when I reminded her that I'd been hundreds of miles away for the past half year and more. I left the next morning, well before dawn, after a long and bitter argument with my father that ended with his threatening to disown and disinherit me if I didn't come to my senses. I never saw Inez again. But I learned that she had gone to visit an aunt in Charleston, South Carolina, and then later married a Yankee and left North Carolina. Her family never mentions her name."

"I wonder what became of her. Poor young woman." Prudence's face, which had felt stiff and as though the skin were about to crack open, regained some of its softness. A hint of color crept back into her cheeks. Why was it the woman or girl who always suffered and never the man who'd seduced her and made promises he never intended to keep?

"I met today with a distant cousin who teaches at the university in Washington Square," Geoffrey said. One more piece of information he had to reveal to the woman he hoped would still marry him. The most difficult disclosure of all. "Inez has lived in New York City since she married her Yankee husband. She's a widow now. Has been for a number of years."

"Here? Inez is here?"

"That's what I was told."

"You're sure?"

"There's no reason to doubt my source."

Prudence said nothing for as long as it took the one small heap of coal to fall apart and send a burst of sparks up the chimney. Then she reached for Geoffrey's hands, entwining her fingers with his, smiling as though the most difficult story she'd ever had to hear had been no more consequential than a discussion of the weather.

"Then we'll have to find her, won't we?" Her eyes twinkled with the brightness of the Tiffany diamond she wore. "But I don't think we're obliged to invite her to the wedding."

CHAPTER 9

A note was delivered to Nathaniel Hunter's Washington Square townhome shortly after Geoffrey Hunter had left.

The writer of the note sat at her large parlor window more afternoons than not, a small dog lying curled in her lap. She was a great one for clocking her neighbors' comings and goings, though she seemed to believe that the men and women strolling the square for their daily constitutionals could not see through her imported Belgian lace curtains. She was wrong, of course. Everyone knew she passed the lonely hours of her widowhood as an observer of life rather than a participant.

In the early days, before her husband died, Inez had often entertained Nathaniel at tea, her voice rising into a soprano Southern belle register as she nibbled at crustless sandwiches and frosted cakes that sometimes left traces of pink-and-white icing on her lips. When she thought he wasn't looking, her tongue snaked out and guiltily licked them away.

She'd done her best to speak as the Four Hundred did, in the icy monotones that condemned everyone who wasn't one of them. But with Nathaniel, Inez fell into the soft melodic cadences with which southern women mesmerized the men they set out to ensnare. She'd been born and trained to be a flirt, but life had dealt her a hand she hadn't counted on and a name that morphed into a discordant and much-hated sobriquet. Nezzie. Even as a child, it made her shudder every time she heard it. When she learned that Caroline Astor was known as Lina to her intimate friends and family, Inez—Nezzie—began refusing to answer to anything but Ina. It sounded much more refined, less Southern. In the end, it did her little good. She never received one of the coveted invitations to Caroline Astor's annual January ball. She remained on the outside fringes of New York society. Looking in, but always and forever excluded.

It was both worse and better after she buried Henry. She was a wealthy widow, without the constant worry that her husband's mistress of the moment would succeed in engineering one of those shameful and financially destructive divorces that had begun to divide even the best families, but she toppled from her pedestal of married woman into the slough of widowhood. A dark and gloomy place where it was supposed she would be content to remain for the rest of her days. In mourning. For a man she had never loved. Hardly even liked.

The dogs were her only comfort. Swirling around her skirts, barking in high-pitched explosive yaps, messing on the rugs when she forgot to remind one of the maids to take them out to relieve themselves in the patch of grass at the rear of the house. Grown especially for that purpose. Toy spaniels like you saw in the portraits of the British King Charles II. The Merry Monarch, son and successor to the king who'd had his head cut off. Inez bought her first pair of spaniels because Henry hated dogs. Despised them. By the time he died, she had at least five of them in the house.

Somehow, she'd missed the occasional society column stories about Miss Prudence MacKenzie and her handsome ex-Pinkerton partner, who had quite scandalously opened a private inquiry agent partnership. There were days when the morning's newspaper lay strewn about on the floor in hopes of absorbing pee puddles before they soaked through into the expensive Turkish carpets. How appropriate to imagine spaniel urine watering Geoffrey Hunter's name.

She'd read the engagement announcement in the *Times* though. Ground her teeth and drunk her way through a nearly full bottle of fine Spanish sherry. Fallen asleep that night with tears on her cheeks. Geoffrey was supposed to have married her. The deceitful, cowardly, shifty, untrustworthy, false-hearted bastard. He'd deserted her when she most needed him, forced her into a painful and mortifying ordeal from which her mind and body never fully recovered. Not a detail of what she suffered forgotten or forgiven. In her mid-thirties, she had already been relegated to the trash heap of women misused, spurned, and left to fend for themselves.

She hadn't thought Geoffrey was physically close enough to feel her wrath. Had imagined him riding his family's acres on a high-stepping stallion or drifting from one European capital to another. Mostly she'd tried to erase him from her heart and her head the way he'd blotted her out of his life. She'd succeeded, until that awful day when the spaniels didn't need the *Times* and she'd had the bad—or the good—luck to read the society column.

She'd disposed of one man. With only happy consequences. All it would take to ruin another was a plan. And money. She was clever enough to come up with the former and had plenty of the latter. She had the patience to wait for the right moment. And the sense to recognize when it loomed on the horizon.

She knew what would bring him to Washington Square, and she didn't hesitate to make it happen.

It only took one day. She watched him stroll by her front door—so close she could have raised a window and called out to him. Tall, still the handsomest man she'd ever met. Elegant. Distinguished. Turning heads and earning admiring glances as he strode toward the far end of the Square where Nathaniel Hunter lived. This older Geoffrey was different in the flesh from the younger man. So much more desirable.

He appeared again an hour later, this time walking in the direction of Fifth Avenue. Moving faster, as if he'd learned something important and needed to act upon it. She half expected him to glance toward where she sat, but he didn't. He didn't appear to know she was there. Good. She wasn't ready for him yet. Soon. She'd know when.

Despite her best efforts, an all-consuming curiosity nearly sent Inez tearing bonnetless down her front steps to race along the sidewalk and pound on Nathaniel Hunter's door. She forced herself to walk calmly to her desk and pen the note that would bring the academic to her parlor for a late-afternoon tea. *It has been such a long time since we've spent a pleasant hour together.* She knew just how to word the invitation. The niceties of social interaction had been drilled into her from childhood.

She remembered that Nathaniel didn't care much for dogs. So while she waited for him, Inez shut the five of them into her bedroom. Upstairs. Where, from the parlor, the yapping couldn't be heard. She had questions to ask and she wanted answers.

Nathaniel Hunter had never married because women of his own social rank terrified him. They were not at all the same creatures as the maids, housekeepers, and shopgirls who were no kind of threat. Ladies—females of high social rank—had a steel edge to them that could cut as quickly and deeply as one of the ceremonial swords he hung on his walls. Something about the way they were instructed from birth in the razor-sharp niceties of polite social intercourse. He'd always wondered whether that allowed for physical abandon in another type of intimate contact. Couldn't imagine it. Had decided after his years at Oxford—and rather too close acquaintance with females of the British aristocracy—that he would not ruin his private life with the company of a wife. He often congratulated himself on the wisdom of the choice.

Now this complication with the former Inez Rankin. Widow of Henry Purcell, gentleman investor. Ina, as she had instructed her late husband and new Yankee acquaintances to call her.

How long had it been since Henry died? Nathaniel couldn't recall exactly, but he knew he'd jotted down copious notes about the accident when it happened. A circumstance so bizarre and unusual that he'd never heard the like.

He found a description of the incident in one of the journals he'd meticulously kept since childhood. Inez—Ina—could wait another half hour or so while he jogged his memory with the horrific details of poor Henry's unexpected demise. Here it was, on a page written shortly after he'd returned from comforting the widow. His hand had shaken so badly that tiny specks of ink had flown from his pen.

A black widow spider in his bed. More than one. Several, perhaps as many as half a dozen, judging by the number of bites on Henry's neck and face. The only reason the doctor who'd been called to his bedside offered that peculiar diagnosis as the cause of death was that two of the creatures—shiny black, long-legged, bearing the distinctive bright red hourglass on their abdomens—had been found on their victim. He must have felt something and reached out to swat whatever he thought was biting him. Too late.

The doctor explained that while a single black widow spider bite was unlikely to cause death to a grown man, multiple bites around the head and neck could certainly result in muscle spasms, difficulty breathing, chest pains, hallucinations, the inability to call out for help. How the creatures had found themselves in Henry Purcell's bed—he and his wife occupied separate bedrooms, as was appropriate—could only be hypothesized. Had there been some sort of deep cleaning recently that might have disturbed them in their attic webs? Could a sheet have been hung to dry in the attic on a rainy day and then been used to make up the master's bed? Without the maid noticing the infestation, of course.

The doctor who attended Henry spent his summers on a wooded estate north of the city. It wasn't a generally known fact, he informed the shocked and grieving Mrs. Purcell, but the venom of a black widow spider was many times more poisonous than that of a rattlesnake.

Every item of bedding and furniture in the dead man's bedroom was burned. The attic was cleaned out and swept so many times that not a speck of new or old dust remained. A cat was installed for a few months to ensure that no spiderlings had escaped notice. When it was removed to the basement kitchen, the cook reported a significant diminution in the rodent population. The cat eventually died of a surfeit of arsenic-laced mice.

Nathaniel had faithfully recorded all this and more. He wrote every evening by candlelight—for inspiration—and with a decent whiskey to speed the flow of words. He wasn't sure what he intended to do with his journals, only that he counted on living long enough, and with sufficient warning of impending death, to burn them eventually.

In the meantime, Inez was waiting for him. Nezzie, as she'd been known in childhood.

Ina. He mustn't forget to call her Ina.

"I insist on knowing what Geoffrey Hunter was doing in your house today," Inez began, having forgotten that she had intended to coax the story out of Nathaniel gradually and without his realizing what she was doing.

The tea service sat undisturbed on a low table. Inez had begun drinking sherry as soon as she'd caught her first glimpse of the man who had failed her. When Nathaniel seated himself in her parlor, she handed him a crystal glass and a decanter of whiskey. She knew he liked his drink as much as she did hers. It was a mutual secret never to be mentioned aloud.

"Well, first off, I outright lied to him," Nathaniel said, savoring the whiskey, probably a holdover from the late Henry Purcell's excellent cellar. "I told my dear cousin that an acquaintance from our ancestral neck of the woods kept up with your whereabouts and had informed me that you were widowed and living in New York City. I'm not sure what he would have done had I told him the truth. That we saw one another frequently and that we both lived on the Square. Not more than five or six minutes apart. Geoffrey was a boy and a young man of impulse. I suspect he hasn't changed much, despite the passage of years."

"Not that many years," Inez chided. She didn't like being bundled in with older widows and ancient grannies.

"I did think to ask why he'd suddenly decided to inquire about you."

"What did he say?"

"He avoided the issue, though not completely. Something about finding a necklace recently that reminded him of one you'd worn one of the last times he saw you. He seemed to feel he'd let you down somehow. I've rarely heard my cousin fumble for words, so this was unusual. It was only a matter of a few seconds, so I suppose he could hope I hadn't noticed his hesitancy. But anyone who teaches literature is also a historian by trade. The smallest details are often the stuff of the most important truths." He thought he detected frantic barking and scratching from somewhere on the floor above where they sat.

"Did he describe this necklace?"

Nathaniel shook his head. "Perhaps I should have made myself clearer. He barely mentioned it, and then immediately scrambled to change the subject. I didn't refer to it again. It's quite possible he'll manage to convince himself that he never spoke of the necklace at all. Difficult conversations are like that. Full of holes where we've deliberately leaked out what we don't want to remember. Don't you find that to be true?"

Nathaniel was thinking of the days immediately following Henry Purcell's death, when everyone except Inez was speculating on the oddity of black widow spiders in the man's bedding. She alone never brought it up, and she alone squashed guesswork and conjecture whenever someone else voiced the issue. From lack of nourishment, the gossip had died more quickly than might have been expected. He wondered if she ever thought about those spiders as she sat drinking her sherry night after night in a silence broken only by the yips and snuffling of the little dogs.

"He's to be married." Nathaniel decided that Inez by herself would never broach the topic.

"I read the engagement announcement in the *Times*."

"The wedding is to be held in Trinity Church."

"Naturally." Inez refreshed her glass of sherry.

"In about three weeks."

"I know the date. September sixteenth. It's a Wednesday."

"Will you go?" Nathaniel found he was holding his breath for her answer.

"I haven't received an invitation."

"I'm sure to be sent one in the next few days. Geoffrey can't pretend I don't exist. Invitations like that are generally extended to the invitee and one other person. *Mr. Nathaniel Hunter and guest.* You could come as my guest."

"Why would I want to do that?" The sherry she'd been about to swallow caught in Inez's throat. She coughed, set down her glass, and realized with a bit of a shock that she was as close to being tipsy—drunk—in the afternoon as she'd ever gotten.

"Just imagine the look on Geoffrey's face when he sees you there. Seated beside me in one of the front rows reserved for family." Nathaniel peered nearsightedly over his whiskey glass, wishing he could read her face a little more clearly.

Inez heard herself laugh in a most unattractive way. She stoppered the decanter of sherry and contented herself with draining the dregs of her glass. She prided herself on self-discipline, the mark of a true lady. Which she never doubted for a moment she was.

"That might be rather amusing," she agreed, trying to picture herself in one of her many black-feathered hats.

"And you could see the new bride in all the splendor of her wedding gown. You won't have to wait for a *Times* reporter to describe it in the next day's society column."

Inez scowled. Rang for a maid. "Go upstairs to my bedroom and let the dogs out," she instructed. "They've been cooped up long enough. Mr. Hunter is just leaving."

Nathaniel would have stayed longer—Inez was so easy to torment—but the thought of having his expensive gray trousers attacked by a pack of yelping spaniels was more than he could bear.

"I'll let you know when the invitation comes," he said, stooping to kiss Inez's flushed cheek. "You can make up your mind then."

He thought he caught a glimpse of something like tears in her eyes, but Nathaniel had never seen Inez cry. Not even when her husband died.

He decided he'd drink some of his own whiskey when he got home. Reread that interesting journal entry about the black widow spiders. Apply the principles of literary and historical research to the conundrum of how they'd come to bite poor Henry's flesh in precisely the most sensitive areas of his body. Hypothesize a bit, the way an academic allowed himself to do when he had a few facts—but not many—and huge holes in a documented narrative that begged to be filled with reasonable conjecture.

He wondered, if Geoffrey contacted him for help in locating Inez, whether he would lead him to her door.

Chapter 10

"I'll be at Madame Régine's to approve the final sketch of the new wedding gown."

Prudence had come into the office early on this Monday morning, curious to find out if Amos Lang had managed to get a fix on Brenda Leavitt's beau. She'd found the ex-Pink standing morosely in front of Josiah Gregory's desk, dictating the names of the saloons he'd visited and the sums he'd spent at each. Whenever possible, Amos avoided putting pen to paper. He'd once explained to Prudence that even the jotting down of notes could be incriminating. The spoken word evaporated as soon as it left a speaker's lips.

Josiah nodded, his pen flying over the account he was creating and would recopy into a meticulously kept ledger.

Amos appeared not to notice she was there.

Geoffrey hadn't appeared yet, which meant he was either pursuing a lead he wouldn't mention unless it panned out, or he'd given in to the lure of a leisurely breakfast in the Fifth Avenue Hotel dining room.

Monday was always a slow starter, as if Sunday's freedom

from scheduled work sapped normal energy and derailed ambition.

"Madame Régine may know when Brenda Leavitt's funeral will take place. I'll send word so we can put it on the calendar."

Josiah's pen didn't hesitate, but he gave a quick bob of the head that told Prudence he'd made a mental note not to plan anything in the next few days that couldn't be postponed.

No one at Hunter and MacKenzie had known Brenda when she was alive, and technically it was Madame Régine who was their client, but both Prudence and Geoffrey believed firmly in the adage that a murderer often appeared at the burial of his victim. To gloat? To glory in his accomplishment? Or simply because the seduction of the blood he'd spilled couldn't be denied? Nobody really knew. But it was a truism few experienced investigators questioned.

"I'm not sure whether Madame Régine has a telephone, but if she does, I'll get the number." Prudence paused, giving Geoffrey another few minutes to appear. He didn't.

Josiah again gave the cursory nod that indicated he'd made one more of the mental notes he never forgot.

Prudence left, closing the office door on Amos Lang's staccato recitation of his expenses.

Madame Régine's face looked tired and drawn, yet she was impeccably dressed and faultlessly coiffed. She hadn't finished the final sketch Prudence had come to look over until well past midnight, but a flicker of pride brightened her reddened eyes as she laid the work before her client. She was a relentless critic of her own creations, but this wedding dress was truly spectacular. A thrill of satisfaction coursed through her every time she looked at it.

"Pure white silk, of course," she explained. "And the pearls are those we matched to the material. But as you can see, I've altered the neckline from the original, increased the height of the ceintured waist, and slightly altered the flow of the skirt. Lace has been added as a background to the pearls and an overlay to the silk."

"It's beautiful," Prudence said, unable to take her eyes from the penciled creation she would be wearing in slightly more than two weeks' time. "I don't think I've ever seen anything quite so elegant. Every bride-to-be at Trinity Church will want to beat a path to your door."

"That's part of it." Madame Régine had decided on first meeting Prudence that she could never be anything but honest with her. "But I wanted—above all else—to make it up to you for what happened to the first gown."

"You're not to blame for that. No one could have predicted such wanton destruction. Or so savage a murder." There were moments, like this one, when Prudence had to remind herself of the nightmarish scene she had witnessed in this workroom only three days ago.

All trace of Brenda Leavitt's final moments had been erased. Unless one of the busy seamstresses looked up from her work and allowed her eyes to glaze over for a moment, it was as though the loss of life amidst blood and a flurry of ripped silk had never happened. It had to be that way, if those left behind were to pick up the threads of their existence and carry on with life.

No matter how deeply she felt loss—as she did every time she had to force herself to study the face and wounds of a victim of violence—Prudence knew she could not allow those emotions to surface. She was a professional inquiry agent and a member of the New York State Bar, though she'd attended no formal training for either profession. Geoffrey had been her instructor for the Pinkerton tactics she'd had to learn, and her father had made her the attorney he'd always imagined a son could be. Both careers demanded self-discipline.

Keep it close to your chest, Judge MacKenzie had insisted. It had taken years and more than a few difficult cases to understand fully what he meant. Prudence forced her face to remain as expressionless as possible. Society women were as rigidly determined as Pinks and lawyers to safeguard what others did not need to know. To be weak was to court failure.

Prudence wasn't the salon's only client that Monday morning, she realized as she finally dragged her eyes from the sketch of her wedding gown.

A very blond, not very slender young woman balanced herself on a stool while a bevy of seamstresses attacked her with pins and tape measures. The dress whose final details they were adjusting was a pale buttermilk color, enlivened by embroidered flowers that exactly matched the sunshine yellow of the girl's hair. It was a day dress, appropriate for at-home wear or for making calls on a warm late summer day. Beautiful, though the young lady wearing it was not.

Lovely hair and skin, Prudence noted, but the nose was a trifle long for a female and the chin had the resolute jut of a dogged determination. Unremarkable eyes, except that they were a clear blue. And really, she needed to slim down. A corseted waist defined female elegance, but it also cruelly revealed extra girth that couldn't be squeezed and pinched into the desirable hourglass figure fashion demanded.

"I'll introduce you." Madame Régine handed the wedding dress sketch to the senior dressmaker.

"Is that the girl you told me about?" Prudence asked. "The one who's going to accompany me from one dreary afternoon at home to another?"

"It might help to think of her as the other half of what we're counting on to save my reputation and keep my salon open." Madame Régine could be curt when necessary, and Prudence immediately recognized the comment for what it was.

She might be Madame Régine's client as far as her wedding dress was concerned, but the designer was Prudence's client in the matter of the break-in that had resulted in Brenda Leavitt's murder. Tit for tat. Quid pro quo. Prudence shrewdly concluded that although she was an immigrant's daughter from the tenements, Madame Régine had never met anyone whose equal she couldn't become. The fact that she had allowed herself to make a tart comment was testimony to the breakdown of social barriers between the two women.

Much like being a MacKenzie, the De Haan name marked Katja as unmistakably as a racehorse brand. She was a Knickerbocker, related to Caroline Astor, one of the many descendants of the original Dutch New Amsterdammers. And like many of them, shunted aside as newer money trampled over them and then realized—too late—that blood didn't budge when it came to defining who was socially acceptable and who was not.

"I think our mothers may have been cousins of some sort," Katja remarked after Madame Régine's introduction. "Father says we're all related somehow or other."

Prudence felt the gaze that she instinctively knew was cataloging her features, ticking off those that might be proof of a shared lineage. Every woman in the Four Hundred had mastered that intent look. Prudence knew she herself was guilty of it. Hard to escape when you were raised to be endlessly aware of the juggling of position and influence.

"I'm delighted to meet you." Prudence reminded her inquiry agent self of the role she had to play. "And I'm pleased to have your company for the next two weeks. There are more at homes and teas to attend than I want to contemplate having to get through alone." She let her eyes slide over the buttermilk dress, lingering on the embroidered yellow flowers. "You'll have every woman's eyes on you, Katja. You and Madame Régine will be setting a new standard for summer gowns."

Katja blushed, tendrils of bright red snaking along the pale skin of her face.

It was, Prudence decided, not terribly attractive. Hadn't the girl's governess taught her how to control allowing her emotions to show? Then she remembered that this young woman had probably not had the tutelage of a governess past the earliest years of leaving the nursery. Prudence added the title of duenna to that of inquiry agent and attorney. The wedding and the tour of Europe with Geoffrey couldn't come soon enough.

And then she immediately regretted what she was thinking. A woman who worked hard to earn a meagre living was dead. A designer hoping to establish herself in New York's competitive fashion world was running the risk of failure and ostracism because her salon was where the murder had taken place. And Prudence's own wedding dress was at the center of the crime.

The first thing Prudence would do when she went home to the mansion at the corner of Fifth Avenue and Twelfth Street would be to answer every one of the dozens of invitations crowding her parlor mantelpiece. Cards she usually swept away without opening them. She hated the round of empty hours women passed in one another's company. But for Madame Régine, for Katja, and for the memory of Brenda Leavitt, she'd get through every one of them with a smile on her face.

And Katja by her side.

A lady in black sitting close to the far wall in Madame Régine's workroom nodded approvingly as the regrettably plain Katja De Haan was almost transformed by the buttermilk dress. Almost, but not quite. The hair needed to be rinsed with vinegar and brushed until it shone like candlelight, various shades of powder could be discreetly applied to the planes of the face, and the attractively shaped lips could be reddened just enough to draw the eye.

From where she sat, Madame Jolene couldn't detect whatever fragrance Leopold De Haan's daughter was wearing, but it was certain to be too flowery by far. Men responded to duskier notes, not unlike the incense-tinged sandalwood shaving lotion and cologne Geoffrey Hunter wore. She'd never had the pleasure of his intimate company, but he'd stepped in to save her house and her business when a murderer stalked her girls. Madame Jolene had not forgotten either the ex-Pinkerton skills or the sheer ruggedly handsome appeal of the man who'd never treated her with anything less than perfect manners.

She liked Prudence MacKenzie, also. Probably the only woman of enviably high social rank in New York City who had ever sat in a brothel, comfortably sipping tea in the madam's parlor.

Any moment now, she expected the bride-to-be to glance her way. It might take her a few moments to recognize Madame Jolene under all the extra veiling, but she would. Prudence MacKenzie was almost as good at what she did as Geoffrey Hunter. And that was very adept indeed.

It had been a bit imprudent to risk being recognized going into Madame Régine's salon this morning, but Madame Jolene had insulated herself enough to take the chance. Her brothel serviced powerful New York City police and political figures as well as men of incalculable wealth. Almost nothing and no one could touch her. Except for a murder that couldn't be hidden because nosy journalists and bungling patrolmen had arrived on the scene before the fix could be set into motion.

A killing very like the one that had disrupted Madame Régine's salon had threatened to close down Madame Jolene's house not too long ago. It was at least one of the reasons she had offered to help erase the inevitable stigma of violence. Regina had been a very competent working girl who gave her madam no problems, but she was also more than symbolic of what a woman could become if she set her mind to it. In her own way, and on a much higher social level, so was Prudence MacKenzie. Not that Madame Jolene believed for a minute that either she or Regina Healy would ever approach the lofty MacKenzie perch. But it wasn't unreasonable to congratulate herself—and Regina—on having and achieving aspirations.

Madame Régine, she corrected herself. Best not to forget that a successful transformation required constant vigilance.

* * *

Prudence recognized Madame Jolene as soon as she spotted the figure in black not very inconspicuously ensconced in one of the workroom's corners. But since the madam gave no sign of acknowledgment, neither did she. Madame Régine had explained the situation behind the De Haan girl's sudden elevation into the world of high fashion. Both women had smiled, raised perfectly plucked eyebrows, and agreed that the less Katja knew of a lady of the evening's involvement, the better. It was never wise to count on the ability of the young not to disclose what an older women would intuit had to be kept secret.

As soon as Katja had been helped down from her stool, divested of the buttermilk gown, and led away to be reclothed in the very ordinary dress in which she'd arrived at the salon, Prudence made her way across the workroom. A second chair had been placed beside the one in which Madame Jolene sat.

"Congratulations on your upcoming marriage, Miss MacKenzie."

Madame Jolene raised her veil for a moment, just long enough for Prudence to catch a glimpse of the still flawless white Irish skin that no amount of face cream could recreate. You had to be born with it.

"I understand you're financing young Katja's foray into the marriage market," Prudence said. It wasn't that she disapproved. She didn't. Young women without financial resources or steely ambition found refuge from the world in wedlock. It usually wasn't a bad bargain.

"Plain as a pikestaff." Madame Jolene judged. "But Madame Régine's creations and the lady's maid I've hired for her will make all the difference."

"We can't forget for a moment that an innocent, hardworking seamstress was murdered here," Prudence said. "Finding the person who took her life has to be more important to us than anything else."

"I've dealt with murder before," Madame Jolene reminded her. "It's how I met your future husband. And you, too, for that matter."

"I remember," Prudence said.

"The police don't value very highly the life of a member of my profession. Don't consider it of any consequence at all, if you want the bald-face truth of it. But I do. I worked my way up, but I've never lost track of what it was like when I was just starting out."

"Are you insinuating something about Brenda Leavitt?" Prudence considered mentioning the man Amos Lang was trying to find. Decided against it. Not yet.

"Isn't there always a two-legged male somewhere in every woman's background? A girl who hasn't had a bad time at the hands of one of the nastier brutes is all the more likely to fall for whatever story a fancy man spins her. That's my experience. And it's considerable."

"There has to be a motive. Something other than killing a witness who's caught him in the act of whatever he broke into the salon to do."

"Did you know that every now and then a girl will sell one house's secrets to another?" Madame Jolene asked.

"I don't understand." Prudence really didn't.

"I'm talking about what makes one brothel more popular than another with clients of a certain persuasion," Madame Jolene explained. "Tricks of the trade, so to speak."

Prudence stared at the face she could barely make out behind the black veil.

"Never mind. You'll find out soon enough. Unless I miss my guess, a certain Southern gentleman has a lot to teach you. Now don't get all in a dander," Madame Jolene added as Prudence stood up so quickly, she nearly dropped her reticule. "Sit back down, my dear."

Reluctantly, Prudence did so.

"Madame Régine—damned if I don't want to call her just

plain Regina—has talent and a good eye. She didn't waste a moment of the time she spent in Paris. What was it? Two years? Three? My guess is that she came back to New York because she was convinced without a shadow of a doubt that no American female would be able to make it on her own in the French fashion world.

"She's smart enough to know when to cut her losses and leave a game. But she's ambitious enough to want to play where winning counts. That would be in Caroline Astor's territory. Someone—we don't know who yet, but we will, eventually—could have a mind to stop her. Sees her as competition so good she's likely to win whatever prize is at stake. So this person hires or bribes a seamstress—the late Brenda—to bring him sketches of what Régine is developing. He means to steal her style before she has a chance to launch it. That would make her a copycat, a laughingstock, something from which it's harder to recover than a murder.

"I don't know what Brenda did to earn the kind of killing she got, but she was expendable from the first moment she agreed to spy on New York City's latest designer. As simple as that, Miss MacKenzie. Believe me. I'm in a business that's as cutthroat as anything an Astor or a Rockefeller could come up with. I know that jealousy breeds violence. Always. There's no getting away from it."

"My wedding dress was cut into tiny pieces and scattered like snow over the body," Prudence said.

Madame Jolene shrugged. "Purely for effect."

"We found a necklace in the closet where the dress had been stored."

"Someone is having a laugh at your expense."

"It's worth thinking about," Prudence admitted.

"If either you or your handsome Mr. Hunter are worth the ink on your business cards, you've already thought of it." Madame Jolene chuckled. "Don't waste too much time on young Katja. That's a dead end. Take her where she needs to be seen but let loose the leash as soon as you can. Trust that Régine's gowns and the De Haan name will carry the day. Brenda Leavitt's killer won't be easy to find, not if he's got the money to cover his tracks. Which I suspect he does."

"I'll tell Geoffrey what you've said."

"You've got a good man there. Don't take him for granted." Madame Jolene settled her hat and smoothed her skirts. "If you need any advice of a private nature, you've only to ask. By rights, your mother should be having a talk with you round about now, but I know she's not here to do that. The consumption, wasn't it?" She waited. "I don't mind standing in for her. Seeing that I'm more than qualified. My girls are the city's best, and I was the one who taught them."

When Prudence didn't answer, Madame Jolene swept past in a rustle of black silk and disappeared from the workroom.

Every seamstress at every worktable stole a quick glance at the woman whose second wedding dress Madame Régine had vowed would be even more splendid than the first.

Prudence glanced up. Blushed to the tips of her ears.

Madame Jolene hadn't bothered to lower her voice at the end of their conversation.

The seamstresses had heard every word.

They all knew exactly what kind of instruction the city's most famous madam was offering.

And every one of them wished she'd been given the same opportunity.

Not a single married or unmarried woman in that workroom would have turned it down.

CHAPTER 11

"I'm sorry I haven't asked how the investigation is going," Madame Régine apologized. She ushered Prudence into her office, scribbled her initials onto an order for more dressmaker-grade pearls, and rubbed itchy, red-rimmed eyes. "Taking on a whole new wardrobe for Katja De Haan was almost certainly suicidal, but it seemed a good idea at the time."

"I think you and Madame Jolene came up with a scheme that's more certain to guarantee your reputation than anything else I could have thought of," Prudence said, taking the wedding dress portfolio from Madame Régine and laying it carefully on the designer's desk. "I've asked one of your staff to bring tea and sandwiches. When was the last time you ate anything? Or got off your feet for a few minutes?"

"I have no idea." Madame Régine stood stock-still in the middle of her private retreat from the bustle of workrooms and the demands of temperamental clients. "You're right, Miss MacKenzie. If I don't stop for a moment, I'll be no use to anyone. Myself included."

"I thought we agreed on first names," Prudence said, smiling broadly as the normally elegant designer flopped wearily into a chair.

"That's not at all comme il faut." Madame Régine fluffed her skirts and rubbed throbbing ankles against each other.

"Neither of us is exactly comme il faut," Prudence declared. "Caroline Astor supposedly gave up on me a couple of years ago, but I think I secretly amuse her. The idea of a genuine Knickerbocker flouting all the rules and getting away with it is both repulsive to her notion of how society should be structured and more than a little enticing. It means freedom for women who haven't enjoyed much of a commodity men profess to value so highly."

"Did anyone ever call you Pru?"

"Let's not go that far." Prudence shuddered. A tentative knock announced the arrival of the refreshments she'd requested.

She took a laden tea tray from one of the uniformed maids who usually served clients in the fitting and display rooms. "We'll see to ourselves, thank you."

The girl dared a quick, curious glance at Madame Régine stretched out in her chair like an ordinary person, then beat a quick retreat.

"The tea's hot and the sandwiches look delicious," Prudence cajoled, pouring two cups and placing crustless buttered triangles of cucumber and ham on delicate serving plates.

"Now that I've confessed to being so heartless as to allow myself to be distracted from the inquiries you're making about poor Brenda, I hope you'll tell me how things are progressing." Tiny sandwiches disappeared almost as quickly as Madame Régine emptied her cup.

"We haven't discovered much of anything." Prudence sighed. "Our best ex-Pink operative has been assigned to track down the man Brenda was meeting in the park. He's going from one saloon to the next, trying to find someone who met him, drank with him, spent any kind of time talking to him. It's the only lead we have, but it hasn't taken us very far."

"I wonder if the sister knows more than she told us," Madame Régine mused. She opened a desk drawer and took out a bottle of whiskey. Pulled out the cork and tilted it over Prudence's cup.

Prudence hesitated, then shook her head. "I have to be careful." She glanced at the hand that had been severely burned and still bore the scars of that experience. There were days when a vague yearning restlessness seemed to course through her veins instead of blood. This was one of them. She'd learned not to try to take the edge off it with even the most innocent glass of wine let alone stronger spirits.

"Laudanum?" Madame Régine asked. She'd designed the wedding gown with tapered sleeves that ended in a pearl-encrusted diamond shape just above the fingers, effectively hiding the scar without drawing attention to it. The only way someone like Prudence MacKenzie could have borne the pain of what was obviously a severe burn had to have been by frequent doses of the liquid opium.

"It's more dangerous to some of us than to others," Prudence confirmed.

Madame Régine poured herself a stiff shot of whiskey, then returned the bottle to her desk drawer. "It's best not to do this on an empty stomach," she said, draining half a cup of doctored tea at a single swallow and following it with the last of the sandwiches. "At least when there's work to be done."

"I think I'll pay another call on Brenda's sister." Prudence sipped her tea, trying not to smile at the designer's evident enjoyment of her whiskey. It was very unladylike. "You're probably right to be curious about whether she was altogether frank with us."

"If someone had asked me about my dead sister, I certainly

wouldn't have told them things I knew she'd want kept secret. It's bad enough the neighbors will talk about Brenda's having been murdered. Nessa won't want them speculating about the why of it, especially not if there's a man involved."

"Surely you don't think . . ." Prudence tried not to look as shocked as she felt.

"That's the first thing anyone assumes about a young, unmarried woman who meets a bad end. Remember, it's always the female's fault, never the male's. It's been that way since time began."

"That's because men make the rules," Prudence said.

Madame Régine's hand stretched out to the drawer containing the whiskey bottle, but she pulled back before the fingers could come to rest on the handle.

"How much younger than Brenda is Nessa?" Prudence asked. "Do you know?"

"Why?"

"Wouldn't Brenda want to keep anything like that from a much younger sister? Especially one who's obviously so ill."

"She never mentioned Nessa's exact age," Madame Régine said. "The consumption makes young victims look old and wipes color off the faces of those more advanced in years. They all turn frail and transparent at the end. And yes, Prudence, I'm speaking from experience. It runs through this city's tenements like water down a drain."

"My mother died of consumption." Prudence set down her teacup. "I remember how long it took. How she seemed to fade like a piece of clothing left outdoors too long to dry in the sun. The weakness. The coughing. The blood she and my father tried to hide from me."

Madame Régine took a pale lavender crocheted shawl from the coatrack beside the door. "I made this myself, when I first arrived in Paris and had time for the needles because no one would hire an American who didn't speak French."

"It's beautiful." Prudence's fingers wandered lightly over the intricate design of the stitches.

"This was the workmanship that got me my first job," Madame Régine explained. "The head seamstress where I applied took her time examining it, but I read appreciation in her eyes when she looked up at me and nodded. That was the beginning of what you see all around you."

Madame Régine folded the shawl into a neat square, wrapped it in tissue paper, tied the bundle with a broad white satin ribbon, and handed it to Prudence. "Give this to Nessa. It will warm her bones at the end. It doesn't make up for losing Brenda, but it's all I can do for her. Justice will have to be your gift."

"I thought we'd go to lunch at Delmonico's," Geoffrey said as he ushered Prudence from Madame Régine's salon into Danny Dennis's waiting hansom cab.

"That's a wonderful idea." Prudence settled the tissue-wrapped shawl onto her lap. "I need to make a stop first. Is there time?"

"You're earlier than I expected you to be, so yes, we've plenty of time." It didn't matter when they arrived. Even without a reservation, the headwaiter would lead them to one of the more desirable tables. Prudence was known to be part of Caroline Astor's circle and Geoffrey had never entered a restaurant where the bills he slipped the maître d' didn't immediately make him welcome. It was the way things were done.

"I have a present for Brenda's sister. From Madame Régine. It's one of the most beautiful shawls I've ever seen. She crocheted it herself, in Paris, when she was just starting out."

"This is the girl you told me about? The one with consumption."

Prudence nodded.

"If the shawl is valuable, the mother will sell it as soon as her daughter is gone." Geoffrey hadn't met Mrs. Leavitt, but he'd heard enough from Prudence to recognize a type.

"I know. I told Madame Régine that. She said that if the mother needed money, she was welcome to it."

"Are you sure about this?"

"The shawl isn't why I'm visiting. Régine and I both feel that the sister may not be telling us everything she could."

"Régine?"

"Madame Régine and I are modern women, Geoffrey. We're on a first-name basis."

"What do you think this consumptive sister knows that she's been trying to hide? She won't say a word if her mother is in the room." He thought modernity was only one of Prudence's many charms.

"That's where you come in. Your job is going to be to distract Mrs. Leavitt. I don't care how you do it, but you've got to make sure she doesn't hear whatever her daughter decides to tell me."

"I'll think of something." He leaned over and kissed Prudence on the tip of her modern woman's nose.

As it turned out, Geoffrey's assignment was easier than he had anticipated. Mrs. Leavitt had taken her basket to the corner grocer's. The potatoes she had saved for the evening's stew had blackened in the damp of the cellar.

"Like what happened in Ireland that made all those poor people come to America so they wouldn't starve to death," Brenda's sister told them. "Can you imagine?"

"That was a blight that spread over the entire country." Prudence's father had insisted she study the history tomes in his library. Novels were all very well for dipping into just before bedtime, but daylight was meant for serious study. "I imagine the potatoes in your larder were almost too old to be edible when an untrustworthy grocer sold them."

"Mother does like to save the odd penny here and there."

"I want you to meet my fiancé, Geoffrey Hunter. Geoffrey, this is Nessa, Brenda's sister."

He nearly dropped Prudence's package.

"Nessa," she repeated, enunciating the name, drawing out the *s* sound. It wasn't until she'd felt his reaction beside her that she remembered he'd once been very close to a woman called Nezzie. A woman Prudence had joked didn't need to be asked to their wedding.

Nessa smiled and held out a thin, nearly translucent hand.

"I have a gift for you from Madame Régine," Prudence said, deftly covering what felt like an awkward moment. She set the package on Nessa's lap, being careful not to nudge the wheelchair.

"Such a beautiful ribbon. I almost hate to undo the bow."

"You can save it to tie up your hair," Prudence suggested.

Nessa breathed a sigh of utter contentment when the tissue paper slipped away from the lavender shawl. "I've always wanted something this color," she said, resting her hand on it. "And this soft."

"And now you have it." Prudence draped the shawl around Nessa's gaunt shoulders. It sank over the girl's frame as though it had always belonged there, softening the angular outlines of her illness, disguising the underweight body that was rapidly approaching emaciation and death.

"Mother will say it's too good for me."

"I'll make sure she understands that it's not." If Geoffrey had his way—and he'd make sure he did—Nessa would be buried in the shawl that had given her what he felt was probably one of the few moments of pleasure in a hard and unappreciated life.

"I don't want to disturb you, Nessa," Prudence began as the girl continued to stroke the shawl as though it were the softest cat who'd ever crawled onto her lap. "But Madame Régine and

I felt you might have more to tell us about Brenda than you were able to manage the last time I was here."

"Is that why she sent me the shawl?"

"No. Not at all. It's yours to keep even if you don't say another word about your sister."

"Mother will be home soon. She never lingers over her errands."

"We thought Brenda might have told you more about the man she met in the park than you thought it proper to share," Prudence said. She sat back in her chair, moving away from Nessa, trying her best not to appear demanding or threatening.

"Brenda didn't dare keep a journal." Nessa wound some of the shawl's fringe around her fingers. "Mother went through her armoire every day while she was at work. She said a girl couldn't be allowed to keep secrets from a parent. I think she looked under the mattress, too."

"I don't suppose there's much privacy in a boardinghouse," Geoffrey said, apropos of nothing.

"Not if my mother is the landlady." Nessa laughed, a slight, tinkling sound that set her coughing.

Prudence held out her handkerchief, but Nessa waved it away. She fumbled at the cushion on which she sat, withdrew a large square of white cloth, and sat clutching it for a quiet moment. "Some days are easier than others. I've hardly coughed at all this morning."

"Can I get you some water?" Prudence asked. A pitcher and glasses stood on a nearby table.

"Just a sip."

Prudence poured and handed Nessa the glass. Set it back on the tray when Brenda's sister had drunk from it. She didn't see any traces of the blood that had stained her mother's cups toward the end.

"He dropped this," Nessa said, holding out what Prudence and Geoffrey could now see was a man's handkerchief. "Brenda told me he didn't notice it had come out of his pocket, so she picked it up when he turned away. I think this must have happened on the last day he walked with her. She brought it home and gave it to me to hide. When our mother wasn't here, I'd bring it out and Brenda would sit where you are, Miss MacKenzie, and hold it to her face. I knew what she was doing. She was smelling him. That's why she never washed his handkerchief."

Nessa handed it to Geoffrey, who passed it briefly beneath his nose. "Bay Rum cologne," he said, "St. John's Bay Rum, I think. It's stronger than some of the other brands. You can smell the Jamaican bay leaves."

"I want you to have it." Nessa glanced toward the parlor window. "She's coming along the street. Mother. I can see her. She mustn't know anything about this. Promise me you won't tell her."

Geoffrey folded the handkerchief neatly, enclosed it in his own handkerchief to preserve what was left of the Bay Rum scent, then slipped the two squares of white into his coat pocket. He nodded at Prudence to signal that it was best they leave right away. A slight hint of the stranger's fragrance hung in the air.

"I'll tell your mother that the shawl is a gift from Madame Régine in remembrance of Brenda," Prudence said, leaning over to kiss Nessa lightly on the forehead. Some people said it was dangerous to touch a consumptive, but whether it was or not, this young woman needed comforting.

"I'll make sure she lets you keep it." It wouldn't be proper for Geoffrey to do more than nod in Nessa's direction. He'd have to content himself with putting the fear of God into the girl's mother. Brenda's sister would be buried in pale lavender cashmere, or he'd know the reason why.

At the very last moment, as they heard the click of the front door opening, Nessa again reached under the cushion of her wheelchair. This time she withdrew a small, flat cardboard slipcase. Just visible at the scalloped top of the slipcase was what looked like a dark maroon notebook, so thin it couldn't possibly contain more than a few pages. It almost fell from Nessa's trembling fingers as she pressed it into Prudence's hand.

"I warned her not to trust him. But she was persuaded that he cared deeply for her. I wasn't surprised when he stopped meeting her. I expected it." Tears appeared in Nessa's eyes. "Hide it in your reticule. Don't let my mother see it."

"What is it?" Prudence whispered.

But Nessa shook her head. Over Prudence's shoulder she could see her mother's face. Mrs. Leavitt wasn't at all pleased to have come home to unexpected visitors.

There was a flurry of brusque but polite exchanges. Mrs. Leavitt didn't close the front door after herself or express regret that she hadn't had the opportunity to share a cup of tea with her daughter's callers. It was clear she wanted them gone.

When they turned for a last glimpse of Nessa Leavitt, they saw a wistful smile on the thin face and hands that stroked the soft shawl as though each strand of cashmere brought peace and healing.

Prudence waited until Danny's cab had turned the corner before undoing the string tie of her reticule and taking out the cardboard slipcase. "It's a bankbook, Geoffrey," she said, pulling out the stiff cardboard folder inside which she could see figures written in ink and pencil. "I can't make out all the dates. It looks like the ink wasn't always dry before the bankbook was closed and hidden away, but I think the record of deposits goes back at least a month or more. There don't seem to be any withdrawals." She handed him the bankbook and the slipcase. Neither of them had the slightly softened feel that cardboard acquires with extended use.

"Brenda Leavitt." Geoffrey read the name inscribed in a clerk's formal, curlicued style at the top of the first page. He flipped back to the cover. "Bank of the City." He tapped on the sliding door in the roof of the hansom cab, slid it back, and called an address up to where Danny was perched at the rear of the vehicle.

"I'm not sure Nessa meant to give this to us," Prudence said. "Until she saw her mother coming down the street and that suddenly made up her mind for her."

"Consumptives always know toward the end that they haven't much time left." Geoffrey reached for Prudence's left hand, held it gently in his, raised it to his lips. "The closer they are to death the less they try to fool themselves. She probably realized this might be our last visit. It was give the bankbook to us now or not at all. And if she died with it hidden in the wheelchair, her mother would find it. I think all of that flashed through her brain in a matter of moments. She made the only choice she could."

"Have you ever known anyone who was cured of the consumption?" Prudence asked.

"Never. Some live longer than others, and I've heard that miracles occasionally occur in mountain sanitoriums, but I've never personally met anyone who could testify to the truth of those claims." He knew the story of Prudence's mother's death. It was hard to imagine how a young child could sit at the foot of her mother's bed or couch day after day and listen to her cough her life away. Watch the light fade from her eyes.

"This changes things, you know. It would seem that Brenda Leavitt was being paid for passing on Madame Régine's designs and perhaps also the names of her clients. It was her misfortune to fall in love with the man who was manipulating her."

"And might have killed her." Geoffrey evaluated suspects without emotion or sympathy. People made choices. He believed they should be held to account. Himself included.

"We're going to the bank?"

"Unless you'd rather put it off until after Delmonico's?"

"Delmonico's can wait," Prudence said. "We'll always be able to get a table, no matter when we arrive."

She said it matter-of-factly, without boasting, perhaps not even realizing how such an assumption set her above most of the population of New York City. It was one of the many things about Prudence that Geoffrey loved.

He held tightly to her hand as Danny urged Mr. Washington to a faster trot.

CHAPTER 12

The Bank of the City was located in Union Square, well within sight of the statue of George Washington on horseback around which circled traffic from Broadway and Fourth Avenue between Fourteenth and Seventeenth Streets. The redesigned Union Square Park had been open to the public for less than twenty years, but its trees and wide sidewalks had always attracted a faithful following throughout the day. Where better to eat your noontime sandwich than beneath the shade of a towering London planetree?

Danny Dennis drove around the Square, past Tiffany, then guided Mr. Washington to the curb in front of the five-story red brick building where the Bank of the City was headquartered. Small, as banks went, but undeniably elegant, the red brick was faced with carved limestone detailing around its windows and main doorway.

"I'm coming in with you," Prudence said, gathering her skirts in one hand as she stepped from the hansom cab. She'd never been inside a bank building. Ladies of her social rank did not usually frequent centers of commerce except for the most exclusive shops of the Ladies' Mile.

"Of course you are."

It never failed to amuse Geoffrey when Prudence set out to explore new territory. She had a determined set to her jaw and a purposeful gleam in her gray eyes.

The hush inside the bank was akin to the sacred silence of a cathedral, but instead of incense, it was the fragrance of money that permeated the air. Printers' ink and paper and the sharp tang of gold, silver, and copper coins.

Barred wooden cages lined one wall and a narrow row of tall tables supplied with inkwells and green-shaded gooseneck lamps bisected the huge, high-ceilinged room. The floor was marble, the lofty windows shaped like gothic arches inset with Tiffany stained glass. Everywhere a customer looked, sculptures and paintings adorned the walnut-paneled walls. The Bank of the City had been designed so that its every inch told you it was a serious place in which to do business. Proceed with dignified awe, preferably with a substantial transaction.

Opposite the row of caged tellers was a space separated from the main area by a low railing, behind which clustered desks that had been arranged to guard entrance to inner offices where important bank personnel served their most valued clients.

That was, of course, the direction in which Geoffrey headed. He walked with the stately stride of a man whose slightest wish is never denied.

Prudence paced beside him, looking neither to the left nor to the right. *Curiosity is a characteristic of the ill-bred.* Or so went the dictum every governess worth her salt imposed on her charges.

The vice president who answered Geoffrey's inquiry was polite, deferential, but firm enough to pass muster should a superior observe his handling of a potentially difficult situation. The deposits about which the gentleman was asking had been made in cash. In person. By the individual whose name was inscribed in the bankbook. Miss Brenda Leavitt. An unmarried female, whose account had most probably been opened for her by a father or a brother. That checks were not involved was evidenced by the small notations in the margins of the bankbook. Inscribed by the cashier who received and recorded the deposits. He pointed them out with a manicured forefinger.

And that was that. Cash, so there would be no record of who had paid Brenda Leavitt the money she deposited. No mystery, though there was one uncomfortable moment when the young bank executive questioned how the bankbook came to be in the gentleman's possession.

"My sister is indisposed," Prudence explained. Just that and no more.

But the inference was clear. As long as neither she nor Geoffrey attempted to withdraw funds, the bank would remain neutral. The one important question that was not asked was whether the indisposed Miss Brenda Leavitt was actually still alive. Perhaps because no death certificate was produced, the bank vice president—of whom there were many—did not raise the topic. But he did follow them with speculative eyes as Geoffrey and Prudence left his desk and walked toward the Union Square entrance.

"Is he watching us?" Prudence asked as they neared one of the tall desks. She paused to inspect the inkstands, giving Geoffrey the opportunity to glance behind them.

"I think he's decided we're relatively harmless family members trying to find out the size of an upcoming inheritance. He's gone back to shuffling through the paperwork he set aside to answer our questions." Geoffrey reached for a pen in one of the inkstands, as though he needed to write a note or fill out a deposit or withdrawal slip.

"What next? Delmonico's?" Prudence asked. She was just hungry enough to think about lunch.

"Wait." Geoffrey's hand hovered over the inkstand, then extracted the gold watch in his vest pocket. "Keep your head down," he whispered, bending over the watch as if peering nearsightedly at its numerals.

"What is it?" Prudence's face was half-hidden by her wide brimmed feathered hat, but her voice breathed excitement.

"Don't look up yet."

All she could see was the marble floor on which she was standing. She tapped one foot impatiently as the seconds ticked by.

"All right." Geoffrey snapped closed the watch he'd been studying, replaced it into his vest pocket. Ran his fingers over the gold fob to straighten it. Kept his voice to a whisper. "The man standing at the cashier's window. Third window on the right. No one else in front of or behind him."

"I see him. What am I looking for?" Prudence asked.

"Brown hair, nondescript suit. Look at his cheeks, his chin."

"He's not bearded." Prudence had no idea what else she was supposed to notice.

"Not now," Geoffrey said. "I'd bet every penny in Brenda Leavitt's bank account that he shaved it off this morning."

"How can you tell?"

"Did you ever see your father right after he'd used a razor?"

"He never grew a beard. At least not that I remember."

"Look at that man's cheeks. See how reddened they look? The skin hasn't seen the light of day in months. His neck, too. Taking off a beard is a lot harder than growing one."

"Is that the voice of experience?"

Geoffrey nodded. "Ask any ex-Pink. He'll tell you a razor is as useful as every other weapon in his arsenal. Look around you. Most men who grow a beard keep it."

"Why now?" Prudence asked. "If that's the man we're looking for—Amos, too—why did he wait until now to shave off his beard? Why not right after he stopped seeing Brenda?"

"We'll have to ask him," Geoffrey said. He shrugged one shoulder, settling his Colt .45 in its holster.

Prudence shifted her reticule to her left hand, noting the reassuring weight of the double-barrel derringer she carried.

"Not here. We don't want to cause a scene. If he's walking, we'll split up. You on one side of the street, me on the other."

"And if he hails a cab?"

"Danny can follow a shadow through the darkest halls of hell. He and Mr. Washington will hang back, but they won't lose him."

"What if he's not our man after all?" Prudence asked. "Just because he's recently shaved off a beard and he's obviously familiar with this bank doesn't make him Brenda Leavitt's mysterious man in the park."

"Two out of three."

"What's the third?"

"He confesses to the murder." Geoffrey pushed open the heavy exterior door, bringing them back out into the dappled sunlight of Union Square. He nodded at Danny Dennis, waiting patiently in the high rear seat of his hansom cab. The Irishman touched a finger to the bright green feather in his top hat. He didn't need verbal instructions to know what to do.

"Now what?" Prudence asked.

"We wait until he comes out," Geoffrey answered. "Then we follow him."

The fellow they were trailing was in no hurry to get to wherever he was going. Fifteen minutes after leaving the bank, he came to a halt in front of St. Patrick's Cathedral where he climbed up the steps and stood looking northward along Fifth Avenue. Like a tourist who'd heard of but never dreamed of actually seeing the mansions that stretched toward Central Park. It was as though he were waiting for someone to join him.

Prudence observed from the opposite side of the street, Geoffrey from half a block directly behind their quarry.

Abruptly, the man descended the cathedral steps, walked briskly to the corner, and disappeared down Fifty-first Street. By the time Geoffrey reached the intersection, the brown-haired gent in the off-the-rack suit was no longer in sight.

Moments later, Prudence stood peering down the narrow street that ran alongside the length of the cathedral. The Vanderbilts had decreed that Fifth Avenue and its palatial homes remain purely residential, but shops and office buildings had begun springing up on the side streets almost before the last European antiques had been hauled from the docks to the new ersatz palaces. Not so close to Fifth Avenue as to challenge society's dictums, but close enough to presage what the future would bring.

"I think we've lost him," Geoffrey said as they walked along Fifty-first Street, moving farther and farther away from the cathedral. Litter began appearing in the roadway and on the sidewalk. Every corner boasted a pile of horse manure waiting to be picked up by a nightsoil wagon. Barefoot urchins wielded brooms bigger than they were, adding to the mounds of steaming ordure. Shops open to the pavement advertised and sold everything from household staples to cheap jewelry that looked suspiciously like brass instead of gold. Fifth Avenue lay behind them, quiet and elegant. They'd reached one of the many neighborhoods that made up the beating heart of the city. Loud, alive, smelly, and crowded.

"I hate to admit failure," Prudence said. She thought she'd stepped in something sticky that was making her boot cling to the sidewalk.

"He moved away from St. Patrick's too quickly," Geoffrey said, scanning the street in front of, behind, and on either side of them.

"What do you mean?"

"I think he knew he was being followed. I'm not sure when he picked us up, but it was probably after he'd left Union Square."

"My hat?" Prudence touched one hand to the multifeathered concoction that was an unmistakably fashionable creation. Expensive, too. It was one of the reasons she'd walked well behind and on the opposite side of the street from the man they were tracking.

"Couldn't be helped," Geoffrey reassured her. "You can't very well go around looking like one of your own servants."

"I don't think anyone would mistake the young lady for anything but the gentlewoman she is," said a voice from the shadow of a narrow alleyway. "You'd best follow me."

The man who stepped out onto Fifty-first Street winked at Prudence and tipped his bowler hat at Geoffrey, then took off at a quick stride toward the warren of small shops and narrow, five-story buildings where most of the activities of a New Yorker's daily life took place. He paused to allow them to catch up, nodded to the grocer who called out to him in Italian, and led them up a dark flight of stairs to a corridor lined with half-paned doors. A steady hum of voices and what sounded like thc clack of typewriter keys floated over open transoms into the hallway.

It wasn't as prosperous a building as the one in which Hunter and MacKenzie had its headquarters. From another floor drifted the smell of something stewing in a pot. Prudence thought it might be cabbage.

The office they were invited to enter consisted of two rooms, the outer one empty of everything but a bare desk and a single wooden chair. No secretary.

The inner office was only marginally more furnished. A larger desk, three chairs, fireplace in which no fire was laid, table piled with stacks of paper, and a single cabinet for stowing away files. A telephone had been attached to the wall behind the desk, new by the looks of it.

The letters stenciled on the frosted glass of the office door spelled out *Anthony Nichols, Confidential Inquiries.*

Geoffrey laid his business card on Nichols's desk. "I see we're in the same profession," he said, seating Prudence and then himself in the client chairs that he forebore from dusting with the gloves he'd taken off.

"You're good, Mr. Hunter," Nichols said, reading from the

business card he'd picked up. "I didn't catch on to you for quite a while after leaving the bank. Your companion, however, isn't as skilled in the art of not being noticed. No offense, Miss MacKenzie." Again he read from the card.

"None taken. If I'd known we'd be following someone, I would never have worn this hat." She smiled her most conspiratorial grin. *Use your feminine wiles,* she reminded herself. *They work every time.*

They sat for a while in silence—the three of them—working out who would speak first, playing advantage against disadvantage, deception against half-truths.

"We're working the Brenda Leavitt murder," Geoffrey said at last. These power games could get annoying if they went on too long.

"I see." Nichols touched the spot on his chin where he'd been used to stroking a beard.

"Walter Duncan proved to be a difficult man to track down."

Nichols acknowledged the compliment with a smile.

"Did you know Brenda had a sister?" Prudence asked.

Nichols seemed to debate with himself whether or not to answer the question. He picked up a file that lay on the desk and ruffled through its pages. Sighed. Opened one of the desk drawers. Put the file inside. Closed the drawer. Lit a cigarette. Made up his mind.

"She often spoke of her," he said, blowing smoke rings above his head as he leaned back in his chair. "The sister and her illness were what made Brenda vulnerable. She wanted to take Nessa to a sanitorium she'd read about. In the mountains of western North Carolina. That's what the money was for."

"I don't suppose you're at liberty to tell us who you're working for?" Geoffrey asked.

"Were working for," Nichols corrected. "The case is closed. I've been paid."

"And Brenda is dead," Prudence said. She waited for an acknowledgment to flit across his face.

"Most unfortunate. But nothing to do with me or my client."

"I find that hard to believe," Geoffrey said. Just that and no more.

Prudence glanced at her partner. Added nothing to the statement he'd made. Despite the tobacco smoke, she thought she detected a hint of Bay Rum aftershave lotion.

They waited.

Nichols finished his cigarette. Extinguished it in an already-full metal dish that spilled ashes onto the desk. He brushed them off with one hand, flicked them onto the floor. "I can't give you a name or a monetary figure. But I can reveal that the job had very precise stipulations. My client wanted to know the details of what Madame Régine was designing in her workshop, the names of her most important customers, and what it would take to shut her down."

"What brought your client here?" Geoffrey ran his eyes over the battered desk and file cabinet, the bare floorboards, the lack of anything decorating the walls. Dirty window overlooking the street. No secretary. No clients in the reception room. No envelopes or flyers lying on the floor beneath the mail slot in the office door. "Was it a referral?"

"I have a reputation," Nichols said, studying the pack of cigarettes he pulled from his pocket. He counted how many remained, put the pack away without lighting one. "Maybe not the kind of status usually associated with how certain people pretend they like to do business, but I get results. I don't ask embarrassing questions. I do the job, take the money, and disappear until the next time I'm needed."

"In this case, you decided that the best way to get inside Madame Régine's atelier was to court one of her seamstresses," Geoffrey said. Matter-of-factly. Nothing accusatory in his tone of voice.

Nichols shrugged. "It worked, didn't it?"

"Why did you stay on at the boardinghouse after you'd got what you wanted from Brenda?" Prudence asked. Amos's most recent report had been brief and to the point. He'd found the boardinghouse and learned the alias that had been used, but the suspect himself had slipped through his fingers.

"The room was paid for. It was comfortable and the landlady is a good cook. The client didn't ask for details when I presented my bill."

"And you were having a few financial difficulties at the time," Geoffrey said. It was a guess, but a good one. Nichols looked like the type of man who would always be skating on thin ice. Always absconding from one boardinghouse to another in the middle of the night.

A brown leather satchel stood beside the file cabinet, half-hidden in the shadow and by a coat that had been thrown over it.

"Moving on?" Geoffrey asked, nodding in that direction.

The discovery of a body in Madame Régine's studio had made Saturday's newspapers. A small item buried on one of the back pages, easily missed but just as easily dangerous. Today was Monday. Two days later. Time enough for a client to decide that the only person linking him to the couturiere's salon needed to disappear. One way or the other.

"Like I said, I do a job, pocket the fee, and get lost."

"Baltimore? Philadelphia? Chicago?"

"Could be. Maybe. Maybe not." Nichols stood up, reached for the satchel, slung the coat over one arm. Opened the desk drawer and took out the file he'd been reading earlier. Slipped it into the satchel and refastened the strap. "Don't bother looking for me. You'd be wasting your time."

"Did you kill her?" Prudence asked. He'd already told them that neither he nor his client was responsible for Brenda's death, but she wasn't ready to believe that. She thought the blunt question might catch him off guard.

"Like I said, Miss MacKenzie. Nothing to do with me. Murder is expensive, usually not worth what you end up getting paid." Nichols gestured a noose around his neck.

"You dropped this in the park. Brenda picked it up." Geoffrey held out the Bay Rum-scented handkerchief but pulled back his hand when Nichols reached for it.

"Keep it, if you like. It's not initialed. There's no proof I ever owned it. A handkerchief lost in a park doesn't signify anything."

Then he was out the door, down the stairs, and disappearing into the crowd along Fifty-first Street before Prudence realized how fast he'd moved.

"He wasn't going to tell us anything else." Geoffrey didn't seem the least perturbed or surprised. He folded the handkerchief again, placed it back in his pocket. "I'll send for Amos to go through the paperwork our erstwhile investigator left behind, but I don't think we'll learn anything useful."

Prudence walked over to the window. "I don't see him," she said.

Geoffrey brushed a tendril of hair from the back of her neck. Kissed the lovely, soft skin. "Delmonico's?"

"Lobster bisque, I think, to take away the taste of failure."

"We haven't failed, Prudence. We're just going to set off in a different direction."

"What direction is that?"

"We'll decide after lunch, my love. It's never a good idea to make plans on an empty stomach."

CHAPTER 13

Prudence and Geoffrey lingered at Delmonico's over a very long, very late lunch, then returned to the office to dictate details of the odd meeting with Anthony Nichols. Amos Lang joined them in the conference room and Josiah kept everyone awake and working with pot after pot of coffee.

"I couldn't shake the feeling that he was a professional," Amos said more than once. It was embarrassing to be given the slip by a suspect, but almost understandable when the target was a fellow inquiry agent.

"It was pure chance that he happened to be at the bank closing out his account when we decided to investigate Brenda Leavitt's passbook." Geoffrey laid the document on the conference room table and flipped it open to the list of deposits the dead woman had made.

"So sad," Prudence said. "He told us that Brenda wanted to take her sister to one of those sanitoriums in the North Carolina mountains. That's why she sold Madame Régine's secrets."

"It doesn't explain why she fell in love with him." Amos had long ago decided that love was the most dangerous emotion to which a person could become victim.

"She was lonely," Prudence explained. "Browbeaten by her mother, exhausted by the extra hours she worked, facing the probable death of the only person in the world who loved her. The sister she was trying to save. When Anthony Nichols approached her, she was ripe for the plucking."

"Heartless cad." Josiah stirred another lump of sugar into his coffee.

"He was on a job." Amos shrugged.

"He took advantage of a desperately sad young woman," Josiah insisted.

"How else was he going to do what he was being paid to accomplish?" Amos understood Anthony Nichols. He'd been in many a similar situation himself. What he didn't comprehend was why Brenda Leavitt had let down her guard so quickly and so completely. Loneliness and disappointment were things you got used to. Endured as you carried on with the daily business of living.

"It's too late now," Geoffrey said, smoothing over the discussion that was threatening to turn into an argument. "Brenda took her secrets with her to the grave and Nichols is on a train to a destination he wouldn't share with us."

"I thought that was one of the oddest things about him," Prudence said. "You would have thought that being successful with this investigation would lead to more cases, more clients. But he ups and leaves town to start over again somewhere else."

"Possibly under a different name." In Geoffrey's experience, some ex-Pinks changed their names as frequently as other men did their suits. He didn't think Nichols was a former Pinkerton, but you couldn't always tell. The agency had high standards, and didn't allow for mistakes. Even a man who washed out usually had the benefit of some training.

"Whoever hired him was prepared to make sure he never

discussed the case he was working." Amos fished around in one of his pockets for the tobacco tin into which he spat his chaws. Josiah's coffee was good but couldn't compete with a plug of rum-soaked Virginia leaf.

"He put a good face on it, but you're right. He must have known his days could have been numbered if he stuck around," Geoffrey said.

"So his client, in addition to stealing business secrets, is capable of murder to get what he wants." Prudence picked up the bankbook, adding the deposits in her head. Her tally agreed with the figure Brenda had written beside the most recent payment into the account. "Or at least, so Nichols believed."

"We don't know who the client is," Geoffrey said. The scent of Amos's chaw reminded him that he hadn't had his postprandial cigar after Delmonico's. But a gentleman didn't light up in a small, unventilated room when a lady was present.

"Whatever the client's business is," Prudence mused, "it has to have some connection to Madame Régine's salon."

"A competing dress designer?" Amos spat into his tobacco tin. "I don't see it."

"Railroad and oil tycoons don't think twice about trying to destroy a rival. Why should dress designers be any different?"

Josiah stared at Prudence as though he couldn't believe what she'd said. His pencil skipped over his stenographer's pad, leaving unintelligible animal tracks behind. Only he could decipher them.

"I think we should ask Madame Régine what it's like to work in the Parisian fashion world," Geoffrey said. "She spent years there learning her craft. She'll know better than any of the rest of us what goes on in the various salons."

"All I can tell you is that when a woman goes for a fitting, she's treated like a queen. Champagne or tea, bonbons and little cakes, maids and seamstresses cluck-clucking over her as though she were the most precious client they've ever had. No one mentions price, of course. That would be unutterably vulgar."

Prudence's aunt had taken her to Charles Frederick Worth's Paris salon to introduce her to the famous designer whose clients included the Empress Eugénie, Empress Elizabeth of Austria, and untold numbers of British nobility and wealthy Americans. Worth had transformed the world of women's fashion, single-handedly raising it to the level of what had become known as haute couture.

"If there's money involved, it's a cutthroat business. Take my word for it," Amos said. "No matter what the product is, someone will gladly slit a competitor's throat to get him out of the way."

It was an unfortunate comment, Prudence thought. The mental picture of Brenda Leavitt's body lying in rivulets of her own blood was so vivid an image, she knew she would never forget the sight of it. Nor of the snowflakes of wedding dress, some of them stained red. She let the conversation flow around her as she toyed with Brenda's bankbook. Josiah's coffee was making her jittery. There was something dancing at the edge of her brain, but she couldn't quite bring it into focus.

She'd told Geoffrey that she thought she'd make an early night of it. He didn't object, taking in at a glance the strained pallor of Prudence's face and the droop of her eyelids. Before she left the office, he kissed her gently on the forehead and the tip of her nose—a favorite spot that usually elicited a soft laugh that was almost a giggle—and wished her a relaxing and uncorseted evening in the quiet of her boudoir.

Geoffrey assigned Amos Lang to search Anthony Nichols's office in the morning, then gave him the night off. But that didn't mean there wasn't an ex-Pink concealed in the shadows opposite Prudence's mansion. Not that Geoffrey expected anything untoward to happen, but he preferred being overprotective to being caught off guard.

Uriah Pritchard was nearly as good as Amos at disappearing. He'd worked a recent case for the agency and made himself available several times on short notice. If he needed to get in touch with Geoffrey, one of Danny Dennis's urchins could carry a message. Two of the homeless boys, wrapped in horse blankets from the stable, would be sleeping in the dubious shelter of a nearby doorstep. Day or night, they could run faster than a carriage horse through the city streets to the Fifth Avenue Hotel. Prudence was as safe as Geoffrey could make her without actually being at her side. It would have to do.

Regina Healy had grown up in the tenements, where concealment was a tenet of survival. She spotted the shadow that was Uriah Pritchard as soon as she turned the corner from Fifth Avenue. She knew that if he was keeping watch, a couple of Danny's ragamuffins would be nearby.

She wasn't sure why she'd decided that no one except Prudence needed to find out about the letter she'd received earlier that evening or where she had been urged to present herself. But she hadn't hesitated when she made up her mind to go to the alley behind Madison and Fortieth Street—as directed—nor had she contemplated taking anyone with her but Prudence MacKenzie. The note hadn't said to come alone.

Like most of the other old mansions on lower Fifth Avenue, the MacKenzie home still had a stable yard behind the main house, with access into the alley that ran the length of the street. No one seemed to be watching the rear entrance, whose massive gate was locked and barred from the inside. Not much of a deterrent to a woman who as a child had scaled rickety fire escapes and jumped from one tenement rooftop to another with as much grace as a wild mountain goat. Skirts hoisted up to her waist and securely knotted, Régine was up and over the carriage gate before anyone could have spotted her. The kitchen door gave way under the same type of picklocks that Prudence always carried.

Silent and dark, the lower regions of the house had been tidied and then emptied by early rising servants eager for their beds. There had been one light on the second floor visible from the corner of Fifth Avenue. Prudence MacKenzie's bedroom, since she was the only family member living in the house. Servants slept in the attics.

Régine made her cautious way up the main staircase, inching along the second-floor corridor, alert to any sudden noise, or the movement of air that would indicate someone else was sharing her space. But it seemed as though the entire MacKenzie household had retired for the night. Except for its mistress.

Prudence had fallen asleep over her book, a not uncommon occurrence. A small fire had been banked, the last vestiges of heat emanating from its covered coals. Always on her guard, Régine locked the bedroom door behind her, tiptoed to the side of Prudence's bed, and laid a hand firmly across the sleeping woman's mouth.

"It's me," she whispered—unnecessarily—slowly removing her hand as Prudence's eyes registered startled recognition.

"What is it? What are you doing here?" Prudence scooted up against her pillows, braided hair coming undone and tumbling over her shoulders.

"Is your maid nearby?" Some women insisted that a maid sleep in a dressing room, to be available if needed during the night.

"Colleen has a room in the attic, with the other female servants." Prudence palmed her eyes and tried not to yawn in Régine's face, which was still inches from her own.

"Are you awake?"

"Of course I'm awake."

"Good." Régine handed Prudence the note she had been shocked to receive. "Read this."

Thick, expensive paper. Bold black ink. *Madame Régine* written in a fine female hand below the fold. A broken wax seal. Prudence's eyes flew to the signature. *Mrs. C. Donovan.* "Is this who I think it is?"

"There's only one Catherine Donovan in New York City

who would be contacting me like this," Régine said. "Her husband's name is Charles. *Mrs. C. Donovan.* It's how she labels all of her creations."

"I've never been to her salon," Prudence said as she scanned the message, then read it again, more slowly. "I've heard it said she's as good as Charles Frederick Worth himself. Until you opened your salon, she was the only dressmaker society women would patronize when they couldn't get to Paris. She's a New York institution to some people."

"Though not much less expensive than Worth. Except for the transatlantic voyage to France. She imports dresses from his and other Paris ateliers and sells them here in New York—with alterations, of course. A client can see what a dress looks like on her—pinned all across the back to fit—before she makes a final decision. Very innovative and extremely popular."

"Why does she want to see you? Why the secrecy? '*Come to the tradesmen's alleyway entrance at ten o'clock this evening.*'"

"Her living quarters are above the salon," Régine said.

"You've been there?"

"No. But I've heard descriptions from some of her clients who've decided to see what I can create for them. At a more reasonable price. Probably at the request of a husband whose wife's dressmaker bills give him apoplexy."

Prudence folded the note and handed it back to Régine. She glanced at the clock on her bedside table. "It's almost ten now. Unless I'm entertaining, the servants all go to bed soon after nine. Who let you in?"

"No one."

"You picked a lock?"

"Your kitchen door. It's how we'll have to leave, too. Someone—probably Mr. Hunter—has stationed a man out front to keep an eye on the house."

"He never said a word to me about doing that." Prudence didn't know whether to be furious at this infringement on her privacy or grateful that Geoffrey had thought it necessary to protect her. There was, after all, the matter of her shredded wedding gown strewn over Brenda Leavitt's body. "What do you mean by *we*? Where are we going?"

"I'm not creeping alone down a back alley to rendezvous with someone I've never met," Régine said. "You're the private inquiry agent."

"But this time Danny Dennis or Geoffrey won't be standing by to get us out of trouble," Prudence protested. Purely for form's sake.

"If we're careful—there's two of us, after all—we won't need to be rescued."

"What do you suppose she wants?"

"We won't know unless we do what she asks. Aren't you going to get dressed? We don't have much time." Régine marched over to Prudence's armoire. Arms akimbo and shaking her head, she surveyed its contents.

"There's a secretary's suit at the far end," Prudence directed, climbing out of her bed. "It's dark gray."

Régine handed her a corset. "Turn around while I lace this up."

"I'm not wearing that thing," Prudence said. "We may have to make a run for it." She laughed at the shocked look on Régine's face. "Don't pretend you haven't wanted to spend a day without your stays. There's a group of women who want to abolish them. It's called the Rational Dress Movement. No corsets, no tight lacing. Bloomers for bicycle riding."

"Of course I've heard of it. Very bad for my business." But after a moment of indecision, Régine tossed Prudence's corset onto a chair, then handed her the gray secretary's suit and a pair of sensible walking boots.

They hailed a hansom cab on Fifth Avenue and directed the driver to let them off at the corner of Madison and Fortieth Street. If he was curious about why two ladies would be traveling to an address he knew to be the salon of Madame C. Donovan, he didn't comment on the lateness of the hour and the certainty that the salon would be closed.

"Wait until he's out of sight," Prudence directed. "We don't want him to know we're sneaking down an alleyway. I take it Madame Donovan has her own good reason why we shouldn't climb her front steps and ring the doorbell like normal visitors."

"It's ten o'clock at night," Régine said.

"For some people in this city, the night is just beginning," Prudence reminded her. "Private parties at Delmonico's often don't begin until around this time. Or even closer to midnight."

"Working people have to get up in the morning," Régine snapped.

"He's well away," Prudence said, leaning out into the roadway to be certain she could no longer see their hansom cab. "Let's go."

"We should have brought a bull's-eye lantern," Régine grumbled. "It's dark as pitch back here."

"We only have to take a few steps," Prudence reminded her. "It's a corner house and she'll have left the alleyway gate open for us. There's enough light from Fifth Avenue so we can tell where we are."

"I'm stepping on all kinds of rubbish. It's as bad as being back behind one of the tenements."

"Don't exaggerate. Try to enjoy the adventure of it." One of the reasons Prudence had so often gotten herself into dangerous predicaments was precisely because she'd developed a taste for daring escapades. She devoutly hoped marriage wouldn't put an end to them.

A cat ambled along the alleyway and paused to study the strange creatures who had invaded its territory.

"Here we are. The latch is off, just as I said it would be." The gate didn't make a sound as Prudence inched it open. Recently oiled, she thought. Madame C. Donovan knew what she was doing.

They walked quietly along a swept garden pathway between beds of fragrant flowers. A light bloomed in what Prudence thought must be a kitchen window as a nearby church bell tolled ten o'clock. A door opened, silhouetting the shape of a woman.

"Right on time," Catherine Donovan said as she ushered them inside. "That speaks well of you." She raised a finger to her lips. "We'll go up to my private parlor on the second floor where no one will hear us and we won't be disturbed."

The kitchen light flicked off and the hallway was illuminated when Madame Donovan turned a pair of key-activated switches on the wall.

"Electricity," Régine whispered. "My next investment."

Madame Donovan turned for a moment, then shrugged and continued leading them down the hallway and up the stairs to the room where she entertained special guests and enjoyed her few moments of privacy. Except for the presence of electricity, the parlor was as elegantly Victorian as money and good taste could make it. All burgundy and deep green velvet, gold- framed mirrors and paintings, a carved marble fireplace in which well-fueled flames leaped.

"Please make yourselves comfortable," Madame Donovan instructed, indicating a deep cushioned love seat and two plush armchairs grouped before the fire. "I've set out sherry and tea. Whichever you prefer."

Prudence held out a gloved hand. "Madame Régine asked me to accompany her, Mrs. Donovan. I'm sure you understand that receiving an invitation for a nighttime meeting such as this required more than the usual caution. I'm Prudence MacKenzie, private inquiry agent."

"You may call me Catherine or Madame Donovan. Either

one, Miss MacKenzie. Whichever suits you. And I shall address this very talented young designer as Régine or Madame Régine, whichever she prefers."

"Irish-born?" Régine asked.

"As were you," Catherine Donovan answered. "Tenement-raised and Paris-trained."

"Then I think Régine and Catherine should do us just fine. Unless you like to be called Kate?"

"I left Kate behind a great many years ago." Catherine Donovan poured three glasses of a very fine sherry, then hovered a hand over the teapot. Prudence and Régine shook their heads. Time for tea later.

Régine unfolded the note she'd brought with her and laid it on the table beside the sherry decanter. "You've pricked my curiosity," she said.

"Slainte," Catherine raised her sherry glass.

"Slainte," repeated Régine.

Prudence said something she hoped sounded similarly Irish.

"I asked you here because I had a very interesting and somewhat alarming visitor the other day," Catherine Donovan said, getting right to the point. She picked up an artist's ribbon-tied portfolio she'd tucked between the cushions of the love seat, but she didn't open it. "A Frenchman, looking to join an established salon as a designer. Théodore Augustin Delahaye."

Régine set down her glass. "May I?" She nodded at the portfolio.

"Please do. I think you'll recognize some of the sketches."

None of the women spoke as Régine lifted first one then another drawing, turning them and the interleaved sheets of tissue paper carefully so as not to smudge the pastel chalks or leave fingerprints on the watercolors.

Prudence watched as Régine turned the pages.

"Several of the gowns are quite beautiful. Very original and elegant at the same time," Catherine commented. "Though I don't believe I've seen any of them made up. I usually know what my clients are wearing. Especially if it's not of my creation."

"Some but not all of these are mine," Régine said. "Designed when I was working in Paris. Stolen from me by a man I trusted. A man I loved."

"And who now wishes to destroy you." Catherine Donovan sipped her sherry and stirred up the fire. "I think you'd better tell us about him."

Chapter 14

"Théo is ten years older than I am," Régine began, "which was one of his great attractions. There were so many young designers competing for so few places at the great houses that it was like being surrounded by hungry dogs. All of them speaking French so fast, I often had no idea what they were saying.

"He was different. Already ensconced at House of Worth. Settled. Secure. His talent recognized and rewarded. What I didn't know when we first met was that nothing he drew was original. He reproduced sketches made by others, refining them or translating them into pastels or watercolors to become part of the portfolios shown to clients. Worth had begun displaying his creations on live models—which no designer before him had done—but he also kept voluminous portfolios. Nothing was ever thrown away, in case some minor detail should eventually become important."

"So much has changed since I trained in Paris." Catherine Donovan sighed and sat up straighter on her love seat. "No one dreamed of electricity in those days. Our eyes ached and watered from the candles and the fumes of the oil and kerosene lamps. At the end of a workday, they were as reddened as though we'd been weeping for hours. I suppose that's why I had electric lights installed here as soon as they became available. I've never forgotten the pain of peering at stitches when it was nearly too dark to make them out."

"The electric light in the workrooms was so bright we thought we'd never get used to it," Régine said. "But we very quickly wondered how we'd ever managed to sew a fine seam without it."

"Théo," Prudence said. "What else can you tell us about him?"

"He didn't allow most people to call him that," Régine said. "Only those he considered close friends."

"Which included you."

"We became lovers the night we met. I was as foolish a girl as any I've ever known. But he was so handsome. And he treated me as though I were a fragile porcelain doll. At first. Later on, he changed."

"You said that some of these sketches are yours?" Prudence touched the closed portfolio, bringing Régine back to the present.

"Can you pick out which ones they are, Miss MacKenzie?" Catherine Donovan phrased the question as a challenge.

"They're very early work," Régine temporized.

"Let her try," Catherine urged.

Prudence opened the portfolio, handling the sketches and watercolors as carefully as she had seen Régine do. She set aside the pages she thought her designer friend had executed, ten in all. Exactly half the total of what Théodore Augustin Delahaye had presented to Madame Donovan as entirely his own compositions.

"What made you chose those particular designs?" Catherine asked. "Speaking as a client, of course."

"Something about them—the graceful lines, the way the fabric hugs the female figure but doesn't distort it, the symmetry between the gown and the woman wearing it." Prudence paused, not certain how to explain why the designs spoke to her. "The others seem derivative, as if they were copied from something finer and more original. They're stultifying rather than exciting. I wouldn't want to appear at the opera or at Delmonico's in any one of them."

"Then you understand Régine's talent," Catherine said.

"Are all of these yours?" Prudence asked, pointing to the stack of sketches she'd set aside.

"Every one of them," Régine affirmed. "You obviously have a very good eye, my friend."

"He's trying to pass off your work as his." Prudence returned the sketches to the portfolio, closed it, and retied the ribbon. "He didn't think Catherine would recognize Régine's distinctive style."

"Which is why I sent you the note. Why I asked you to come here after hours," Catherine said.

"Stealing designs goes on all the time. In all of the major salons," Régine said. "The less important ones, too, for that matter. It's why no one is allowed to write anything down during a showing. It's relatively easy for a thief to pass herself off as a client. Very substantial sums are often paid for early purloined copies of a famous designer's new collection."

"Your Frenchman appears to be using his real name," Prudence remarked. "Théodore Augustin Delahaye. Was that what he called himself in Paris, Régine?"

"It's a name with a certain cachet. You'd have to be French to know that the Delahaye family was once noble, wealthy, and very much a part of court life. Before the Revolution. Only a sprig or two survived. None of the estates, and none of the political clout. Nor the title. So while Théo bore a once celebrated name, he was only as secure as his pencil or paintbrush could make him."

"And that's where you came in?" Prudence asked.

"He wanted to move from what was essentially a clerk's or minor artist's position into the rarefied atmosphere of designer. Charles Frederick Worth's two sons, Gaston-Lucien and Jean-

Philippe, turned him down. Not once, but many times. They had their father's talent for what would please a client and turn an ordinary woman into the bewitching creature she'd never dreamed she could be. Théo has always been an excellent draftsman, but nothing he designed caught the imagination.

"I'd gotten a position as an apprentice seamstress, but I moved very quickly up the ranks. When I was promoted into the design department after I'd suggested a few changes that greatly improved one of the gowns I was working on, I thought he'd beat me senseless."

"Théo beat you?" Prudence had met physically battered women in her charity work, but she'd never known any of them in the way she knew Régine.

"Very carefully, so the bruises didn't show. Never on the face, the neck, or the hands. Only in places covered by clothing."

"Did you tell anyone?"

"I was too ashamed," Régine admitted. "I thought it had to be my fault. That I'd done something to deserve it. Then he began taking the sketches I was practicing on at home. They disappeared from my sketch pad and found their way into the salon. I only found out by accident. When I confronted Théo, he threatened to kill me if I told anyone."

"So you left and came back to America," Catherine said.

"I had saved some money, hidden it away where he couldn't find it. I suppose I knew what would eventually happen. I was planning my escape before I allowed myself to believe I needed to break free of him. I burned every sketch he hadn't stolen, and then I crept out of the apartment in the middle of the night."

"Is he here in New York because he knows that's where you are?" Prudence asked.

"He promised that he would always find me if I tried to hide from him," Régine said.

"Finish your sherry," Catherine ordered. "I'll pour you another glass and you'll drink that one down, too."

"If Théo applied to you for a position on your design team, Madame Donovan, he must be planning to come back to learn your decision," Prudence said, watching Régine sip at the sherry that brought a flush to her pale cheeks.

"He didn't want to leave his portfolio, but I insisted," Catherine explained. "I knew that might be the only way to get him to return if he sensed my answer would be no. I praised his work extravagantly, but men can be stupid that way. They're easily persuaded of their own presumed superiority."

"Régine, you said Théo beat you. And that he threatened to kill you if you left him. Think for a moment. Is he capable of committing murder? Could he have wielded the weapon that took Brenda Leavitt's life?" Prudence watched tears flood Régine's eyes as she realized she might have attracted a killer into her salon. "Take your time. Don't answer until you're sure."

The look on Catherine Donovan's face told Prudence that she had been about to ask those same questions. And that, in her own mind, she had already formed the answers.

"I was very afraid of him," Régine conceded. "He became someone I didn't recognize after the first blow. As though feeling his fist on my flesh goaded him into a frenzy. He beat me nearly senseless, then he gathered me in his arms and wept as though his heart were breaking. It was my fault, he begged me not to force him to do what he claimed hurt him more than it did me."

"Is he capable of killing?" Catherine asked.

"No. Yes. Yes, he is." Régine contradicted herself and choked on her answer, as if the words stuck in her throat.

"Do you know if he's ever behaved toward another woman as he did with you?" In Prudence's experience, men like Delahaye rarely limited themselves to one victim.

"I don't know. He was living alone when I met him, when I moved in with him."

"He never spoke of someone else? Perhaps a youthful love?"

"No. It was as if he'd always been alone until I came into his life."

"I doubt that very much," Catherine said.

"It will be your word against his," Prudence said. "From what you've told us, there's no proof that the beatings ever took place or that the sketches he showed Madame Donovan aren't his own. They're not signed, and I imagine it would take a practiced eye to distinguish one designer's work from another's. There again, one person's word against another person's denial."

"If Catherine doesn't hire him, he'll go elsewhere," Régine said.

"Is it possible he doesn't know Régine is in New York? That his presence here is happenstance?" Catherine asked. Then she answered her own question. "No, of course not. The haute couture world is very small. We all know the work of every other salon. The gossip in our workrooms guarantees that no one keeps a secret for very long. Delahaye has to have heard of a young designer recently arrived from Paris whose gowns have the ladies of the Four Hundred all atwitter. He'd know in an instant that it has to be you, Régine."

"I agree," Prudence said. "You may be in as much danger as though you'd never left Paris."

"You've both been too polite to ask why I decided to warn Régine like this, late at night with no witnesses to your arrival here," Catherine Donovan said. "Why I didn't just hand Delahaye back his miserable portfolio and tell him he wouldn't be welcome in my salon.

"It's a very simple answer, Miss MacKenzie. I haven't been unaware of Régine's talent. I know that some of my clients have commissioned work from her, and that the gowns she's designed for them have been at least as good as anything I've ever created. That's the greatest compliment I can give you,

Régine, because we both know that I wouldn't be where I am today if I weren't a match for Charles Frederick Worth himself. As are you.

"I'm sixty-five years old. I made my mark in New York City before the war, and I'll continue to work for as long as I'm able. But someone will eventually have to take my place. I've always known that. I wish it could be my own son or daughter, but my husband, Charles, and I have never had children.

"Until Delahaye walked into my salon, I didn't interfere with what Régine was doing," Catherine explained to Prudence. "There's great satisfaction in building a business entirely on your own, which you must know from your own experience. I know you have a partner in the private inquiry firm, but I also understand that admission to the New York bar was a victory belonging to you alone."

"That's kind of you, Madame Donovan," Prudence said. "There aren't many of us yet, but I believe that someday there will be others who successfully swim upstream."

"That's a lovely metaphor," Catherine said. "Irish salmon are well-known for their ability to survive. So are Irish women." She chuckled. "But to get back to Régine's situation. Delahaye is a brutal and evil man. New York City has its fair share of them. I see their handiwork every day. I can't stop that kind of violence. But this stealing—what he's doing—I won't ignore because I can put an end to it. That's why I've pushed my way into your life and your livelihood, Régine. Uninvited. Perhaps unwanted. But I'm here now, and I'm stubborn enough not to go away."

"I wouldn't want you to," Régine said, reaching out both hands to clasp one of Catherine's.

"Nor would I," Prudence agreed.

How was she ever going to explain tonight's adventure to Geoffrey?

Then she realized that Catherine Donovan was exactly the type of woman he most admired. The tricky bit was why Prudence had felt it necessary to sneak out of the house and evade the ex-Pink he'd set on guard to keep her safe.

Inez had considered soaking handfuls of pearls in an arsenic concoction until she realized that none of her research was instructive enough to guarantee success. Should powdered arsenic be put into water or alcohol? At what concentration? How long did the pearls have to remain in the liquid to absorb enough poison to kill? And most vexing of all, how would she get them into Madame Régine's salon and onto Prudence MacKenzie's wedding gown? It had been a lovely plan, but, she finally admitted, highly impractical and almost certainly doomed to fail.

There were no more black widows haunting her attic or spinning webs in the glass apothecary jars in which she'd raised them. They had provided a spectacular end to a vexing situation, and the loveliest part of the operation was that it had begun quite innocently. A black widow she'd sighted in the attic one day when she'd gone up to hide one of her journals in a small traveling trunk. There it was—perched on the brass lock—in all its shiny black and scarlet glory. She'd captured it in an overturned jelly jar. The plan was hatched at that very moment, though it took months to acquire enough black widows to ensure an opportune outcome. They were all gone now, and one should never use the same stratagem twice. That smacked of pattern, which was how so many famous murderers were eventually caught. Lack of imagination.

Flowers. Could a deadly blossom be slipped into the bride's bouquet? Henry Purcell had devoted an entire section of his extensive library to the sciences—botany among them. But nothing Inez read suggested as simple a task as clipping a deadly flower and inserting it among the violets, roses, and decorative greenery favored at most weddings. Plants, she learned, could be very deadly, but they had to be harvested, pounded into pulp, boiled, dried to a paste—difficult to accomplish under the circumstances and hardly worth the effort since bridal bouquets were seldom eaten.

Such a shame that Prudence MacKenzie had chosen to be married in white. The bright green gowns that could only be achieved through arsenic-laced dye had carried off many a dressmaker and foolish young woman back in the day. Some women continued to drape themselves in emerald even after the dangers of that particularly vivid dye had been proven and publicized.

She thought about painting a poison on the teeth of one of the spaniels but couldn't come up with a way for the dog to bite her victim. Spoiled oysters delivered to the MacKenzie kitchen? Chocolate-covered cherries into which hemlock or cyanide had been injected? An electrical switch that gave off a heart-stopping shock? A hansom cab veering onto the pavement at precisely the right moment?

Inez fell asleep in her chair, the dogs puddled at her feet. Thinking about murder was an exhausting business, especially when nothing she came up with seemed promising. She'd try again tomorrow. Surely there was a solution to her problem somewhere in Henry's library. It was just a matter of finding it.

Chapter 15

Régine insisted on hailing a hansom cab when they finally left Catherine Donovan's home and salon shortly after midnight.

"We're both too tired to walk," she maintained.

Régine was right, of course, but Prudence stopped the hansom half a block away from the corner of Fifth Avenue and Twelfth Street. "I'll have to tell Geoffrey about tonight, but I'm not up to it yet, and I don't want to take a chance on his man catching a glimpse of me sneaking back into the house."

"I'll walk you down to the alleyway," Régine offered. "I'm sure the hansom driver will be willing to wait—for a price."

The man nodded. Set the cab's brake. Reached under his seat for the bottle every cabbie carried on night runs.

"I'm taking Katja to an at home," Prudence said, linking arms with Régine as they stuck close to the building fronts to avoid the pools of lamplight along Fifth Avenue. Within a few minutes they'd reached the mouth of the alleyway where Prudence had left the rear stable gate off the latch.

"I'll have the dress she's to wear delivered to the De Haan house by midmorning," Régine promised. "The lady's maid has already been hired, so there isn't anything more to do."

"Then everything's going according to plan."

"Not quite," Régine reminded her.

"Madame Donovan will take care of Théo," Prudence said.

"For the time being."

"She's more than a match for him. And by bringing him into her salon she'll be able to keep him so inundated with design work that he won't have time to threaten you." Prudence knew it wasn't a foolproof scheme, but it was the best they'd been able to come up with.

"I said I thought he was capable of murder, but the more I think about it, the less I'm able to picture him killing poor Brenda. She was struck so many times with that heavy glass weight, Prudence." Régine shuddered. "He likes to use his fists on women. In places that won't show. That's not at all the same thing."

"We're buying time. Or rather, Catherine Donovan is buying it for us. We'll deal with Théodore Augustin Delahaye. He won't get away with what he did to you and what he's trying to do now. But murder? We have nothing we can use against him."

Prudence watched Régine walk to the end of the alley, turn to wave, and then disappear around the corner onto Fifth Avenue. She lifted the well-oiled latch, slipped into the stable yard, and remembered to lock the gate behind her.

By the time one of Danny's urchins thought to tell Uriah Pritchard that he might have seen someone—could have been a woman, but he was taking a piss and wasn't sure—in the alley behind the MacKenzie mansion, Prudence was upstairs in her bed.

Serious thought had been given to where Katja De Haan would be introduced to the feminine side of New York City's Four Hundred. From among the several ladies who were at home on Tuesday afternoons Prudence chose two. Lillian Osborne was a close friend of Caroline Astor, but she was also one of the kinder women in society. Always encouraging to the shyest or least popular of the debutantes. Eleanor Eaton, the oldest of Lina Astor's intimate circle, was by far the most grandmotherly. Another good-natured woman of impeccable lineage who could be counted on to understand and forgive any slight social error made by a newcomer. Once Mrs. Osborne and Mrs. Eaton put their stamps of approval on Katja, the rest would follow.

It wasn't as though either the girl or her family were strangers on the scene. The De Haans and Katja's mother's family were Knickerbockers of such long standing that they were automatically included on every important invitation list. The once-elegant brick house on Twentieth Street two blocks west of Fifth Avenue was not quite ramshackle yet, but even a casual passerby could tell that it was in need of the kind of ongoing repair that keeps a time-honored home from appearing rundown. It was obvious to those who knew him that Leopold De Haan's gambling debts had siphoned funds away from the once-proud edifice built by a stern, uncompromising, and hardworking Dutch grandfather.

A lady's at home didn't begin until three in the afternoon, which meant that no matter how many obligations Prudence found to fill her morning and after-luncheon hours, there was no possible way she could avoid informing Geoffrey about Monday night's adventure. Régine had insisted that he be told the whole truth, which was that she—Régine—was responsible for Prudence's nighttime excursion.

"So Madame Donovan is going to hire Delahaye?" Geoffrey skipped without comment over Prudence's explanation of how she came to be at the salon at ten o'clock at night, having eluded the watchful eyes of Uriah Pritchard and two of Danny's boys.

"She'll pretend she doesn't know about his connection with Régine, or that fully half the sketches he showed her weren't his creations. But she'll insist that all of his design work be completed at her atelier and that none of it leave the salon for any reason whatsoever."

"Is that how it's normally done?"

Prudence shrugged. "If it seems odd, Delahaye will probably assume that Americans do things differently than French designers."

"We'll need to search wherever he's staying."

"Madame Donovan didn't have that information yet, but she'll get it."

"The sooner the better. The behavior of men with a penchant for violence usually escalates with every successful assault."

"We don't have any proof that Delahaye is responsible for Brenda Leavitt's death." Prudence was doing her best not to assume guilt without hard evidence. It was something Geoffrey maintained was essential to good detecting.

"Did you tell Régine about Anthony Nichols?"

"There wasn't time." Prudence didn't want to admit that waking up with Régine's hand over her mouth had driven all thought of Nichols right out of her head. That and the extraordinary interview with Catherine Donovan.

"She needs to know that someone hired him specifically to get information about her designs and clientele."

"The impression I got from Régine and from Madame Donovan is that neither of them would be surprised to learn there was a spy in their workrooms. It's apparently as much a part of haute couture as threading a needle."

"Nevertheless, as soon as he reports in, I'm sending Amos out to search Nichols's office." It was already midmorning, late for someone like Amos who rarely slept a whole night through. Geoffrey knew about Amos's use of laudanum, but since the ex-Pink appeared to have it under control, he made a point of not mentioning it. He'd also decided that he'd ignore Prudence's most recent escapade. It was over. She'd come through it safely. That she'd managed to give the slip to Uriah Pritchard was worrisome, but in a few more weeks she'd be sleeping at Geoffrey's side.

There was no way in the world she'd ever creep from their bed without his knowing it.

Amos Lang expected to have to break into Anthony Nichols's office; he never went anywhere without his picks. Mr. Hunter hadn't mentioned engaging the door lock when he and Miss Prudence left, but a cleaning lady would certainly have seen that everything was secure once she finished sweeping and emptying wastebaskets. She hadn't scoured the corridor, though; dust balls had nestled against the baseboards and dirt from the street crunched underfoot.

It was hot for the first day in September, muggy and smelly in the hallway. Gamey. Like someone in the cheap apartments on the top floor was boiling a knob of tough beef that had gone off a bit and therefore become affordable. If you cooked it for three or four hours, then doused it with horseradish, hot mustard, and some fermented Worcestershire sauce, it almost became edible. Good way to doctor up the barreled salt pork and horseflesh that was used as ballast on incoming ships and often sold dockside.

The moment Amos opened the office door, he realized the tainted smell wasn't coming from upstairs. A man's body lay sprawled on the floor, a cloud of flies hovering over him. A gun lay beside his right hand, but Amos knew instantly that this was no suicide.

Anthony Nichols hadn't taken his own life. Amos didn't have to have witnessed the event to reconstruct what must have happened. Nichols had watched outside until he saw Miss Prudence and Mr. Hunter walk back toward Fifth Avenue, then he'd returned to his office to retrieve something he'd forgotten or to wait until dark when presumably he could hoof it to Grand Central without being seen. Except it hadn't worked out that way. Someone, perhaps whoever had hired him, had guessed he'd be leaving town and decided to make sure he didn't.

The cops would probably take a quick look at the setup and buy it. Less work, and who cared if there was one fewer two-bit private inquiry agent in the city. He wasn't real law enforcement. Private dicks mostly worked skip artists and cheating spouses. Drank as much or more as the hustlers they chased down.

Amos could let Nichols lie there until a building tenant investigated the worsening smell or he could pass along word of the body to a beat cop. First things first, though. The files. He had no idea what he was looking for. Mr. Hunter had said he'd know it when he found it. Which was pretty much how most of the inquiry business worked. You rooted around until you nosed up something that didn't sit right.

The file drawers were less than half filled. Either someone had gone through them or Nichols had had very few clients. Easiest thing to do would be to toss what remained into a bag or a box and take them back to the MacKenzie office. A lot more pleasant to read through them without the ripe odor that was settling into his hair and clothing. Amos stacked the files on the desk, then wrapped them in a coat he found thrown over a chair, tying the bundle tightly with the coat sleeves.

Nichols's body had to be searched, though Amos knew the killer had almost certainly taken anything of value. Empty pockets, not even a box of matches or a pack of cigarettes. No loose folding money or coins. No handkerchief. No wallet. No comb. Someone who knew what he was doing and wasn't bothered by stealing from the dead had taken everything Nichols might have been carrying. Why be so thorough? Why take his time?

Hadn't the bullet that had entered Nichols's mouth and come out through the back of his neck made enough noise to bring someone running? There'd been talk for years about inventing something you could clamp on to the barrel of a pistol to deafen the sound of a pulled trigger. But so far, nothing like that had become available. Amos kept up with the world of firearms. It was worth his life to know what was new, what was more effective today than had been around yesterday.

When he got back to the office, Amos would take a better look at the coat he'd bundled around the files. Could be the killer had folded it over a few times and shot through the layers of fabric. Muffled the sound enough so as to make it less recognizable. Forgotten to take it with him after he'd rearranged the body.

Nothing in the desk drawers. Not so much as a pencil stub. The phone on the wall wasn't working. Disconnected? An unpaid bill?

The last thing he did was take off the dead man's shoes. Under the interior lining and beneath the heel were the two best places to hide something small and valuable.

He wasn't disappointed. A grimy piece of paper had been wedged beneath the right heel. Writing on it that Amos couldn't make out in the dim light coming through the dirty window. He shoved the paper into one of his pockets, then ran his fingers under the lining of both shoes. Nothing but a sweaty smell that clung even after he'd wiped his hand on the corpse's coat.

Back on with the shoes. Leave the gun where it lay, but remember the position, the make and model, the way the right hand had been folded around the handle. Much too neat. A man who'd shoved a gun into his mouth and pulled the trigger wouldn't still be holding the weapon. It would have fallen to the floor, perhaps to lie under the collapsed body.

Amos pictured Nichols on his knees, face upturned to beg for his life. The execution happened quickly. No time to lunge toward his killer and try to wrest the weapon from his hand. Muzzle in the mouth, pull the trigger, step back. There might not even have been blood stains on the murderer's clothing.

Amos had locked the office door behind him, so when a knock sounded on the glass pane, he simply froze in place. There wasn't enough light in the room to cast a shadow, but he couldn't take a chance that movement might still be detected.

Whoever was in the hallway knocked again, rattled the doorknob, knocked a third time. Louder, more impatiently. Then apparently gave up and turned away. Footsteps sounded on the stairs.

Moving quickly, Amos flattened himself against the wall to one side of the window that overlooked Fifty-first Street. He'd expected to see a man exit the building, but a woman came out, paused for a moment on the sidewalk, then began to walk toward St. Patrick's Cathedral and Fifth Avenue.

Miss Prudence would have been able to assess the woman's exact place in society by the clothing she was wearing. Amos memorized the dark skirt, fitted jacket, wide-brimmed hat, gloved hands, polished boots. Her face was turned away from him, but her posture had that special straight spine stiffness that Amos knew every society female learned from her governess. Therefore, not a woman of the working classes.

He would have followed her, was about to open the office door, in fact, when three men came down the hallway and paused to argue about something. Amos could hear their voices and make out their shoulders and bowler hats through the pebbled glass. They stood there, apparently in no hurry to move on, while Amos fumed and cursed silently on the other side of the door. If he'd been a few seconds faster! He could have been gone before they appeared. But he had no choice. He had to wait them out.

There was no way he could explain away the body on the floor.

Katja De Haan had been transformed. The girl Prudence had first seen being fitted for a yellow gown in Madame Régine's salon no longer wore her hair in a style that had gone out of fashion years ago. The beautiful skin had been highlighted with nearly invisible brushstrokes of peach-colored powder along the cheekbones, and the eyebrows thinned and shaped into perfect semi-circles. The blue eyes sparkled, and the perfectly shaped lips glowed. She was still heavier than fashion dictated, but the gown Madame Régine had designed for her hid every small flaw and emphasized the generous curve of an outstanding bustline.

"Magnificent!" Prudence clapped her hands spontaneously, amazed at the metamorphosis.

The lady's maid who handed Katja a pair of matching yellow silk gloves and an embroidered reticule smiled conspiratorially at Prudence. Both women were well aware of the impression the girl would make the moment she entered Lillian Osborne's parlor. The ladies of Caroline Astor's circle could assess a debutante's effect and probable success in the marriage market within seconds of the girl's first appearance on the scene. They would still take note of the somewhat long nose and the less-than-delicate chin, but these small defects would be far outweighed by Katja's impeccably styled afternoon gown.

The De Haan name would once more be known in society for something other than a wastrel's gambling addiction.

CHAPTER 16

"I left the office door cracked open so the first person to pass by would report the body," Amos Lang told Geoffrey as he piled the files and coat on the conference room table. "Someone's found him by now."

Josiah took rapid notes until the old blood smell from what Amos had brought made him put down his secretarial pad and raise a window in the outer office.

"Mulberry Street will send a pair of detectives as soon as the beat cop calls it in." Geoffrey stacked the files neatly to one side and spread out the coat.

"I thought the killer might have used the coat to muffle the sound of the shot," Amos said. "But there's no sign of a bullet passing through." He ran a hand over the material. "No hole. No powder burns."

"Which may mean the execution was done after the other offices in the building were empty for the day. Possibly after dark. Trains leave Grand Central at all hours. If that's where he intended to go," Geoffrey speculated.

"Earlier rather than later," Amos said. "Rigor had just about passed. Judging by the temperature inside the office, I'd put the time of death at shortly after you and Miss Prudence left the building yesterday afternoon. The blood on the floorboards had dried solid."

"You said there were apartments on the top floor. One of those tenants might have heard something."

"I doubt it. It's an old brick building, but sturdy. Ordinary sounds don't carry from story to story. If someone was standing out on the stairs or a landing, maybe. Otherwise, no." Amos spoke like a man who'd already considered and rejected that possibility.

"A shot could be mistaken for a slammed door," Josiah volunteered. A draft of fresh air followed him back into the conference room.

Amos thought that extremely unlikely, given the type of tenant likely to be renting in that building, but he was reluctant to contradict Josiah. The secretary had proved too useful in past cases. He might not be professionally trained in the science of investigation, but he was unquestionably loyal and more than a little courageous.

"There's nothing in Nichols's office that could point to a connection with Hunter and MacKenzie," Amos said. "But someone has the business card you gave him. That's a bit troubling."

"The file he was referring to and put in his satchel isn't here." Geoffrey had opened each of the folders Amos had brought, thinking that the dead man might have deliberately hidden papers by misfiling them. But that would only have happened if he'd spied his killer from the window and suspected that he might have very little time left.

"No satchel," Amos confirmed. "It's circumstantial at best, but I'd venture to say that whoever paid him also decided to get rid of him. Either personally or by another hire."

"And took away whatever evidence could point in his direction."

"Or hers," Amos said, reminding them that it had been a

woman he'd seen exiting the building after the preemptory knocks he hadn't answered.

"A woman can handle a gun as easily as a man," Josiah agreed. "They're not that heavy."

"We don't know whether the gun left by the body was Nichols's weapon or if the murderer brought it with him." Geoffrey shook his head. "And we're not likely to be able to find out. Guns don't have to be registered as private property," he explained to Josiah.

"That's ridiculous," the secretary said.

"Someday. Maybe. But years and years too late to do us any good." Amos was privately of the opinion that a man who owned a gun wouldn't bother conforming to a law that inconvenienced him. If such a law were ever passed.

"I'll hold this over the teakettle spout," Josiah said, smoothing out the bit of paper that none of them had been able to read. "Heat makes old ink get darker. Usually." He glanced at Amos, who looked as though he were about to say something. "Don't worry. I won't hold it in the steam long enough to make it run. I do know what I'm doing. I've done this before."

"Let's check the coat again," Geoffrey suggested. "Nichols put a presumably important piece of paper in the heel of his shoe. It's not beyond the realm of possibility that he created hiding places in the lining of his coat. We're not looking for a bullet hole or powder burns this time."

To the music of the teakettle beginning to steam in Josiah's outer office, Geoffrey and Amos concentrated on feeling every inch of the dead man's coat. Tapping. Listening for the rustle of paper. Searching for the slightest indication that something might have been slipped beneath the thin, worn lining and the outer layer of threadbare wool.

"He had this coat for a while," Amos commented. "The question is why he didn't replace it."

"We know he was short of funds," Geoffrey said, continuing to run his fingers over every seam and buttonhole.

"Yet he had a bank account. You said that's what he was closing out when you followed him from Bank of the City." Amos was slicing open the coat's thick collar.

"If Nichols had a bankbook, it's disappeared, and so has any cash he might have withdrawn. I'm guessing that whatever he had in the bank was an emergency fund, not to be touched for ordinary expenses. His getaway stash."

"He'd be more likely to blend into a certain type of crowd if he wasn't wearing a brand-new overcoat." Amos was a master of disguise and a connoisseur of clothes befitting a man down on his luck. "Which to me indicates that when he did decide to run, it wouldn't be to anywhere posh."

"I haven't given up yet on this wreck of a coat," Geoffrey said. "There's still the sleeves to pull apart." He snapped out the blade of a pocketknife and began cutting through the stitching of the sleeve closest to him. "Good strong thread. I'd guess it's not original to the coat. Much newer."

A many-times folded piece of paper fell onto the table.

"It's a statement from a bank in Boston," Amos said, spreading out the paper. He whistled softly as he read the figures. "Our man Nichols might have been poor as the proverbial church mouse here in New York City, but he had a healthy nest egg in Beantown."

"Same name?" Geoffrey asked, attacking the other sleeve.

"Anthony Nichols," Amos read aloud. "This time there's an address on the statement. But I'm not familiar with the city neighborhoods in Boston so I don't know where it puts him."

"We'll have Josiah consult a directory. That's the kind of information he loves to chase down."

"What's that?" Josiah appeared in the conference room doorway, waving the damp piece of paper they'd taken from the inquiry agent's shoe. "It's hard to read, but I made out what he wrote. It's not going to do us any good."

"Why not?" Amos handed over the Boston bank statement. "Can you find out what part of the city this address is located in?"

"It might take some time." Josiah slipped the bank statement into one of the file folders he was never without and set the steamed paper on the table. "Brenda Leavitt's name and address. And the name and address of Madame Régine's salon. That's all. No notes. No other names."

"We know the name on his office door is probably the one he was born with, and we have a bank statement and an address in Boston. That's already more than I think Mr. Nichols wanted anyone to find out about him."

"Do you think he meant to catch a late-night train to Boston?" Amos folded up the coat now that they'd extracted all the information it was going to give them. "I'm thinking that's why he went back to the office when he assumed the coast was clear. To hide out for a while until it was time to go to Grand Central."

"That's a logical deduction," Geoffrey agreed.

"I've never been to Boston," Amos said.

"You can remedy that oversight this afternoon."

"I have a New York to Boston train schedule in my desk drawer," Josiah volunteered.

Neither Geoffrey nor Amos was surprised.

"And the water's still hot in the kettle. Tea or coffee?"

"I don't have any calling cards," Katja suddenly realized. She was sitting as straight and still as she could manage as Prudence MacKenzie's carriage made its way up Fifth Avenue through the traffic snarls of fashionable women calling upon one another.

"I'll order some for you as soon as we finish our rounds," Prudence promised. "We'll use mine in the meantime. You'll be my guest and protégée. No one will say a word."

"I do know the basics of how to act, Miss MacKenzie. I may not have come out properly, but my father claims that kind of knowledge is born in the blood."

"He's probably right to a certain extent, but for the finer points you need to be under someone's wing. Mine, in this case.

Remember, we'll only stay for fifteen minutes. I could stretch it to thirty since my mother knew all of these ladies, but I think it best not to presume. We want you in and out as quickly and gracefully as possible, leaving behind an impression that will be impossible to ignore or forget."

"Won't they consider me competition for their daughters or nieces?" Katja asked.

"Not coming out during this winter season may work in your favor because it means you will automatically be excluded from a great many entertainments the others will attend. They won't see you as much of a threat. Any debutante who didn't attract a serious suitor last year will be desperate. No girl wants to have to brave the marriage market rush for a second time. If she and her mama haven't already ordered a new wardrobe from the Paris salons, our task is to convince them that remarkable gowns can be had right here in New York City, either from Madame Donovan or from Madame Régine."

"I almost forgot why we're doing this."

"I advise you to do precisely that. When someone is obviously selling something, no one wants to buy."

"I've never worn anything this beautiful before," Katja said. "I think I've managed not to wrinkle the skirt."

"You've been as still as a plaster mannequin," Prudence said as the carriage pulled to the curb in front of the Eaton mansion. "Now it's time to smile and sip tea, mention Madame Régine's name when your gown is praised, and otherwise answer questions so vaguely that no one learns anything you don't choose to reveal. Can you do that?"

"My mother—if she were alive—would probably say that's what Knickerbockers do best." Katja ventured a timid smile.

"Being one myself, I most heartily agree. I hope Eleanor Eaton is serving a decently strong British tea today. I'll need it to stay awake."

Katja, knowing it wasn't polite to ask personal questions, didn't inquire why Miss Prudence was in need of a restorative.

And Prudence certainly wouldn't tell her about the late-night escapade for which Geoffrey—for some unknown reason—had chosen not to berate her. It was puzzling. Could a husband be more understanding, more forgiving, than a business partner who also happened to be a fiancé? She supposed she'd find out, but in the meantime, there was tea to drink and a young girl to chaperone through the thorny thickets of feminine society.

Katja's buttermilk dress with yellow embroidered flowers was an instant success. It breathed summer warmth and sunshine.

"Miss MacKenzie introduced me to Madame Régine," she informed a young woman who asked for the name of the designer. "Papa said that going all the way to Paris at this time of year was out of the question."

Heads nodded sagely. Fathers and husbands could be uncooperative when it came to fashion.

"Mrs. Donovan is considered to be nearly as good as Worth," someone else volunteered. "But I don't think she's taken on many new clients in the last few years. There's always a traffic jam of carriages outside her salon, and it takes weeks, sometimes months, to arrange an initial fitting. It's like waiting for someone to die so a pew becomes available at Trinity Church."

"I have a grandson who might suit your Katja very well," Eleanor Eaton told Prudence quietly. Comparing dressmakers had captured the attention of every other woman in the room. "He's rather studious and a bit dull. Doesn't dance very well or sail his own yacht, but he's fond of animals. A gentle soul, as out of place in society as I gather she is. Not having a decent dowry wouldn't be a problem."

"It sounds like a match worth pursuing." Prudence smiled as she sipped her tea. Eleanor Eaton was living up to her reputation as the most grandmotherly of Caroline Astor's close friends.

"I must tell you, Prudence, that I admire the way some of you young women are taking risks and claiming independence." Eleanor's smile was as genuine as the wrinkles on her face and the gray in her untinted hair. "I was fortunate to have a happy marriage—though rather short—but if I had my life to live over again, I might make some very different choices. My generation was never allowed to study serious subjects, you know. Embroidery and polite French phrases were thought quite taxing enough for our weak womanly brains."

"The world is changing." Prudence glanced toward Katja. Their fifteen minutes of conversation were nearly up.

"Faster than many would like. The vote is next."

"Do you think so?"

"Something major, nearly earth-shattering, will have to happen before important change can occur, but the small steps are not to be ignored. Did I congratulate you on being admitted to the bar?"

"I've yet to try my first case in open court." It was a sore spot that rubbed Prudence the wrong way every time she thought about it.

"You will. In the meantime, you're doing private inquiry work. Allan Pinkerton broke through that barrier when he hired Kate Warne, but the momentum has stalled. I know about the body found in Madame Régine's salon. Everyone does. I assume, since Katja is wearing one of her creations, that you're working the investigation."

"Very perceptive," Prudence said.

"Being in society one's whole life does teach a few useful skills, the most important of them being able to read between the lines, so to speak. Madame Régine is talented. She deserves your help." Eleanor smiled. "I'll make sure my grandson is introduced to Katja, and I predict they'll immediately recognize themselves to be kindred spirits. In the meantime, be very careful, Prudence. I knew your mother, and that dreadful sister of hers. Lady Rotherton, as she became. You rather resemble your aunt, but for your dear mother's sake, watch where you go, what you say, and what you do. Now give me a kiss on the cheek and be on your way."

"Your face is slightly flushed," Prudence remarked as she and Katja climbed into the waiting carriage. "Are you ready for at least one more visit?"

"I've just never before gotten so much attention," Katja said, feeling the warmth of her skin through the light silk summer gloves that were the exact shade of buttermilk as her dress. "No one has ever seemed to care what I had to say or what I thought."

"That's going to change," Prudence predicted.

Then she settled back in silence as the carriage rolled toward Lillian Osborne's mansion. She wondered how many women felt the way Eleanor Eaton did. That if they had their lives to live over again, they would do so very differently.

CHAPTER 17

There were more private inquiry agents in New York City than the ordinary citizen would have suspected. The wealthy spied on one another.

Wives hired agents to follow their husbands and learn the names and addresses of their spouse's latest mistress. Without access to a beloved's bank account, it was the only way to judge approximately how much of one's dowry was being spent on a usually younger, almost always less socially acceptable rival. Actresses, dance hall dollies, secretaries, and shop girls were to be expected and considered largely unthreatening, but it was quite a different story if a man took up with a wife's friend or social equal. That type of affair simmered away quietly, though there were always rumors. Everyone knew that someday, someone would smash the social mold and leap into a scandal from which there would be no recovery.

Husbands snooped on their wives, but more for the satisfaction of learning how vulnerable the women's public faces were than for any real intent to be rid of them through a financially draining and embarrassingly public divorce. As tightly drawn as nearly all marriage contracts were, there was always a bevy of high-priced lawyers willing to take on their most annoying provisions. But—and on this most husbands agreed—it was easier to send a wife off to a country retreat where laudanum immobilized her than to wade into marriage legalities. If a rest home cure did not suit, a man could content himself with hiring someone to accumulate enough evidence to blackmail his other half into submission. The profession of private inquiry agent was entirely unregulated; they were vastly cheaper to employ than attorneys.

Prudence MacKenzie did not suspect she was under surveillance. It didn't occur to her that every outing would be of interest to anyone but herself. Geoffrey might have warned her, based on his years of Pinkerton duplicity. It was second nature for him to watch his own back and to assign ex-Pinks to try to keep Prudence from being harmed when she was recklessly pursuing a lead. But he failed to remind her that inquiry agents could be prey as well as predator.

The man who had been hired to write detailed reports on where Prudence went and whom she met did not know the identity of the individual who hired him. A lawyer, acting for a client, engaged him, gave instructions, received the reports, and paid the agreed-upon fees. A bit unusual, but not the first time a deep-pocketed customer with a recognizable name had chosen to remain in the shadows. It actually lessened the danger for the inquiry agent and could lead to additional work, since confidentiality was a rare commodity.

He sent a telegram detailing the afternoon's itinerary, as revealed when the subject's butler informed the subject's chauffeur. First to the Eaton residence, and then on to the home of Mrs. W. Osborne. Lillian Osborne, not to be confused with her Osborne daughters-in-law. Miss MacKenzie would be accompanied by Miss Katja De Haan. The ladies would be driven in Miss MacKenzie's carriage by her coachman. Name of Kincaid.

Were there additional instructions other than to observe and report? Receiving no answer to his telegram, the agent had to assume there were not. While lucrative, this assignment was turning out to be considerably more boring than most of his work.

With only fifteen minutes in which to complete a social call—if one was not a close relative and therefore entitled to perhaps half an hour's formal visit—it was imperative to arrive a few minutes ahead of one's quarry and to secure a seat with a good view of one's hostess. Courtesy demanded that each new arrival greet the lady of the house before ensconcing herself on a love seat or chair for the delightful pastime of exchanging gossip. The whole process was as carefully orchestrated as a minuet. Any display of ignorance of the rules guaranteed that the offender would subsequently be ostracized.

Inez Rankin Purcell had taken great care with her appearance. Though a widow, she was no longer obliged to wear the somber lilacs and grays that replaced the black garments of the first year of mourning. Henry Purcell had been dead long enough for his bereaved spouse to have remarried without opprobrium, but Inez had long ago decided that one wealthy marriage was quite enough, thank you.

She'd never seen the witch who had stolen Geoffrey Hunter's affections. The closer it got to the wedding, the more impatient she became. Southerners were famous for producing women of astounding beauty. Some said it was the climate that did it, since it was too hot to brave the sun and risk one's delicate complexion. Others maintained that intermarriage of cousins refined good looks, thinned the bones, and enhanced a graceful sway of the hips. Whatever the reason, it was difficult, if not impossible, for Inez to believe that a Yankee female could compete with one of Geoffrey's own kind. Someone like Inez herself. She'd known Yankee women who could be termed attractive, but she'd never acknowledged that true beauty could exist above the Mason-Dixon line.

She had to see for herself. Hence a lawyer she'd never used before and an inquiry agent who would never learn her name.

The plan didn't go quite as intended.

The timing was off, for which Inez blamed the inquiry agent who sent the telegram, the lawyer who advised her of Prudence MacKenzie's itinerary, and the Western Union delivery boy who wasn't fast enough on his bicycle.

Inez barely made it to the De Haan residence before the MacKenzie carriage pulled away. She caught only a glimpse of the two women she'd come to spy upon, more a flurry of skirts than a good look at the faces half-hidden by the tall coachman who blocked her view.

Annoying. And Inez hadn't brought along one of the small dogs whose fur she pulled out by the handfuls when she was too angry to do anything else.

To make matters worse, Inez's idiot of a coachman didn't negotiate the Fifth Avenue traffic with half the skill of Prudence MacKenzie's man. By the time her carriage arrived at Eleanor Eaton's residence, the empty MacKenzie vehicle was drawn up at the curb where its passengers would expect to find it in a quarter of an hour.

Inez—now pinching and pounding at the fine fabric of her carriage's interior—could only wait in solitary splendor. She had left a calling card at the Eaton home years ago, but it had never been accepted, which meant a butler or footman would not admit her to his employer's parlor. The etiquette of the calling card was as strict as any of the customs governing the lives of New York City's elite.

It had always enraged Inez to be excluded by all but a few of the women whose husbands could not afford to snub Henry Purcell. As soon as Henry died, invitations dried up like one of the cracked summertime cotton fields back home, and there hadn't been a thing Inez had been able to do about it. She could count on the fingers of one hand the foyers where her calling card had been accepted. The number would never increase. The only good thing about the process was that those few women who had welcomed her would not snub her—unless she was stupid enough to bring scandal down upon her head. Which she was careful not to do.

Inez sat in her carriage outside the Eaton mansion for exactly thirteen minutes. Then she instructed her coachman to drive to the Osborne home. She would be inside, settled into the parlor, when Prudence MacKenzie and Katja De Haan arrived.

Inez might have to extend her stay for slightly more than the acceptable fifteen minutes of polite conversation, but she meant to make the most of the time available to her. Nor for a second would she take her eyes off the wanton hussy who had ensnared her Geoffrey.

The plan was back in place.

Prudence took a few moments to remind Katja of what she needed to do at Lillian Osborne's at home.

"Mention Madame Régine's name and salon at least once, more if several women comment on your gown. Don't answer any questions on why you didn't come out last season. If anyone asks about your father, mention very quietly and sadly that you fear his health isn't what it should be. Sip your tea, but don't empty the cup. Nibble at one sandwich and take a single bite from a petit four. Smile your appreciation at your hostess's refreshments, but don't finish anything or you'll be branded a glutton. Any questions?"

"I heard some of what you and Mrs. Eaton were talking about," Katja said. "When am I supposed to meet her grandson?"

"Congratulations. You have excellent hearing. That will stand you in good stead when people start whispering about you."

"Miss MacKenzie?"

"I imagine Eleanor will let me know when she's arranged something," Prudence said. "It will have to be very informal since you're not out in society. You mustn't seem overeager."

"Life with my father hasn't been easy." Katja sighed.

"And you'd like to get out from under his thumb?" Prudence had hesitated for a moment before asking the question.

"Does that seem terribly unfilial?"

It struck Prudence that Katja De Haan must be very lonely, living in a once-grand house now visibly neglected and an eyesore to its neighbors. No governess for several years at least, her only parent rarely home. Her father spent his days gambling and his nights whoring while she read or did needlework by candlelight or the flames of a small fire that barely took the chill off a room. Marriage must have seemed like an improbable dream, Eleanor Eaton's unknown grandson as close to a Prince Charming as she would ever get.

Prudence reached for one of the buttermilk-gloved hands. "Mrs. Eaton won't forget you," she promised.

Katja's hesitant smile lit up the interior of the carriage. She nodded her thanks.

Prudence paused on the threshold of Lillian Osborne's parlor, a quick look around assuring her that she'd chosen their arrival time well. One didn't want to be part of too large a gathering, nor was it a good idea to be either the first or last guest.

With only fifteen minutes during which to make an impression, she guided Katja directly to their hostess, performing the introduction as she allowed Lillian to greet her with a light kiss to the cheek.

"My dear Prudence, I am so delighted to see you this afternoon. You don't make a habit of calling as often as you should,"

Mrs. Osborne chided. "I refuse to believe you spend all of your days in a dreary office or racing about town pursuing criminals."

"Not every moment of every day." Prudence smiled mischievously. "But I do fill empty hours with legal briefs and untangling the activities of men and women who should know better." She drew Katja forward. "Have you met Leo De Haan's delightful daughter, Katja?"

"I do know your father, my dear, but I fear he's been hiding you longer than he should have. I hope all is well with him."

"Perhaps not as well as one would hope," Katja replied, her rather throaty voice pitched low and sad, exactly as Prudence had instructed.

"Then you must sit here beside me and tell me everything," Mrs. Osborne cooed. "That's a lovely dress, by the way. It suits your coloring admirably."

"Do you know Madame Régine's salon?" Katja asked. "She's rather recently arrived from Paris where I understand she was one of Charles Frederick Worth's most talented designers."

Attention turned Katja's way at the mention of haute couture's most famous name.

Prudence glided toward the sideboard where an array of cakes and sandwiches was being served by two maids in black uniforms and starched lacy white aprons and caps. She had an excellent view of Katja explaining to a rapt audience how Madame Régine considered each client's wishes and turned them into masterpieces of design.

As she lifted a cup of Darjeeling to her lips, Prudence felt an odd tingling at the nape of her neck, a sensation she rarely had but never ignored. It meant someone somewhere was watching her with more than casual interest. Geoffrey claimed it was a perception that was like a sixth sense to the best inquiry agents. A lifesaver when a bullet was about to be fired or a knife hurled. Prudence thought he exaggerated the idea to make a good story out of it, but she had never managed to explain why she herself had often found it to be true.

The important thing was not to let on that she knew someone was studying her. Not dangerous here in Lillian Osborne's parlor, but it was a most impolite thing to do. She let her gaze wander, ticking off in her organized, lawyerly way the names of the women she knew, which was nearly every one of them.

There, over by the windowed French doors that opened onto the garden, sat a woman conspicuously alone, balancing a teacup from which she didn't appear to be drinking. Prudence judged her age to be in her early thirties, perhaps as old as thirty-five. She was dressed in the height of fashion, as was every other lady in the room. The wedding ring she wore on her right hand indicated widowhood, some years in the past to judge by the pale blue of her gown. Like Caroline Astor, who was known to be overly fond of her magnificent jewelry, this woman had bedecked herself a little too garishly for afternoon. Not crossing the line into tasteless ostentation, but close. Very close.

She didn't appear to have noticed Prudence. Her eyes were focused on Lillian Osborne, Katja, and the small group around them who were enthusiastically discussing the state of fashion design in the city. But as soon as Prudence turned back to the sideboard to consider the array of crustless sandwiches, she felt that tingling start up again on the back of her neck.

That did it. Prudence had quickly mapped the position of everyone in the room. No one else could be staring at her. She couldn't approach and speak to the woman, as they hadn't been properly introduced, so she decided to do the next best thing.

Turning toward the French doors, she ambled as casually as she could in that direction. It took her out of the woman's direct line of sight, brought her, in fact, to a spot behind and to one side. Lillian Osborne's garden was an explosion of color framed by the French doors. Prudence was able to seem to be appreciating its beauty while discreetly scrutinizing the visitor who had now piqued her interest.

She watched as the lady in blue set down her teacup and prepared to leave, presumably because her prescribed fifteen minutes of formal call were over. As she approached Lillian Osborne to make her goodbyes, Prudence followed. Geoffrey always said you could learn a great deal about a person by listening to their voice. The accent. The choice of words. The structure of a sentence.

"So nice of you to drop by, Mrs. Purcell," Lillian Osborne said without a trace of warmth or sincerity. "Do come again."

And then the woman was gone, not having uttered a word that Prudence could make out. What she did pick up, however, was a rather odd cadence, one not heard frequently in New York. It reminded her of when Geoffrey occasionally lapsed into sounding more Southern than he realized.

Inez thought that Prudence MacKenzie was one of the least becoming creatures she'd ever seen. Slender, of course, with light brown hair, rather pale gray eyes, skin untouched by wind or weather. But with an air of belonging that only came after generations of family wealth and a superior place in society. You were born with that kind of assurance. It was bred in your bones and then fine-tuned by a strict governess.

Inez knew all about that look. She possessed it herself. So did Geoffrey. The two of them had grown up on plantations and in city townhomes where no wish was too outlandish to be denied, and servants far outnumbered the family members they served. So Inez supposed that if the MacKenzie girl hadn't awakened a romantic love in her fiancé, she had at least shown herself to be eminently suitable since he seemed determined to remain in the North.

That did not for one moment mean she accepted the fact of a marriage that was only two weeks away. Now that she'd seen the bride for herself, Inez knew that disrupting the wedding was not only desirable, but very feasible. Geoffrey had made a bad decision when he'd refused to marry her when she most needed him. It was Inez's opinion that men often did not realize what was best for them. It fell to the women in their lives to instruct them or—if instruction failed—to manipulate events to their desired conclusion.

She began to plan even before the carriage reached Washington Square.

CHAPTER 18

The address on Anthony Nichols's bank statement brought Amos Lang to the most beautiful residential street he'd ever seen. A Boston neighborhood called Back Bay.

Redbrick- and limestone-faced brownstones lined both sides of Commonwealth Avenue. Down the center ran a tree-lined park dotted with benches and statuaries. He stood in the cool, quiet shade of the park, wondering how such a refuge could have been built in a city famous for its busy, noisy port and sprawling industrialization.

He consulted the bank statement more than once, finally matching the address with the crisp black numerals on a four-story home nearly in the center of a block of attached single family dwellings. He figured it would be years yet before the area began to be invaded by waves of immigrants, its middle-class houses divided into tenement-style apartments and single-room rentals. If he'd learned only one thing by living in a city, it was that nothing remained the same for very long.

Judging by what he'd seen of Anthony Nichols's office, the dead man had definitely come down in the world. Men left their roots and their families for any number of reasons, most of them having to do with alcohol, opium, gambling, or women. He wondered which of them had ruined the private inquiry agent's life. And whether he'd had a respectable profession before deciding to delve into the squalid minutiae of other people's mistakes.

He noticed that the front stoop of the Nichols house had been swept and scrubbed that morning, its black iron railings cleaned of dust and grime. That spoke of an organized, well-run household staffed by trained servants and overseen by a conscientious housekeeper. The maid who opened the door to his knock and took the card he held out to her was obviously Irish by the few words she spoke. Young, pretty, her apron spotlessly clean. He wondered if every well-to-do household in Boston had a recently arrived Bridget on its staff.

Somewhat to his surprise, Amos wasn't left standing outside while the maid checked to see if her employer was at home. A polite euphemism that allowed unwelcome visitors to be easily rebuffed. She showed him into a small vestibule, then disappeared down a shadowed hallway, returning a few moments later to take his hat and lead him to the main parlor that faced the street and its distinctive park.

Two women who resembled each other so closely they had to be sisters waited for him. One of them held his card in her hand. The other crossed to the doorway, said something he couldn't hear to the maid, then waved him to a well-upholstered chair. In the moment of silence before introductions began, he looked around him, taking in gallerylike ranks of paintings hanging on the walls, fragile china figurines atop every table, the thick Turkish carpet underfoot, and a fragrance of fresh flowers from several Chinese vases. He tried and failed to picture Anthony Nichols alive and well in this setting.

"You wrote our brother's name on the back of your card, Mr. Lang," one of the sisters said. Her dark hair was lightened by strands of gray. Face powder that smelled like violets had been liberally applied over spidery wrinkles. "We would not have received you otherwise. I am Miss Martha Nichols."

She nodded toward the woman sitting beside her.

"I am Miss Delia Nichols." The woman placed Amos's business card on the low table before her and folded her hands in her lap. Like her sister, she was slightly portly, as though she'd enjoyed too many slices of cake with her afternoon tea. "May I ask what brings a private inquiry agent to our home?"

"If Anthony Nichols is your close relation, I'm afraid I have sad news to impart," Amos began. It wasn't the first time he'd revealed the death of a family member, but it never became easier, especially when ladies were involved.

"I assume our brother is dead or in police custody." Miss Delia's jaw muscles tightened and her eyes hardened. Her fingers tightened around one another.

"My condolences on your loss," Amos offered.

"I suppose we should be grateful he lived as long as he did." Miss Martha accepted the formal acknowledgment of death without surprise or emotion. "Even as a young boy he was impossible to control. Our father despaired of him, and he broke our mother's heart." She stiffened her back and raised her head to look straight ahead at a portrait hanging on the opposite wall.

"The circumstances of his death?" Miss Delia asked.

Amos hesitated.

"Please don't think to spare our feelings, Mr. Lang," Miss Martha said. "Before he left our home, Anthony's misdeeds had introduced us to more than one police officer. And several clergymen, when he was still in his early manhood and believed to be redeemable. Our father hired lawyers to keep him out of jail and repay what he owed to a number of claimants. Despite the promises he made, Anthony never changed."

Miss Delia's lips pursed. "We have always anticipated the worst from him. And have seldom been proved wrong."

"Mr. Nichols was found dead on the floor of his office in New York City," Amos began. "He had been shot. Murdered."

"We didn't know he'd left Boston," Miss Delia said.

"We should have guessed," Miss Martha told her sister. "When we didn't hear a word from him. He didn't come begging for money or to sleep off his liquor. No policemen knocking at the door. It should have been obvious, but I think we tried not to think of him at all. It had become too painful."

"When did the authorities find him?" Miss Delia was asking for details.

"I was the one who found him," Amos said. "In the course of an investigation." The card he'd given the Nichols sisters bore only his name and profession. No mention of Hunter and MacKenzie, Investigative Law. "He was working as a private inquiry agent."

"I don't understand," Miss Martha said. "He had no training for that kind of job. None that I know of. Why is one inquiry agent looking into the affairs of another agent? I assume that's what you were doing."

"He was part of a case with which I'd been charged." Amos picked his words carefully. He needed to learn all he could while giving away as little as possible.

"You said our brother was shot, Mr. Lang?" Miss Delia's voice was as steady as though she'd asked about the weather.

"The killer tried to make it look like suicide. It wasn't." Amos looked from one sister to the other, anticipating tears. There were none.

"What do you want from us?" Miss Martha asked. "You didn't have to come to Boston to deliver the news of Anthony's passing. You could have telegrammed."

Amos took the bank statement from the inner breast pocket of his jacket and handed it across the table. Miss Martha found her sister a pair of spectacles. "You read it, Delia."

"It's a bank statement." Miss Delia adjusted the spectacles on the bridge of her nose.

"Father's missing funds?" Miss Martha asked.

"Possibly. The sums seem about right."

"Anthony made a habit of filching money from various accounts our father set up for personal, travel, and household expenses," Miss Martha explained. "Never enough to cause immediate alarm, but the withdrawals and false checks added up to a significant amount over the years."

"Is that what led to his estrangement?" Amos asked. He'd phrased the question as gently as he could.

"He told Father that he'd spent the money to settle gambling debts," Miss Delia explained. "It was finally too much for a man with a weakened heart."

"We believed Anthony when he claimed he'd changed. And that he blamed himself for Father's sudden death. Mother had been gone for several years by then, so it became just the three of us." Miss Martha reached for her sister's hand.

"Six months later, we closed our hearts and our home to him." Miss Delia choked back a sob, as though the effort to appear unaffected was breaking through the barrier she'd built around her feelings.

"It's a considerable sum," Amos said, pointing to the bank statement.

"The money isn't important." Miss Martha turned to her sister. "Shall I?"

"Yes. Tell him," Miss Delia said.

"When our brother was still in school, he began bringing home abandoned animals he found." Miss Martha averted her eyes.

"He went out looking for them," Miss Delia added.

"He tortured and killed them, Mr. Lang. Down in the basement. We none of us knew what was happening until one of his victims got away from him. We heard the cries and at first our father thought a rat had been caught in the traps he sometimes set. But that wasn't it at all. What he found shocked him. I remember when Anthony came home from school that day our father took him into his study. They stayed there together for a very long time. I think Papa took off his belt and beat him."

"Anthony wrapped the animals in a cloth so they couldn't scratch him. Then we think he broke their necks or smothered them, Mr. Lang. With his bare hands." Miss Delia stared down at her fingers. They'd curled themselves into a tight circle.

Amos felt himself grow still and cold. Brenda Leavitt's skull had been fractured by repeated blows from a heavy object. Was there a correlation between that and snapped bones?

"Eventually he killed a woman, the same way he destroyed all those animals. Anthony swore it was an accident. Said she'd sold him her body and then attacked him when he refused to pay. Our father arranged to have the police investigation halted. There were no more incidents for several years. It was as if our brother had nearly succumbed to a mortal disease, then miraculously recovered. We all became hopeful again."

"Mama died. Our father was never the same without her."

"As I said before, it ended up being just the three of us." Miss Martha took a deep breath. "I can't tell you exactly why, but we became afraid of Anthony. Afraid of our own brother. It wasn't one thing he did or said, just the feel of him."

"I'd catch him staring at me," Miss Delia said. "And my throat would begin to hurt. I'd have trouble catching my breath."

"Did he threaten either of you?" Amos asked.

"Not in so many words. But his eyes followed us everywhere we went." Miss Delia shuddered. Of the two nearly identical sisters, she was slightly smaller and paler.

"We couldn't force him to leave," Miss Martha said. "It was as much his house as ours."

"You were so clever. I would never have thought of the solution you came up with." Miss Delia smiled for the first time since Amos had begun asking questions.

"I invited a cousin of ours to come live with us," Miss Martha explained. "We had an extra bedroom, and she was a widow struggling to make ends meet."

"She and Anthony clashed the first week she was in the house. They hadn't gotten along as children and couldn't much tolerate each other as adults. As time passed, the quarreling got more frequent. She never gave in to him, not an inch." Miss Delia smiled again.

"One day he packed his bags and left. He said he couldn't stand living any longer in a household of cantankerous womenfolk," Miss Martha said. "We never thought he'd leave Boston; we got used to the idea that he was somewhere in the city but choosing not to call on us."

"Does your cousin still live with you? Would it be possible for me to talk to her?" Amos asked.

"She remarried. Quite unexpectedly, but very happily. Anthony must have read the wedding announcement in the newspapers, but he made no attempt at reconciliation."

"She'd never had any children with her first husband, so when she found out she was in a delicate condition, she was overjoyed. She would have made such a good mother." Miss Delia touched a memorial locket at her throat, the kind that contained a lock of hair of a departed spouse, child, or—in this case—perhaps a cousin. "She and the child both died. Her husband sold up everything he owned and went west."

It seemed to Amos Lang that every time he thought he was on the verge of cracking open the mystery of Anthony Nichols, something or someone vital to the case would disappear like a puff of smoke.

"Is there any way to verify where the deposits your brother made came from?" he asked, picking up the bank statement to study it more closely. "Were these monies taken from your father's accounts or could they represent payments made to him by clients he worked for here in Boston or perhaps in New York City? The dates should give us an indication."

"I didn't look at when the deposits were made," Miss Martha said, borrowing her sister's spectacles to peer more closely at the statement she'd only glanced at before handing it to Miss

Delia. "The sums look reasonably close to what our father complained was missing, but I can't be certain."

Miss Delia rose from the sofa she shared with her sister and opened the top of a small Windsor rolltop desk. From one of the drawers she withdrew several leather-bound notebooks, each of them tiny enough to fit inside a lady's reticule.

"Our governess taught us to keep meticulous records of outings and correspondence," she said, returning to the sofa, spreading the notebooks on the table. "One must always send thank-you notes within twenty-four hours of an obligation. If we look up the dates of the deposits, we should be able to remember whether Anthony was living here at that time. It's so much more accurate to depend on the written word than on one's memory."

Fifteen minutes later Amos had his answer. A very few of the deposits had been made during the lifetime of Nichols's *père*, but by far the larger number dated to the period after Anthony had declared himself quit of irritating, petulant women. But before he had leased the dingy office in New York where he had been killed. Josiah had been able to confirm with that building's owner that Nichols had been a tenant for slightly less than two years.

"He was earning money here in Boston," Miss Martha decided. "He had to have been able to walk into this bank, cash or check in hand, and do business with a teller. That's the type of bankbook this is. I can't tell you how he earned what he accumulated because he hadn't been trained for a profession. But he was doing something that seems to have been relatively lucrative."

"He closed a bank account in New York the day he was killed," Amos said. "Whoever shot him took the cash and whatever papers he might have had on him. One theory is that he was intending to slip out of the city without anyone being the wiser. Obviously, he wasn't quick enough."

"Is being a private inquiry agent a dangerous occupation?" Miss Delia asked.

"It can be. Most of the time it's about as dangerous as clerking." Amos was thinking of the hundreds of hours spent watching hotel doors, waiting for errant husbands or wives to leave a place of romantic assignation.

"I was wondering if Anthony had already begun to work as an investigator before going to New York City. Perhaps he left Boston because he thought his life was in jeopardy," Miss Delia said. "And he might have decided to come back here for the same reason."

"I'm not following you." Miss Martha shook her head in apparent confusion.

"If enough time had elapsed between whenever he quit Boston and when he felt himself in peril in New York, he could have thought it safe to return. Perhaps he'd even decided that he missed the family life we could provide for him."

"That's a very far-fetched notion," Miss Martha snapped. "Have you forgotten how relieved we were when we didn't have to deal with him every day? How something about him frightened us?"

"He always maintained that killing that woman was an accident," Miss Delia insisted. "He's not the only man of our acquaintance who's taken a life. Carriage collisions are not uncommon. We're always reading in the newspapers about someone who's stepped into the street and under the hoofs of a horse. That happened to one of our own relatives. He wasn't driving, of course, but he was the owner of the rig."

"That's not at all like what Anthony did." Miss Martha glared at her sister.

"The woman you told me about," Amos interrupted. "The one your brother claimed to have killed in what he made sound like self-defense. How did she die?"

"How?" Miss Delia looked bewildered.

"He strangled her," Miss Martha said. "Placed both hands around her neck and squeezed until there was no more breath in her body. The autopsy also revealed a broken neck." There wasn't a hint on her face of compassion for her brother.

Miss Delia flushed red and then blenched nearly as white as the handkerchief she held to her eyes.

"You may forgive him, sister, but I never shall." Miss Martha leaned toward Amos. "If Anthony *had* come back here, I would have refused to take him in."

"What he left behind in his room is still in the basement." Miss Delia folded her handkerchief into a small triangle. She remained pale, but she'd fought off tears, and now she sat up straight again, seemingly determined to see this conversation through to the end.

"Some of your brother's things are in the basement?" Amos asked.

"We packed them into trunks when it became obvious he'd left for good. I thought that way it would be easier to send them on to wherever he settled. But he never asked for them." Miss Martha thought for a moment. "I have the keys."

"I wonder if I might take a look at the contents of those trunks." Amos tried to make it sound as though it wouldn't matter whether his request was granted.

"Why?" Miss Martha asked. "What can it matter now?"

"Was your brother in the habit of keeping a journal?" Most women did, but Amos knew that men were less likely to confide their innermost thoughts to a page someone else might read.

"Not that I know of," Miss Delia said. "But he did scribble notes to himself on bits of paper that he stuffed into his pockets. Our father said it was a very unorganized way to live one's life. He was never very happy with whatever Anthony did. Or tried to do."

Miss Martha took a ring of keys from the desk where the

small datebook diaries had been stored. She held them tightly, as if undecided what to do with them, then laid them on the table atop Amos Lang's business card.

"Don't expect either of us to go down there with you, Mr. Lang."

He wondered if the basement held memories too disturbing to risk reviving?

Chapter 19

"I want to start you off in the salon," Madame Donovan said, leading Théodore Delahaye into the showroom for clients who would choose from gowns worn by live models, an innovation borrowed from Paris fashion houses.

"I'm not a greeter, Madame Donovan. I'm a designer."

He was insulted. Under different circumstances he would have stormed out the front door—portfolio in hand—never to return. Delahaye had a temper; explosive fits of pique cowed seamstresses and eventually exasperated the purveyors of haute couture who hired him. Parisian salons had only put up with his outbursts because he was an exceptionally talented draftsman. Faster with drawing pencils and pastels than anyone else in the industry. *Doucement, doucement,* he crooned to himself. *Gently, gently.* His options here in New York City were far more limited than in France. He couldn't afford to burn any bridges.

"If you are to join and perhaps someday head my design department, Monsieur Delahaye, you must familiarize yourself with every aspect of the business. That includes learning the names and preferences of my American clients. They are not like the French women with whom you are accustomed to dealing." Madame Donovan had decided that placing Delahaye in the salon would allow for the closest scrutiny of his behavior and the least amount of harm to her product line. He had a way about him guaranteed to charm old and young clients alike. The allure of a handsome Frenchman's accent and manners guaranteed it.

"Of course, madame. If you insist." He had learned long ago that appearing to agree with a woman was the foundation on which all future wooing could be built. He thought Madame Donovan was probably old enough to be his mother, but Théodore had courted many a lady *d'un certain âge.* They were often pitifully grateful for the attention. He had schooled himself not to shudder at the old skin that looked and felt like wrinkled tissue paper.

Madame Donovan introduced him to the cadre of senior salesladies who saw to a client's comfort at every stage of her couture experience. "Champagne and petits fours which Delmonico's delivers every morning. The finest in the city. Teas are imported from England, as are the cups and saucers from which they are drunk. Linen napkins, whisked away as soon as a patron has finished her initial refreshment. Nothing must distract once the models enter the salon."

He nodded. So far Madame Donovan had faithfully copied the best of the French houses of haute couture. Ladies could not help but compare what she offered to that of the incomparable Charles Frederick Worth. Unlike many of his imitators, Madame Donovan was proving herself to be a worthy competitor.

"We are expecting Mrs. Purcell very shortly," one of the salesladies said. "She has ordered a gown to wear to a society wedding. It's a bit of a rush, but nothing we can't accomplish. Mrs. Purcell has been a client for a number of years."

It was clearly a warning that Delahaye had better perform at his best if he wanted to advance to the design department where he believed he belonged. "Do we have a portfolio of gowns she's ordered from us in the past?" he asked.

The saleslady handed him a beribboned folder. "This is everything," she said.

Delahaye caught himself just in time, moments before he would have turned his back on her and walked away to study the client's selections. "Merci, madame." The slight brush of his mustache on the back of her hand brought a blush to the saleslady's cheeks. He smiled at her, causing the blush to deepen. Even in a new city in an uncouth country, Delahaye thought, he could work his magic. Madame Donovan would be no match for the Delahaye charisma.

"If we consider launching Katja De Haan into society in order to save Madame Régine's salon from ruination, then this afternoon's calls were successful." Prudence had returned Katja to her home and continued on to the Hunter and MacKenzie office at the foot of Broadway and Wall Street near Trinity Church. "You'd think every woman we met today was a dear and trustworthy close friend. My teeth hurt from the cloying sweetness of it all."

"I don't suppose you'll want a cup of tea?" Josiah asked.

"If I were a man, I'd smoke a cigar to get the taste of sugary compliments out of my mouth."

"It's a good thing you don't pay afternoon calls very often." Geoffrey tried to keep from smiling. Prudence acting like a petulant child didn't happen very often. "Tell us about it."

"There really isn't much that would interest you," Prudence said. She glanced at Josiah, who was hanging on her every word. "Everyone loved the gown Katja was wearing, so she praised Madame Régine's salon and made sure to emphasize the individuality of each dress she creates and the expertise of the workmanship. It's no secret that Madame Donovan isn't expanding her client list as much as she did in her younger years, which means that Charles Frederick Worth's designs are in greater demand than ever."

"Most men, including husbands who pay the bills, have a difficult time understanding women and their obsession with what they wear," Geoffrey said.

"One cannot be seen in the same gown twice in one season," Prudence reminded him. "And if a gown does have to be worn again, it must be refurbished so as to seem new. That doesn't really fool anyone, but we pretend it does."

"Go on, Miss Prudence," Josiah urged. "You were telling us about the calls you made."

"Nothing out of the ordinary, except that there was one woman at Lillian Osborne's home whom I haven't met before. Her name was entirely new to me, and she sat apart from everyone else, as though she'd accidentally turned up in a place she hadn't intended to be."

"Maybe she's unaccustomed to the ladies of New York society," Geoffrey said. He'd once described to Prudence how his mother and her North Carolina friends spent hours in one another's company, sipping cool beverages and gossiping in the shade of one of the plantation house verandas. Servants—slaves before the war—stood behind their mistresses, fanning the sultry Southern air.

"I didn't get that impression. She's a widow, so perhaps she's not ventured out much since the loss of her husband."

"Surely she wasn't still in mourning?" Josiah sounded shocked.

"Not even half mourning. Lillian Osborne—when I asked—told me the lady's husband had been in business with Mr. Osborne, so of course when she left her card, Lillian was obliged to accept it. I gather that was some years ago. Lillian was rather surprised that Mrs. Purcell showed up today, but of course she didn't let on that she barely remembered her."

"Say that name again." Both of Geoffrey's hands rested against the edge of his desk, as though he'd caught himself in the act of abruptly standing up.

"Mrs. Purcell," Prudence repeated. "Lillian didn't tell me her first name. It doesn't matter because I doubt I'll meet her again. She really didn't seem at ease; I imagine she'll shrink back into her widow's seclusion. Some women never manage to rejoin society, especially if their doctor has introduced them to the comfort of laudanum. The medical profession has a lot to answer for."

"Mr. Hunter?" Josiah barely managed to move out of the way as Geoffrey surged to his feet and stepped away from the desk.

"I'll get a hansom cab down by Trinity Church." Hat on, gloves in one hand, cane in the other, Geoffrey paused in the office doorway. He looked like a man who'd forgotten something. "I don't know what time I'll be back. You can close up for the day, Josiah. Make sure to call for Miss Prudence's carriage."

"Kincaid is waiting for me downstairs," Prudence said. "But you're welcome to take the carriage if you need it. I can always call on Danny Dennis." She expected him to explain what had caused the sudden leave-taking, but he didn't.

"That was odd," Prudence said, walking to the window that overlooked Broadway. Geoffrey was nearly out of sight already, walking quickly toward Trinity Church where hansom cabs could usually be found waiting for a fare. "Do you know where he's going, Josiah?"

"I haven't a clue," the secretary said.

"I wonder what set him off?" Prudence mentally replayed their conversation. "I was telling the two of you about the calls Katja and I made this afternoon, and the rather odd woman I met at Mrs. Osborne's."

"Mrs. Purcell, you said." Josiah closed his eyes and wrinkled his forehead. "The name doesn't ring any bells." He didn't need to add that he read all the society columns at which Prudence barely glanced. His knowledge of who was who in New York society was encyclopedic.

"When is Amos expected back from Boston?" Prudence asked.

"I think it depends on what he's found there. Could be late tonight or sometime tomorrow. There's no point waiting for him. Amos shows up when it suits him." Josiah cleared his desk and put the cover on the typewriter he was still learning to use and still distrusting. His penmanship was excellent. Why bother with a machine that often got the letters mixed up and left blotches of ribboned ink on the page?

"Geoffrey did say to close up the office for the day." Prudence picked up her gloves and reticule. "Socializing is exhausting. And not nearly as interesting as following a suspect or digging up clues."

"Are we really no closer to finding out who killed Miss Brenda Leavitt?" Josiah asked.

"Not only that. We have no idea who murdered Mr. Anthony Nichols."

"I suppose we can't expect to solve every case."

"I wouldn't say that aloud where either Mr. Hunter or Amos Lang could hear you, Josiah." Prudence stepped out into the hallway. She knew better that to ask the Hunter and MacKenzie secretary if he wanted to share her carriage. Josiah lived an intensely guarded private life.

As she walked down to where Kincaid waited, Prudence wondered again what had set Geoffrey off. Something he suddenly remembered he had to do? Something she'd said? She supposed he'd eventually get around to telling her. In the meantime, there was no use fretting over it. She was certain there was another pile of RSVPs waiting for her at home. It wasn't the done thing to have personal mail sent to one's business address. Too bad. Josiah would have loved wading through all the invitations. Perhaps she'd bring them—unopened—to the office tomorrow.

Every hansom cab driver in the city knew the location of the building where Danny Dennis stabled his horses and stored his carriages. He lived upstairs, in a small flat that was grander than anything he'd known in Ireland. Bedroom, sitting room, kitchen, indoor bathing and hygiene facilities. Just up a narrow staircase from Mr. Washington, Flower, and the ever-changing crew of street urchins who slept in the straw. No one had ever asked how he'd been able to afford setting up his business—recently off the boat as he'd been—and he'd never volunteered any information except his name. Which wasn't the one he'd been given at his baptism. Nor was it the one the British authorities had on their books for him.

The cabbie who dropped Geoffrey Hunter at the stable door lingered for a moment before pulling away from the curb. Just in case Danny himself stepped out onto the sidewalk to give him a nod of thanks. But he didn't. The red-gold dog with the plumed tail stood in the doorway, not barking, plainly delighted to greet the visitor. Beside and behind her popped up three or four tousled haired orphan boys who made do living on the streets. Danny always had work for them and a free spot in the hay for the asking. Food, too. They were perpetually hungry.

Geoffrey scattered pennies as he walked into the stable, stopping to run a hand down Mr. Washington's neck. "Is himself here?" he asked, automatically sinking into the Irish phraseology he'd picked up over the years from Danny and the boys.

"Upstairs," one of the children said. He couldn't have been more than seven or eight years old. Barefoot, wearing ragged short pants and a tattered shirt. "I'll fetch him for ye." He disappeared as soon as the last word was out of his mouth. You learned to be as fast as the wind or you didn't survive a parentless childhood in New York City.

"I need to know someone's address," Geoffrey said when Danny had come down and sent the boys out to buy sausages from a street vendor. Flower went, too, just in case one of them dropped something.

"I'll need a bit more information than that," the Irishman said. "No matter what some people believe, I don't read minds."

"Henry Purcell is the name."

"The only Henry Purcell I know of is dead. Has been for years. Bitten in his own bed by black widow spiders. It made all the newspapers at the time. People in every neighborhood of the city cleaned their attics."

"What else do you know about him?" Geoffrey asked.

"Wealthy. Married. No children. Banking, properties, invested in the cotton market at one time." Danny reeled off Henry Purcell's life statistics as easily as if he were reading them from a printed page.

"Cotton market? Was he a Southerner?"

"He was from somewhere in New England. Came to New York with a small family inheritance to make his fortune. But his wife came from your part of the country. So I was told. I've never driven her." Danny's eyes had begun to sparkle with curiosity.

"But you drove Purcell?"

"He had his own carriage, but he took hansom cabs when he didn't want his wife to know where he was going. I drove him more than a few times. He made a point of telling me he liked the idea of using a cabbie who could keep his mouth shut. He tipped too well for his outings to be entirely legitimate."

"Gambling or a mistress?"

"Mistress. He wasn't the kind of man who liked to take chances with his money." Danny paused. "Where are you going with this?"

"There may be a tie to a case we're working."

"Tie to a dead man?" Danny asked.

"It's complicated," Geoffrey said.

"Henry Purcell lived in one of those townhomes that face onto Washington Square Park," Danny said. "I remember him complaining about the little dogs his wife kept. Said they tore out the front door every time someone opened it. A servant had to chase the runaway through the park. Neighbors didn't like their yapping." He searched his mind for the number of the house. Found it. "There's no guaranteeing the widow still lives there. If that's who you're looking for."

"I owe you one, Danny." Geoffrey touched his hat brim with his cane.

"I'll put it on your tab," Danny said. He watched Geoffrey leave the stable and nodded Little Eddie to his side as the boys came tumbling back through the door, all of them smiling and smelling of sausage. "Follow him," he said. "Let me know how long he stays where he's going."

Little Eddie tipped his cap and scampered out onto the street. He was as fast a runner as Flower, and a lot less noticeable.

CHAPTER 20

Afternoon was shading into early evening when Geoffrey walked into the green oasis that was Washington Square Park. The day's warmth cooled as tree shade became shadow. Workers and walkers turned toward home and dinner while students packed up their books and papers. Benches gradually emptied, and the sidewalks grew silent. Here and there a child's toy lay abandoned or forgotten on the grass. A nighttime peace slowly enshrouded the park.

The town house whose address Danny Dennis had given Geoffrey was on the north side of the Square, in a section popularly called the Row. He stood for a moment beneath the branches of a massive oak tree, reconnoitering as he had often done during his Pinkerton years. Unlike the other homes on either side of it, in the Purcell town house he saw no gaslights burning in the rooms fronting the green space, though small plumes of dark gray smoke spiraled upward from the building's chimney. The drapes had not yet been drawn across the curtained windows, as they would certainly be once true darkness fell. He listened but heard no one playing a piano or a harp. No raised voices beat against the walls. There weren't even any tantalizing food smells drifting from an open window in a hot kitchen.

If the woman Prudence had described and named as Mrs. Purcell was the Inez Rankin Geoffrey had known so many years ago, she had had more than enough time to arrive home from Lillian Osborne's mansion. He couldn't remember ever feeling this flummoxed at the prospect of confronting a suspect, but it had to be done. He had to wade into the muck of his past if there was to be any hope of a bright future with Prudence.

He hefted the gold curb and bobble link chain in one hand, then returned it to his coat pocket. If—by some miracle—the chain did not belong to Inez, was not the one he'd seen her wearing at their last dinner together, then she couldn't have caused it to be left at the scene of Brenda Leavitt's murder. The string of coincidences that had led him here this evening would be just that—a series of unrelated happenstances that cruelly mimicked cause and effect.

He left the concealment of the oak tree's canopy and crossed grass and sidewalk to the front door of a dead man named Henry Purcell. Raised his cane and knocked with gentlemanly restraint. Took a step back so as not to be staring a butler too closely in the face and waited for his rap to be answered.

It wasn't. He heard no sound of approaching footsteps, saw no hall light switched on.

Geoffrey counted to ten, then knocked again.

This time he heard the rustling of skirts, the skittering of toenails against a wood floor, and the sharply cut-off yelping of more than one small dog's high-pitched bark. Someone stood on the other side of the door, deliberately not acknowledging his presence, waiting him out.

It was a game two could play, and one at which Pinkertons excelled.

Geoffrey descended the town house steps to the sidewalk, stood for several long moments studying the home's façade, then turned and walked away. Slowly proceeded toward the

Fifth Avenue entrance to the park, drifting out of sight of anyone looking out a parlor window. When he was sure he could not be seen, he stepped into the park again, moving through the growing darkness from one tree to another, careful not to cast a shadow, until he reached a spot deep within the park but in line with the oak tree opposite Inez Rankin Purcell's front door. Sometime in the next fifteen to thirty minutes, that door would crack open and his quarry would step outside. She wouldn't be able to resist peering down the empty sidewalk to assure herself that he was well and truly gone.

He'd wait. It wasn't the first time.

The basement in the Nichols house was nearly as clean and neatly organized as the upstairs parlor. Anthony's trunks and boxes had been stacked to one side of the rear entrance where deliveries were made, as though his two sisters had expected them to be speedily taken away. That hadn't happened. For whatever private reason, the brother had neither contacted Miss Martha and Miss Delia to arrange for their removal nor informed them of his decision to leave Boston for New York City.

Amos had keys to the trunks, but he also had a key that unlocked the small storage room where Anthony—as a boy growing into manhood—had created a retreat for himself that he grandly called his laboratory. This was the place where his father had discovered whatever remains of cruelty his son had practiced on the small animals he found in the streets and brought home. Unsure of how much time the sisters would allow him, Amos decided that his first investigatory stop had to be the so-called laboratory.

A small lantern stood on the lowest basement step, but the area was also lit by gas fixtures that cast a murky, yellowish glow over the dirt floor and brick walls. Assuming that the lantern had been placed there because the gas feed was undependable, Amos struck a match and held the flame under the mantel. From the way the sisters had reacted when he'd asked to be allowed into the basement, he didn't think the lamp had been used recently, but aside from a brief sputter, it burned steady and true.

Anthony's private space was at the far end of the basement. Amos supposed that it had originally been used to store wood before the house converted to gas heat. The key turned easily in the lock. Shelves lined the walls, and a long rectangular worktable took up most of the room's central space. The servants who had packed up the young master's bedroom had apparently been spared the ordeal of clearing out his laboratory. Glass jars and fish tanks crowded the shelves, some of them empty, many containing dried-out specimens that were sometimes difficult to identify even on close inspection. Labels were printed in what Amos decided was handwriting that had evolved from childish printing to the beautifully formed calligraphy of an adult bent on creating a collection worthy of admiration.

He saw no evidence that small animals or reptiles had been tortured. Could the young Anthony's family have misunderstood his admittedly unusual hobby? Was it biology that fascinated the boy rather than pain? What about the cries that had supposedly led Nichols Senior to investigate the basement room where his son spent so much time? Could the specimens the young investigator brought home have already been wounded? Could they, in fact, have been casualties of the city streets, on the point of death when he picked them up?

As Amos paced along the shelves, occasionally reaching out to touch or hold one of the collection jars, he wondered about Anthony Nichols's choice of career. Nothing he was seeing pointed to an interest in private inquiry work. On the contrary. A young man who was this meticulous in amassing test subjects would have been expected to pursue one of the sciences, probably at Harvard, Boston's premier college. Something had steered Anthony away from academia. Or perhaps something he'd done had slammed that door in his face, forever locking him out of a life of research and scholarship.

One of the sisters said her brother had killed a woman, the inference being that their father had paid not to have charges brought. Could it have been that act—presumably covered up as it was—that had ruined his chances for an academic career? Had that been the reason he'd turned toward the private inquiry field despite its dubious reputation and the whiff of scandal that inevitably hung over its operatives?

Conspicuously missing from Anthony's laboratory was any record of the experiments he performed there. No notebooks, loose papers, not even a stray pencil on any of the shelves or lying forgotten on the table. While the room was an engrossing hint at the dead man's early personality and interests, it contained nothing that would explain why someone had murdered him and contrived to make it look like a suicide.

The trunks were filled with neatly folded garments, everything from socks rolled together in pairs to pressed shirts and a box of men's jewelry. If he'd left this much behind, what had Anthony taken with him when he stormed out of the house after declaring he could no longer live with contentious women?

The journal that Amos had been counting on finding either did not exist, had been destroyed, or been tossed into the bag Nichols carried with him to whatever lodging he'd procured. One thing you learned early on in a Pinkerton career was not to let disappointment slow you down or distract you from the main thrust of your investigation. Amos had known from the moment he stepped off the train in Boston that he was unlikely to find the kind of clues that every inquiry agent dreamed of. But so far, except for what he'd learned about Anthony from his sisters, he'd come up close to zero. Nothing concrete. Nothing visible. Nothing at all that deserved to be called evidence. He went back to the laboratory for one more look around.

"You won't find anything down here that explains what happened to young Master Anthony. The upstairs maid had a listen at the parlor door. She told me what you've come for." The woman who stepped into the dusty, abandoned former storage room was tall and as broad-shouldered as a man. Wisps of gray hair escaped the cook's mob cap covering her head; she wore a white apron that reached to the floor. "I've been the Nicholses' cook for more years than I like to admit to. I was here when that poor child was growing up." The skin on her face had been disfigured by the smallpox and permanently reddened from steam and oven heat.

"Poor child?" Amos gestured at the racks of specimen jars with their ghostly contents floating in the preservative liquid that he supposed must be what was also used to embalm human bodies.

"You'd best take a read of this," Cook said, taking a small leather-bound diary from her skirt pocket. "Them two up there would have burned it if they'd found it. He left it behind the day he tore out of here like the hounds of hell were after him. He never came back for it."

Amos opened the diary to the first page. Anthony Nichols's name and birthday were inscribed there in round, childish handwriting.

> *I found a sick kitten today. Out by the trash bins. I brought it home and Cook gave me milk and meat from the soup bones. I'm making it a bed in a storage room in the basement. It's a boy. His name is Max. I've decided that I'm going to be a doctor even though I know Father wants me to follow in his footsteps and manage his businesses. He'll be angry, but I don't care.*

"His father accused him of torturing small animals and beat him for it," Cook said. "But he never asked what Anthony was really doing down here. The boy had himself a hospital for the creatures who were sick and dying in the streets. He tried to cure them, and when they died, he preserved their bodies in those jars you see. Master Anthony was the loneliest child I've ever known. He grew up to be an unhappy young man."

"I was told he killed a woman," Amos said, tucking the diary into his breast pocket for safekeeping. He didn't think Cook would ask for it back, but he didn't want to take any chances.

"He always claimed it was an accident, that she attacked him and he was defending himself. Nobody but me believed him. He'd started drinking, you see, so he couldn't remember the details of what happened. He was always a rebellious lad, but never cruel. Not that I ever saw. But Master Anthony changed after that, as if he knew he'd never get what he wanted in life. Closed up the basement, stopped bringing in sick animals. Drank some nights until he passed out."

"Did he keep in touch with you after he moved out of the house?" Amos asked.

"Not a word. But I heard things. He got a job working for an inquiry agent who was hiring on the cheap, but it didn't last very long. Then he left Boston. Went to New York City. I guess he figured he'd disappear into the crowd there. Start over, if you know what I mean." She stepped out of the laboratory and filled her apron with potatoes and carrots from the cold bin that stretched along an outer wall. "You can keep that diary," she said, gesturing toward Amos's chest. "Nobody else in this house has ever cared a whit about Master Anthony. At least now somebody besides me will read what he wrote about himself."

She slowly climbed the basement stairs, holding the sides of the apron tightly so the vegetables wouldn't cascade out. Amos heard a murmur of voices, then steps moving toward the back of the house, where he presumed the kitchen was located.

He relocked the trunks, restacked the boxes, and locked the

basement door behind him. A maid waited at the head of the stairs, hand outstretched for the keys he'd been given.

Neither of the sisters left the parlor to bid him goodbye.

Amos concluded that they'd allowed him in their home only because he could tell them the details of their brother's death and confirm for them that he was really and truly gone. There was no love lost here, not even a hint of sadness that Anthony Nichols was no longer among the living.

The sisters hadn't inquired about claiming the body. Their brother would not be coming home to Boston. In all probability he would join the hundreds of unwanted and unidentified corpses buried in the trenches of Hart Island.

Only the cook would remember him as she sat at her worktable drinking her afternoon cup of tea.

Geoffrey made himself comfortable on one of the wooden benches of Washington Square Park, grateful that it seemed relatively clean and free of splinters. An hour passed. If not for the periodic tolling of a nearby church bell, he might have dozed off.

Inez must have decided that he'd left the area because lights were turned on as she or a servant moved from room to room, closing draperies and presumably performing whatever rituals formed the backbone of her evenings. Dinner, perhaps a book to read by the light and warmth of a sitting room fire. She had dogs, so at some point before she retired to her bedroom, they would have to be let out to relieve themselves for the night. He supposed that would take place in a back garden or alley, but he wasn't ready yet to give up his scrutiny of the front rooms of the house. He was certain that the most prized bedroom would overlook the park. He might even catch a glimpse of Inez's shadow against the window.

His plan—although he hesitated to call it that—was to wait until he was sure the household had settled in for the night.

Then he would rouse them by a brisk knocking on the front door. Inez was bound to send a maid or her butler to answer it. An unexpected summons after dark always presaged some form of disaster.

He wouldn't leave until she emerged from her bedroom and agreed to talk to him. It was a scheme to match any of Prudence's risky, ill-thought-out plots. And since her machinations always seemed to work, it seemed logical to expect this plan to be successful also.

Chapter 21

The downstairs lights in the Purcell town house were extinguished one by one, except for a dim lamp in what Geoffrey decided must be the formal front parlor. He continued watching as the upstairs lights also went dark. When the last candle in an attic window was blown out, he knew the servants were abed.

The parlor light continued to burn, and above it, a light in what had to be Inez's bedroom.

In the silence of the park, Geoffrey heard the snick of a door being eased open. He stood, waited for a moment, then walked slowly across the grass, as silent in his approach as though he were gliding through the North Carolina woods in search of a deer.

He hadn't been mistaken. Inez's front door had been unlocked and cracked just wide enough to allow a thin shaft of feeble lamplight to pool on the steps.

He was expected.

Inez wore virginal white, a silk dressing gown with froths of handmade lace on its long, loose sleeves and running from neck to hemline down the front. Diamonds sparkled in her ears and on her fingers. Pale blond hair that was usually confined in upswept curls hung loose across Inez's shoulders. Her bare, unstockinged feet rested inside low-heeled white satin slippers.

"I knew you'd be back," she said, not rising from where she sat in an elaborately carved Louis XV armchair upholstered in blue velvet to match her eyes. Small dog beds were scattered around the room, but there was no sign of the animals who usually curled up in them.

Geoffrey didn't wait for an invitation to sit down. This wasn't an informal call between two people who had continued to be friends over the years. "You were watching from behind the windows when I knocked earlier this evening."

Inez exuded barely suppressed anger. And another emotion also, one Geoffrey recognized from long ago. Possessiveness. The firm conviction that something had been taken from her that was rightfully and forever hers. Him, of course. He knew he must be one of the very few of Inez's belongings—human or otherwise—who had managed to escape her acquisitive control. He suspected she was intent on making him pay for it.

"You were at Lillian Osborne's tea this afternoon." Geoffrey wanted this conversation over with as quickly as possible. If that meant being blunt and combative, he was more than ready for the challenge. "Why?"

"Surely your mamma didn't raise you to have the manners of a Yankee." Inez pursed her lips and shook her head at his descent into uncouth social behavior. "You haven't even asked how I'm doing, Geoffrey. Which, for your information, is very well, thank you. Widowhood doesn't have to be nearly as sad a period in a woman's life as it's often depicted. Once a lady is out of deep mourning, she can rejoin the world, but on her own terms. Wives are chattels, wealthy widows belong to no one but themselves."

"I asked a question, Inez. I'd appreciate the courtesy of an answer." He'd listen to her prattle, but not allow it to distract him.

"I wanted to meet your Yankee bride, of course. Or at least look her over from head to toe before the great day arrives. She must have a large dowry. She certainly has very little else to recommend her."

Geoffrey's back stiffened. If Inez had been a man, he would have slapped her across the face to provoke a duel or beaten the lout into insensibility with well-aimed fists. He said nothing, holding himself in check. The Inez of his young manhood had never been able to tolerate more than a few moments of silence.

"I didn't stay long enough to compel Mrs. Osborne to introduce us." Inez tapped one foot impatiently, then stopped abruptly as she realized what she was doing. "So your fiancée and I didn't engage in conversation. She'd brought a wretchedly ugly young woman with her, though the gown the creature was wearing was quite acceptable."

"I didn't realize until recently that you were living in New York City," Geoffrey said.

"Would you have called on me had you known?" Inez asked. "I doubt it, so don't bother lying. You left me alone and bereft when I most needed you. That was hardly the act of a gentleman."

"I wasn't responsible for the dilemma in which you found yourself." He kept his voice measured and low.

"Everyone expected us to marry. Don't try to deny it. You had a duty to me, and you walked away from it."

"What happened, Inez?" He suspected but had never known for certain.

"You forced me to do something that nearly killed me and ruined the rest of my life. You stole away any hope I might have had of decent motherhood. The husband I eventually married never understood why we had no children. He blamed me, which was quite true, but he didn't know why I never quickened. I couldn't tell him. No woman shares that kind of experience, but it marks her. She never forgets or forgives the man who made it necessary."

Inez's cheeks flushed with righteous anger.

"I wasn't the father of the child you didn't want," Geoffrey said.

"The child I couldn't have, you mean. Not without the loss of everything else in my life. Family, reputation, fortune. My parents would have cast me out without a second thought. I had a small inheritance from one of my grandmothers, but that wouldn't have lasted long. The worst existence a woman can suffer is that of poor spinster. That was the future I was looking in the face when you refused to marry me, Geoffrey."

"You married someone else."

"I found a husband who would take me out of the South and the possibility of what I'd done being discovered. I went into exile," Inez said. "And I've never forgiven you for destroying every dream I ever had."

"Did you hire Anthony Nichols to ruin Prudence's wedding dress?"

"Never heard of the man."

"A seamstress was killed in the dress designer's studio."

"No concern of mine." Inez shrugged.

"Nichols was a private inquiry agent. He's dead. Whoever killed him tried to make it look like suicide."

"You're wasting my time, Geoffrey. I don't know what you're talking about, but I'm sure your bride will manage to secure another dress." Inez refused to say Prudence's name aloud. It would be like vinegar in her mouth.

"There's this," Geoffrey said, taking the gold curb and bobble link chain from his pocket. It shone a deep, warm ochre color in the lamplight. "This is yours, Inez. I've never seen another one like it. You wore it at that dinner when everyone apparently expected our engagement to be announced. And then again the night you told me I had to marry you and pretend another man's bastard was my child." He watched her face carefully as he spoke, deliberately using a word no man should utter in a lady's presence.

Inez didn't flinch.

"It was left in Madame Régine's workroom, where we also found Prudence's wedding dress cut into tiny pieces and strewn over Brenda Leavitt's dead body. Did you pay off a hired killer with the necklace, Inez? Very foolish, if you did. Was he supposed to pawn it?"

Inez said nothing.

"The only other alternative is you killed Brenda Leavitt. You broke into the workroom out of some insane compulsion to shred Prudence's dress—as if that would cancel the wedding—and were surprised there by the seamstress. She threatened to call the police, so you killed her. You picked up one of the heavy glass weights used to hold down fabric while it's being cut and flung it at her head when she turned away from you. She fell, but she was still alive, so you used the weight to fracture the back of her skull. Is that what happened, Inez?" The bald accusation of murder would sidetrack whatever game Inez had intended to play with him.

"I'm a lady, not a killer, Geoffrey."

"Everyone is capable of killing, given the right circumstances. As I recall, you were almost as wild as we boys before your mother put a stop to it. Many a night you crept out of your bedroom window and joined us in the woods, as good a shot as any one of the rest of us. Remember? You were tough and nimble enough to climb the tallest tree without help. Are you still strong and fast on your feet, Inez?"

"I think it's time for you to leave." Inez stood, the silk and lace of her nightrobe falling around her in graceful folds. It had been years since those unladylike childhood exploits. So like Geoffrey to taunt her with a past she'd gone to great pains to hide.

"The police don't know about you," Geoffrey said. "But they will. I can promise that."

Inez pointed to a servants' call button embedded in the floor beside the chair in which she'd been sitting. "This rings in the servants' hall downstairs and in the upstairs attic bedrooms.

The entire staff will be down here in minutes if I summon them. I'm sure you don't want to be found in a widow's parlor at this time of night."

"We're not finished. This isn't over, Inez." He stood and started to take a step toward her.

She moved a satin-shod foot closer to the button.

Furious, but painfully aware that she'd outmaneuvered him, Geoffrey directed a mocking bow in Inez's direction, turned, and was out the front door before she could carry through on her threat. He heard the soft click of the lock behind him as he hurried down the sidewalk. No one had seen him enter the town house and no one saw him leave.

Inez scooped up the gold curb and bobble link chain from where it had fallen soundlessly to the carpeted floor. Men hardly ever noticed the little things that made up a woman's world.

It was time to put the next stage of her plan into motion. Geoffrey had to pay for what he'd done to her.

Amos Lang couldn't sleep.

He'd caught an evening train back from Boston, too late to report to Geoffrey Hunter about what he'd learned at the Nichols house, too early to climb into the bed that became a battlefield without increasingly large doses of laudanum. So he walked, as he did most nights when he chose to fight the specter of opium before finally surrendering to it.

He knew every house and every street in the neighborhood in which he lived, where he'd finally put down roots after vagabonding for most of his life. He'd never spent much of what he earned, so when the time came, he'd been able to buy a small, attached brownstone that wasn't too run-down. He planned to work one room at a time to bring it back to something approaching its former glory. Sand the wooden floors, repaper or replaster the walls, scavenge furniture from secondhand shops. So far he'd only managed to redo his bedroom.

All that work was part of Amos's private sobriety plan to

stay busy during the empty hours when he was alone. Surprisingly, it worked better than anything else he'd ever tried. He had Tyrus Hayes to thank for that. The octogenarian former slave who sweated, cajoled, and threatened his employer through frequently recurring bouts of addiction loved the man he served as though he were his own natural child. That love extended to Ned Hayes's friends, of whom Amos was one of the closest.

Ned and Amos had gone through one of the famous Dr. Leslie Keeley's Institutes together. Amos remembered every miserable moment of the regime. Dr. Keeley's patients received four daily injections of chloride of gold, drank a secret tonic every two hours, ate a special diet, and were isolated from friends and family for a minimum of thirty-one days. The theory was that if an addict returned to his drugs of choice after suffering through the Keeley program, it was not because he hadn't been cured. He had deliberately chosen the path of illness and dependency. Ned was among Keeley's many failed graduates.

"I reckon no tonic and no needle in the world gonna cure a man of dope and drinkin'," Tyrus acknowledged after the spectacular binge with which Ned had celebrated his release from the Institute. He then tied his beloved master to a chair to get him through the worst of the withdrawal tremors and hallucinations, worked him like a professional boxer when Ned was strong enough to stand on his own, fed him good Southern cooking to put on weight and muscle, and watched him like a hawk.

When the thirst got too much to bear and being sober bored him to tears, Ned always managed to slip Tyrus's leash.

An ex-New York City Police detective, Ned was as safe in the city's streets, slums, taverns, and opium dens as a man could be. Once, years ago, he'd saved the life of Billy McGlory, the most famous hoodlum of his day. In so doing, he incurred the wrath of his fellow police officers, who had him maligned and fired.

That's when Billy McGlory began protecting him. On pain of incurring McGlory's wrath, which was legendary, bloody, and as certain as the sunrise, Ned Hayes would come to no permanent harm, alcohol and opium use excepted. Somebody always deposited the unconscious ex-cop on his doorstep, rang the bell, and disappeared as soon as Tyrus opened the front door.

Tyrus and Billy McGlory weren't the only ones having a care for Ned Hayes. Geoffrey Hunter looked out for him, hired him, depended on him when he needed to go into places from which he might not be expected to emerge alive. Prudence thought of him as the wayward brother she'd never had. Once upon a time, they'd hoped Ned would mend his ways for the love of a good woman, but it proved to be too much to ask. Lately, he'd drifted back into isolation and darkness.

Was Ned sober tonight? Amos didn't know. Just as he wasn't sure why his long walk through the darkness had brought him to the street on which Ned and Tyrus lived. Except that he often ended up here when he didn't know where else to go.

The trip to Boston and the conversation with the Nichols sisters, what he'd found in their basement, and the encounter with their cook had unsettled him. This case—and it wasn't the first time he'd felt this way—was the oddest combination of circumstances he'd ever come across. He felt as lost as though he were a rank beginner instead of a seasoned ex-Pinkerton.

He needed someone to talk to, but he didn't want to lay all of his doubts and uncertainties on Geoffrey Hunter. He'd fill him in on the Boston trip, to be sure, but it wouldn't be right to add all the twists and turns he couldn't figure out. The man was getting married in two weeks' time, for heaven's sake. He owed him a clean, well-thought-out solution to what had started as a relatively straightforward murder.

Women got their skulls bashed in all the time, for all sorts of reasons. Husbands, lovers, break-ins, being in the wrong place at the wrong time. But what killer worth his salt would take the time and trouble to cut up a wedding dress and scatter the pieces over the body? A professional knew to leave the scene as soon as the victim hit the ground.

Gaslights were burning in the Hayes residence.

Amos rang the bell.

CHAPTER 22

Tyrus didn't seem surprised to find Amos Lang on the Hayes doorstep as midnight pealed from a nearby church belltower.

"Mister Ned be mighty pleased to see you, Mister Amos," he said, leading the visitor toward an empty parlor whose prewar furniture had been pushed back against the walls to accommodate a professional poker table placed squarely in the middle of the room. "He's gettin' tired of me winnin' just about ever' hand he deals out. Lord knows, I try to lose, but Mister Ned make it awful hard."

"He's a good card player, as I recall, Tyrus."

"It ain't the drink, and I sure don't let him out of my sight to buy any opium or get him a couple of bottles of laudanum. Might be the headaches he been gettin' but you know Mister Ned don't believe in complainin'. He went out to the kitchen a couple minutes afore you got here. I'll go fetch him."

Amos wandered over to the poker table as Tyrus disappeared toward the back of the house. Chips lay in neat stacks in a horizontal casino-style holder. Next to it were two decks of cards, one battered from use, the other still in its elaborately decorated cardboard box. He pictured the octogenarian ex-slave facing off against his pale, skeletally thin master beneath the hissing gas lamp that hung above the table. It wasn't difficult to imagine the two of them locked in deadly earnest competition for hours on end, interrupted now and then by an annoyed cook who had learned never to serve a meal until her employer was sitting at the table, his manservant at the ready to coax him to eat. Coffee by the gallon, and all day long.

It had been almost a year since Amos had seen Ned, longer than that since they'd worked together on a Hunter and MacKenzie case. Ned had a way of sliding close to death, then scrambling back from the edge of his own mortality long after everyone who cherished him had given up hope. He'd been a handsome man—once—but years of drink and opium had ruined the good looks and left him a phantom shell of his former self. Amos, like Prudence, Geoffrey, and Billy McGlory, expected the worst whenever Ned chose to make contact. They were seldom disappointed. It was best to be prepared. You didn't want Ned to read on your face the shock, horror, and grave sorrow you were feeling as you shook his bony hand and tried to smile.

"Did this old man Tyrus tell you what he's been putting me through?" Ned's voice was as hollow as his malarial cheeks. For many veterans of the war, disease had been as dangerous as cannon fire, and harder to avoid. He stood in the parlor doorway, swaying as though a wind were whipping through the house. "You're a sight for sore eyes, Amos Lang."

"I was passing by and thought I'd stop in." It was the only quick explanation Amos could come up with.

Tyrus skirted the two men and knelt to place more logs on the fire. He manhandled Ned into a baggy gray wool sweater and gentled him into a large leather chair where the heat from the flames would warm his legs. He held out a knitted cap, but Ned waved it away. His once-thick blond hair had thinned and begun to turn silver, but wearing a hat inside the house was something only old men did.

"Passing by and thought you'd stop in? I don't believe that for a minute." Ned waved his visitor to a comfortable armchair opposite his own. "You've never done an unplanned thing in your life, Amos. You've got a reason for being here, and you'd better tell me what it is. Otherwise, it's the poker table, and Lord knows you don't want to be sitting there the rest of the night. Or morning. Whichever one it is."

A pot of coffee and a plate of apple cake slices appeared on the low table where Ned's pipe had spilled out tobacco ash. Tyrus poured and handed cups to both men, then faded into the drapery, as if he were a domesticated ghost who would reappear when needed. The only time he took his eyes off Ned was to run them over Amos's pockets, searching for the telltale rectangular shape of a bottle.

"I'm working a case that doesn't make any sense," Amos began. The more he studied Ned, the more he realized that his friend didn't look as bad off as he'd expected. True, he didn't look healthy, but neither did he resemble the corpse he'd often been thought to be. He'd put on a few pounds; his clothes no longer hung scarecrow-like from an emaciated body. Amos thought it possible that Ned was on his way back from whatever most recent hell he'd dropped himself into. He'd resurrected himself from the abyss so often, his friends had gotten used to finding out he was still alive when they'd thought he'd surely died.

"You'd best tell me about it." Ned's blue eyes sparked beneath half-lowered lids, then he fixed a professional interrogator's gaze on his visitor. There was nothing more challenging, more likely to stir the cold coals of a wasted life than joining forces with an equally talented colleague to decode a seemingly unsolvable puzzle.

Tyrus kept the fire going and the coffee poured as Amos told the story, beginning with the discovery of Brenda Leavitt's body on the floor of Madame Régine's workroom. It was like watching the flickering images of a zoetrope. Amos had a gift for remembering and recreating every conversation he'd been a part of, overheard, or was told about. His descriptions of the places he'd been and the people he'd seen were equally detailed and as vivid as though his listeners had been there themselves. By the time he'd finished, Ned Hayes was no longer a stranger to Hunter and MacKenzie's most recent case.

"Does Geoffrey know you planned to come see me?" To Ned's mind, Geoffrey might well be an ex-Pink and a lawyer, but he was first and foremost a fellow Southerner. A brother exile in Yankee land, a son of the South to the marrow of his bones and the depths of his soul. Like Ned, forever unable to make a life for himself in a homeland that still cherished slavery despite the war fought to end it.

"I didn't know it myself until I got here." That was as close to the truth as Amos was willing to come.

"All right, then. We'll keep this collaboration to ourselves—unless and until we need to fess up." Ned could be as stubborn as a schoolboy when it came to guarding a secret. "He's got his sights set on marrying Miss Prudence, so we'll just let him coast along."

"Mr. Hunter never coasts," Amos said. "He's set on cracking this case before the wedding, and so is Miss Prudence."

"Remind me when that is." Ned glanced at the mantel where he'd seen Tyrus set out the invitation. He'd opened and read it, of course, but lately things like dates and numbers had a way of slipping out of his memory. He couldn't recall, for example, when he'd first heard Tyrus call him *Mister* Ned after a lifetime of *Master*.

"Two weeks from now." It was the first time Amos could recall having to remind Ned of anything.

"Two weeks? That should be more than enough time. Two bodies means twice as much of a chance to make a mistake. You and I both know that however clever a killer believes himself to be, he's going to make more than one miscalculation. The slightest blunder has to be covered up, and every time that happens, it creates another clue. Murderers just think they can get away with taking a life."

"I've seen many a killing go unsolved," Amos argued. "And so have you."

"Not because the perpetrator of the crime was too intelligent to be caught, but because the police were too lazy or too stupid to track him down. Or they'd been bought off." Ned had very little respect for the department of which he'd once been a part.

"There's a good chance Anthony Nichols killed Brenda." Amos wasn't entirely convinced, but this conversation was less about defending a theory than it was about trying to eliminate competing possibilities.

"How do you figure that?" Ned knew how he would argue that prospect, but he was curious about what Amos's approach would be. "He denied to Geoffrey and Prudence that he or his client had anything to do with her death."

"Exactly what you'd expect him to do." Amos sat back in his chair and stretched his legs toward the fire. "I had a lot of time to think about this on the train back from Boston."

"And?"

"I think it's possible Nichols had accomplished what he'd been paid to do. He got copies of some of Madame Régine's designs and learned how she ran her business. Brenda told him about the seamstresses Madame Régine employed, and probably a lot more. Who her fabric and notions suppliers were, for example. Important, because what she was creating had to be of the highest quality. A society woman can tell with one feel whether the silk that's been used in her gown is worth what she's paying for it. She can spot cheap goods the minute she sees them. And so can every other woman in her circle."

"Go on."

"The key to Nichols lies in what the cook told me about him. He had compassion for the animals he found in the streets. He wanted to be a doctor, wanted to heal people. His father would have forced him into the banking and investment business. So Anthony hid his passion down in that cellar, where his father—and eventually the rest of the family—cruelly misunderstood what he was doing. Labeled him a monster."

"Which he wasn't," Ned agreed.

"Far from it. I think that what could have happened is that he was on the point of leaving New York permanently and decided to see Brenda one last time. Perhaps to ask forgiveness for deceiving her, perhaps just to say goodbye. He didn't dare risk going by her house, so he went to the only other place where he knew he'd find her." Amos paused, allowing Ned a moment to join the narrative.

"Madame Régine's studio."

"Exactly. Early in the morning, before any of the other seamstresses could be expected to be there. He knew, because she'd told him, that she was always the first one at her machine. So he broke in. Probably picked the lock on the delivery door that opens onto the alley. Went upstairs and waited."

"I thought you maintained he wasn't a killer," Ned reminded Amos.

"He wasn't guilty of premeditation. But anyone can kill given the right circumstances."

Ned closed his eyes, the better to visualize what Amos was about to describe.

"He surprised her. She couldn't have expected to see him again. He might have tried to explain. We'll never know. But at some point Brenda attacked him. The years and years of being her mother's dogsbody and caring for the sister she knew was dying had built a volcano of rage that suddenly erupted. I doubt she knew what she was doing, but I imagine she picked up one of those large shears they used to cut fabric and lunged at him. Nichols fended her off, but he couldn't make her drop the shears. So he grabbed one of those heavy glass weights you see on the tables where they stretch out material, and he swung at her to make her let loose of the shears. But he used more force than he meant to, and maybe she moved out of where he'd been aiming. The glass weight smashed into the side of her head. Maybe she turned away and tried to run. Nichols had been abused and wronged by his entire family—everyone he'd ever loved. The first blow became a rain of strikes, and I don't believe he knew what he was doing any more than Brenda had when she picked up the shears. Afterward, when the blood lust had played itself out and she lay at his feet, he had a single moment of clarity. His instinct for self-preservation took over. He had to change the dynamics of the crime. So he cut up Miss Prudence's wedding dress and flung the bits over the body. Then he left, taking the shears with him. Why, I don't know. Maybe he didn't realize he was still holding them when he left."

"One important thing you've omitted from that story. The curb and bobble link necklace that you say Geoffrey picked up, put in his pocket, and didn't tell the police about."

"It's not a perfect theory," Amos admitted.

"I like some parts of it." Ned reached for a slice of apple cake. "The whole thing reads a bit like a penny dreadful."

"You have a better take on the two murders?" Amos knew the hypothesis wasn't perfect, but to compare it to the plot of a penny dreadful was insulting.

"That's my first point. You've only accounted for Brenda's death. Who killed Nichols?"

"Whoever hired him."

"Why?"

"He knew too much."

"Your second point?"

"The necklace. Obviously. One of three people brought it to that workroom. Brenda and Nichols are both dead, so we won't get a confession from either of them. That leaves a third, unknown individual."

"I was afraid you'd complicate this case."

It was what Amos had been thinking all along but was hoping couldn't be true. "We have no idea who hired Nichols. We've gone through his files and searched the clothing he was wearing when he was shot. Dead ends, both of them."

Tyrus, laying more logs on the fire, grimaced. He seldom bothered to hold his tongue when it came to keeping Mister Ned in line and not laughing at his bad jokes, but Amos Lang wasn't a Southerner. Best to stay silent.

"So Josiah and Miss Prudence learned about the necklace from a retired Tiffany gold worker." Ned jumped back to the necklace. "Geoffrey had already recognized it. He could have told Prudence and Madame Régine right away that he'd seen it before, but he waited. Why?"

"He's hiding something?" Amos didn't like what he'd forced himself to say.

"Or someone. Protecting a woman from his past. I'd say that fits right in with his notion of what it means to be a gentleman. A Southern gentleman. What we don't know is whether he's told Miss Prudence who this woman is."

"We need to find out who hired Nichols," Amos insisted, trying to bring Ned back to how a detective usually went about solving a case.

"Identify the woman you saw leaving his building, and you'll have your answer." Such an obvious conclusion that Ned wondered why Amos hadn't already taken steps in that direction.

"She apparently paid him in cash."

"Which I would assume she conveniently took back after she shot him. Very economical of her. My guess is that after she shot Nichols, she came back to the office because she remembered something that might have incriminated her. While she was there she glanced out the window, saw you coming, and hid in the upstairs hallway until after you'd found the body." Ned's vision clouded over for a moment. A fierce pain exploded behind his eyes. His head dropped forward onto his chest.

Tyrus pounded him on the back and pulled his neck up straight. "He do this when he get tired, Mister Amos. Some kind of fit. Best I get him up to his bed."

"Has he seen a doctor?" Amos reached out to help haul Ned to his feet, but Tyrus motioned him away.

"Mister Ned don't hold with no doctors. He gonna sleep like a baby for the rest of the night and be fine in the morning. You come back then, Mister Amos. I'll cook us up some grits."

"Tell Mister Ned I'll be in touch." Amos felt about grits the same way he did about tea. Fine for women and sick people, but not something he'd voluntarily eat.

He sat for a while enjoying the warmth of the fire, listening to Tyrus maneuver Ned up the narrow staircase to the second floor. He didn't doubt that Tyrus was right about Ned being fine in the morning. Amos had known him to make remarkable, almost legendary recoveries. He wasn't sure whether they'd made any headway to solving this case tonight, but of one thing he was certain. Ned never did anything by half measure. Like Amos, he didn't believe there was such a thing as a murder that couldn't be solved.

With the two of them working together, they'd have the answer well before Geoffrey and Prudence pronounced their vows in Trinity Church.

A wedding present. The best one Amos could think of. He didn't care much for linens or silver. He didn't think Ned did, either.

Chapter 23

One thing society woman were well trained for was organizing. The daily running of a household, a masquerade ball, an entire social season, or the seemingly accidental meeting of a young woman and a suitable young man. Prudence MacKenzie was no exception.

She instructed her butler to send a message to the home of Miss Katja De Haan and informed her coachman to ready the landau for an early morning ride through Central Park. Then she put on her best black riding habit and directed the housekeeper to send a maid up to the attic where she'd find a riding habit that had been worn by one of her several governesses. That governess had been on the plump side. So was Katja.

"I remember that we put it in one of the storage trunks when Mademoiselle left," the housekeeper said. It wasn't her place to ask why Miss Prudence wanted it.

"You'll have to come with me, Colleen, for propriety's sake. Just in case Mrs. Eaton isn't able to bring her own maid."

"I'll run upstairs and put on my hat." Colleen wasn't sure exactly what Miss Prudence intended doing, only that it was bound to be more exciting than her ordinary lady's maid duties. Thank goodness that as a lady's maid she didn't wear an ordinary maid's uniform that always included an apron and cap.

"Meet me downstairs. Hurry!"

"Miss Prudence, you haven't had a bit of breakfast." The housekeeper held out a cup of steaming black coffee. "Shall I send word to Mr. Hunter that you've gone to Central Park?"

Prudence thought for a moment. "No, not this morning. If he telephones, you can tell him I've taken Miss Katja riding. I'll explain later what it's all about." She swallowed a mouthful of coffee, then checked the pins in her hat. It wouldn't do to have it fly off onto the riding path. She tucked Eleanor Eaton's note into her jacket pocket in case she needed to read it again, then sped down the stairs and out into the stable yard at the back of the house.

Kincaid had hitched the pair of matched bays to the landau and donned a spotless and perfectly pressed dark green coachman's uniform. Colleen, the former governess's riding habit neatly folded beside her, sat straight and apple-cheeked in the coach. Today would be the first time she'd taken a carriage ride with society folk in Central Park. It was all she could do to keep from grinning like an excited child.

"Miss Katja De Haan's home," Prudence told Kincaid. "We were there yesterday."

"I remember, miss." Kincaid helped her into the landau and made sure the lap robe was within reach should she need it. Minutes later, to the sound of hoofbeats on cobblestones, they were on their way.

"Do you have a riding habit?" Prudence asked.

Katja, slightly dazed and very much surprised, stood at her modest dining table, one hand clutching a linen napkin. She hadn't bothered to do more than put on a dressing gown before coming downstairs this morning. Far too early for her father to put in an appearance. What was Miss Prudence doing here?

"More to the point, do you ride?"

"Of course I ride, Miss Prudence." She'd been trained to be polite, no matter the circumstance. "May I inquire why you ask?"

"I'll take that," Prudence told the maid who didn't quite know what to do with the plate of toast she'd just carried up from the basement kitchen. Or who the strange lady was who'd appeared out of nowhere.

"One slice will have to do, but it's better than nothing." Prudence took a bite of the toast and grimaced. Day-old bread masquerading as newly baked.

"Miss Prudence?"

"I had a note from Eleanor Eaton this morning. She tells me that she and her grandson will be riding in Central Park. If we hurry, we can accidentally run into them. Not literally, of course."

"My riding habit is a bit outdated," Katja said, catching on immediately to the scheme Prudence was hatching. "But it fits, so I suppose it'll have to do."

"I had Colleen, my lady's maid, bring along another habit, just in case, but it's better that you wear your own." Prudence wasn't quite sure how to say that Katja had more flesh on her bones than the well-padded governess. She hadn't quite realized how much flesh.

"I'd never be able to fit into anything of yours." Katja smiled and suddenly looked almost beautiful. "I'm very sturdy. It's the Dutch blood, you know." She laughed, and really was quite pretty.

"I'll sit here and eat all your toast and drink your coffee while you go upstairs and dress." Prudence consulted the small gold watch she wore pinned to her jacket. "Ten minutes, no more."

She decided not to tell Katja that the riding habit she'd brought for her to borrow hadn't been Prudence's own, but rather belonged to a governess who'd left it behind because she hated horses and having to chaperone her charge's riding lessons.

Maybe a spoonful of jam would make the stale bread more palatable.

Prudence had Katja mount Geoffrey's horse and together they set out along the riding trail that wound through Central Park. It was a beautiful morning, the second day of September, but still so early that only the most dedicated riders were out. The landau followed close behind them and off to one side, where a carriage track paralleled the horse path. Later today, the afternoon riding and carriage parade would bring out a genteel, exceedingly well-dressed crowd. For the moment, however, the park was nearly empty, its green lawns sparkling under a thin blanket of dew. The trees, still fully leafed out and not yet turning color, stood tall and silent, waiting for a breeze to cross the island from one of the rivers.

"You ride very well," Prudence said, noting Katja's straight back, tucked-in elbows, and good seat. Geoffrey's horse was a bit large for a woman, but Katja was handling him well.

"My mother loved to ride. She made sure I did, too."

It was on the tip of Prudence's tongue to ask how old Katja had been when her mother died, but she bit back the question. It would be easy enough to find out, and she didn't want a memory of past loss to dampen the spell she hoped would be cast. If Eleanor's sense of timing was correct, they should encounter her and her grandson very soon now, possibly not far up ahead where the trail bent just enough to conceal whoever might be coming toward them.

She glanced behind to see how Colleen was doing all by herself in the landau. If she hadn't been wearing a simple black dress and unfashionably small hat, the maid might have passed for a lady far above her station. No, Prudence decided, after a second good look. Colleen was too obviously Irish, too red of hair, and blue of eye, with pale freckled skin that was as good as an announcement that she'd just gotten off the boat.

"I see Mrs. Eaton," Katja said. "On the black mare. She's just ridden around the bend."

"You've better eyes than I." But Katja was right. Eleanor Eaton's calculations had been spot-on. "That must be her grandson, there, coming up alongside her."

"Do you know his name?" Katja asked. She tightened her already irreproachable riding posture and checked the veil that discreetly shaded her face.

"No, I don't. I didn't think to ask. That was careless of me." But even at a distance, Prudence could tell that Mrs. Eaton's grandson was as she had described him. A bit bookish looking, with a pleasant rather than a handsome face. And not at all the arrogant set of shoulders so many wealthy young men cultivated.

If everything went well in the next half hour, Katja's life would change. For the better.

Inez Rankin Purcell wore a loose-sleeved morning gown of summery white, the better to highlight the bruises encircling each of her wrists. No bracelets to distract the eye from the vividly purple skin.

Detective Stephen Phelan was always uncomfortable in the homes of New York's wealthy elite. Their chairs weren't large enough and the carpets were likely to snag on a copper's boots. The rooms were always too well heated for someone who'd grown up in the cold damp of a tenement, and he knew without a shadow of a doubt that their servants both feared and despised the police. "Your note read that you had important information about the recent killing in Madame Régine's dress salon."

"I appreciate your coming so quickly." Inez toyed with the lacy edge of one of her sleeves.

Pat Corcoran, Phelan's much younger partner, stared openly at the evidence of physical assault, then scribbled something in the narrow notebook that fit into his inside jacket pocket.

"Perhaps you'd like to tell us what you think you know." Phelan knew the subtle insult wouldn't go unremarked, but he really didn't care. Society women annoyed him even more than their sumptuously decorated homes and high-handed husbands.

"Last night, when I was about to go upstairs, a man forced his way into my parlor." Inez had practiced every line of her speech until she thought she'd gotten it pitch perfect.

"Your servants will testify to this?" Phelan asked, signaling to Corcoran to take down what Mrs. Purcell was saying.

"They were already in their rooms. I doubt anyone saw him enter or leave. However, that shouldn't be an issue. I'm telling you he was here."

"Did you open the door to him, Mrs. Purcell?" Phelan asked. If he had to prompt every revelation with a question, he and his partner would be here for hours.

"I knew him, you see."

"Name?"

"Geoffrey Hunter."

Corcoran's pencil stub rolled across the carpet. He scrabbled after it, red-faced and confused. The only Geoffrey Hunter he knew of was a lawyer and private inquiry agent. Detectives Phelan and Corcoran had worked several important cases with him. The man Corcoran knew and rather liked was marrying a society heiress in a couple of weeks. Miss Prudence MacKenzie. Phelan despised her, though Corcoran had never figured out why. He himself thought she was a lovely woman. And intelligent, too. What was Mrs. Purcell going on about? Could there be another Geoffrey Hunter in the city?

"I think you'd better start at the beginning." Phelan leaned forward in the chair that was much too small for his bulk. "Take it slowly, but don't leave anything out." He glared at Corcoran, who quickly touched the pencil stub to his tongue and prepared to take notes.

"I've known Geoffrey since we were children. Our families

lived on adjoining properties, and it was always intended that we would marry." Inez had almost slipped and said *plantations*, but she'd caught herself in time. Yankees had peculiar notions about Southerners. "He gave me a beautiful antique gold necklace as an engagement gift. Curb and bobble link design. Very distinctive." She touched the pocket of her gown. Not yet. "I returned it to him when I broke the engagement. He was furious, of course, but I had discovered flaws in his character that would have made him a most unsuitable husband. Fortunately, my parents agreed." She paused, waiting for Phelan's question. He did not disappoint her.

"What flaws were those?"

"Geoffrey Hunter is a licentious womanizer." She thought Phelan looked like a dog panting hungrily after a bone.

"That may not be a desirable trait, but it's hardly a crime. Was there something else?"

"A great deal more, Detective Phelan, but delicacy and propriety prevent my speaking of his most depraved characteristics."

"Then why are we here, Mrs. Purcell?"

She decided he really did resemble one of her dogs salivating after a treat being withheld.

"I heard that a necklace was found in the workroom where Madame Régine's seamstress was murdered. Apparently, Geoffrey Hunter scooped it up, put it in his pocket, and told Madame Régine not to mention it to the police."

Phelan glanced at Corcoran, who shook his head.

"We don't know anything about a necklace. How did you get this information?"

"We women have our sources," Inez said. She batted her eyes coyly and lowered them to the hands resting in her lap. The bruises on her wrists seem darker than just a few moments ago. "The point is, Detective, I saw him loitering in the park just opposite where we are now sitting. I was terrified, of course, but he had once loved me a great deal, and I thought he couldn't bring himself to do me harm. I was wrong. I let him in when he knocked."

Phelan let out a great sigh. He sat as far back in the uncomfortable chair as he could. "Now we're getting somewhere."

"He killed that seamstress because he was having an affair with her and she threatened to tell his fiancée. He'd given the woman the necklace he'd once given me, and when she refused to return it to him, he snatched it from around her neck and then killed her. Unfortunately for him, his inquiry agent partner insisted on taking it to Tiffany. As I said before, it's a very distinctive piece. But I'm the only one who could link it definitively to him. I'm the only one who knew its true history. He threatened to kill me if I said anything. His fiancée is a very wealthy woman. Geoffrey needs that marriage." It was awkward, but Inez still couldn't bring herself to pronounce Prudence's name aloud.

"Where is the necklace now?" Phelan asked.

Inez took as long as she dared to draw it from the pocket of her gown. She held it out, tantalizing the two detectives with its bright gold curb and bobble link design. She doubted they'd ever seen anything quite like it. Certainly, they'd never be able to afford so beautifully crafted a piece of jewelry. When Phelan reached for it, she let the links curl into his outstretched palm.

"He had the nerve to threaten me with it. He promised that he'd wind the necklace around my throat and strangle me with it if I thwarted him. He was angrier than I've ever seen him. When he grabbed my wrists and shook me, the necklace fell to the floor, on the carpet. He didn't notice he'd dropped it." Inez smiled.

"If he was so furious and so threatening, how did you get rid of him, Mrs. Purcell?" It was the first question Pat Corcoran had asked. Stephen Phelan was fondling the twenty-two-carat links and seemed not to have heard.

Inez stood, placed one foot near a bell embedded in the floor, then slid open the drawer of the small table beside her chair. "I'm a Southern woman, Detective. I keep derringers and Colts in every desk drawer in my house and rifles hidden behind the drapes. We ladies learned during the war that we had to take care of ourselves. A lesson passed down from mother to daughter and never forgotten. If I'd stepped on that bell, every servant sleeping in the attic would have rushed downstairs. I'm a very good shot with both handguns and rifles. Geoffrey's seen me shoot. He knows I never miss."

"So he left? Just like that?" Phelan sounded pleased but disbelieving.

"Not before he admitted what he'd done. Geoffrey thinks he's some sort of mythic creature who can't be harmed. He's wrong, and now I've given you the evidence."

"What time during the night did all of this take place?" Pat Corcoran again, trying to fill in the holes in Inez's story.

"I really don't know, Detective. Except that it was late. He was out the door and through the park as soon as he understood that I'd cornered him. I sent you the note this morning because as soon as he realizes he no longer has the necklace, he'll be back. I know that as sure as I know the sun rises in the east. I don't intend to be here then. Unless you arrest him?" She'd practiced that rising inflection until she was sure she got it right. Not telling the detective what to do, just suggesting it. Men didn't like to be bossed around.

"We'll pick him up within the hour, Mrs. Purcell. You've nothing to be concerned about. Geoffrey Hunter will be sitting in a jail cell before you've drunk your midmorning cup of coffee. You have my word on that."

"I knew you'd believe me. I knew I could count on the New York City Police to protect me." She held out her hand. "I'll take my necklace now, Detective."

"It's evidence, Mrs. Purcell," Phelan said.

"My necklace, Detective. I wouldn't want it to get lost as I understand can happen rather easily when valuable items are stored in your precincts."

Inez wouldn't yield, and Phelan knew it. He held back a sigh as he returned the beautiful gold chain to the woman who would help him give Geoffrey Hunter his comeuppance. Best not to cross her. Pat Corcoran noted that the item had been returned to its owner.

Inez watched from her parlor window as Detectives Stephen Phelan and Pat Corcoran disappeared down the sidewalk. She stretched her arms over her head, wincing just a little as her hands curled around her wrists. She'd always bruised easily, but it had taken a lot of painful squeezing and pulling on her skin to bring on the purpling. All the way around each wrist, as though a man with large hands had grabbed her. Just as she'd described.

Maybe she'd go back to bed for a while, have one of the maids bring up a tray. Pat the bedcovers until all five of her spaniels lay curled up around her.

She'd never been locked in a filthy jail cell, but she'd seen the punishment shacks left over from slavery days. Geoffrey would hate the noise, the dirt, the smells, the confinement.

He should have married her when he'd had the chance.

Little Eddie had run so hard and fast down Fifth Avenue to Danny Dennis's stable that he couldn't catch his breath enough to talk when he got there. He'd never cried in his life but drops of something wet and salty trickled down his cheeks. Danny pounded him on the back and splashed water on his face. The boys who had spent the night curled up in the hay of empty stalls joined in enthusiastically.

"The coppers nabbed Mr. Hunter," Eddie finally gasped, bending over to keep from passing out under the barrage of small fists and sluices of water scooped from Mr. Washington's trough. Bits of straw and horse saliva lodged in his hair and stuck to his face. "They had him handcuffed like he was some sort of criminal. Mr. Hunter!"

"Everybody stop jumping around," Danny ordered. "Get back from Little Eddie. Give him room."

One by one the boys inched away, whispering among themselves until Danny's glare silenced them. They hadn't had this much fun in a long time.

"Now tell us what you saw, Eddie. Start with why you were at the Fifth Avenue Hotel in the first place."

"I was helping Timmy the Gimp sell his papers. He nearly got run over by a carriage the other day, so he's not walking too good."

"He never could walk good," one of the boys contributed. "That's why he's a gimp."

"Enough," Danny said. "Go on, Eddie."

"I'm out on Fifth Avenue, with an armful of papers. I'm yelling out the headlines like Timmy told me to do and all of a sudden I see these two policemen pulling a man out of the hotel. He's got his hands cuffed behind his back. Trousers and a shirt, but no jacket. So as soon as I recognize that it's Mr. Hunter, I go running over to him, but the cops push me away. They're not in uniform, so I know they're detectives. Mr. Hunter starts to say something to me, but one of the detectives cuffs him across the mouth. Tells him to shut up. There's a Black Maria parked at the curb, and that's where they start dragging him. Timmy the Gimp falls down right in front of them. Newspapers all over the place. So while the coppers are yelling at him to get out of the way, I get close enough to Mr. Hunter to ask him what he wants me to do. 'Tell Danny,' he says. He has to whisper or that detective will punch him in the teeth again. His mouth was all bloody, and it looked to me like maybe he put up a fight when they arrested him."

"Who were the detectives, Eddie?"

"That mean one, Stephen Phelan. His partner, Pat Corcoran."

"Corcoran's decent enough, but Phelan's a disgrace to the name." Danny had known men like Phelan back in Ireland, but most of them were British. Fair game on a dark night. "Now here's what I want you to do, Eddie. Find Amos Lang and tell him what you just told me. He's likely to be still in bed at this time of the morning. Bang on his door as long as you have to. Just make sure you wake him up."

"I know where he lives." Danny might not come right out and say it, but Little Eddie figured Mr. Lang took laudanum to help him get to sleep at night. That's what the banging on the door was all about. People who took laudanum were hard to wake up. Sometimes they didn't.

"Two of you go see how Timmy the Gimp is doing. Bring him back here if he's hurt. One of you go with Little Eddie in case he needs to send back a message." Danny put a couple of nickels into eager hands, watched the four youngsters tear out of the stable, then turned to where Mr. Washington stood patiently waiting to start the day.

Somebody had to tell Miss Prudence.

CHAPTER 24

Detective Stephen Phelan ordered Geoffrey Hunter to be locked into one of the ground floor cells of the Tombs, the one in the far corner of the sinking building, where noxious effluent from the malfunctioning sewer stood an inch deep on the floor much of the time. The heavily cross-barred cell door allowed little light and less ventilation into the dank space that measured six feet by nine feet. An open latrine in one corner added another layer of stench to the air. There was nothing to sit on, and a narrow row of slanted wooden slats served as a bed. No table, no chair. No pillow, no blanket. Inedible meals were served on tin plates. Prisoners ate with their fingers.

The arresting officers had manhandled but not beaten Geoffrey. That would come later, when Phelan gave him the third degree. But transport in the Black Maria had done its work. It was a sport in the police department to whip up the horses pulling the Maria over the cobblestoned streets of lower Manhattan. The manacled prisoner inside the vehicle slammed against its walls and benches. Unable to steady himself, with nothing to hold on to, he was flung to the bare floor where he rolled back and forth over his chains, emerging from the Black

Maria bruised, bloodied, and barely conscious. No doctor to treat his wounds, no sympathy from guards. His only hope was to stay alive until a relative could visit or his trial began.

It wasn't Geoffrey's first visit to the Tombs, but it was his initial stay there as an inmate. He'd been through some harrowing experiences during his Pinkerton years, but nothing to match the filth, the noise, the choking smells, and the crushing despair of New York City's Halls of Justice and House of Detention.

Phelan had hustled him out of his apartment in the Fifth Avenue Hotel without giving him time to finish dressing that morning. He wore pants, a white shirt, and shoes without socks. That was it. No watch, which would have been confiscated and stolen anyway, no cigar case, no clean handkerchief. Not a single coin in his pockets. His sole ray of hope as the cell door clanged shut was that he'd seen Little Eddie running down Fifth Avenue as if the devil himself was chasing him.

Geoffrey had powerful friends and former clients in the city, as well as allies among the crafty denizens of the streets. He reminded himself that as long as someone knew where he was, there was a chance he'd eventually be released.

Eddie would tell Danny Dennis, Danny would inform Prudence, and then all holy hell would break loose. Geoffrey would have smiled except that his jaw hurt and his teeth felt as though a giant hand had tried to shake them loose.

Every element of whatever plan they came up with to free Geoffrey from the Tombs had to run like clockwork. Danny had been in enough raids and assassination squads in Ireland to know that improvising was never a good idea. Nor was setting out on a mission without sufficient personnel to carry it off. Many a twosome in the old country had ambushed a soldier relieving himself in his outdoor privy only to find themselves surrounded and bullet ridden when a barracks door slammed open before the echo of the kill shot faded. Acting on your anger and despair was a sure way to court disaster. Rescue and revenge had to be served up cold.

He sent a boy to Miss Prudence's house to find out if she was home. He knew she and Geoffrey often went for an early morning ride in Central Park. She might have gone alone today or be waiting there for him. "No gossiping." He pressed a nickel into the messenger's hand. "Just ask where Miss Prudence is, then find me. I'll wait at Amos Lang's house until you bring me word." He didn't ask the boy if he knew where the ex-Pinkerton lived. A street urchin who needed directions wasn't worth beans.

Little Eddie was still pounding on the front door when Danny pulled up to Amos's attached brick town house.

"Don't bother," Danny said, taking a set of lock picks out of his pocket. "Here, you need the practice. I'll time you."

Little Eddie grinned. His grubby fingers hovered over the row of picks, then selected exactly the right one. He held his breath as the slender piece of metal glided into the lock. Moments later he let out a great sigh as the lock clicked and the door swung open.

"Not bad." Danny took back the canvas-wrapped package of picks before Little Eddie could squirrel them out of sight. "Amos's bedroom will be on the second floor. Let's go."

The rooms on the ground floor were empty of furniture. Paint and plaster buckets, brushes, trowels, and canvas cloths lay scattered in neat piles. It didn't look as though Amos's refurbishments had progressed much beyond the assembling of materials.

The upstairs was no better, except for the room in which Amos lay snoring, his head wrapped in a scarf to keep out the street noises that penetrated his leaky windows.

"Laudanum," Danny said, picking up the telltale small brown glass bottle from Amos's bedside table. "My guess is that last night he took a few drops more than he should have." He put down the bottle and slid his hand under Amos's pillow to find the gun he was certain lay there within easy reach.

Then he yanked the covers off the sleeping man and grinned at the outburst of profanity with which Amos greeted the day.

Detective Stephen Phelan didn't have an office at the Tombs, but he did have a room set aside for interrogating prisoners according to the third-degree protocol set up by Chief of Detectives Thomas Byrnes. It couldn't match the sumptuous private office setting in which Byrnes personally conducted interviews known throughout the police department for their success and their casual cruelty, but it was the best Phelan could commandeer under the circumstances.

As Byrnes was known for doing, Phelan sat behind a large desk, the surface of which was empty except for a square glass ashtray from which rose the thick smoke of an expensive cigar. A chair was set to one side, but that was to be used only if the prisoner cooperated or his legs gave out. Otherwise, the man stood before the desk, hands cuffed behind his back, a policeman on either side to catch him if he fell. The first fist to the face usually broke the prisoner's nose, sending blood flowing into his mouth and down his chin. Often the eyes were next, swelling shut and turning purple under repeated blows. Teeth fell to the floor where a heavy boot crushed or kicked them aside. And that was just the beginning.

Geoffrey Hunter was not your ordinary prisoner. Phelan knew he had to leave as few marks as possible on the Southerner's face. Well-aimed punches to the stomach, the kidneys, and the scrotum could be just as painful despite the lack of visible blood. A pail of water stood in one corner. The prisoner was not to be allowed the sweet oblivion of unconsciousness. A blindfold and a pair of thumbscrews lay beside the pail. Phelan had observed that a prisoner who could not see what awaited him often caved faster than one who knew what was coming next. He'd found the thumbscrews to be particularly effective.

"Bring him in," Phelan ordered two of his subordinates.

They were big, beefy men with a ferocious lust for cold-blooded savagery written on their scarred faces. Drunk or nearly so most of the time, but useful when there were miscreants to be questioned or done away with. It wasn't often they witnessed a toff being given the third degree. Not that the bastards didn't deserve it. But money talked. Rich men seldom, if ever, saw the inside of the Tombs.

"We need someone with reliable contacts inside the police department," Amos said, hoping the coffee Danny had given him would stay down. He figured he'd had maybe three or four hours of sleep at the most, not nearly enough time for the laudanum to wear off.

"Most of the force is Irish but born in this country. It's not the same." Danny topped off Amos's coffee and handed the cup back to him. "Chief Byrnes doesn't tolerate disloyalty or failure among his detectives, and I can't think of anybody who'd go up against Phelan anyway. When Pat Corcoran was on his honeymoon, Phelan had to work without a partner because nobody else would put up with him."

"I know someone who's not afraid of Phelan or Byrnes or even the mayor, for that matter." Amos splashed cold water on his face, ran a comb through his hair and over the mustache he grew or shaved off depending on the job he was doing. He stank a bit but there wasn't time to do anything about that except slap on some Bay Rum cologne and hope it did the trick. He picked up his hat, checked the gun strapped to one ankle, and the knife to the other. A gun holstered under each arm, brass knuckles in both coat pockets, change for Danny's boys, and he was ready.

"Who's that, Mr. Lang? Who's not afraid of the coppers?" asked Little Eddie, chewing the heel of bread Amos hadn't finished.

"Ned Hayes," Amos said. "Former detective and friend of Billy McGlory. There's not a crook in New York City would lay a hand on him, and not many a cop, either. They ran him out of the police department, and probably would have liked to kill him, but Hayes became untouchable. He's a pariah in some circles, but he can't be done away with."

"He's doing that all on his own." Danny hurried them downstairs where Mr. Washington waited patiently, occasionally stomping a hoof or chomping at his bit. "The man has a hollow leg for whiskey and veins that scream out for morphine. The only reason he's still alive is because Tyrus refuses to let him die."

"I talked to Ned last night." Amos climbed into the hansom cab and held a handkerchief to his mouth and nose. Smells that usually went unnoticed crept down his throat and coiled into his stomach like restless snakes. "That's why I was still asleep this morning. This case we're working on isn't going anywhere, and I'm damned if I can figure it out."

"Was he sober?" Danny asked. He waited for an answer before vaulting up into the driver's high seat.

"Dead sober. And not too happy about it, either." Amos understood the feeling.

"Then that's where we'll go before we tell Miss Prudence what's happened. Ned Hayes had a reputation for being the best detective the city ever had before he made the mistake of saving Billy McGlory's life. He chose not to fight the police department when they turned on him, but he knows where all the bodies are buried. If anyone can rig a deal to get Mr. Hunter out of the Tombs, Ned Hayes is the one to do it."

"Not too fast, Danny," Amos pleaded. A rough ride over

cobblestones could send a man's stomach right up into his head and out his mouth.

Danny Dennis and Mr. Washington paid him no mind. Time wasn't on Geoffrey Hunter's side this morning.

"Mister Ned don't go nowhere without me," Tyrus declared, enveloping his employer in the gray cloak Ned had once worn as a young officer in the Army of the Confederacy. It was only September, but the ex-NYPD detective was always cold.

"Miss Prudence told her butler she was going riding in Central Park." Danny's waif had just brought the news, intercepted halfway up Fifth Avenue and led to Ned's house by another of the stable urchins.

Tyrus handed the youngsters pieces of fried, sugared cake and cups of hot chocolate. He remembered what it was like to be small and run off your feet. There wouldn't be a crumb or grain of sugar left on the boys' ragged shirts and shorts. Hungry fingers could move as fast as ants.

"You want us to run on ahead, Mr. Danny?" Little Eddie asked. He'd naturally taken on the role of self-appointed leader of the pack.

"I may need you boys to spread out once we get into the park. You keep me and Tyrus company up top until then." Danny thought about sending one of the boys back to the stable to get Flower, but the dog hadn't been her usual energetic self that morning. She ate all manner of street garbage and there were times when the bits and pieces of rot caught up with her. Best leave her where she was and let her recover.

Ned Hayes squeezed in next to Amos, realized what the handkerchief was for, and inched away from him as much as the narrow seat would allow. Thankfully, it wasn't far to the entrance to Central Park. "Let me know if I need to get out of your way," he muttered.

Amos nodded. With the aroma of Mr. Washington's broad

white haunches in his face, he couldn't quite trust himself to answer.

Phelan put on a pair of black leather gloves, just like the ones Chief of Detectives Byrnes wore during an interrogation. He gripped his cigar between his teeth and grinned, blowing smoke into Geoffrey Hunter's face. Everything he was about to do was legal, or close enough that it didn't matter. People wanted results. They usually didn't care how the police got them.

"We know you were having an affair with Brenda Leavitt. Did she threaten to tell Miss MacKenzie? Is that why you killed her?" Phelan stood so close to Geoffrey that drops of his spittle sprayed across the prisoner's face.

Geoffrey didn't answer. He'd learned during his Pinkerton years that nothing he said would be believed or make a difference when a bully like Phelan had the upper hand. The cuffs on his wrists were tight and solid. He'd already tried every trick he knew to free himself, but only succeeded in bloodying his skin. His shoulders ached from his arms being pulled behind his back and his stomach growled. Ridiculous to be remembering that he hadn't yet sat down to breakfast when Phelan shoved his way into the hotel suite that Geoffrey called home.

"I asked you a question. I expect an answer." An unholy light flashed in Phelan's eyes, telegraphing what came next.

Solid one-two punches to Geoffrey's gut. Bile forced its way up into his mouth and mingled with blood from where he'd bitten his tongue. He spit the mess out onto Phelan's shoes and the bottom of his trousers. The detective hadn't stepped back fast enough.

Heavily muscled arms held him up while Phelan clenched his fists and slammed his knuckles into Geoffrey's kidneys. The pain was bad enough to propel him into unconsciousness, but Geoffrey refused to let go. By sheer force of will, he stayed aware if not entirely awake, though his knees buckled and only the grip of Phelan's two cop helpers kept him on his feet.

Phelan dragged the chair to the center of the room. His assistants threw Geoffrey onto the splintery wood and tied a rope around his chest to hold him upright. One of them kicked his feet out of the way, hobnailed boots stomping on delicate bones and nearly shattering his ankles.

Phelan would have loved to use the thumbscrews, but he couldn't figure out a way to break Geoffrey's fingers without the damage showing. He had no illusions about how long an important attorney and inquiry agent would be left to his tender mercies. As soon as the MacKenzie woman found out where her fiancé was—*if* she found out—she'd contact one or more of her dead father's friends, probably another judge as prominent and powerful as the late Thomas Pickering MacKenzie had been. If Phelan hadn't made him confess by then—in front of witnesses and in writing—he'd have to let the Hunter bastard go.

He nodded, and one of the gorilla-sized cops upended the bucket of wastewater over Geoffrey's head. There was nothing a man under duress wanted more than cold, clear water. Nothing was fouler than what a jailer could supply from the cells. Phelan watched closely as the slops poured down his prisoner's face and firmly closed lips. Detainees had been known to sicken and die from what they choked on and swallowed.

"I'm going to ask you again, and this time you'd better answer if you know what's good for you. We know you killed Brenda Leavitt." Phelan grabbed a shock of Geoffrey's hair and pulled his head back as far as it would go. He took the cigar out of his mouth and spit brown saliva into Geoffrey's eyes. "Go ahead and blink all you want. I've got the whole rest of this cigar to chew on. You'll be blind, or wish you were, by the time I finish with you, Mr. High and Mighty Hunter. Now nod that proud head of yours and I'll have one of my boys fill the bucket with clean water. You killed Brenda Leavitt, didn't you? Just nod yes and this can all be over."

Geoffrey's bile and blood-laced spit landed square on Stephen Phelan's face.

The detective beat him with both black leather gloved fists until Geoffrey passed out.

"Take him back to the cells," Phelan ordered. "Tell the turnkey on duty that I don't care whether he ever wakes up or not."

Geoffrey's name had not been entered into the roster of prisoners being kept in the Tombs.

Nobody knew he was there.

CHAPTER 25

"That's her up ahead. That's Miss Prudence," Danny Dennis shouted down to Ned Hayes and Amos Lang, who were below him in the hansom cab's open passenger compartment.

The four riders who sat their mounts to one side of the riding path turned toward the sound of Mr. Washington's heavy hoofs pounding along the carriage track in their direction. Miss Prudence's carriage, containing a single passenger, moved out of the way of the fast-moving hansom cab. Kincaid, the longtime MacKenzie family coachman, had recognized Danny and realized that something important must have happened to bring him and Mr. Washington into Central Park at a near gallop.

Moments later Prudence had brought her horse to the side of the cab. She thought Amos Lang looked like he'd been out drinking all night. She hadn't seen Ned Hayes in months, but his eyes were bright and clear, so at least he was sober. She glanced up at Tyrus, who tipped his cap to her. Danny's emerald-green feather bent in the early morning breeze as he touched one gloved hand to his top hat.

"One of you had better tell me what's going on," she said. Four pairs of eyes stared at her, but nobody said a word.

Ned took a deep breath and wriggled uncomfortably under the heavy Confederate gray cloak Tyrus had wrapped him in. "Stephen Phelan has arrested Geoffrey. The bastard. My apologies, Miss Prudence."

"No apology necessary, Ned." Prudence tightened her grip on the reins she'd allowed to lie loosely across her sidesaddle. Her trained lawyer's mind swung into action. "Details. I need to know everything you've managed to find out. Danny?"

"Little Eddie was outside the Fifth Avenue Hotel helping Timmy the Gimp sell papers when Phelan and Pat Corcoran hauled Mr. Hunter out and shoved him into a Black Maria. Little Eddie said it looked as though they hadn't given him enough time to get properly dressed."

"What else?" Prudence's horse sidestepped restlessly as it sensed its rider's rising tension.

"Phelan will have him taken to the Tombs," Ned contributed.

"What was the charge he arrested him on?" Prudence asked.

Ned shrugged. "No charge needed to get detained at the Tombs. At least not right away. Phelan will have the legal paperwork done before Geoffrey has to appear in court, but I wouldn't count on being able to get much information until then."

"If he's in the Tombs, then that's where I'll go," Prudence said. "I'm his lawyer. They have to let me talk to him."

Ned shook his head at Prudence's naiveté. It was obvious to him—and probably to Amos, as well—that she was an attorney who had never handled a criminal case in New York City's notoriously corrupt judicial system. "That's not the way things work in the Tombs, Miss Prudence. There are five or six decent cells kept empty for important detainees, but the rest of them are death traps. My guess is Phelan would throw Geoffrey into the worst of them. Money and influence are the only two things that count once a prisoner gets locked up."

"You and I both have influence, Prudence." Eleanor Eaton had nudged her horse close to the hansom cab, listening intently to what was being said. "Your father was one of the city's most respected judges. His colleagues on the bench will do everything they can to stand by his daughter. You have only to ask." She smiled confidently. "I've at least two old beaux in judicial robes. Either of them can have Geoffrey out of the Tombs by the end of the day."

"What can I do to help?" Katja asked, kneeing her horse forward to join the group. Beside her, Eleanor's grandson looked over at her admiringly.

"Katja can come with me," Eleanor offered. "I may need a hand."

"I'll come, too," Gerhard Eaton said. He was a quiet young man, but like his grandmother, high principled and steady in resolve.

"I'm going to the Tombs," Prudence repeated. She was about to remind Ned that she and Geoffrey had once visited a client imprisoned there, so she knew what awaited her, but the ex-detective interrupted.

"You'll need someone with you who knows how the system operates," Ned Hayes said. "That's me."

A voice from the roof of the hansom cab echoed down through the trapdoor that Danny Dennis had opened. "I be there, too, Miss Prudence. Ain't no place Mister Ned go that Tyrus don't go right along with him."

Amos climbed out of the cab, then helped Prudence down from her horse and into the seat beside Ned. "We need to find out why Phelan felt he could arrest Mr. Hunter. I'll go to the office and tell Josiah what's happened. He'll have a list of the people Mr. Hunter recently saw and the places he went. That might tell us something."

Prudence nodded. She ticked off the elements of what was shaping up to be as organized a rescue plan as could be devised at short notice.

"Let's get going," she said. "We haven't got a minute to waste."

The intake sergeant ran an ink-stained finger down today's registry page. "Not here, miss. No Geoffrey Hunter. It's still early, though."

"What does that mean?" Prudence asked.

"Well, if he got picked up, he might still be riding around in a Black Maria. They don't like to drop off just one prisoner at a time."

"I'm his lawyer." It was the second time Prudence had identified herself as a member of the bar.

"So you say. But if he's not in my book, he's not here. Could be in one of the local station houses, until somebody there gets a chance to bring him over."

"I understand there are special reserved cells in case someone important gets arrested." Prudence laid a two-dollar silver coin near the sergeant's hand. It disappeared almost before it touched the wooden counter.

"Don't make no difference what cell somebody gets put in. Like I already told you, if his name isn't in my book, he's not here. Why don't you go on home and check back later?" The sergeant's tone had softened a bit, but he hadn't relented.

"We'll go around the corner to where visitors get their day passes," Ned said quietly as they turned away from the intake desk. "I wouldn't put it past Phelan to deliberately delay putting Geoffrey's name in the register."

"He can't do that," Prudence asserted. "That's got to be breaking some police department regulation if it isn't against the law."

"Phelan does whatever he wants. And gets away with it, too. Most of the time." Ned ushered her out the door, down the block, and around the corner toward the visitors' entrance. "Follow my lead here. If Geoffrey's name isn't in the prisoner registry, there won't be a record of him in the visitors' log, either."

"Then who do we say we're visiting?" Prudence asked.

"We don't. I know one of the keepers. We're going to pretend he's promised to give us a tour of the prison."

"That makes it sound like a museum," Prudence said.

"In a way, it is." Ned nodded toward the line of poorly clad men, women, and children that had formed along the sidewalk. "We'll be out of place, so just do your best to try to blend in. Tyrus, stay close to me."

"Ain't going nowhere by my lonesome, Mister Ned."

Within minutes, another dozen prisoner friends and relatives appeared behind Prudence, Ned Hayes, and Tyrus. One of the shawled women was studying Prudence's elegant riding habit as if trying to figure out who on earth this girl was and what she was wearing.

There was no getting through the barred door to the interior of the prison unless the desk sergeant writing down names in his book handed over a visitor's token. And there was no getting a token without naming the prisoner being visited. Everything had to match, coming in and going out.

"I wonder if Mickey Shanahan is on duty today," Ned asked quietly when they finally reached the desk where the visitors' log was being kept. Anything noisy or out of the ordinary could attract attention, and that was the last thing he wanted. "We worked together more years ago than I care to remember. He said to stop by, and he'd give us a tour." Another silver coin glinted briefly then disappeared.

"Sweet Mickey? He's at the women's prison this morning. Getting on in years, you know," the desk sergeant said. "Not quite up to keeping some of our men in line anymore."

Two bright silver coins found their way onto the wooden counter.

"Tell Mickey I said he can show these folks around." The desk sergeant handed over three visitor tokens and waved them toward where a guard waited to collect his cut of that morning's bribes.

"You've got women held here?" Prudence was doing her best to follow Ned's lead and act like a harmless, curious newcomer to the Tombs.

"We got women's cells, boy's cells, and out in the yard we used to have the hanging scaffold." The desk sergeant looked thoughtful. "In my opinion they should have left it up, as a warning, you know. And people always ask about it. But as soon as they started using that electric chair up at Sing Sing, down came the noose. Kind of a shame, if you ask me. It always got nice and quiet around here when an execution was scheduled."

"Who is Mickey Shanahan?" Prudence asked as soon as they'd passed into the courtyard around which the prison buildings had been erected.

"Used to be a beat cop." Ned paused for a moment, as if looking for the spot where the scaffold had once stood. "He helped me save Billy McGlory and I repaid the favor by not letting anyone know what he'd done. Kept his name out of the report I wrote. Mickey doesn't have what it takes to be a cop in this city."

"What does that mean?"

"I don't think he's ever used his billy club on anyone, and I know for sure and certain that the women he had to arrest were always safe with him. He got the nickname Sweet Mickey because he handed out candy to all the kids on his beat. He might be a little soft in the head. He probably should have been a priest."

Behind them, Tyrus huffed. He didn't trust priests, who were always white and babbling prayers in a language nobody understood anymore.

Prudence set off at a fast pace toward a blocklike building with rows of very small windows. "I've got a good idea where Phelan put Geoffrey. The cells on Murderers' Row in the men's prison are damp, filthy, and smelly all the time. It's so wet down at the far end that even the rats don't like to nest there."

"Miss Prudence, how you know where you going?" Tyrus took hold of Ned's arm as they both tried to keep up. "How you know so much 'bout this place?"

"Not quite three years ago, Geoffrey and I had a client here. Tim Fahey was his name. Phelan arrested Tim on no evidence at all, beat him senseless to try to get a confession for a murder he hadn't committed, destroyed any record that he'd ever been in the Tombs, and made him disappear. You were on that case with us, Ned. Do you remember it?"

"I do." Ned wasn't entirely sure he'd be able to recall the details of what he'd helped Hunter and MacKenzie uncover. "Now that you remind me, I do."

Tyrus looked doubtful, but for once decided not to ask the obvious question. It was hard to remember all the times his employer had fallen off the wagon with no memory of what he'd done after that first drink.

"Phelan has to know you'll move heaven and earth to get Geoffrey out," Ned declared. "And that things won't go well for him once you do. He may think Chief of Detectives Byrnes will protect him if he goes too far, but men like Byrnes never do anything that's not to their advantage. He'll let Phelan swing in the wind if it comes to it."

"How we gonna get in that building, Miss Prudence?" Tyrus asked. "And how we gonna get back out again? We supposed to be on a tour. I don't see no keeper showin' us around."

Prudence held up her visitor's token. "We just show this little gem and pair it with a few coins. When Geoffrey and I came to see Tim Fahey, visitors were bribing the guards to open the cell doors, and you could hardly squeeze your way through the crowds on the catwalks. Money talks as loudly here as anywhere else I can think of."

She was right. Their passes and a couple of coins got them into the men's prison without incident. It was still early morning, but visitors were already standing outside many of the cells.

"Everything's exactly the same," Prudence whispered, staring down the dark corridor lined on either side with one-man cells that usually held two or more prisoners. Sound traveled to every corner of the overcrowded cellblocks—rumblings of discontent, harsh snores, shouted threats, the thwack of fists on flesh, contraband weapons being run back and forth across the bars.

Even as they took their first steps into the Tombs's version of hell, the stench became unbearable. Ned tied his handkerchief over the lower part of his face and Tyrus hitched his shirt up over his nose. Prudence took a miniscule bottle of scent from the jacket pocket of her riding habit, poured some on one finger, and rubbed the perfume into the skin above her upper lip.

"There's no point asking the guard if he knows what cell Geoffrey is in." Ned felt something of the detective he used to be come flooding back. "If the intake sergeant is right about his name not being in the register, he doesn't exist."

"Down there." Prudence pointed toward the far end of the corridor, where a puddle of scummy water spread from a cluster of cells out onto the central walkway.

Hands reached through heavy bars as they made their way toward where Prudence remembered Tim Fahey had been kept. She'd never forgotten her horror at seeing what had been done to him, and the terrible fear that once the prison door closed behind her, it might not ever open again. Despite the families all around her that day. Despite the visitor's token she'd clasped in her hand, trying not to panic as she imagined losing it.

"Don't look," Ned counseled as they walked past the cells where desperate men shouted obscenities or sullenly watched them pass. "You won't sleep tonight if you do."

"Almost there, Mister Ned. You hold on to me good now." Tyrus had been brought north with Ned Hayes's mother when she married a Yankee, well before the war. He had almost no memory of what it had been like in the pens of slave auction houses, but he thought it could hardly have been much worse than the Tombs.

Two white hands gripped the bars of the last cell on the right. A faint whiff of sandalwood cologne drifted over the stench of slops.

"I wondered how long it would take you to find me." Geoffrey tried a smile, but all he could manage was a grimace. At some point in the beating, his shirt had been ripped open, the buttons torn off. It hung over his chest and stomach like a sad flag of surrender, while beneath the linen an expanse of dark, mottled skin testified to the viciousness of Phelan's fists.

Maddened by anger as Phelan had been, he'd managed to keep the worst of his blows from raining down on Geoffrey's face. When the prisoner appeared in court to enter a plea and have his trial date set, there would be no visible evidence that he'd suffered the third degree.

"We're getting you out of here." Prudence pressed her face against the bars, hands reaching into the cell to comfort the man she loved.

"It won't be easy," Geoffrey said. Escapes weren't unheard of at the Tombs, but Geoffrey was certain that Phelan had spread the word about him. Marked him as one of his special cases. As laconic and easily bribed as most of the keepers were, none of them would dare incur Phelan's wrath by letting his prize prisoner slip out through the visitor throng.

"We're going to need Mickey Shanahan's help. The sooner the better." Ned gave Tyrus a handful of coins and sent him off in the direction of the women's prison. "I doubt Mickey's keys will do us any good in this building, but we can use him to create a distraction. I don't suppose you've got a set of lockpicks with you, Miss Prudence?"

"No, but I've something almost as good." Prudence reached under the veiled top hat every fashionable woman wore with her riding habit and pulled out a wickedly long, sharp pin.

Ned unfastened the clasp of the Confederate cloak Tyrus had insisted he wear into the damp chill of the Tombs.

"Not yet," Geoffrey urged. He thought he knew the outlandishly simple plan Prudence had dreamed up, and he couldn't help but believe it was so ridiculously obvious that it just might work. Worth a try, anyway. They needed more time, more people outside the cells, before the cloak changed wearers. "You only have three visitor passes," he said.

"That's why we need Shanahan." Ned was guessing at what Miss Prudence intended to do. He thought there was no more than an even chance it would work, but that was probably why she hadn't talked out the details on their way here. She'd more than once gotten herself and others in trouble over a scheme no ex-Pinkerton in his right mind would have attempted.

"Keep talking," Prudence said. The sound of her hatpin working the lock on Geoffrey's cell door was slight but distinctive to any keeper who might walk their way.

"Amos has gone to the office to track down who you saw and talked to in the past few days." Ned edged closer to the cell, talking to Geoffrey all the while he angled his body to conceal what Prudence was doing. "He figures he might be able to find out if one of them put Phelan up to arresting you."

"I know who's responsible for this," Geoffrey said. "That's all I've been thinking about ever since they threw me in the Black Maria."

"You got a name?" Ned asked.

"A certain lady who held a grudge long after I'd forgotten her."

Prudence straightened, her hands stilled as she remembered

the story Geoffrey had told her about a long-ago sweetheart. "Inez?" she whispered.

"I did something stupid. I went to talk to her, to find out how the curb and bobble necklace ended up in Madame Régine's studio."

"You should have told me, Geoffrey. We said we weren't going to keep secrets from one another." Prudence's right hand began its tiny movements again, but her eyes bored into Geoffrey's.

Ned couldn't tell whether Miss Prudence was very disappointed or very angry. It might not matter in the end, as long as she got the lock picked and opened.

They heard Officer Shanahan before they saw him.

"Stand aside, stand aside."

Then the sound of a billy club against cell bars. Not violent bangings, but loud and rhythmic enough to announce that authority was on the scene, so anyone thinking to break the visiting rules had better think again.

Behind him came Tyrus Hayes, looking for all the world as if he belonged in one of the work crews hired to supplement the prisoner cleanup details. He was wearing a dark blue jacket that reached to his knees and a billed cap with what looked like a variation of the NYPD insignia on it. Carrying a pail and a mop.

"You're looking fine, Mickey." Smiling warmly, Ned Hayes clapped the newcomer on the shoulder.

"I'd say the same about you, Ned, but you wouldn't believe me." Another of Mickey's personality traits that had gotten in the way of promotion. He had an unwavering addiction to telling the truth. "This fellow here tells me we've got another job to do together." He gestured toward Tyrus.

"An injustice to set right before it's too late." Ned urged him forward, closer to the cell door. "This fine lady working away on one of your best locks is Miss Prudence MacKenzie, attorney-at-law and private inquiry agent. The man in the cell is her business partner and soon-to-be husband. Geoffrey Hunter."

Mickey stuck out a stubby-fingered hand and Geoffrey reached through the bars to shake it. Prudence nodded but didn't turn her attention from the hatpin that was doubling as a picklock.

"Phelan been at it again?" Sweet Mickey asked.

"How did you guess?"

Mickey turned toward where Tyrus stood as if awaiting orders. "It's a bit of a walk from the women's prison. I think I found out just about all I need to know."

"Got it!" Prudence's whisper, though soft, sounded triumphant.

Ned sidled in front of Shanahan, whose broad back effectively hid the cell door from a casual onlooker.

"Wait until I give the word." Shanahan turned to face the row of cells and the corridor that now held at least a dozen groups of visitors. He smacked the billy club against one outstretched hand. The few faces looking in his direction quickly shifted away. "All right now. Be quick about it."

Prudence eased the cell door open just wide enough for Ned to squeeze through. He took off the gray Confederate cloak, draped it over Geoffrey's shoulders to hide his ripped and bloodied shirt, and secured the neck fastening. Then he handed him one of the precious visitor's tokens, without which there was no leaving the Tombs.

They walked out of the men's prison building and across the courtyard to the waiting room where visitors were checking in. The crowd had grown as the morning wore on.

"Stay behind me," Sweet Mickey ordered. "Don't say a word. Let me do all the talking."

He launched into a droning spiel about the history of the women's prison as he led them into the waiting room and waved at the desk sergeant. "Now don't let me catch you in one of my cells, little lady," he said to Prudence, holding out one hand for her token. As Geoffrey and Ned turned over their passes also, Tyrus dropped the bucket he was carrying. Filthy, marginally soapy water poured out.

"Here now, clean up that mess," shouted the desk sergeant, taking the numbered tokens Shanahan handed him and checking off the three names written in his ledger next to those numbers. The guard standing beside the outer door pushed and shoved against the people breaking out of what had been an orderly line, sidestepping the mucky water, some of them obviously thinking they were going to be denied entry. Arms waved in the air, women screamed out that they weren't leaving no matter what, and children jumped up and down in delighted excitement.

Tyrus energetically plied his mop, splashing as much of the dirty water as he dared.

Prudence, Ned, and Geoffrey—anonymous in the Confederate gray cloak—slipped out onto the side street and around the corner where Danny Dennis and Mr. Washington waited for them.

"Tyrus said not to wait. Shanahan will see he gets safely out once the commotion has died down." Ned smiled in satisfaction at a job well done. If only he could lift a glass to toast their success.

"I think Phelan managed to crack a couple of ribs." Geoffrey held himself as straight as he could. Bending or breathing in too deeply hurt like the devil.

"Five Points, Danny," Prudence called up through the trapdoor. She wrapped one arm around Geoffrey to steady him. "We're taking you to Charity Sloan's clinic. Not even Stephen Phelan will be able to figure out where you've gone."

"The bastard," muttered Ned.

CHAPTER 26

"Read this." Josiah thrust a piece of paper at Amos as soon as the ex-Pink stepped through the office door.

"I've got more important news. Stephen Phelan arrested Mr. Hunter." Amos held the paper Josiah handed him, but he barely glanced at it. "This looks like a bill from a florist."

"He can't arrest him." Josiah had been standing behind his desk when Amos arrived. Now he fell backward into his chair as though the breath had been knocked out of him. "Mr. Hunter hasn't done anything criminal. There must be some mistake."

"That's why I'm here. Miss Prudence and Ned Hayes have gone to the Tombs to get him out—if they can—and I need to learn who squealed on him. Phelan had to be acting on a tip from someone who's out to frame Mr. Hunter. There's no other way the arrest could have happened. Someone's accused him of something he didn't do." Amos flung the unimportant florist's bill onto Josiah's desk. "I need a list of everyone Mr. Hunter's talked to here in the office or gone to see somewhere else. Start with the last couple of days. We'll work our way backward until something clicks."

Josiah picked up the florist's bill and slid it into a folder marked *Wedding*. "He's got a personal diary in his office, and I keep track of his and Miss Prudence's business appointments out here." An expensive, leather-bound calendar held pride of place on the secretary's desk. Appointments were meticulously noted in a beautifully formed calligraphic hand: beginning and end time of the visit, client's name, case reference if applicable. That day's page was noticeably empty. "They've both cut back on active casework so as not to have anything interfere with the wedding."

"You said Mr. Hunter keeps a personal diary in his office?"

Josiah nodded and started to get up.

"Stay where you are. I'll get it." Amos was back before Josiah could protest, a smaller version of the secretary's office calendar lying open on his hand.

"I'm not sure we should be prying into his personal affairs," Josiah said.

"Don't be ridiculous. If we don't get him out of the Tombs before Phelan gives him the third degree, he'll have too many broken ribs to be able to walk down the aisle at Trinity without crutches."

Josiah blenched.

Amos laid the two calendars side by side, turning matching pages slowly, muttering aloud the names of clients, restaurants where Geoffrey had met someone for lunch or dinner, tailor's appointments, reminders to buy another suitcase, to check on the steamboat tickets, other bits of daily life easily forgotten without a written note to oneself.

"Nothing," he said, closing Geoffrey's personal diary but leaving Josiah's large office calendar open. "I don't see anything or anyone suspicious. How good was Mr. Hunter about keeping track of things, Josiah?"

"I've never looked at his personal calendar before." Josiah plainly thought what Amos had done was a serious breach of etiquette. He opened the folder marked *Wedding.* "Now will you look at this?"

"The florist bill?" Amos checked his pocket watch. "I don't have time for things like that, Josiah. Not when Mr. Hunter is locked up in the Tombs."

"The florist sent a bill for the wedding flowers that he says have been canceled but will have to be paid for anyway because they've already been ordered."

"Say that again." Amos picked up the florist's statement, this time reading it with the careful attention he'd been trained to give every clue, no matter how small or seemingly insignificant. "But the wedding hasn't been called off. What does this mean?"

"That's what I've been trying to figure out. I'm the one who placed the original order, and only after a long discussion with the florist about what's available at this time of year. We discussed the placement of every single bouquet, basket display, and white ribboned bow. It was a masterpiece of design, if I do say so myself." Josiah preened like a barnyard cock for a moment. Then his face fell, and his fingers picked at the fancifully embroidered vest that was one of his favorites.

"If you didn't cancel the flowers, who did?" Amos rocked back on his heels, hands tucked into his pants pockets.

A shadow fell across the glass in the office door, followed by a sharp rap. A Western Union delivery boy opened the door without waiting to be invited in, one hand holding the familiar piece of folded pale-yellow paper. "I need a signature," he said, twisting on his heels, clearly eager to get the telegram delivered and be on his way. A heavy canvas bag hung from one shoulder.

Amos reached for the telegram and signed the delivery boy's receipt book.

"I'll take that," Josiah said, as the door slammed shut and the clatter of hurrying feet echoed from the staircase. He opened the flimsy carefully, using the brass letter opener that was part of the beautifully polished desk set Prudence had given him on the first anniversary of Hunter and MacKenzie, Investigative Law.

"What is it?" Amos asked. He had a bad feeling about this entire day.

"It's from the office of the rector at Trinity Church. Acknowledging the cancellation of the wedding of Prudence MacKenzie and Geoffrey Hunter. The deposits for the church, the choir, and the organist won't be refunded." Josiah set the telegram next to the florist's bill and stared at them. He looked as though he couldn't believe what he'd just read.

"Get your hat," Amos ordered, stuffing the bill and the telegram into one of his pockets.

"Where are we going?"

"First to the florist's shop and then to Trinity Church. We need to find out who's determined to call off this wedding."

"I can't leave the office empty," Josiah protested.

"Lock up," Amos ordered. "You're the one who placed the orders, so I need you with me to ask the right questions. Let's go."

"Miss Prudence . . ."

"You know she'd ask what you're waiting for."

Amos was right. Miss Prudence was always one for action. Josiah made up his mind. Settled his hat on his carefully combed hair, snugged his hands into his gloves, and locked the office door behind them.

He caught up with Amos as they left the building and turned down Wall Street in the direction of Trinity Church and the busy florist favored by its high-society parishioners. Whatever it took, he'd have the wedding back on everyone's books within the next hour or two or know the reason why.

He'd almost forgotten that Geoffrey was a prisoner in the Tombs.

"You've got a couple of cracked ribs and a lot of deep bruising," Dr. Charity Sloan said as she wound a heavy cotton binding around Geoffrey Hunter's torso. "But no bones are broken, your lungs weren't punctured, and your spleen wasn't ruptured. I'd say you were a very lucky man."

"Who needs a place to hide out for a few days." Prudence eyed the bandaging critically, knowing she might have to duplicate Charity's expertise if Geoffrey couldn't be accommodated at the Friends Refuge for the Sick Poor. It was a clinic Charity had founded to offer healing and a safe place of concealment for the abused women of the Five Points area, but it never turned away a sick or needy patient, regardless of sex or age.

"I can put him in one of the basement storage rooms," Charity offered. "The upstairs dormitories are for women and children only."

"Could he make it across the bridge to Brooklyn without doing more damage to himself?" Prudence asked.

"Brooklyn?"

"I was thinking of taking him to hide out at Ben and Lydia Truitt's house. You know how obsessed Clyde Allen is with keeping Ben safe. He'd do the same for Geoffrey."

Charity thought for a moment. "Clyde Allen has a wicked knife. And as far as I can tell, he doesn't sleep more than a couple of hours a night. Would Danny Dennis be able to get Geoffrey there without being followed?" Every cabbie in New York City knew Danny's huge white horse, Mr. Washington.

"He'll figure something out." Danny had spent half a lifetime running from the law in Ireland. He'd cultivated a new identity in America that no one had managed to crack. So far.

"Let me know when the two of you have finished planning my future." Geoffrey swayed on the examining table, barely managing not to fall to one side. His skin was pale and clammy, beaded with sweat.

"Laudanum," Charity said, mixing a few drops of the liquid opium with water and holding the glass to Geoffrey's lips. He shook his head, but Charity pinched his nose until he finally gave in and swallowed the dose. "You need sleep and relief from the pain," she said matter-of-factly. "I've given you a minimum amount, under the circumstances." She handed the small brown glass bottle to Prudence. "Make sure Lydia doesn't give him more than two or three drops at a time, and not more than twice a day and then again just before bedtime."

"That's not too much?" Prudence had overcome a nearly overwhelming addiction to laudanum. She was terrified of the drug, but also resolutely determined not to let fear rule her life.

"For you, yes. For Geoffrey, no. Trust me, Prudence." Charity turned her attention back to her patient. "You're in worse shape than you want to admit, my friend. If you intend to marry this beautiful young woman in two weeks' time, you'll follow doctor's orders. To the letter."

"I need to talk to Prudence before this damn drug knocks me out." Geoffrey's voice was strained and tremulous. His shoulders had begun to shake.

Charity wrapped a blanket around him. "I'll go out to where Danny's waiting and give him instructions. Lie down if you start to feel like you're about to pass out. Don't worry about it. We'll manage to get you to where you need to be." She didn't add that she and her staff had handled more cumbersome drunks in their time than she cared to remember.

"I told you I went to talk to Inez, but I didn't tell you all of it," Geoffrey began.

"Save your strength," Prudence said. "Just give me what I need to know. We can talk later about whatever else there is to discuss."

"She's bitter. Blames me for the ruination of her life. Inez couldn't have children after she got rid of the one she wanted me to pretend was mine. That's my fault, too. She claims she's never heard of Anthony Nichols, but I don't believe her. Where Inez is concerned, lies and fabrications and half-truths are so mixed up that I don't think even she can unravel them."

"She can't stand the idea of your being happy." Prudence tightened the blanket around Geoffrey's shoulders. "She doesn't want you to marry. She must hate me nearly as much as she still loves you."

"Loves me?"

"Loves you enough to commit murder to keep you away from anyone else. Women can be very dangerous when they're crossed, Geoffrey. We know that from my stepmother. She wanted to kill me, just the way she killed my father. Inez is no different."

"Be careful, Prudence," Geoffrey pleaded. "I can't be there to keep you safe. Stay away from Inez. Whatever else you do, make sure she can't get near you."

"You've taught me everything I know about detecting. Have some faith in me and your expert tutelage." She framed it as a jest, but Prudence was deadly serious.

"One other thing." He could feel the laudanum creeping toward his brain, numbing his senses, interfering with his speech.

"What is it, Geoffrey?"

"The curb and bobble necklace."

"What about it?"

"It wasn't in my pocket when I got back to the Fifth Avenue Hotel. I must have dropped it in Inez's parlor. I took it out because I wanted her to identify it as the one I often saw her wear. She refused to admit it was hers. I was angry. That's when it must have slipped from my fingers. A few minutes later I was back out in Washington Square Park, still furious. I should have gone back for it, but I didn't. I gave her something to hold over me. Half the seamstresses in Madame Régine's workroom must know we found the chain there and didn't tell the police. The witch outsmarted me, Prudence."

"That's because you're not a woman, my love. It takes one to know one."

The dress was one of the most beautiful creations Inez Rankin Purcell had ever worn. At the final fitting, Madame Donovan herself came into the private mirrored room to inspect her latest inspiration.

"Incredible," she said. "The gown and its wearer are both breathtakingly splendid. I know we designed it for a daytime social event, Mrs. Purcell, but I really think it would be suitable for late afternoon or early evening as well. Informal evening, of course." Catherine Donovan waited for her client to reveal the important function she would be attending, but unlike most of the women she clothed, Inez Purcell was frequently close-mouthed.

White wasn't often worn by older women, but Mrs. Purcell had been obstinately unshakable in her choice of fabric and color. The shade of ivory silk she'd insisted on was close to what a spring or summer bride might have preferred, especially in the years since Queen Victoria had married in white satin and lace. Madame Donovan had had reservations about whether the ivory silk would flatter Inez or overwhelm the woman's pale skin and silvery blond hair, but for once, she had underestimated a client's ability to triumph over what could have been a poor choice. Something about the way Mrs. Purcell preened and pirouetted in front of the mirrors reminded Catherine of bridal excitement, but that was ridiculous, of course. No one wore white to a wedding nowadays except the young lady who was about to be married.

"A promenade around the grand salon, perhaps?" Madame Donovan suggested. "Just to check the sweep of the skirt. There are no other clients there at the moment."

She led Mrs. Purcell out to the room that was nearly a duplicate of Charles Frederick Worth's famous main salon, a gloriously decadent space furnished with gilt-framed mirrors, satin drapes, Aubusson carpets, and imported European antique sofas, fainting couches, spindly-legged chairs, and marble-topped tea tables. Several of her most experienced saleswomen, all of them dressed entirely in black, gathered to see the impromptu show.

And one impressively tall, handsome Frenchman.

"Monsieur Théodore Augustin Delahaye." Catherine introduced her newest hire and repressed a smile as Delahaye bowed gracefully over Inez Purcell's hand, bringing it to within an inch of his lips. One didn't actually touch the skin, but there was the seductive sigh of gently exhaled breath. Warm, slightly damp.

"*Enchanté,* madame. And may I say that you are a vision no one who has the good fortune to see you will ever forget."

His English was alluringly accented, but not at all difficult to understand.

"Monsieur Delahaye's portfolio contains the latest Parisian styles." Catherine would be only too happy to turn the sometimes difficult-to-please Mrs. Purcell over to the Frenchman. Judging from the effect he seemed to be having on the mercurial Inez, he would very soon become one of the house's prime attractions.

"I should like to see Monsieur Delahaye's portfolio." Inez twirled slowly, listening appreciatively to the swish of the silk skirt. "But not today. And not here."

"I shall hold myself ready at madame's convenience," Delahaye purred.

If Madame Régine was right, and Delahaye's only talent was as a draftsman, a copyist, he would soon lose some of the glamorous fascination of good looks and French manners. Catherine had not forgotten that the main reason she had hired him was to keep him under observation and away from Régine Healy's workrooms. He might be a thoroughgoing cad, or perhaps a more dangerous creature, but as long as the House of Donovan kept him on a tight leash, it was unlikely he could do any harm.

Or so it was hoped.

CHAPTER 27

Trinity Florists had just opened for the day, its unlatched door spilling a wave of fragrance onto the sidewalk where the season's favorite blooms beckoned to passersby. Pails of bright pink peonies stood before tall stalks of deep purple delphiniums. Sprays of white bridal wreath set off bouquets of crimson roses. Scarlet carnations nestled amidst sheaves of deep green ferns and Italian ruscus. To the busy denizens of lower Wall Street who paused before the display, it was like being absorbed for a moment into one of the famous gardens of romantic literature. Visitors to Trinity Church's venerable cemetery often stopped to purchase a small bouquet to place on Alexander Hamilton's grave before wandering along the pathways bordered by less well-known dead.

Josiah frequently spent a quiet lunch hour reading the epitaphs on new and old Trinity gravestones, but today he was all business and righteous anger.

"Mr. Brightwing," he announced, closing the shop door firmly behind Amos, who was unobtrusively following the Hunter and MacKenzie secretary. Josiah snapped down the window shade, turned the OPEN sign to CLOSED, and snugged shut the door lock. "I want to know the meaning of this." He flung the bill he had received that morning onto the counter where it teetered atop bits of cut stems, dethorned rose stalks, and odd bits of greenery.

"The order had already been placed before I received your cancellation request." Philip Brightwing dealt with disgruntled and demanding customers every day. Josiah Gregory, smartly tailored in his black suit and colorfully embroidered vest, might intimidate a lesser shopkeeper, but not Brightwing. A florist who spent his life catering to brides and the bereaved grew a very thick skin. "My suppliers informed me that it was too late to rescind. Some of our growers are located in remote areas and cannot be contacted on a whim. We did discuss deadlines, Mr. Gregory, and your financial responsibility at every stage of the wedding preparations."

"The ceremony has not been canceled, and neither has the order for the flowers we discussed." Josiah slammed his hand against the counter and tried not to wince as thorns dug into the palm of his hand. He had insisted to Amos that he, Josiah, could handle this problem without any help, thank you very much, so now he had no choice but to see it through. Amos melted into the surrounding foliage as though he were a woodland elf.

"Your secretary was most explicit," Mr. Brightwing said. "She stood right where you are today and explained that due to unforeseen circumstances the bride and groom had broken their engagement and would therefore not be getting married after all."

"I don't have a secretary," Josiah said. "I *am* secretary to Miss Prudence MacKenzie and Mr. Geoffrey Hunter, and they are very definitely intending to become husband and wife in exactly fourteen days' time."

"That's as it may be, but I'm sure you understand that even though I have already begun to secure new purchasers for some of the flowers, I shall certainly incur a substantial loss."

"Nonsense," announced Amos Lang, stepping out from behind a fully leafed *ficus lyrata* growing in a wooden tub. "It's too late to cancel the order, the flowers will arrive, and you, Mr. Brightwing, will see that they are placed in Trinity Church as per Mr. Gregory's previous instructions. Problem solved."

Philip Brightwing blinked, as if uncertain how this oddly unremarkable fellow had materialized in his shop. "I can't cancel on the new purchasers I've already contacted. I have a reputation to uphold."

Amos made a swishing motion, as though flies buzzed around his face. He reached casually into one of his concealed shoulder holsters and withdrew a Remington New Model Police revolver, which he used to brush the cut stems, rose stalks, and other greenery from the counter. The subject of the flowers had been dealt with. No more argument on that score. "Please describe the woman you claim to have spoken to."

Brightwing made a mewling sound, like a cat who's about to be jumped by a jaw-slobbering dog.

"How old was she?" Amos asked. To get him started.

"I couldn't tell. She wore a big hat with a veil that reached all the way down to her chin."

"Stylish clothes?" Josiah thought that anything else would stand out as not belonging in this part of town.

"Stylish. Yes. Not what a working woman could afford, come to think of it. Not off the rack." Brightwing tried not to stare at the Remington, but his eyes kept glancing down at the gun despite his best efforts to pretend it wasn't there.

"Did she come in a carriage?" Amos asked. He laid a hand on the revolver's grip, one finger inching toward the trigger.

"Carriage? No. No carriage." Drops of fear sweat popped out on Brightwing's forehead.

"Hansom cab?" Amos allowed a hint of amusement to creep into his voice.

"No. No cab."

"She walked then. From what direction did she come?"

"I was in the back seeing to the morning's deliveries when the shop bell rang. She was already standing at the counter when I came out."

"Did she sign a cancellation request?" Josiah thought he understood the drift and purpose of Amos's questions. Anything that could identify her.

Brightwing fumbled through his order book, nearly tearing a page or two in his hurry to get this distressing conversation over with and these frightening men out of his shop. He turned the book around so that Josiah could read the page that detailed the Hunter and MacKenzie order and its cancellation. "Right there." He pointed at an illegible scribble.

"I can't read that." Josiah was incensed. He would never have permitted a client to get away with such a scrawl. The full legal name would have been printed beneath the abominable longhand. "What name did she give you?"

"She didn't say." Brightwing suddenly realized he had been duped. He pulled a handkerchief from his pocket and mopped his face. "She identified herself as secretary to Miss MacKenzie and Mr. Hunter, but she never spoke her own name."

"Useless." Amos picked up the Remington and slid it back into the concealed shoulder holster. He walked to the shop door, stood there for a moment in case Josiah had another question to ask, then turned the CLOSED sign to OPEN, and slid back the bolted lock.

"I was upset, so I watched where she went when she left." Brightwing was desperate to provide any piece of helpful information. The last thing he wanted was for the strangely ordinary man with the gun to come back.

"Where did she go?" Josiah wondered what the florist would do after he and Amos left. Pass out? Drink from the pocket flask he undoubtedly carried? Close down for the day?

"Straight across the street to the church." Brightwing nodded vigorously. "Not the graveyard. She went right to where the church offices are located."

"You saw her go in?" Josiah felt they were finally getting somewhere.

"I watched the door close behind her." Brightwing suddenly sat down on the stool behind the counter. He'd reached his limit. Not an ounce of strength left in his legs.

"Remember," Josiah said quietly. Forcefully. Leaving no room for discussion or dispute. "We are back to the original MacKenzie-Hunter order. Everything as we planned it. No alterations. Is that clear, Mr. Brightwing?"

The florist nodded.

"Then we'll say good day." Josiah prided himself on being polite in even the most trying circumstances.

"Judge Ingram is a friend of many years' standing." Eleanor Eaton angled the top hat of her riding habit so it tilted just the slightest bit over her still-youthful blue eyes. They'd always been her best feature. "He's a widower now, a vulnerable state for a man who's grown used to the comforts of a loving wife and a well-run household."

Katja tried to look shocked, but only managed to seem amused. She glanced at Gerhard Eaton, who didn't appear the least bothered by his grandmother's artifice.

"The secretary will be back out in a moment," Eleanor continued, looking around appreciatively at the well-decorated waiting room outside the judge's chambers. "Let me do the talking. You two are here as window dressing. Consider it your task to look distressed, unsettled, whichever word suits you best. What you have to convey is a conviction that only Judge Ingram's intervention can save an innocent Geoffrey Hunter from a fate worse than death."

"This reminds me of the time you visited my school when the headmaster was determined to expel me." Gerhard chuckled, not looking the least bit despairing.

"What did you do to get yourself expelled?" Katja had never been to school. Her entire education had been with governesses who seldom stayed very long before moving on to positions that paid better and more regularly.

"Stabled a goat in the chapel belltower and then broke the lock so the door couldn't be opened. The smell was so bad the chaplain couldn't hold services there for a week or so after it was all over."

Katja pictured heaps of hay and goat dung above the not-so-innocent heads of mischievous schoolboys and grinned. She wondered what else Gerhard Eaton was hiding behind the glasses and the equable demeanor of a gentleman of impeccable manners. "Why did you do it?"

"A dare. I was the only one caught. Fortunately, my grandmother came to the rescue."

"An expensive outing, but well worth it." Eleanor gave a quick nod as the door to Judge Ingram's private chambers opened. "Ready? Here we go."

They'd decided that neither Prudence's carriage nor Mr. Washington could be used to take Geoffrey into hiding in Brooklyn. Danny produced a pair of nondescript sorrels and a larger than average four-wheeled carriage he rented out for weddings and special occasions. Dr. Sloan supervised the placement of pillows and blankets to support Geoffrey's bandaged ribs.

"Send for me if you have any sudden, sharp pain in that area," Charity ordered. "If a rib is cracked badly enough, it can splinter. Then you're really in trouble."

"I'll tell Lydia he's not to be allowed to walk by himself or without someone at his side in case he needs help." Prudence had a grim set to her lips that meant she was not to be trifled with.

"I brought Flower along," Danny said, stroking the dog's

red-gold fur. "She'll stay with him night and day and bark if he's in discomfort or takes a fall."

Or someone approaches the Truitt house who has no business being there, Prudence thought. She couldn't for the life of her remember whether Detective Stephen Phelan was aware of the close relationship Prudence and Geoffrey had cultivated with Ben Truitt and his daughter. Having on guard a dog as intelligent and alert as Flower would add significantly to their defensive tactics.

The carriage rolled away from the clinic with Geoffrey propped up like an oriental potentate, Prudence keeping a sharp eye out for any expressions of pain on his face, and Flower pressing her beautifully shaped head and long silky ears against his legs.

If everything worked according to plan, Prudence would return to Manhattan after Geoffrey had been put to bed at the Truitt home. Eleanor Eaton had promised to send word if she'd managed to persuade a judge to look into what was surely a warrantless arrest and detention. Amos Lang and Ned Hayes were to report whatever they'd managed to discover. With Geoffrey down for the count, Prudence would make it clear to all of them that she and she alone would direct the investigation that had begun in Madame Régine's salon.

It was Madame Catherine Donovan's idea to entrust Théodore Delahaye with Inez Purcell's gown.

"We have our own delivery people, of course, and an entire department devoted solely to ensuring that our clients' orders arrive at their homes in perfect condition," she told the Frenchman. "But I did notice the immediate rapport that developed between you and Mrs. Purcell. Whenever possible, we like to extend an extra courtesy if a garment is delayed after what was to be a final fitting. Normally, I would send one of our senior salesladies to wait on Mrs. Purcell, but I thought you might relish the opportunity to deepen what I'm confident will be a warm relationship with a valued customer."

She made it sound as though he had a choice, but of course he didn't.

"I'll order one of our carriages for you."

"Madame does me a great honor." Delahaye didn't for a moment like being treated as if he were a delivery boy, but he'd survived this long by being endlessly adaptable. He'd been in New York for several months longer than he'd led Catherine Donovan to believe, but it hadn't been until he'd met Brenda Leavitt and discovered who she worked for that his plans had gelled. It had taken time for the agent he hired to persuade Brenda to steal designs from Régine's salon, then hours of painstaking work to create the sketches that would make them his own. He had modified the designs only enough so they did not exactly resemble what Régine had envisioned. It would take the eye of a professional to understand what he had done. Delahaye had known a moment of angst when Madame Catherine Donovan opened his portfolio, but the unease had passed the moment she clucked her tongue in appreciation.

Since the two Donovan carriages were occasionally used for the convenience of clients, they were as luxuriously appointed as any of the rooms in the salon. Far from the narrow confines of the hansom cabs Delahaye had been forced to hire when he'd spent nearly every franc he'd brought with him from France on that buffoon of a private inquiry agent. At first, the man had seemed to know what he was doing, and it was true that he had a natural way with women, or at least with the one woman Delahaye was paying him to court. Théo himself did not dare attempt to bedazzle the seamstress with his charms. He could not disguise his Frenchness, and he could not risk impressionable Brenda letting drop a careless boast about a handsome European suitor. So he'd contracted the job out. An expensive investment, and one he'd had to terminate rather messily, but the result was more than satisfactory.

Now he stretched out his long, well-muscled legs, settled back into the comfort of the carriage's extravagantly appointed interior, and planned the seduction of the woman whose absurdly expensive cream-colored gown lay wrapped in white muslin on the seat opposite. He preferred his conquests to be younger, but Inez Purcell was a wealthy widow. Just what he needed.

For the moment.

CHAPTER 28

Inez had aways preferred dark-haired, dark-eyed men to the brownish-blond, blue-eyed cousins and brothers of friends she'd grown up with. The mother of the man who'd gotten her pregnant had been a Louisiana Creole beauty, and Geoffrey Hunter—who should have married her—had eyes so deeply black she'd often felt spellbound when she looked into them.

No doubt about it, Geoffrey was handsomer than this Frenchman who'd delivered her Madame Donovan gown and accepted an invitation to sip tea in the parlor. Much better looking, but absent. The Frenchman—Monsieur Théodore Delahaye—had a Gallic arched nose and wasn't broad enough through the shoulders, but he was there, seated across from her, smiling in a manner that struck her as both slightly indecent and deliberately suggestive.

She'd had lovers over the years, both before and after her late husband's unfortunate encounter with the cluster of black widow spiders that had invaded his bed linens. For the most part, the partners she chose were content to agree to her terms. No commitments, no promises, no love talk. Purely physical trysts that might or might not be repeated.

She preferred married men. They were less likely to be demanding, always aware that an anonymous letter could upset or destroy the comfortable tranquility of the home and marriage they were blithely jeopardizing. When the lovers met in a social setting—as happened occasionally—they bowed, chatted politely, and went on their separate ways, sometimes with a telltale gleam in the eye had anyone known how to read it.

Seeing Geoffrey again, listening to his voice, smelling that special aroma of mingled body fragrance and sandalwood cologne, had reawakened the lustful girl in her. There had been an incident the year before that might have spelled the end of her reputation had it come to light, and for one of the first times in her life, Inez had decided that casual coupling might not be worth the risk it entailed. So she'd restrained what was an unladylike appetite and amused herself with the dogs and long walks in the park.

Then had come the engagement announcement in the *Times*. She'd boiled over, lost every ounce of the control she'd prided herself on mastering. Inez's fingers twitched as she reflexively counted off the men she'd shocked with the violence of her lovemaking. One of them had even accused her of being a professional.

The frenzy died down, as bouts of delirium inevitably will. She'd abstained. She'd planned. And now here was a delicious tidbit of a Frenchman who almost certainly thought he controlled the situation. Sometimes it amused her not to disabuse the ephemeral lovers who preened like peacocks, believing themselves to be the fulfillment of every woman's dream. One or two encounters. Never more than that. Men had a tendency to grow demanding and possessive.

"Did you think to bring your portfolio, Monsieur Delahaye?" Inez asked.

"I did, madame." He'd chosen ten of the designs Brenda Leavitt had sketched for Anthony Nichols, gowns that were different enough from what other salons were producing to be on the cusp of being called audacious. Daring. Bold. But of such classically beautiful lines that even the most conservative matrons of the Four Hundred would be drawn to them.

Inez smiled and patted the cushion of the settee beside her. Invitingly. She played the seduction game as a seasoned participant, with just enough implied attraction to be beguiling. The trick was to captivate yet still persuade the quarry that he was in charge. The afternoon stretched before her, empty of engagements. The evening, also.

"Do show me what you have," Inez crooned as Théodore Delahaye installed himself on the settee and opened the leather portfolio. She laid a gentle hand on the muscle of his thigh, felt a ripple of response course through her fingers, and decided to think of him as Théo. She'd made a mistake about a man only once. But she was remedying that slip. She thought the Frenchman's eyes were almost as dark as Geoffrey's. And if she closed her own eyes when it counted most, she could nearly believe Delahaye wasn't Delahaye at all.

"Her name is Inez Purcell," Prudence told Ned Hayes and Amos Lang. "Inez Rankin when Geoffrey knew her. She believed they had an understanding that no gentleman could deny, and that he would gladly throw away his life to save her reputation."

"Southern women can be like that." Ned sipped the aged bourbon Prudence kept in the library for Geoffrey. Tyrus had gone down to the kitchen to brush clean the Confederate gray cloak that had gotten stained during its brief sojourn in the Tombs. Ned knew there would almost certainly be hell to pay when Tyrus saw him with a glass in his hand or smelled the bourbon on his breath, but he'd promised himself not to fall too far off the wagon. And this bourbon was worth whatever price Tyrus would exact.

"We couldn't get a good description of the woman who ordered the cancellations," Amos said. He, too, was drinking

Geoffrey's bourbon, but in his case, it was hair of the dog. He needed it. "Fashionable clothing, wide-brimmed hat with a thick veil. An air of confidence about what she was doing. That was the best we could get out of the florist, and it wasn't any more detailed at the church office. I felt like asking them if they always canceled weddings on the word of anyone who walked in off the street, but I kept my mouth shut, Miss Prudence."

"Everything's back as it should be." Ned sank farther into the comfortable chair from which he could appreciate the late Judge MacKenzie's library. It was as lavish and masculine a room as any to be found in the string of Fifth Avenue mansions where the powerful men of New York City's elite continued the work begun in their offices. Judge MacKenzie had created a personal library as filled with legal tomes as any judge's chambers, and Prudence had kept every volume. She looked poised and regal as she sat in the leather chair from which her father had once instructed her, the riding habit she'd worn to the Tombs replaced by a dark blue silk afternoon gown from Madame Régine's collection.

She knew Geoffrey was safe, guarded by a man who knew how to wield a knife, a woman who was a crack shot, and a dog who would lay down her life for him. All that remained was to identify and lay hands on whoever murdered Brenda Leavitt and Anthony Nichols. Inez Purcell was a tempting suspect, but there was no evidence to link her to the crimes. They couldn't even accuse her of trying to interfere with the wedding. No one had seen the face of the woman who had visited the florist's shop and the Trinity Church office. All they could lay at her feet was a long-ago passion for a man who refused to marry her. Nothing branded her a murderess. Not even the shocking death of her husband.

"What next, Miss Prudence?" Ned devoutly hoped whatever it was would leave him enough time to make substantial inroads on the Jack Daniel's that smelled and tasted of charred oak barrels and the South.

"Start at the beginning." Prudence dipped a pen in the crystal inkwell in front of her and took a piece of embossed MacKenzie stationery from one of the desk drawers. "Again."

"Which means trying to identify who the real target has been," Amos said. "That's what's been bedeviling me all along. It could be Miss Prudence, Mr. Hunter, or Madame Régine. Or all three of them."

"Or none of them." Ned set down his bourbon, hesitated a moment, then poured another two inches into the almost-empty glass. "Brenda Leavitt might have been killed by someone who broke into Madame Régine's salon to steal whatever he could find there. No connection whatsoever to any person we've named. We know that Anthony Nichols had clients who were probably more dangerous than the people they hired him to find or investigate. He was getting ready to leave town when someone put a bullet in him. That killing didn't have to have anything to do with Brenda Leavitt's death."

"Damn." Amos took a chaw of tobacco from his pocket, then reluctantly put it back. "Sorry, Miss Prudence."

"We've all said worse things, Amos." The ink had dried on the nib of Prudence's pen. She set it down. "I refuse to give up, but I don't know which direction we should be going. We're running out of time, and we can't afford to make a mistake."

"Back to the beginning." Ned picked up the bottle of Jack Daniel's, hesitated, then banged in the cork with enough force to ensure he wouldn't be able to ease it out again.

"Let's talk about what you and Mr. Hunter saw at Madame Régine's salon that morning," Amos suggested. It was what detectives always did when they faced a brick wall. Pick apart the clues and the crime scene, one tiny piece at a time.

Over and over again until something broke free.

Nathaniel Hunter had been avoiding Inez. When she sent a footman down with an invitation to tea, he'd had his housekeeper inform the man that Mr. Hunter was indisposed. Hint-ing, but not actually claiming that on doctor's orders, he was confined to his bed. The truth of the matter was that he'd seen something he knew no one was meant to observe. He didn't know quite what to make of it, but the longer he thought about it, the more the fear of God crept into the marrow of his bones. To be more precise, the fear of Inez.

It had happened just a day ago, so late at night that the park was invitingly quiet and empty. He'd been too restless to sleep, and he hadn't turned on any lights when he'd come downstairs from his bedroom. Thinking a touch of moonlight might settle his nerves, he'd shrugged on a dark coat over his very British pajamas and stepped outside for a moment. Down the steps he'd gone, slipper silent, and across the sidewalk into where the mist shrouding the trees was like entering an enchanted forest. He thought of Arthur, Excalibur, and the Lady of the Lake, murmuring lines from Malory's *Le Morte d'Arthur* as he passed beneath branches heavy with moisture. Nathaniel's happiest moments had always been when he could lose himself in literature.

He sat on the bench opposite his front door for a while, and only got up to go back to his bed when he felt himself begin to nod off.

At first, he thought the glimpse of movement he caught deeper in the park must be someone's dog let out for a last moment of natural relief. But then the shadow grew to the height of a man, and he knew he'd been mistaken.

He froze.

Watched as the figure made its way from deep in the trees to Inez Purcell's front door. Pushed soundlessly on the painted wood, then disappeared inside. But not before he recognized his cousin Geoffrey's distinctively tall stature and facial features in the moonlight that bathed Inez's front steps in silver.

What happened the next morning—today—puzzled and frightened him even more. He'd just about convinced himself that he was brave enough to march up the sidewalk to Inez's front door and ask her point-blank what Geoffrey Hunter had been doing at her house in the middle of the night.

He'd gotten as far as the halfway mark between the two townhomes when he ran out of courage. Sat himself down on a park bench and asked himself what business it was of his if Inez the spider lady had secretly taken up with Geoffrey, the soon-to-be-married. Real people were far more unpredictable than the heroes and heroines of the classic works of fiction he had taught to hundreds of university students. Perhaps it was time to request a sabbatical. Take refuge in the civilized cloisters of Oxford while his cousin and the woman he was supposed to have taken as his wife all those years ago worked out whatever had reignited between them. Dalliance? Liaison? *Affaire de coeur*? He didn't know what to call it except *trouble*.

If he hadn't overheard them talking, Nathaniel wouldn't have known the two men walking toward Inez's house were policemen. They looked ordinary enough, but then he realized they also appeared very Irish, dressed in off-the-rack suits and brown derbies. When one of them opened his coat to check his pocket watch, Nathaniel saw the butt of a gun and the gleam of handcuffs. He thought for a moment he would tip over on the bench and slide to the ground in a dead faint.

He reminded himself that men of the Hunter family were all made of sterner stuff. Followed the coppers with his eyes as they passed in front of him, and heard one of them say something about the third degree. Everyone in New York City knew what that was. There'd been articles aplenty in the newspapers about Thomas Byrnes, Chief of Detectives, and how he was revolutionizing the apprehension of the criminal class. The consensus was that violent lawbreakers deserved whatever they got. But why were the Irishmen knocking on Inez's door? Why did they stay inside her house for at least an hour? And why was the older of the two policemen smiling broadly when they came out? Like someone who'd just received the greatest gift Almighty God could have bestowed on him?

Nathaniel went home, drank more coffee—liberally spiked with whiskey—and very nearly convinced himself that he had no part to play in whatever was happening. But he knew better. Geoffrey was blood; Inez wasn't. It was as simple as that. He might no longer live in the South or consider himself much of a Southerner, but when family honor was at stake, a man didn't have a choice.

It took him most of the morning to find the business card Geoffrey had left him. He'd stuck it between the pages of a novel he intended to start reading, then absentmindedly buried the book in a pile of volumes stacked haphazardly behind a chair he rarely sat in. Pretending to himself that he'd forgotten where he'd put the book was procrastination, putting off the moment of action for as long as he could. He knew it and despised himself for being cowardly. Over the years, he'd created a comfortable, unchallenging life for himself. It wasn't easy to face uncertainty and danger when you'd lulled yourself into complacency.

When he finally held Geoffrey's business card in his hand, he knew he was out of time. Almost. There was lunch to eat because Cook had prepared it, and clothes to change because he couldn't appear in public in what he'd worn that morning to walk to Inez's house. By the time he left Washington Square Park to find a hansom cab to take him to Wall Street and Lower Broadway, it was already past midafternoon.

And it was too late. The office of Hunter and MacKenzie, Investigative Law, was closed.

Nathaniel pounded on the door just in case someone was working in an inner room, but the door remained locked. He took the stairs down to the street and started toward the corner, where he saw a hansom cab pulled to the curb.

"Who ya lookin' for, mister?"

A filthy street urchin tugged at his sleeve.

Nathaniel pulled a penny from a pants pocket and waved the barefoot boy away. The boy whistled, and seconds later, Nathaniel found himself looking down at half a dozen dirty faces.

"Who ya lookin' for?"

"Get away." Nathaniel threw a handful of pennies onto the sidewalk. One of the boys scooped them up, but the rest didn't move a muscle. They stared up at him as though he should know they wouldn't leave until he'd answered the question.

"The office I was going to is closed," he said. He didn't understand what these ragged children wanted. He'd given them all the pennies he had.

He didn't feel the hand that crept into his jacket pocket and extracted Geoffrey's business card.

"Here ya go."

The card passed from hand to hand. It was obvious none of the boys could read, but it was also undeniable that they recognized the logo printed above the firm's name.

"Whadda ya want with Mr. Hunter?" One boy did all the talking.

Nathaniel looked up and down the street for a beat cop. They were never around when you needed them.

"I'm Mr. Hunter's cousin," he said, reaching to take back the card.

"Yeah? What's his first name?"

He had no choice but to play their game. "Geoffrey. Geoffrey Hunter."

One of the boys took off at a run. He leaped onto the rear of the hansom cab, clambered toward the driver, and seemed to be telling him something, waving his arms and pointing toward Nathaniel.

The boys were like a persistent herd of small but determined goats, shoving and pushing Nathaniel toward the cab. No explanation from the driver, but he tipped his hat and opened the vehicle's half door. Moments later the cab pulled away from the curb, its stupefied passenger hemmed in on both sides by the smelliest street urchins he'd ever encountered, all of them chattering away in what he knew was English but was nevertheless completely incomprehensible.

Except for one name.

"Miss Prudence."

CHAPTER 29

Chief of Detectives Thomas Byrnes was not a man to waste time. He summoned Stephen Phelan and Pat Corcoran to his office as soon as he arrived back at Mulberry Street Headquarters from Judge Ingram's chambers. His ears were as red as though they had been more than verbally boxed and his stomach felt like a legion of devils were using their pitchforks on it. Clouds of cigar smoke swirled above his head as he paced.

An hour passed with no sign of either Phelan or Corcoran. No one knew exactly where they were, although rumor had it that Phelan was in as explosive a temper as his commanding officer. Something about a prisoner escaping from the Tombs. No paperwork to prove the man had ever been incarcerated there in the first place, but the third degree had been mentioned. Winks and knowing looks were exchanged. Hard as it was to believe, Stephen Phelan was reputed to be tougher with his fists than Thomas Byrnes when persuading an accused that it was in his best interests to confess.

By the time Phelan knocked on Chief Byrnes's door, it was late in the afternoon, but none of the detectives at Mulberry Street had thought for a minute about leaving for the day. Despite his enviable record of arrests and convictions, none of the men who worked with him liked Stephen Phelan. They shared office space with him, grudgingly solved cases with him, and occasionally bellied up to a bar with him, but they didn't trust him. A man who could beat a suspect nearly to death with his fists could just as easily turn on his brothers in blue to save his own skin.

Coppers didn't live an easy life; they lumbered through each day knowing they wore targets on their backs. So they took bribes and kickbacks, leaked upcoming raids to dance hall owners who paid well for the warnings, and drank as hard as the lushes sleeping off their booze in the drunk tanks. Once in a while someone like Stephen Phelan got what was coming to him. Nobody wanted to miss the party.

Thomas Byrnes didn't say a word when Phelan finally stood in front of him, Pat Corcoran off to one side. He snarled when Phelan sank into a chair without being invited to sit down, and he dismissed Corcoran with a wave of a scarred fist.

The two men were alone. No witnesses.

"You arrested someone this morning without a warrant," Byrnes began. He spoke quietly, with the careful intonation and purring cadence of a priest in the confessional. "Threw him in the Tombs without adding his name to the registry. Put him through the third degree. The man you dragged out of the Fifth Avenue Hotel in front of onlookers is a lawyer. More importantly, he's somebody with influence and friends on the bench. I just heard from one of them."

Phelan pulled out a cigar from his waistcoat pocket. He and Byrnes had lit up together many a time. Phelan was part of the Chief's inner circle, privy to many things best left undocumented.

Byrnes leaned across his desk, tore the cigar from Phelan's hand, and flung it to the floor. "You've gone too far this time, boyo. I can't haul you out of this bog even if I wanted to."

Phelan knew there weren't many in New York City who

would stand up to Byrnes; it took real power to challenge him. Tammany Hall controlled the police, just as it kept a tight rein on every aspect of the city's political life. Byrnes's introduction of the third degree and his ruthless pursuit of the unaffiliated criminal class could never have been done without Tammany's consent. But even Tammany respected the power that still resided in the wealthy Dutch-descended residents known as Knickerbockers. Political bosses came and went; old money and old names were harder to dislodge.

From Geoffrey Hunter to Prudence MacKenzie to a judge friend of her late father was a logical leap. That and Byrnes's remark about friends on the bench. It had to have been a judge who ruined Thomas Byrnes's day and now threatened Phelan's own career. He had no doubt the Chief of Detectives had been ordered to fire the offending detective on the spot. The ex-Pinkerton's escape from the Tombs had only fueled Byrnes's already volatile anger. It might have been an illegal arrest, but for any prisoner to break out of the Tombs was a slap in the face the police department would be hard-pressed to live down.

The trick was going to be to convince Byrnes that he—Phelan—was not to blame for what had obviously been a humiliating experience the Chief was ill-prepared to accept. The two of them were Irishmen, accustomed to slurs on their religion, their names, their looks, and the country from which they'd had to flee. The judge, whoever he was, would have treated Byrnes as some sort of inferior insect who needed to be crushed beneath his foot and swept out of the way. Phelan knew the feeling and he also knew that the only way to deal with it was to fight back.

"The warrant and the registry are easy to fix," Phelan said. They were. Documents were created after the fact so often that no one bothered to remark on it. "Hunter won't want his name in the papers, so he'll stay quiet. So will the MacKenzie woman. The only one who's likely to cause us trouble is the judge they or a friend of theirs got to."

What he was saying made sense. He could read it on Byrnes's face. The Chief and his preferred detective had cleared up many a mess together. They were expert at manipulating witnesses, threatening reporters, buying off victims, and destroying evidence. They also knew that Tammany had no use for politicos who let an honest judge win a round in the never-ending struggle for control of the city.

"Judge Ethan Ingram." The name came out on an exhalation of cigar smoke, a steady stream this time as Byrnes considered the intricacies of what Phelan was suggesting. Blackmail was tricky at best, but it was often a guilty man's only defense. If Judge Ingram could get Phelan fired, he'd go after Byrnes next. All the rest of what had happened today was no more than a series of minor annoyances.

"What do we know about him?" Phelan asked. He knew that once threatened, Byrnes wouldn't go down without a fight.

"Rich. Knickerbocker. Widowed. No adult children. Owns a box at the Met. Apparently enjoys the social scene. Has a reputation for being knowledgeable and fair on the bench."

"A man like that usually has a mistress he's hiding." Phelan spoke from experience. He'd hushed up many a disturbance that could have caused the kind of scandal Caroline Astor wouldn't tolerate. Alcohol and a woman could turn the most cultivated gentleman into an unregenerate libertine.

"Find out who she is." Byrnes ground out his cigar in the cut-glass ashtray that was as heavy and dangerous a weapon as could be found anywhere in the building.

Phelan nodded.

"This stays between the two of us." Byrnes stood up, walked toward the office's only window, and turned his back on Phelan.

Dismissed him.

Prudence thought that Nathaniel Hunter resembled every caricature of an academic that she'd ever seen. His suit was obviously bespoke, but the jacket hung awkwardly from narrow shoulders and gaped over a pouchy pot belly. The wrinkled trousers sagged as though they had too many pockets. If he'd begun the day wearing a hat, he'd managed to lose it somewhere. He stood in the library doorway as though he might at any moment turn and make a run for it. If he didn't collapse first.

Cameron had reluctantly allowed Nathaniel Hunter to enter the house after a whispered conversation with the hansom cab driver who'd brought him there. The sight of four of Danny Dennis's street urchins snugged tightly on either side of the cab's passenger had further reassured Prudence's butler that his employer would indeed want to hear what this odd Mr. Hunter had come to tell her.

"Thank you, Cameron. I think we could all use some tea." Prudence rose gracefully to her feet as Cameron prodded forward the obviously unnerved guest and then left the library, closing the door noiselessly behind him. She called up her most hospitable hostess smile. "Geoffrey did tell me that he had a cousin living in the city. Welcome."

Ned turned in his seat and stared. Amos took in every detail of the stranger's appearance, cataloging him the way he did all the men and women he met or followed.

"I didn't know what else to do, Miss MacKenzie," Nathaniel stammered. "I thought you should know."

"Do sit down." Prudence guided him to a chair opposite Ned and Amos, neither of whom said a word. "Now tell me what it is you think I should know."

"Geoffrey came to see me last Saturday. He was looking for someone. A mutual acquaintance." Nathaniel's voice strengthened as he spoke. If he concentrated on what he'd come to reveal instead of what it all meant, he'd be able to make it through.

"Inez Rankin," Prudence said. "Yes, I know. He told me about her and the necklace we found. He also told me that they were never formally engaged although both families took it for granted they would marry someday. Then Inez found herself in compromising circumstances. They quarreled."

The two men to whom Nathaniel had been introduced but whose names he couldn't remember raised their glasses as if in a toast. Miss MacKenzie had very effectively taken the wind out of his sails. And they hadn't been very full to begin with.

"Did he tell you he went to call on her? Secretly? Alone? At night?" There. He'd learned over the years how to subdue a classroom of undergraduates and protect himself from predatory women. All he had to do was control the narrative.

"I think you'd better explain yourself, Mr. Hunter." Prudence's voice dripped icicles. Ned and Amos clutched their whiskey glasses until their knuckles turned white.

Nathaniel described the park, the moonlight, the shadow he'd seen, and the moment when he recognized his cousin Geoffrey sneaking in through Inez's unlocked front door. He deliberately left out the part about waiting to see him leave and then giving in to the fear of being discovered as he scuttled across the sidewalk to his own front steps. He didn't know how long Geoffrey had remained with Inez, but his silence on that point was insinuation enough.

"Is that all?" Prudence felt her instinctive dislike for this man growing by the minute. He so obviously enjoyed wallowing in what he thought would surely be embarrassing to her, if not actually hurtful. She wondered what the rest of Geoffrey's family could be like.

"Just the beginning." Nathaniel looked toward the drinks table, but nobody offered him anything. "This morning, early, I saw two policemen arrive at Inez's door. They were inside with her for at least an hour. When they left, they were both in a hurry, and one of them was smiling."

"Geoffrey was arrested at the Fifth Avenue Hotel this morning. Taken to the Tombs." Prudence spoke with as much emotion as she might have shown reading a newspaper headline.

"I didn't know that." He really hadn't. Nathaniel had just suspected that Inez had been up to something. Respectable people didn't usually deal with the police.

"She lied to a detective who holds a longstanding animosity toward Geoffrey. And who doesn't like me very much, either. I assume your cousin has told you about our private inquiry agency."

"He gave me your business card. I went to the office, but it was closed."

Prudence crossed to her desk, picked up a piece of stationery, and handed it to Nathaniel. "Write down Inez's address. And your own. Are either of you on the telephone?"

Nathaniel shook his head. He didn't much care for modern inventions, though he supposed electricity and indoor plumbing had their advantages. "She hates him, you know. But oddly, I think she's also never fallen out of love with him." He tried to think of a literary heroine with the same dilemma. Most of the characters he recalled killed their erstwhile lovers and sometimes themselves. Another reason not to marry.

"The cab is waiting outside to take you home. Unless, of course, you've something else to tell us?" Prudence folded the piece of stationery and slipped it into a pocket hidden in the folds of her skirt.

"Only that Inez is a dangerous person to confront. I wouldn't dare do it myself. Her husband was bitten by dozens of black widow spiders who somehow managed to nest in his bed linens." Now that he'd done what he came to do, Nathaniel was strangely reluctant to leave.

"Are you insinuating that she murdered him?" Prudence knew it wouldn't be the first time a wife disposed of a troublesome husband, but this was certainly among the most inventive methods anyone had come up with.

"I wouldn't dream of it," Nathaniel said. "Inez is every inch a fine Southern lady."

"That's warning enough." It was, Prudence thought, something Geoffrey himself might have said.

Prudence hadn't rung the bell, but Cameron was one of those butlers who had an instinct for knowing when a guest should leave. Or an exceptionally acute ear for what went on behind closed doors. He escorted Nathaniel Hunter out onto the street and into the hansom cab where Danny's boys were gobbling enormous ham and cheese sandwiches with one hand, while holding on fiercely to pieces of chocolate cake with the other. Their grubby fingers would have removed every crumb from Nathaniel's clothing by the time they reached Washington Square Park.

Geoffrey's cousin decided he might think twice before answering if duty and honor called again. He didn't much care for disruptions to his quiet life, especially when they involved street urchins who smelled like wild animals and society women who barely troubled to conceal their dislike for him.

"Inez is behind Geoffrey's arrest," Prudence declared.

Neither Ned nor Amos contradicted her.

Cameron lingered in the library doorway for a moment, nodding to let Miss Prudence know that Nathaniel Hunter was on his way back to Washington Square Park. He sensed what was coming next, and she didn't disappoint him.

"Tell Kincaid to hitch up the bays," she ordered.

"Amos and I are coming, too." Ned put down his glass even though it wasn't quite empty. "We're not letting you face Inez alone."

"You'll want the brougham then, miss?" It was the largest of the MacKenzie carriages.

"I rather think so." Prudence hadn't made up her mind yet what she would do once she got to Inez's house, but she wasn't averse to threatening force if that's what it was going to take to make the woman confess that she'd framed Geoffrey. She'd worry about the consequences after Inez had sworn before

Eleanor Eaton's judge friend that her statements were entirely false.

Before he went out to the stables to let Kincaid know he'd be driving Miss Prudence and her two guests this evening, Cameron stopped in the basement where a telephone hung from the wall of his butler's office. With Mr. Hunter convalescing in Brooklyn, someone tough, experienced, and reliable should know what Miss Prudence was up to. Mr. Lang was an ex-Pink and Mr. Hayes had once been a New York City detective, but Cameron had someone less scrupulous and more street smart in mind. He put a call through to Danny Dennis. Then breathed a sigh of relief.

Chapter 30

Inez yawned and stretched with the delicacy of a satiated cat. Delahaye lay beside her, deeply asleep in the rumpled tangle of linen sheets and nothing much else. She almost never thought of or addressed her lovers by their given names, preferring to hold them mentally and emotionally at arm's length even while enjoying the intimacy of their flesh.

He had shown himself an adept lover, as she suspected he would be. She wondered if Frenchmen ever proved to be a disappointment and smiled to think that what was commonly believed about them was probably true. God's gift to women. Delahaye had certainly upheld that high standard.

She slipped out of bed and into a silk dressing gown that was like cool water on her skin. They'd opened a bottle of champagne from her late husband's well-stocked cellar, nibbling at one another between sips of the golden bubbly liquid. It had been one of the better encounters of the many Inez had enjoyed in this room over the years. For the space of a few hours, she'd managed to forget Geoffrey Hunter and the unprepossessing young woman he had thought to marry. Said wedding would not now take place, not with flowers and church canceled and the groom languishing in a cell in the Tombs. Everything had worked out exactly as Inez had planned.

Now she had to decide who to frame for Brenda's murder when she engineered Geoffrey's release from New York City's most notorious prison. There was no doubt in her mind he would be so grateful for his freedom that what had once bloomed between them would blossom again. She had no idea who was really responsible for the killing, but it didn't matter. If you added up the number of crimes reported in the newspapers and compared that to arrests that were made public, it was obvious the New York City Police were incompetent. Whoever killed the seamstress had probably broken into Madame Régine's salon looking for money or whatever could be pawned. He'd never be caught. Whomever Inez chose to sacrifice for Geoffrey's freedom would languish or die in prison. Too bad. She'd turn her fertile mind to the problem once she'd rid herself of the Frenchman in her bed.

She swayed gently from side to side, imagining herself in Geoffrey's arms—where she belonged—as he slowly lifted the silk from her shoulders and showered kisses on skin that had been awaiting his touch for years.

"You look like a well-contented woman," Delahaye said, raising himself to lean on one arm, the other outstretched to beckon her back to the bed. "Shall we try for *very* well contented?"

"It's past time for a respectable gentleman to leave the home of a husbandless lady." Inez softened the dismissal with a smile. She wasn't one for spending time in idle chitchat once the purpose of a visit had been accomplished. She wanted the afternoon tea she'd missed—crustless ham, cucumber, and butter sandwiches; slices of apple cake; a petit four; and perhaps two or three chocolate-covered cherries. Cook knew what she liked in the empty hours before a proper dinner, and Inez had no intention of sharing it with this new, albeit accomplished lover. She relished her privacy.

"Perhaps you're right. We wouldn't want a neighbor to get the wrong impression." Delahaye had a knack for knowing when to insist, when to let a woman have her way. He had found Inez to be a practiced athlete of the bedchamber, but whenever possible, he preferred younger women whose skin had the feel and scent of youth. Not that Inez was *d'un certain âge* yet; he judged her to be in her mid- to late thirties and well preserved, so perhaps the best word to describe her would be *mature*.

"I'll be sure to tell Madame Donovan how pleased I was that one of her designers delivered my dress himself," Inez said.

"And did such an outstanding job of it." Delahaye took his time putting on the clothes he'd draped over Inez's bedroom furniture. Even in the throes of passion, he was first and foremost a connoisseur of fine garments. "Madame Catherine does like to satisfy her clients."

"Don't forget your portfolio." Inez handed him the flat leather case as she escorted Delahaye to the top of the staircase leading down to the town house's front door. There wasn't a servant in sight. They knew to keep their distance when their mistress was entertaining a particular type of visitor.

Delahaye paused for a moment at the foot of the stairs. He bowed to Inez, taking his leave as the dandified French gentleman he was, confident that this afternoon's romantic rendezvous would be the first of many. He carried her answering smile with him as he stepped out into Washington Square Park.

Inez slid the sketch she'd taken from Delahaye's portfolio out from under one of the dog beds where she'd hidden it while he slept. Something about the gown he'd drawn in pastel chalks had struck her as familiar when he'd shown it to her in the parlor, but she hadn't been able to place what it was. Not then. Not until later had she recalled the exceptionally graceful drape of the skirt Katja De Haan had worn to Lillian Osborne's afternoon tea, an especially flattering way of concealing what even a tightly laced corset could not always sufficiently diminish. The ladies clustered around their hostess and her young guest had remarked on the buttermilk silk dress Katja told them had been designed by New York City's newest French import. Madame Régine was her name.

Madame Régine. Inez was familiar with both the woman's name and her salon. She'd sat in the luxurious parlor where clients sipped champagne or pale India tea and viewed the latest styles inspired by what was being shown in Paris this season. And not just the parlor and the fitting rooms. Inez had also expressed an interest in the workrooms where the actual task of creating beauty was carried out.

Few clients cared about the seamstresses who sewed their gowns, but Inez was both curious and generous. One of the younger salesladies led her up the back stairs and showed her the many windowed space where sewing machines whirred and women old and young bent over their needles to do the complicated handwork. She'd seen the bridal dress on which Brenda Leavitt would sew hundreds of pearls and asked to whom it belonged, though she thought she already knew. It was why she'd come to Madame Régine's salon. The engagement item in the society column had hinted that the bride-to-be had decided on a new couturiere to design her gown. When the saleslady said she wasn't at liberty to divulge that information, a few more coins bought a name. Miss Prudence MacKenzie, soon to wed a handsome Southern lawyer, Mr. Geoffrey Hunter.

Another piece fitted itself snugly into the puzzle of Inez's plan to reclaim the man who rightfully belonged to her.

It was already dusk when Prudence's brougham entered Washington Square Park and drove along the carriageway that fronted the row of exclusive brick townhomes. Kincaid kept the bays to a walk so as not to attract unwelcome notice. A few residents of this side of the park were enjoying the golden light of day's end as they walked their small dogs, but most had already retreated into the comfort of their homes where they sipped aged sherry or cask-distilled whiskies, bathed, and changed for dinner. Life here was luxurious, rhythmic, and predictable.

As the carriage neared Inez Purcell's home, Théodore Delahaye descended its front steps and swung jauntily along the sidewalk, clearly a man without a worry in the world. Tall, handsome, debonair as only a Frenchman can be. Although she'd never met him, Prudence immediately realized who he was. Both Madame Régine and Madame Catherine Donovan had described Delahaye with all the identifying characteristics that women attuned to fine details could put into words.

"That's the sketch artist Madame Régine was involved with in Paris," Prudence pointed out to Amos and Ned as the brougham rolled slowly past Delahaye.

"Handsome devil," Ned commented.

"Definitely someone with ambition," Amos said. "The handsomer the man, the more he has to hide."

"What does that mean?" Prudence asked.

"Only that he should be watched. He has a lot to gain here in New York, and a great deal to lose if he has to slink back to Paris and the attic workroom of a minor salon." Amos could as easily picture a subject's future as he could recreate his past.

"Catherine Donovan has her eye on him. That's why she's hired the fellow. And she reports that he hasn't stepped out of line so far. Except for trying to pass off Régine's designs as his own. Which we can't prove." Another annoying obstacle, Prudence thought, to an intensely exasperating case.

"It's only a matter of time before he tires of playing the perfect gentleman," Ned predicted.

"It may have already happened." Amos scribbled something into the notebook he'd started carrying when he began to suspect that the years of laudanum and whiskey might be gnawing at the edges of his once-prodigious memory. *Find out about Inez Purcell's love life since the death of her husband* read the note. "Mr. Hunter's old flame is a very wealthy widow. Could be that Delahaye senses romantic opportunity there."

"Then Inez may have met her match," Prudence said. It was not an unpleasant idea. "Perhaps they deserve one another."

"We're coming in with you," Ned stated flatly as Kincaid pulled the carriage to a halt, engaged the brake, and tied off the reins controlling the pair of bays.

"That could be awkward," Prudence protested.

"If we're right that Inez contrived to have Mr. Hunter arrested this morning, she's dangerous." Amos was first out of the carriage, extending a hand to Prudence before Kincaid climbed down from his perch high above them.

"Are you armed?" When he was a young man, Ned had had a curiously naïve opinion of women. Experience and his own mother's Medean nature had taught him to respect the venom of the gentler sex.

Prudence patted the reticule she carried. Geoffrey had insisted that she never go anywhere without an over and under derringer at the ready. "Don't get her riled up by asking too many questions. Women don't like to be interrogated."

Amos snorted. He really didn't give a damn what a suspect—male or female—might or might not like.

The butler who answered Prudence's knock looked a little taken aback at the visiting card she handed him. Like most upper servants, he was an avid reader of the society columns. He knew immediately that Miss Prudence MacKenzie was never refused entry to wherever she chose to appear. "I'll see if Mrs. Purcell is at home," he said smoothly.

"Where else would she be at this time of day?" Amos exerted just enough pressure on the front door to force the surprised butler back a step or two. The visitors were making their way toward the parlor before he realized they'd entered the house.

Ten minutes later they were told that Mrs. Purcell would not be receiving them. She was indisposed.

That should have been the end of it. But Prudence was in no mood to observe the social niceties. Geoffrey had suffered cracked ribs and painful bruises all over his torso, not to mention the hours spent locked in a damp, rat-infested cell that stank of human waste and was devoid of the most basic comforts. He'd been accused of a crime he hadn't committed, and she had no doubt Inez had further maligned his character. Geoffrey had been careful over the years not to push Detective Phelan too far, knowing by reputation how vindictive he could be. Inez had undone that tenuous relationship in a single morning.

"I'm going upstairs. Inez is not going to get away with hiding in her boudoir." Prudence had reached the parlor door before Ned and Amos understood what she was planning to do. "You two stay here. I'm absolutely capable of handling this woman on my own."

She swept out into the hallway and up the stairs to the second floor before either of the two men thought to attempt to stop her. Most of the townhomes in New York City were narrow affairs, rooms opening off a corridor that ran front to back. The exclusive three-story row houses that skirted Washington Square Park were expensive properties, but not particularly large. Prudence assumed that Inez's bedroom and adjoining boudoir would boast a view of the park, so she directed her steps toward the front of the building.

She didn't knock. The door opened easily when she twisted the knob. A cacophony of excited barking greeted her. A pack of five small spaniels swirled around her feet then bolted past her and down the stairs toward where she supposed they were used to being fed and let out to do their business. She stepped into the room and closed the door behind her.

"I'm not receiving." The woman Prudence had seen drinking tea in Lillian Osborne's parlor rose from a chaise longue and reached for the bellpull that would summon a maid.

"I can see that." Prudence closed her fingers around Inez's wrist and squeezed. When the sleeve of Inez's dressing gown fell back, Prudence saw a ring of purple bruises.

"You're hurting me."

"I hope so. You deserve a lot worse for what you did to Geoffrey this morning." Prudence let loose Inez's wrist and twisted her away from where the bellpull hung against the wall. "We're going to have a nice, quiet conversation, you and I. No interruptions. Do you understand?"

For a moment, as their eyes met, Prudence thought she saw a flicker of what might be fear in Inez's stare, but it passed as quickly as it had appeared.

Inez shrugged, tightened the belt of her silk dressing gown, and eased herself back down onto the chaise longue. "I have nothing to say to you, Miss MacKenzie."

"You know who I am?"

"We weren't formally introduced at Mrs. Osborne's tea, but yes, I know who you are."

"Why did you do it? What lies did you tell Detective Phelan that led him to arrest Geoffrey?" Prudence positioned a chair between Inez and the bellpull. When she sat, she placed one hand atop the reticule in which lay the derringer.

"It wasn't necessary to lie. He's been a womanizer all his life, or didn't you know that about him? I merely hinted to Detective Phelan that it wouldn't be unlike your dear fiancé to be consorting with a servant. Southern women aren't ignorant of what has always gone on that no one talks about."

"What exactly do you mean by that?"

"I suggested to Detective Phelan that he would do well to consider whether Geoffrey had taken up with the seamstress. It would have been easy enough. When he demanded that she return the gold chain he had given her in a moment of weakness, she refused. She threatened to tell you about the affair, so he had to silence her."

"That's preposterous. No one in his right mind would believe that story."

"Except that the seamstress had hidden the necklace in the cupboard where your wedding dress was stored between fittings. Geoffrey found it and convinced you and Madame

Régine not to mention it to the police. He brought it with him the night he visited me. Men can be such fools sometimes. He didn't realize he'd dropped it in my parlor. I showed it to the two policemen. That's all it took to convince Detective Phelan that he had good reason to suspect Geoffrey of murder. All I did was supply a bit of information. What followed was inevitable."

"You accused Geoffrey of murdering Brenda Leavitt?" Prudence compressed Inez's ramblings into the one essential accusation.

"Not in so many words. I provided the police with some facts they would not have gotten by talking to anyone else. As I said, I showed them the necklace Geoffrey didn't know he'd accidentally left here. No one had mentioned that lovely little piece of evidence to them." Inez's eyes sparkled and her face flushed pink with the pleasure of what she was reliving.

"Take it back," Prudence demanded. "Take it all back. Geoffrey had nothing to do with Brenda Leavitt's murder, and you know it. Tell the police you made a mistake, that what you told them was just a string of suppositions that you no longer believe to be true."

"He could have been having an affair with the seamstress," Inez said. "He's capable of playing a double game with the women he professes to love. Look what he did to me."

"Geoffrey wasn't the father of your child." Prudence thought that now, finally, they were getting to the sordid heart of Inez's bitterness.

"I didn't have a child."

"No, you didn't. You ended the pregnancy. You've paid for that mistake ever since. The abortionist who performed the procedure left you unable ever to conceive or carry a child again." Prudence paused. "And you've blamed Geoffrey for it."

"He should have married me. We had an understanding. A true gentleman would have safeguarded my reputation."

"There was never an understanding between you two," Prudence said bluntly. She wondered if Inez would recognize the truth when she heard it. Or if she had so distorted her past that she accepted her own lies for unvarnished authenticity.

"You should thank me, Miss MacKenzie. I've saved you from a future of deception and unhappiness."

"You were the woman who canceled the flowers at the florist's shop. Who told the Trinity Church secretary that there was no longer any need to reserve the church or hire the choir."

Inez smiled. "Rather cleverly done, don't you think?"

"Not clever enough. Geoffrey and I will marry in two weeks' time. At Trinity Church and with all the flowers of our original order. Everything is back on schedule. You failed, Inez. Admit it, you failed."

"I admit nothing."

"Did you hire Anthony Nichols to follow me?" It was the only way Inez could have known that Prudence would be attending Lillian Osborne's at home that day.

"I've never heard of anyone by that name. Who is he?"

"Was. He was a private inquiry agent."

"Dead?"

"He and Brenda Leavitt both."

"You're a dangerous person to know, Miss MacKenzie. The seamstress who was sewing your wedding dress dies and so does this inquiry agent who seems to have been involved somehow. I'll make it a point to keep my distance."

A soft knock sounded on the door.

"Are you all right, Miss Prudence?" Amos Lang asked.

"I'm fine. Nothing to be concerned about." Prudence had lost track of time. How long had she been in Inez's boudoir? Obviously long enough to worry her two companions.

"Who is that?" Inez demanded. "One of your ex-Pinkerton bodyguards? Get him out of my house."

"You won't see me again," Prudence said, getting to her feet. "I won't be coming back." Inez had hatched and carried out a ridiculous plot to ruin the wedding plans Josiah had labored over with loving attention to detail, but Prudence could not in all honesty accuse her of the deaths of Brenda Leavitt and Anthony Nichols. This blond Southern woman languishing on her chaise longue was venal, resentful, and vindictive, but her actions had been like those of a petulant child determined to get her own way. Nothing about her screamed *murderess.*

Once again, this beast of a case had slipped the noose.

CHAPTER 31

The more Inez thought about her conversation with Prudence MacKenzie, the more annoyed she became. She prided herself on being a methodical, well-organized individual who, after one disastrous mistake, had devoted considerable time and energy to crafting a life that was devoid of nuisances. She married well and welcomed wealthy widowhood when she tired of the husband she'd chosen. Cheated out of motherhood, she found pleasure in the undeniable devotion of her pack of spaniels. They were a bit noisy and shed enormous amounts of fur, but there was no doubt in her mind that the little dogs were loyal and suitably worshipful. Why, then, had this Knickerbocker snip of a girl managed to ensnare the only man Inez had ever wanted but been unable to capture?

She skipped over the thorny question of romantic love because experience had taught her to be realistic. Emotional entanglements could be just as deceptive as outright lies. She'd loved Geoffrey Hunter once upon a time. Then she'd hated him with every breath she drew and every step she took. There had been moments when her entire body had vibrated with the force of her loathing. He'd betrayed her. After she'd dealt with the inconvenience for which Geoffrey wouldn't take responsibility, Inez's passions had eventually cooled. She'd known the tranquility of calm, uneventful years. Had her Yankee husband not chosen a mistress who became too demanding, she wouldn't have had to risk disposing of him. The simplicity of the operation had surprised and pleased Inez. It proved that a woman was not as powerless as society and her menfolk would have her believe.

Now Geoffrey was back in her life. She supposed she could have ignored the implications of his impending marriage, but Inez believed that turning a blind eye usually made things worse in the long run. She was angry again, drenched with the vitriol of that long-ago rejection. If she didn't do something to exact retribution for what Geoffrey had done to her, the rage would build until it became uncontrollable. That was not something she could allow to happen. So . . .

There had been no mention of Geoffrey's having been released from the Tombs; Inez decided he must still be incarcerated there. Surely if his odious fiancée had managed to engineer his freedom, she would have boasted of it. A few revisions to the plan Inez had originally made, and Geoffrey would once again be hers. Did she still love him? Yes. Of course she did. Did he by rights belong to her? Yes. Unquestionably so. Would she allow him to slip away from her again? No. One defeat was enough for a lifetime. Two rejections was unconscionable.

The most important piece of the scheme was to choose the identity of Brenda Leavitt's killer. Inez thought it likely the seamstress had stumbled across a nameless intruder and unwisely tried to run him off. It didn't really matter who he was. Or why he was there. So be it. But there had to be a living, breathing scapegoat who would take Geoffrey's place in the case Inez had built for Detective Phelan. Someone whose motive for murdering the seamstress would be believable. Who could logically be placed in Madame Régine's workroom, and who wouldn't have an alibi for the time of death.

There was one perfect candidate for the situation. One individual no one would mind losing to Sing Sing or death by the newly invented electric chair. It was a shame, because he was a very good lover, but Théodore Delahaye fulfilled every requirement, and Inez had one of the designs he'd undoubtedly stolen from Madame Régine. The sketch was proof that Brenda could have been blackmailing him.

By the time Inez had worked out all the details of what she would need to do, it was too late in the evening to summon Detective Phelan and his partner. She liked to allow her ideas to simmer overnight before committing them to the light of day, so Inez gathered her spaniels around her and fell blissfully asleep to their snuffled snores and the warmth of their silky bodies.

She knew exactly how things would play out in the morning.

Théodore Delahaye knew precisely where, when, and by whom a pastel had been stolen from his portfolio. What he couldn't at first figure out was why Inez Purcell had taken it. It took several hours and half a bottle of expensive French wine that he couldn't really afford before he settled on her motive. Blackmail. Perhaps not right away, but certainly as soon as she perceived he was tiring of her. He thought he'd made enough changes in the designs Brenda had stolen for him so their origin was concealed, but the more he studied the copies he'd made of what Régine had created, the more he had to admit that her designs could never be mistaken for someone else's work. Not by a professional. The world of haute couture was insular. Everyone knew everyone else's specific look. A couturier's conceptions were as distinctly his as a signature.

Then why hadn't Madame Catherine called him out on what he'd shown her? Perhaps her eyes weren't as good as they'd been in her youth, or maybe she'd decided to ignore a niggling but unprovable suspicion. After months of uncertainty and the expense of hiring that buffoon Nichols, Delahaye had finally begun to settle in to where he had always belonged—a flourishing salon whose owner was nearing the age at which he or she would have to name a successor. Bedding Inez Purcell had been chancy and not part of his original design, but he couldn't risk alienating an important client before he'd managed to sink his talons into Catherine Donovan's shapely figure. The whole situation was knottier than he'd anticipated, but nothing he couldn't manage.

He had to get back the design Inez had taken. Not by threat or force, but by sweet wooing. Whatever her real reason, he had to pretend that he believed it no more nefarious than a desire to study the design at leisure before making up her mind to commission it. She'd blush, stammer, and surrender the sketch, feigning the most harmless of motivations. And he'd profess to believe her. Whatever was said or done during the conversation, he couldn't let the meeting get out of hand the way it had with Brenda Leavitt. Not that it had been his fault. The blame was all on her. She'd already stolen almost a dozen designs for which Nichols had paid her well—with Delahaye's money. When Brenda suddenly developed a conscience and refused to smuggle more drawings out of Madame Régine's salon, Delahaye had told the inquiry agent to break it off with the seamstress, that he wouldn't pay another dollar for the pretend romance.

He couldn't risk being seen in the salon where Régine would recognize him, but as the days passed, Delahaye's hunger grew for more of Régine's work. It had been a moment of extraordinary bad luck that Brenda Leavitt had come so early to work on the very morning that Delahaye had decided to search Régine's salon himself. She'd screamed, and when he tried to convince her that all he wanted was time to copy some of the sketches in the salon's master design book, she'd gotten such a look in her eyes that he knew she had figured it out. Nichols had sweet-talked her, but this stranger was the mastermind behind what she deeply regretted having done. Madame Régine had always been a kind employer, giving Brenda extra time off to care for her sister whenever she needed it.

He'd never forget what she said.

"I'm going for the police."

So when she turned to leave the workroom, he'd picked up one of the heavy crystal weights used on the cutting table and struck her head with it from behind. She hadn't gone down right away. Had stumbled and tried to run. He hit her again. And again. Until finally he knew she would never get up from where she'd fallen. Never reveal to anyone that she'd been a thief because a man had betrayed her into doing his dirty work for him.

Delahaye didn't often dwell on the women who deceived him. He tended to forget them as soon as they had been dealt with.

It would be the same with Inez, though he thought there were still months of cat-and-mouse play to enjoy.

Delahaye picked up the pair of imported French fabric shears that the seamstress had been using to cut a piece of white silk. They were the finest he'd ever seen, perfectly balanced, a masterpiece of forged steel. One of the armoires where client dresses were stored stood open, revealing a white wedding dress that shimmered in the dim light. He used the shears to cut the gown into tiny pieces which he scattered over the body lying on the floor, smiling as the bits of silk drifted down like snow. He thought the scene he created was worthy of the cover of a penny dreadful.

The loveliest part of it was that no one—not Régine, not the police—would have the slightest idea that the destroyed wedding dress had nothing at all to do with Brenda Leavitt's death.

He took the shears with him when he left.

* * *

Inez didn't often leave her house before a comfortable late-morning or early afternoon hour, but she woke up at dawn the day after her tryst with Théodore Delahaye and realized she'd forgotten something. It wasn't like her to leave loose ends dangling. Seeing Geoffrey again after all these years must have rattled her more than she'd realized. Or wanted to admit. If she'd been floating, it was time to come back down to earth. She ticked off on her fingers the steps she'd successfully completed, smiling to herself as she remembered the astonished expression on the florist's face when she canceled the expensive floral arrangements. The Trinity Church secretary hadn't seemed nearly as concerned; she wondered how often engaged couples changed their minds about appearing in front of the altar.

Prudence MacKenzie had been dealt with. She'd said she wouldn't be returning, which Inez took to be a declaration of defeat. Claiming that the wedding would take place as planned had been sheer bravado. Nothing to worry about. Especially when Inez's next step but one would be to engineer Geoffrey's release from the Tombs.

It was that next step that she'd nearly forgotten about. But she was going to remedy what for her was an unusual shortcoming.

She dressed in a conservative walking suit, choosing a narrow-brimmed hat whose veil nicely concealed her face. Nothing to remark or remember about a modestly clad woman going about her business at a brisk but unhurried pace. Just for an extra bit of concealment she took a hansom cab rather than her own carriage. No point giving the coachman something to gossip about when the staff sat down together for their next meal. At the last minute, she decided that a small gift would be a nice touch, so she had the hansom cab drop her off a block away from her destination, arriving at Brenda Leavitt's house with a small bouquet of flowers and a chocolate cake from the neighborhood bakery.

Nessa Leavitt looked as if she were already dead, so thin that her bones pushed against the pale skin of her face and hands, which were all Inez could see. The girl was wrapped in the most beautiful lavender cashmere shawl Inez had ever seen, surely something far too expensive for the daughter of a woman who ran a boardinghouse. Inez's fingers itched to stroke the delicate wool; she imagined the feel of it against her cheeks, softer even than the newly washed fur of one of her spaniels.

"It's very kind of you to pay a call," Nessa said, not quite understanding who this woman was or why she'd suddenly appeared in the Leavitt parlor. "We don't often have chocolate cake from the bakery. Mother is brewing tea, so I hope you'll stay and drink a cup and eat a slice of the cake with us."

"How very thoughtful of you, but I am in a dreadful hurry this morning." Inez hadn't removed her gloves or done more than perch on the very edge of a chair, poised for a quick departure as soon as she could get an answer to the question she'd come to ask. "I wonder if you can tell me whether your dear departed sister ever mentioned a rather special necklace to you. Gold curb and bobble links. Not something you see every day."

"What a strange notion that is." Nessa's body was failing, but her mind had never faltered. Something about this veiled woman made her uneasy. "Brenda often talked about how Madame Régine's clients sometimes brought jewelry with them when they came for a fitting, just to be sure that a neckline was suitably flattering, for example. But usually it was diamonds or pearls. I don't remember her ever mentioning what you described."

"You're sure?"

"I recall every conversation I had with my sister. We were very close. She never hid anything from me." Nessa had lied to her mother so often that not telling the truth to this stranger was almost second nature. "Brenda knew how much I enjoyed hearing about her day and the beautiful clothes she worked on."

"You're absolutely certain that she never spoke of a family heirloom entrusted to her care? That she promised to place with a client's dress when no one was looking."

"What would Brenda do with something like that? Who would give it to her? And why?" Nessa wondered why her mother was taking so long with the tea. Perhaps she should ring the bell that was only used when she desperately needed help. She stretched one hand toward the table where it sat next to the book she'd been reading.

"Nothing to trouble your sweet self about," Inez said. "I appear to have made a mistake. It must have been another seamstress who was matching the gold color to the gown she was sewing." She was on her feet and at the parlor door while Nessa still wore a puzzled look on her face. "I'll be on my way. Give your mother my regards and tell her I'm sorry I wasn't able to stay for the tea."

Out the door and stepping lightly down the block without a single glance back toward the Leavitt house. Inez didn't see the curious face following her progress toward where she would flag down another hansom cab.

She'd paid Brenda Leavitt a decent price to put the curb and bobble necklace into the locker where Prudence MacKenzie's wedding dress hung between fittings. And the story she'd concocted had been so poignantly sad and believable that the seamstress hadn't hesitated for a moment. The necklace was a gift from Geoffrey Hunter's mother to the bride, but because of a family estrangement it had to be given in secret. As soon as Mr. Hunter saw it, he would understand and explain to his bride-to-be that it was a true and valuable token of her new mother-in-law's love and acceptance of her. Apparently, Brenda had slipped the necklace into the locker only a day or two before her unfortunate battering.

If the sister in the wheelchair knew nothing about the arrangement Inez had reached with Brenda, then there was no possible way to explain how the necklace had turned up where the MacKenzie slut's wedding dress was stored other than to assume that dear Geoffrey had given it to his casual mistress who had hidden it there rather than return it to him. Once Inez had tightened the frame around Théodore Delahaye, the necklace would be forgotten and Geoffrey's affair swept under the carpet where men always hid their indiscretions.

Except by the MacKenzie bitch. She'd know that all of society would be laughing behind their hands at her fiancé's having been caught as close to in flagrante delicto as to make no difference whether he denied it or not. She'd messenger back his ring and take herself off to hide in Europe until the gossip died down. Which would leave dear Geoffrey free to marry the woman he should have wed when she first gave him the opportunity.

Inez sank back into the hansom cab's not uncomfortable leather seat. She'd rushed out this morning without even a cup of coffee. As soon as she got home, she'd take off this ridiculously plain walking suit and hat, put on one of her silk dressing gowns, and order a breakfast tray brought up to her bedroom.

After all she'd done, she deserved a few hours to herself before it was time to get back to work.

Chapter 32

"I got nowhere with Inez Purcell yesterday." Prudence drank the strong tea Josiah had brewed and tore a corner off one of the pastries he'd bought at the German bakery. "And now this." She passed a piece of expensive monogramed stationery to Amos Lang, who badly needed his first chaw of the day but doubted the smell of a plug of tobacco would be welcome in the Hunter and MacKenzie conference room.

"She never admitted a thing, but I had the feeling the whole time I was talking to her that she was crowing over me."

"What do you mean, Miss Prudence?" Josiah glanced at Amos, who seemed to be having difficulty reading the letter he'd been given. "The wedding is back on track—flowers and church reserved again. And Mr. Hunter is no longer in the Tombs."

"There's the matter of two dead bodies," Ned Hayes reminded him. His eyes were bloodshot, and his skin looked like old parchment. It was obvious he'd fallen off the wagon again, but he'd managed to shave without nicking his cheeks too many times. Tyrus had fixed huge, disappointed eyes on him and refused to help him dress.

"And this from Mrs. Eaton." Amos threw the piece of stationery onto the table, where it landed on a frosted cinnamon bun. "Read it, Josiah."

The secretary gingerly extracted the letter from the sticky frosting, wiped that fragment of the stationery with a napkin, adjusted the pince-nez on his nose, and began scanning the beautifully penned message. "What does this mean?" he asked.

"Judge Ingram has informed Mrs. Eaton that he will not be able to assist her with the matter she requested he look into. Resolution of her concern rests with Chief of Detectives Thomas Byrnes." Amos really needed that chaw of tobacco.

"I can read," Josiah snapped.

"They've gotten to him," Prudence explained. "My father used to complain all the time about the extent of corruption in the police department. He said that most of the jurists in the city were no better. Judge Ingram has a weakness he's been concealing. Byrnes and Phelan discovered what it is and threatened to blackmail him. It's an old story."

"Probably a woman," Amos said. In lieu of his tobacco chaw, he swallowed more of the sludgy New Orleans coffee Josiah had absentmindedly brewed, forgetting for a moment that Geoffrey was across the bridge in Brooklyn.

"Now what do we do?" Josiah told himself not to give in to panic. No matter how bad a predicament appeared on the surface, there was always a way out of it. The solution just had to be figured out.

"What about going to talk to Byrnes?" Amos suggested. "You, I mean, Miss Prudence. He wouldn't let me through his office door."

"What would be the point?"

"It's tricky," Ned explained, "but since no charges were ever brought against Geoffrey, and there isn't any evidence of his time in the Tombs, it seems to me you've got a good case for the mutual failure of recollection." Ned had known more than a few detectives who were well-known in the division for their inability to remember whatever turned out to be inconvenient.

"The whole thing never happened?" Josiah was scandalized until he realized that nothing could be simpler.

"Phelan won't want to go along with it," Prudence said. "He's had it in for Geoffrey—and for me—ever since the first case we worked where he was the lead detective. He thinks we stepped on his toes, and he's never forgiven us."

"More to the point, he doesn't like a society woman sticking her nose in where he thinks it doesn't belong." Amos looked longingly at the few remaining pastries. It would be a shame to waste any of them.

"So since there were no charges filed, no charges have to be dropped." Ned ticked off the case elements on shaky fingers. "Unless they've already doctored the books, which I doubt they've had time to do yet. If the judge began a formal complaint against Byrnes, that disappears. It never existed. Brenda Leavitt and Anthony Nichols were murdered by person or persons unknown, but not by Geoffrey Hunter. Phelan will convince Inez Purcell not to pursue an accusation that is chiefly gossip. The deaths get relegated to the bottom of whatever heap their files are currently in. *Et voilà. C'est fini!*"

Josiah's nod told Ned that he'd summed it up rather well.

"Geoffrey needs to weigh in on this." Prudence knew where she stood, but she wasn't the one who would be most affected. In all fairness, Geoffrey should have the last word. "I'm going to Brooklyn to talk to him."

Amos wiped the sticky frosting from his fingers and stood up. He'd enjoy a talk and a chew in the Truitts' back garden with Clyde Allen, Ben Truitt's friend and bodyguard, the best man with a Bowie knife Amos had ever met. He nodded at Josiah, who closed the pastry box, emptied the teakettle, and picked up the ring of office keys. Miss Prudence's carriage was still downstairs. They'd all four be in Brooklyn before the end of the daily morning traffic jams on Manhattan's crowded streets.

* * *

Théodore Delahaye hesitated before finally deciding to go back to Inez Purcell's townhome this early Thursday morning. His first meeting with one of Catherine Donovan's clients wasn't until eleven o'clock; society ladies seldom left their beds much before then. There was time, therefore—more than enough time—to coax the plundered sketch from Inez and reassure her that yesterday's rendezvous had not been a mistake. He might be a bit stern with her; most women were accustomed to obeying the men in their lives and were perplexed when a man did not assert his authority.

He dressed carefully, as he always did. Fawn trousers, a cream-colored satin waistcoat, and black long-tailed coat. Gold watch and fob, diamond stickpin—although the stone didn't bear too close an examination—top hat of the finest beaver skin, gloves, and ivory-handled walking stick. If he'd been in London, he would have been described as a dandy. Which wouldn't have offended Delahaye in the slightest.

Just before leaving the miserable apartment he hoped soon to be quitting forever, he slipped into his coat pocket the derringer he seldom bothered to carry in the daytime. Sometimes the sight or feel of the tiny gun was the final persuasive argument needed to convince a stubborn woman to agree to what he was asking.

Delahaye didn't anticipate having trouble of any kind with Inez, but it was always good to be prepared. Women were unpredictable.

Inez's butler hadn't been told to expect Monsieur Delahaye, but he was used to his employer's male callers arriving with only the most casual regard for the proprieties. He recognized her most recent lover from his visit the day before and assumed that arrangements had been made that did not include apprising the household staff that the gentleman was expected this morning.

The butler ushered Monsieur Delahaye into the parlor and would have gone upstairs to inform the lady of the house of her guest's arrival except that Mrs. Purcell and her spaniels were already descending the staircase as the parlor door closed. She flicked an impatient hand, a gesture the butler interpreted to mean the servants were to stay out of sight. She'd ring if anything was needed.

Most inappropriate for a widow lady to receive a male caller while wearing what was clearly the type of morning gown usually only donned for the most familial or private moments. But Mrs. Purcell made her own rules.

The butler shooed the pack of spaniels down the back stairs. They'd be released into the rear garden and then remain in the kitchen until it pleased their owner to allow them upstairs. Judging from past experience that might not be for more than an hour or two. Plenty of time to drink tea, read the morning paper, and enjoy the privacy of the servants' dayroom while ignoring whatever unseemly noises filtered down into the basement from the floors above.

"I wasn't expecting you." Inez hadn't quite decided on the fine points of how she would deal with Delahaye. She certainly hadn't anticipated finding him in her parlor at an hour when no civilized individual paid calls. He'd forced her hand, and she wasn't happy about it.

"You'll have to forgive me. I simply could not go to the salon this morning until I'd kissed your hand and gazed on the beauty of your lovely face." Delahaye's lips brushed lightly over Inez's fingers. His eyes shone with sincerity and his smile was as perfect as hours of practicing before a mirror could make it. He'd learned early on in life that women responded best to a gentle wooing until their blood began to call for something more robust. His plan was to reclaim the sketch she'd taken from his portfolio and be on his way as quickly as possible. He couldn't afford to displease Catherine Donovan by arriving late, especially as he knew he hadn't yet proved his value to her. But neither could he disappoint this rather ordinary-looking woman whose praises he had just sung.

Inez's eyes darted around the room, locating the two long guns hidden behind the window drapes and the single-shot derringer nestled in the tiny drawer of a table that was barely large enough to hold a book and a cup of tea. There were also two revolvers in the parlor, one lying at the bottom of a heap of music in the piano bench and the other burrowed under the cushion of Inez's favorite armchair.

She'd had some notion of getting Delahaye to toast their liaison with a drink of drugged whiskey before shooting him dead, though it would be a shame to spoil the rug with blood that almost certainly couldn't be scrubbed clean. She hadn't worked out all the details of the story she'd tell Detective Phelan, but the gist of it was simple. While drunk, Delahaye had confessed to Brenda's murder, then realized what he'd done and threatened to kill her—Inez—if she didn't keep his secret. Better still, he'd waved a gun at her—the revolver hidden in the piano bench would fit nicely into his dead hand.

Feeling in imminent danger of losing her life, Inez had shot him in self-defense when he turned his back on her. That should be enough to get the charges dropped against Geoffrey. When Phelan informed him of Delahaye's guilt and Inez's role in securing his freedom, she had no doubt Geoffrey would speed to her side, would finally realize that the two of them had always belonged together.

Her face gave her away. The scenes Inez was envisioning were as easy for Delahaye to read as though he were watching an actress playing them out on stage. Not the details, but enough of a conspiratorial satisfaction to convince him that he had misjudged the lady. She was definitely intending to involve him in an intrigue from which he would emerge the loser. Why? He had no idea. All he knew for certain was that he needed to get safely away from Inez before she had a chance to put her plot into action. Whatever it was.

The sketch. She wouldn't have stolen it unless she meant to use it against him. He couldn't leave without it.

"I wonder if you've finished studying the pastel I left you. I think the style would be most flattering, if you should decide to have it made up." Better to pretend he believed he'd absent-mindedly forgotten to put it back in his portfolio rather than accuse her of having taken it without his knowledge.

"It's a beautiful creation," Inez agreed. "And I have no doubt it would suit me very well. But it's not your design, is it, my dear man?" She had a chuckle in her voice and a sneer across her lips that sent a frisson of fear up his spine. What was she up to?

"I don't understand." Stall for time. Try to confuse her.

"I've seen that trick with the skirt before. It's a particular bit of artistry that only Madame Régine has been able to manage. One might say it's one of her trademarks. You stole the design and you're trying to pass it off as your own. Shame on you, Delahaye. You'll be ruined when the truth gets out."

Was she set on blackmailing him? Was that what this was all about? She sensed that their affair would last only until he tired of her, so she was establishing the ground rules well in advance of a rejection. As long as he remained attentive, she would keep his secret. She was clever, this American whose face was already showing her age, but Delahaye had dealt with females who were far more ingenious and much more artful in their attempts to manipulate him. Inez was an amateur at the game. He almost felt sorry for her.

She'd left the sketch on the table where tea was usually served, where, presumably, she'd discovered the resemblance to Régine's innovative way of draping material over female hips. Careless of Inez not to keep the design where he would be unlikely to find it. But then, she hadn't expected him to call this morning.

Delahaye reached for the piece of thick drawing paper, thinking to himself as he did so that the gown he'd copied from a design Brenda had stolen really was a masterpiece. He heard the rustle of Inez's silk skirt as she moved behind him across the room. When he turned, she was pulling a revolver from beneath a chair cushion, aiming it at him with the steady hand of someone who had spent hours of her youth honing the skills of marksmanship.

"Don't!" His voice sounded weak and frightened even to him. "Whatever you want, Inez, whatever you want."

"I'm afraid that what I want is something I'll have to take from you, Delahaye. Sorry. I did enjoy our little dalliance. A shame it won't be repeated."

She pulled the trigger. A bloom of bright red blood appeared in the center of his chest. Inez watched as he fell to the floor and waited for him to stop gasping for breath. Then she turned to ring the bell that would summon her butler, if he wasn't already racing up the stairs to find out what had caused that awful noise in the parlor.

Delahaye had just enough strength to reach into his coat pocket for the derringer he hadn't thought he would need. One shot was all he had. But he was only a few feet away from Inez. One shot was all it would take.

She went down in a flurry of silk and surprise. The last thing she saw before blackness descended was the Frenchman's lips twitch in satisfaction as he, too, breathed his last.

They were both gone when the butler opened the parlor door.

EPILOGUE

The wedding of Prudence MacKenzie and Geoffrey Hunter was the social event of mid-September, especially since the groom's brief stay in the Tombs had somehow leaked out to the popular press. Chief of Detectives Thomas Byrnes refused to be interviewed by reporters, but that only fueled the fires of speculation. They only died down and sputtered out from lack of proof that anything at all untoward had actually happened.

The winter social season would not begin until mid-November and the summer season was ending as the Four Hundred ordered their Newport residences closed down and took themselves off to other climes. London. Paris. Nice. Yachting on the Mediterranean. Perhaps a visit to the pyramids or some other exotic destination made endurable by the comforts their considerable fortunes could buy.

Passing through New York City via their Fifth Avenue mansions, many of Mrs. Astor's coterie made time in their busy lives to reserve a few hours for a wedding in Trinity Church. A magnificent reception in Delmonico's was to follow. It was, all agreed, rather a fitting way to make the transition from one season to another. Hadn't they been gossiping about Judge MacKenzie's daughter for several years now? And wasn't it sensible of her—finally—to trade the indecorous life she'd been living since her father's death for the dignity of a wife? She'd been a bad example for those debutantes who weren't quite in the mold, but thank heavens, that would soon be in the past.

The design of the dress was a great secret. No one knew what to expect from the young Madame Régine, but it was bound to be as revolutionary as the white lace extravaganza Queen Victoria had worn when she married Prince Albert more than fifty years ago. White had become fashionable for brides because Victoria chose white. No telling what new idiosyncrasy Madame Régine would introduce onto the stage of haute couture.

Wednesday, September 16, 1891. Who gets married on a Wednesday?

"She's the most beautiful bride I've ever seen." Josiah blinked away the tears filling his eyes. He'd promised himself and Miss Prudence that he wouldn't cry.

Music boomed from Trinity's massive Henry Erben pipe organ, sweeping down the church's central aisle as guests turned in their seats then rose to their feet.

"Handel," whispered Josiah, just loud enough for Amos Lang, standing beside him, to hear. He was never sure how far the ex-Pinkerton's cultural education extended.

"*The Arrival of the Queen of Sheba*," Amos informed him.

Josiah realized Amos had done something to get rid of the pervasive aroma of chewing tobacco that usually announced his presence. A new suit?

Clyde Allen whispered into Benjamin Truitt's ear, describing what the blind cryptographer could not see. Lydia Truitt, Miss Prudence's only bridesmaid, had taken her first measured steps toward the altar where Geoffrey Hunter waited. Ned

Hayes stood beside him, one hand nervously patting the waistcoat pocket where the wedding ring lay.

It was traditional for the bride's father to escort her to the man who would guide her into a new life, but Prudence MacKenzie was an orphan. The congregation held its collective breath as the Dowager Viscountess Rotherton preceded her niece through the arch of white roses and paused for a moment to ensure that everyone understood what they were seeing.

Gillian Vandergrift, elder sister to Prudence's mother, had been one of the first American heiresses to resurrect the failed fortune of a British aristocrat. The *New York Times* had named them dollar princesses, a sobriquet whose accuracy always brought a smile to Lady Rotherton's lips. She'd been a wealthy beauty in her day, widowed after a year of marriage. Never remarried. Lived in a London mansion exactly as she pleased, one breath away from scandal, but never in danger of social ostracism. The two women loved each other fiercely. And drove one another crazy. Bonkers, as Lady Rotherton was fond of remarking.

Madame Régine had exceeded even her own expectations in the execution of Prudence's gown. Hand-crafted Belgian lace over cream-colored silk fit the bride's arms and torso like a second skin strewn with pearls. More pearls shone and shimmered in a full skirt that flowed decorously behind her, long enough to be graceful but not ostentatious. In her ears and around her neck Prudence wore her mother's pearls. Even Lina Astor was said to envy them. A veil so thin and light that it floated like a cloud finished off the wedding ensemble that the society columns would rave about and all of the next season's brides would yearn to eclipse. None of them would.

Geoffrey was breathtakingly handsome in formal black and white, but nobody except lovestruck younger sisters paid any attention to what the men were wearing as long as it was expensive, bespoke, and suitable to the occasion.

What everyone remembered was the joy in Prudence's voice as she pledged herself to her new husband, and the deeply resonant tones with which Geoffrey wrapped his bride in love and security. Unusual for grooms of his era and social standing, Geoffrey chose to receive and wear a wedding ring.

"They're going to Europe for their honeymoon," one of the guests was heard telling another. "But they're being very close-mouthed about their itinerary."

"Do you blame them?" someone else said.

Josiah had made all the arrangements and not revealed them to anyone but the bride and groom, who were adamant about not wanting to be tracked down by bored New Yorkers wandering the European sights until it was time to recross the Atlantic for the winter social season. They intended staying away at least through Christmas, which they had promised to spend in London with Lady Rotherton.

"Ireland first," Lady Rotherton had insisted. "One of my late husband's nephews has a magnificent estate there. Absolute privacy. Not a chance in the world anyone will bother you."

"I'm not sure I want to spend our first weeks together in an Irish peer's castle," Prudence had protested, imagining a pile of ancient bricks teeming with servants, dogs, the peer's children, odd relatives, and guests invited to hunt the countryside. She thought a luxurious hotel like Claridge's in London would be wonderfully peaceful and private after a week on the Atlantic where shipboard socializing was even more strenuous and suffocating than in New York City. Dressing for dinner every night would be de rigueur, and she was bound to know many of the ship's first-class passengers.

"You're to stay in the dower house," Lady Rotherton informed her. "It's all arranged. Josiah has coordinated everything. Entirely your decision whether you go up to the castle for meals. The dower house is fully staffed, quite large, and at a good distance from the castle. I've been a guest there myself."

Geoffrey's smile told her he didn't mind stopping off in Ireland for a few weeks before going on to England and then the continent. And since it was useless to argue with Prudence's aunt even when she'd made plans without consulting anyone, why bother?

"Ireland it is then," Prudence agreed, hoping it wouldn't rain every day.